EARLY WRITINGS

Early Writings

GUSTAVE FLAUBERT

Translated and with an introduction

by Robert Griffin

University of Nebraska Press

Lincoln & London

Copyright © 1991 by the University of Nebraska Press
All rights reserved
Manufactured in the United States of America

The selections from Flaubert's writings are translated from
Œuvres complètes de Gustave Flaubert, tomes 11 et 12 (Paris, 1973–74),
© Éditions du Club de l'Honnête Homme.
The paper in this book meets the minimum requirements of
American National Standard for Information Sciences – Permanence of
Paper for Printed Library Materials,
ANSI Z39.48 – 1984.

Library of Congress Cataloging-in-Publication Data
Flaubert, Gustave, 1821–1880.
[Selections. English. 1991]
Early writings/Gustave Flaubert: translated and with
an introduction by Robert Griffin.
p. cm.
"Selections . . . translated from Œuvres complètes de Gustave Flaubert,
tomes 11 et 12, Paris, 1973–1974" – T.p. verso.
Contents: A trip to Hell – Portrait of Lord Byron – A fragrance to smell,
or, The clowns – Rage and impotence –
A lecture on natural history – genus: Clerk –
Dream of Hell – Whatever you want – Passion and virtue –
Dance of the dead – Diary of a madman – Smarh.
ISBN 0-8032-1982-2 (cl)
1. Flaubert, Gustave, 1821–1880 – Translations into English.
1. Title.
PQ2246.A25 1991   91-11715
843'.8 – dc20   CIP

Contents

vii
Introduction

1
A Trip to Hell
("Voyage en enfer," from
Art & Progress, *no. 2, 1835)*

3
Portrait of Lord Byron
("Portrait de lord Byron," from
"Narratives & Treatises," *1835)*

5
A Fragrance to Smell; or, The Clowns
*("Un parfum à sentir, ou
Les Baladins," April 1836)*

34
Rage and Impotence
*("Rage et impuissance,"
December 1836)*

45
A Lecture on Natural History—
Genus: *Clerk*
*("Une leçon d'histoire naturelle—
genre:* commis," *March 30, 1837)*

50
Dream of Hell
("Rêve d'enfer," March 1837)

76
Whatever You Want
("Quidquid volueris," October 1837)

103
Passion and Virtue
(*"Passion et Vertu,"* December 1837)

129
Dance of the Dead
(*"La danse des morts,"* May 1838)

161
Diary of a Madman
(*"Mémoires d'un fou,"* 1838)

204
Smarh
(*"Smarh,"* April 1839)

Introduction

Translated into English for the first time, the essays and tales in this collection represent about half of Gustave Flaubert's initial experiments in writing.[1] They rank among his best youthful fiction and foreshadow the techniques and ideas of his mature work. The eleven selections allow the reader to appreciate in perspective some of the comparable yet inimitable themes, character studies, and styles of writing that mark Flaubert's major novels and stories. From the initial schoolboy sketches through "Smarh," the more memorable writing of the young Flaubert reveals the eye of a precocious artist who surveyed the world primarily as material for fiction. His transference of this field of vision into language set the modern novel on a new course.

Until he underwent a near-mystical attack of nerves in 1844, Flaubert's life lacked the emotional trauma or material crisis that is often associated with the genesis of such great art. Unlike the destitute characters in "A Fragrance to Smell," he inherited enough money to avoid the struggle with poverty that supposedly tempered the sensibility of Romantic souls. In assessing the prime influences that helped to shape Flaubert's true sensibility, we should consign this myth to its Romantic origins and instead briefly mention at least three catalytic events and personalities in his emotional and intellectual development, beginning with his home life.

---

1. Because of its increasing acceptance as a standard scholarly apparatus, Œuvres complètes de Gustave Flaubert, 16 vols. (Paris: Club de l'Honnête Homme, 1971–75), is the source of all the translation in this book. The edition is cited throughout these notes by volume and page number.

Introduction

1. Dr. Achille-Cléophas Flaubert was for many years resident director of the city hospital of Rouen and became its chief surgeon at the age of thirty-four. A methodical scientist and laborious practitioner, Dr. Flaubert was purportedly the model for the admirable Dr. Larivière, who (to no avail) came galloping to Emma Bovary's deathbed in 1857. As a heroic projection of Gustave's famous father, however, this picture is troubled by occasional asides in his first stories. In one memorable instance, the narrator in "Passion and Virtue" observes that "there are people who dissect a heart the way they do a cadaver" and completes the idea by adding, "That's the cruelty of an anatomist."

The Flaubert family lived in a wing of the public hospital, where from his childhood Gustave became accustomed to the sight and smell of disease, suffering, death, and operations. His letters reveal that one of his earliest thrills was climbing up to the barred windows of the dissecting room to peer at the corpses stretched out on tables: "I grew up in a hospital and as a child I played in the dissecting room." It was in the hospital quarters that he began to write, outlining tragedies at the age of nine and performing his plays in the family billiard room when he was ten.

Scholars no longer seek a tight link between the scientific milieu of his father's household and the development of Flaubert's own artistic principles. In line with one of the century's early scientific fads, various stories in this collection allude to the effects of galvanic repercussion on personality, decked out in the trappings of popularized science. But Flaubert habitually saw life as stupidity (*bêtise*) because, in his view, the world offered no evidence of evolving according to discernible laws of physics, biology, or psychology, despite attempts in nineteenth-century philosophy and science to establish these kinds of equations.

The family's medical tradition and environment surely did affect Gustave as a young man, and there is plenty of evidence that the awesome presence of Dr. Flaubert made his son tremble. Yet Gustave became less the son of a famous surgeon than the child of his Romantic era, a somewhat belated "child of the century," as he himself portrays Byron. His exaltation of Byron, Victor Hugo, and others is evident in both his initial and mature work, and thus remains a true index of his own nature and temperament. In his early love of heroism and condemnation of God's creation, this son of a middle-class family played the part of a young rebel. He may have attempted to escape from the generation of 1830, but he remained a product of the Romantic age. As his narrator in "Diary of a Madman" exclaims, "I devoured the pages of Byron and *Werther*; with what transport I read *Hamlet*." We should remember that these titles were forbidden reading when Flaubert was a student at the Collège de Rouen (1832–39).

The currents of thought and feeling sweeping through the provinces in the decade 1830–40 carried Flaubert along in their wake. Napoleon was already dead when Gustave was born on December 12, 1821. For Byron, Hugo, and other writers he admired, Bonaparte had epitomized personal strength and the irresistible force of the ego (to paraphrase Hugo's *Hernani*, 1830). But the great general's epic conquests did not weigh on Flaubert's conscience. Some of his characters still meet the Romantic requirement for the superiority of the soul by pursuing exotic conquests, emotional experiences, and dreams of glory; poetry struggles with absolutism in "A Trip to Hell," where a figure who is "young, proud, vigorous, with a Herculean build" resembles Gustave himself. For the most part, however, Flaubert and his postwar generation had little confidence in politics as the great instrument of progress, even less faith in the inviolability of the individual will, and no belief at all in pious abstractions.

Although the first flower of Romanticism was fading in Paris, it was only beginning to blossom in provincial *lycées*. During the school years 1835–36 Flaubert came under the guidance of his literature teacher Gourgaud-Dugazon (Henry Gourgaud) and his beloved history teacher Adolphe Chéruel. Like other passing idealists of his time, he was also drawn to some of Victor Cousin's philosophical speculation on a universal synthesis of feeling and intuition. This minister of public education attracted young disciples by his vocal defense of freedom and his belief that true beauty invites the artist to contemplate an unreachable idea. Desire for absolute certainty impels Flaubert's Almaroës, Smarh, and others after them; the impossibility of attaining certainty is the steady theme of his *Temptation of Saint Anthony*, just as its three versions (1849, 1856, 1874) reflect Flaubert's continual search for perfect expression.

2. Succeeding Achille-Cléophas as the initial dominant person in his life, the second catalytic influence in Flaubert's early years was his schoolmate Alfred Le Poittevin, a kindred spirit with a budding cynicism that mirrored the temper of his age. Flaubert's biographers have become increasingly aware that Alfred was highly instrumental in helping to develop the writer's sensibility and the contemptuous portraits of Philistine bour-

geois values that we find in "A Lecture on Natural History" and "Whatever You Want." Le Poittevin's deep streak of pessimism enabled Flaubert to sharpen the prevailing, crude Romantic notions about modern-day degeneracy. The views of Alfred and Gustave characterized a *second*-generation Romanticism and were shared by their contemporary Baudelaire in *Les Fleurs du mal* (1857). A strange beauty emerges from their sardonic insight, cruel irony, and depiction of life's ugliness, which even in Flaubert's early writings such as "A Fragrance to Smell" and "Passion and Virtue" took the form of varied structures of language, musical richness, and poetic vision.

3. The third and perhaps most decisive imprint on Flaubert's early years was the encounter with Elisa Schlésinger at Trouville during the summer of 1836, four months before his fifteenth birthday. Their meeting was poetically transfigured into the vision of "Maria" in "Diary of a Madman," which Flaubert completed a few months before he was seventeen; Madame Schlésinger was nine years older than Gustave. The narrator's detailed account of the sleepy fishing village with its expansive beaches has led many to read the diary's events as an adolescent's true confession.[2] But one aspect must be stressed for an understanding of its place within the continuity of Flaubert's ideas and fiction.

The tides of Trouville beach never completely effaced Elisa/Maria from Flaubert's memory. The account of their meeting conforms to principles of writing and to mechanisms of the psyche that fascinated him all his life; for example, "When you reduce a woman to writing," he wrote, "she makes you think of a thousand other women."[3] There are nearly a dozen reflections of enigmatic "Maria" types in Gustave's writings up to the completion of the "Diary." Entrancing characters who bear her name continue in later texts, from the prostitute in his first novel *November* (1842) to the saintly Madame Arnoux in *Sentimental Education* (1869). From even random reading through his correspondence, it is apparent that Flaubert

---

2. See René Descharmes, *Autour de Flaubert* (Paris: Mercure de France, 1912), pp.65–69; Algernon Coleman, *Flaubert's Literary Development* (Baltimore, Md.: Johns Hopkins University Press, 1914), pp.2–6; Albert Thibaudet, *Gustave Flaubert (1821–1880)* (Paris: Plon-Nourrit, 1922), p.24. Cf. Maxime du Camp's judgment on "Madame Arnoux, who is the phantasm of Trouville transported into another milieu," in *Souvenirs littéraires* (Paris: Hachette, 1882), 2:469. Currently, the most reliable reference on these and other points is Herbert Lottman, *Flaubert: A Biography* (Boston: Little, Brown, 1989).

3. Cf. "In adolescence, one loves other women because they more or less resemble the first one" (8:266).

viewed this malleable image of woman as a continually revised maternal imprint of sorts on the psyche of modern man.

In Elisa/Maria's obsessive return throughout Flaubert's letters, she is variously portrayed as the captive and captivating queen of his heart and as "all truth." But we should also note, first, that in his correspondence it is "illusion, which is the true truth," and second, that the "all truth" comment came from a letter to Louise Colet, written ten years after Elisa had become the lodestar named "Maria." The explanatory language in that letter comes from the close of section 15 in "Diary of a Madman," where the narrator tells of the last flicker of his affection for Maria, now reduced to "cold ashes." Whereas Flaubert retained the memory of his own affective experience, he admits that when he met Elisa years later, he "had trouble recognizing her." She had already unwittingly modeled for the young artist, and her presence was evidently no longer required. When Flaubert reflected in 1872 on the initial meeting, he finally acknowledged that "the days of yesteryear are recalled in an aura of golden mist." In both letters and fiction, the "golden aura" is Flaubert's metaphor of choice for expressing the poetic alchemy of transforming commonplace objects into *objets d'art*. Later, the imagination of the humble Justin, for example, is graced with the Midas touch: as Justin prepared to polish Emma Bovary's boots, encrusted mud "crumbled away at his touch and he watched the particles float upward into a sunbeam."

This "as if" quality we find in Flaubert's writing—reading the "Diary" as confession, and Flaubert's prose as if we were reading Justin's mind—lies at the heart of his famous "free indirect discourse." Translators and readers alike should remain alert for this quality of ambiguity, as in Mazza's crisis in "Passion and Virtue" when she "gave herself over to a torrent that swept her away . . . [as] when you feel the world slipping away from *you*" (emphasis added). Flaubert uses this kind of language to intimate the plight of Emma Bovary; like the ambiguous "We" that begins *Madame Bovary*, "you" implies a perspective shared by reader and characters which may be outlined but never fully grasped. Similarly, in the narrator's recollection from "Diary of a Madman" we read: "I hear the sound of her steps, I hear her breath when she passed me. I was bemused as if Venus had descended from her pedestal and begun to walk. That's when I felt my heart for the first time, I felt something mystical and strange like a new sense." What remains ambiguous in this account is whether the memory of Elisa/Maria caused the narrator's elation or whether his joy stemmed from altering her into a work of art through his poetic alchemy. The praise of writing added to "A Fragrance to Smell" comparably describes the attempt to compress the world's complexity between the covers of a book, where the growth of an idea can be placed on a pedestal for inspection.

Flaubert was haunted throughout his life by apocalyptic visions of beauty and by the daunting task of trying to make language eternalize fleeting perceptions. His fear of abandoning himself to the vagaries of imagination reflected in turn a fear of compromising his austere ideal of art—the ideal of complete impersonality, which became the essence of his craft.[4] As the young writer began to work toward larger and more complex tableaux, the tension between language and art, medium and ideal, became his dominant theme. The lecture given by the narrator in "Smarh" to no one in particular ("Your impoverished language has been castrated by grammarians, although it is chaste enough by itself") is a succinct variation on the artist's dilemma as it is pictured in the "Diary": "How can speech shape that harmony which rises in the poet's heart or gigantic thoughts which crumple sentences the way a strong and beefy hand tears the glove that covers it?"

THE EARLY WORKS

As Flaubert's disciple Guy de Maupassant put it, "Creating a true picture involves creating the complete illusion of truth, according to the normal logic of facts." The "facts of life" are neither good nor bad, beautiful nor ugly: they simply exist. But while Balzac remains an engaging storyteller, the following selections show that Flaubert does not really tell us a factual story. Instead, he recreates it in order to make his readers *see*, thus allowing them to infer connectives and establish conclusions that his narrative technique of refraction only implies. As the narrator in "Diary of a Madman" states the case, "Each of us has a prism through which he sees the world." Stories proceed through a sequence of visualized scenes where

---

4. E.g., "By trying to understand everything, everything makes me dream" (12:463); (September 1845; 12:463); "Watch out for revery . . . the evil monster that has already devoured many of my resources" (April 1846; 12:471); "I am no longer as much of a dreamer as people think, since I know how to observe like myopics" (January 16, 1852; 13:158); "Each dream finds its own particular form" (June 14, 1857; 13:554).

links are close to the conventional montage of modern film: our lives are a series of loosely connected pictures and detachable images. Marguerite, Mazza, Djalioh, and Smarh are not really motivated by sheer emotions or abstract concepts such as sexual desire or lust for power; instead, they are moved by concrete images that pass before their (and our) mind's eye. Therefore, the writer's job is not to dramatize life or simplify its problems but to help interpret it. Any conclusions about the "meaning" of Flaubert's stories would have to be supplied through the complicity of a reader who completes the tale. The artist should not moralize ("Whatever You Want": "You probably insist on a conclusion, don't you?") but rather try to perfect a vision of the inexplicable complexity of life.

The early texts also demonstrate the breadth of Flaubert's imagination and the density of his prose pictures. The fragmentary "Agonies," for example, is contemporaneous with "Diary of a Madman" and "Dance of the Dead," and it treats similar themes; "La dernière heure" (1837) is merely a preliminary depiction of "Rage and Impotence" (1838); the glorification of death in "The Woman of the World" (1836) is greatly broadened in the last four stories. "Smarh" is a logical stopping point for this anthology, since it was followed by a long silence until Flaubert completed *November* in 1842.

"A Trip to Hell" and "Portrait of Lord Byron" reflect the Romantic enthusiasms that Flaubert never entirely outgrew. The first sketch, which appeared in the literary journal *Art and Progress*, had been polished at school and circulated among friends; "A Trip to Hell" borrows the first two cantos of Byron's semiautobiographical *Childe Harold's Pilgrimage* (1812) and is indebted to Edgar Quinet's Faustian *Ahasvérus* (1833), whose hero thirsted for knowledge. The models for the personified cathedral in "Smarh" came from Quinet's work as well as from Hugo's *Notre Dame de Paris* (1831). French translations of Byron were among the best-sellers of the time, and along with Rabelais's irreverence, Byron's assaults against human pretensions inspired Flaubert's entire generation.

"A Fragrance to Smell" is the first story to display an array of themes that return in Flaubert's novels. The idea that monstrosities are microcosms of creation, for instance, recurs in the geography of the infamous cap of "Charbovari" as in the nightmare visions of Saint Anthony. "A Fragrance to Smell" introduces a misshapen outcast, pitted against society and the world, in a tragic account of the web that binds individual fortune to overarching fate. Flaubert's comments in his travel journals on the decline of the spectacle of tightrope-walking might have come from virtuoso performances he saw at fairs near Rouen. But the play of fate in the outcast's life points to *Notre Dame de Paris* as Flaubert's richest model, while the closing praise of writing illustrates the persistence of Byronic ideas.

Passing from "Rage and Impotence" to "A Lecture on Natural History," the reader can see how easily Flaubert moves from the fantastic genre of the "wild tale" to middle-class caricature in the style of his contemporary Honoré Daumier. "Rage and Impotence" blends personal reminiscences from the young writer's family, where the servant Julie furnished the model for both the faithful servant Berthe and the enigmatic Félicité of "Three Tales" (1876).[5] This Romantic theme of suffocation is reshaped from a reflection on Flaubert's experience; in "La dernière heure," written several months later, the young hero who holds vigil over his dead sister is gripped by an agony equivalent to that of Flaubert himself at the bedside of his ailing sister Caroline.

In a letter to his friend Ernest Chevalier, Flaubert mentions taking the galleys of "A Lecture on Natural History" to the editor of the Rouen literary magazine, *Le Colibri*, where it was published. In this satire on petit bourgeois mentality, Flaubert used Balzac's "Physiology of the Clerk" as a sourcebook for character types. Balzac's office manager, M. Bouvard, resurfaced again in 1880 as an eternal copyist in *Bouvard and Pécuchet* (Pécuchet was the name of one of Flaubert's school friends).

In contrast to the fluid tone of the two previous tales, epic scenes and metaphysical themes imbue "Dream of Hell," which enlarges Flaubert's earlier accusation against God and creation in "A Trip to Hell." Satan's battle for the soul of Duke Almaroës pits the "sublime monsters of Creation" against one another as "two incoherent principles." Their struggle recalls the portrayal in his letters of the composite creatures of myth: "Those monsters explain history to me" (July 15, 1839). Although "Dance of the Dead" and "Smarh" go their separate ways, they too adopt an Olympian perspective in their survey of the world's flaws and the ruins of paradise. The protagonist in "Smarh" is taken on a cosmic voyage through epochs "where embryonic creation first stirred"; following the final battle

---

5. See Lewis Shanks, *Flaubert's Youth, 1821–1845* (Baltimore, Md.: Johns Hopkins University Press, 1927), p.22.

of good and evil, the "monstrous coupling" of the angel of Truth with Yuk assures victory for this embodiment of the grotesque. Thus, from "A Trip to Hell" to "Smarh," the promise of finding an untarnished image of Truth is inevitably dashed. Flaubert's lavish portrait of Nero in "Dance of the Dead" may reflect the heady influence of Chéruel, who had already established Jules Michelet's *History of Rome* as a staple of his teaching at Flaubert's *lycée* in Rouen.

Initiating a collection entitled "psychological studies," "Whatever You Want" is the first of Flaubert's fiction to integrate multiple recollections from his life in descriptive scenes and in the affective response of Djalioh. Djalioh is the noble primate who lives in exile within the social order because of an inability to express his deep feelings in language. In his mammoth work *The Family Idiot*, Jean-Paul Sartre saw Djalioh as an important projection of the seventeen-year-old writer's feelings of inadequacy when confronted by his father; from "A Fragrance to Smell" onward, references in this collection to medical students, dissecting cadavers, and burying a doctor alive shore up the connection. From Flaubert's correspondence we see that, like Djalioh, he was chagrined at not knowing how to dance. But aside from possible echoes from his own memory, the idea of affinities between men and primates was a staple of popular speculation, as in Dumas *père*'s *Antony* (1831), which Flaubert read as background for his story.

The theme of adultery in Dumas's play continues in "Passion and Virtue," which Sartre also discussed at length for Flaubert's inclination to analyze psychological struggle within women characters. His characterization of Mazza appears to contain an embryonic sketch of Emma. The composition history of the tale exemplifies Flaubert's use of everyday newspaper accounts to support his fictional creation with key facts drawn from the environment of his characters. Through detailed study of a given setting and a character's relation to it, he became acutely aware of degrees of (un)suitability of his characters to the world he created: "A castle in ruins seemed suitable to his thought. . . . The castle where the count [Almaroës] lived took on some of the sadness of its inhabitants." Maladaptation is the essential "biographical" fact of Marguerite, Mazza, and Emma Bovary: "That was when the world's symphony sounded discordant and infernal [to Mazza], when nature seemed like one of God's cruel jokes." The "idea" of his novels and stories, then, arose from the tragedy (or comedy) of this maladaptation.

Introduction

TRANSLATING FLAUBERT

Documentation for the readings in this collection is provided in order to clarify textual details that reveal the extent of Flaubert's study of setting and character. The information in the notes is intended to enhance the reader's conversance with aspects of French society in the 1830s, as well as with Flaubert's germinal temperament and attitudes. The main effort of the translation itself has been to safeguard the subtle ambiguity of his *style indirect libre,* as in the comic or tragic tension between the perceiving mind of characters and the world at large.

In attempting to isolate a young writer's thought and retrace it to the root of his story, a translator may occasionally wonder whether the text contains a flash of the writer's insight or merely signals a lapse of concentration, or indeed whether the puzzling textual detail reflects both the writer's blindness and his insight. Flaubert's habits of composition and revision are of little help in resolving this uncertainty because his early manuscripts housed in the Bibliothèque Nationale in Paris and the Bibliothèque Municipale in Rouen reveal an irregular rhythm of writing. The narrators in "A Fragrance to Smell" and "Diary of a Madman" concede that a single sitting might produce a partial page or many pages. But the ink variations (coloration, haste, density, multiple corrections) show that the circumstances of Flaubert's revisions were more complex. His rewriting entails no particular hierarchy of values, so that indicating all his fitful starts and stops would amount to publishing his entire work notes. Instead, the following five discriminations have been used to determine when Flaubert's text should be altered for greater clarity in translation and when it should be left unchanged to convey his delight in "voluptuousness in all its forms."

1. Like criticism, true translation must be a sustained commentary and interpretation of the original rather than a substitute for it, even in the most trivial instances. As a typical example, in "Passion and Virtue" Mazza's emotional turmoil contrasts with her peaceful surroundings: "She saw people going toward the nearest city, on their way to market carrying fruit that was still on the stem and covered with moss to keep it fresh." Flaubert's text actually ends "on the stem and covered with moss." Since nineteenth-century dictionaries do not suggest any peculiar meaning for *mousse* which might be taken into account, the explanatory "to keep it

Introduction

fresh" has been added to prevent an otherwise confusing description from interfering with the primary drama of Mazza's passion.

2. Some textual problems involve only grammatical confusion rather than creative ambiguity. In "Dance of the Dead," for instance, Flaubert's enthusiasm for description outstrips his command of syntax, when one of his characters sits down on shaded moss which the dew has made silvery. After several parenthetical interjections, she/Flaubert evidently loses touch with her grammatical referents and inadvertently has the moss made silvery by water that "gave a green cast to the stones which soak the grass." But while a translator should not attempt to make his subject sound better than he reads, he need not emphasize all similar quirks of language. Since there is no particular density of ideas or meaning in this passage, the morass of syntax has been dissolved by breaking it into two sentences and eliminating the unkempt description.

3. Still other cases entail grammar problems blended with the textual ambiguity of free indirect discourse. Midway through "Smarh," the "Savage Mind" speaks to the Savage about the family he has abandoned to a troubling fate: "A demon took them and made them founder in their hope, like fire dropped into a river." In elucidating the comparison, one could cite numerous passages from Flaubert's complete works where the play of fire and water symbolizes the two potencies of both creation and destruction in the world's major religions. But the analogy cited as proof ("like . . .") confuses what it purports to clarify. The text literally reads "like *those* fires which fall in rivers," where French grammar dictates that the causative *font tomber* makes someone or something fall—those fires make *you* fall into their opposite element?—presumably referring to a known category. Yet on what evidence can we assert that the appeal for recognition is directed to the Savage Mind, to the Savage himself, or to the reader? Any determination must be arbitrary, especially when we consider that the only other time this vocabulary of revelation is used in these eleven selections, it is to portray the unfathomable struggle within Djalioh's fragile heart: "the way a senseless lightning bolt . . . is harmlessly extinguished in a puddle of water." The text resolves none of the uncertainties that it raises.

4. Elsewhere, fragmented clauses cascade for over one hundred words in a grotesque jumble that may actually illustrate an idea which the text

only implies. Near the end of "Smarh," Death plays straight man to Yuk in his tirade on the fullness of the grotesque, which is punctuated a dozen times by "all." Since we are clearly meant to witness a verbal performance, Flaubert's convoluted syntax has been left intact. Translators are on safe ground in making such determinations, since the virtuosity of Flaubert's characters is usually announced by a verbal cue. "Dream of Hell" begins with a conversational pause before listing the prowess of Almaroës ("Well [*Eh bien*], that satanic terror . . ."), and it closes with the defeat of Satanic power ("Well [*Enfin*], after Satan had jumped around and fallen . . ."). Likewise, Mazza's erotic revery is the second part of a symphonic description of nature's melody welling up in her. Her revery is initiated by long paragraphs beginning with "Each day . . ." and "Often. . . ."; her "endless voluptuousness" in the second symphonic movement is subdivided into two sentence-paragraphs totaling 160 words: "And when. . . . And when. . . ." Attention to these cues prevents the translator from overlooking the significance, the "meaning," of the cadence in Flaubert's prose.

5. The medium of writer and translator alike has never been *meaning* per se so much as the linguistic conditions of meaning. Attention to the auditory value of language must be a basic condition for reproducing Flaubert's obsessive search for *le most juste*, the exact word. His final test for his work was always an aural and purely esthetic one: meticulous reading aloud to verify the way sound, rhythm, and especially falling intonation all embody the sense of his work. How else can we explain the arbitrary shift in "A Fragrance to Smell" from the name "Isabella" to the more resonant "Isabellada"? Flaubert used language like an instrument that he was trying to tune to some perfect note sounding in his own mind, like the rapturous music of Djalioh that he alone could fathom. Several efforts were needed before the exact pitch could be attained. The line that Marcel Proust valued for its "beauty stripped of meaning"—Phèdre as "la fille de Minos et de Pasiphaë" (the daughter of Minos and of Pasiphae)—was prized by Flaubert as the most artful in French literature. Racine's verse scans automatically, but its power has less to do with translatable meaning than with the pulse of Phèdre's beating mind, which can never be conclusively translated. Whether one sees a writer's use of language as a betrayal of meaning or as a celebration of its richness, the translator always works in the no-man's-land between the word and its referents.

A Trip to Hell

1. And I was atop Mount Atlas, and from there I contemplated the world, and its gold and its mud, and its virtue and its pride.

2. And Satan appeared to me, and Satan told me: "Come with me, look and see; and *then* you will see my kingdom, my world."

3. And Satan took me with him and showed me the world.

4. And gliding on the winds we arrived in Europe. There he showed me scholars, men of letters, women, fops, pedants, kings, and sages; the latter were the most foolish.[1]

5. And I saw brother killing brother, a mother cheating her daughter, writers who, through the prestige of their pens, were abusing the people, priests who betrayed the faithful, pedants who made students languish, and war which harvests men.

6. There, groveling in the mud, a schemer reached the feet of the mighty

---

1. As was typical of Flaubert's tendency to copy himself and others throughout his life, fragments of this sketch (nos.4–7) emerge at the close of "Agonies" (1838), up to the point where the unfinished manuscript tails off: "There he showed me scholars, men of letters, women, fops, torturers, kings, priests, and sages; the latter were the most foolish. . . . There a king savored his filthy debauchery in the dishonored bed where the lessons of adultery are passed on from father to son" (11:435–36). The end of both phrases may originate in the satirical doggerel of Auguste Barthélemy's *Douze Journées de la Révolution* (1835): "That's the bed where the kings transmitted the lessons of adultery to their sons through inherited taste." In *Sentimental Education* (1869) Deslauriers nostalgically recalls revolutionary days when lawyers gave orders to generals and ragamuffins defeated kings, after which he cites Barthélemy, concluding, "I've forgotten the rest" (3:140; cf. 14:603, 609, 638).

and bit their heels; they fell, and then he quivered from the impact of their heads in the mud.

7. There, on the dishonored bed where the lessons of adultery are passed on from father to son, a king savored the charms of the favorite courtesan who governed France, and the people applauded; they were blindfolded.

8. And I saw two giants: old, bent, wrinkled, and skinny, the first leaned on a gnarled staff called Pedantry; the other was young, proud, vigorous, with a Herculean build, the head of a poet, and golden arms; he was leaning on an enormous club which, however, the gnarled staff had damaged; the club was Reason.

9. And both were fighting vigorously, and then the old man gave in. I asked him his name.

—Absolutism, he told me.

—And your conqueror?

—He has two names.

—Which?

—Some call him Civilization, and others Liberty.

10. And then Satan led me into a temple, but a temple in ruins.

11. And the people were melting coffins to make cannonballs, and the dust there blew away out of bitterness; that century was a bloody one.

12. And the ruins remained deserted. And a poor white-haired man in rags, a man laden with misery, shame, and disgrace, sat there at the foot of a column. He was one of those whose foreheads are wrinkled with cares, and at the age of twenty he contains the ills of a century.

13. And he seemed like an ant at the foot of a pyramid.

14. And he looked at the men for a long time; all looked at him with disdain and pity, and he cursed them all; for this old man was Truth.

15. "Will you show me your kingdom," I said to Satan.

"There it is!"

"How's that?"

And Satan answered:

"Because the world is hell!"

Portrait of Lord Byron

He was one of those men with lofty thoughts, ample and progressive ideas, violent passions, and a soul that was both sensitive and magnanimous—in short, bizarre. Lord Byron was the child of the century.[1]

He believed in nothing, with the possible exception of his faith in all vices, in a living God who exists for the pleasure of doing evil. He believed in nothing, except love of country, the power of his genius, and the fascination of his mistress's eyes. Beyond that, he found the world to be only prejudice, ambition, and greed.

He considered a woman's honor to be a rose whose perfume was for the taking by any passerby before it fades and withers. He had a hundred mistresses but loved only one; and he even mistreated and disdained her

---

1. Written in compliance with the assigned school theme: "Characterize Lord Byron according to his writing and his life," concluding on the formula "Byron, the son of the century." In *Les Débuts littéraires de Gustave Flaubert, 1831–45* (Paris: Armand Colin, 1962), pp.26–27, Jean Bruneau persuasively argues that Flaubert did not actually begin to read Byron in English until around 1837–38. The first two readings in this book show a basic change in French schools after the July Revolution (July 27–29, 1830), when modern French models replaced Latin texts; they typify the rhetorical compositions assigned by Flaubert's literature teacher, Gourgaud-Dugazon (Henry Gourgaud), and his history teacher, Adolphe Chéruel, about whom he speaks with admiration in his correspondence. Both were instrumental in shaping his interests and honing his writing. Under the educational system of the July Monarchy (see note 3 to "A Lecture on Natural History," below) this sort of narrative exercise became a regular component of the trivium (grammar, logic, rhetoric). One of Flaubert's copybooks (dated December 7, 1837) is headed "Natural History: zoology, birds, reptiles, fish, insects, generalities"; see the last paragraph of "A Lecture."

because of her mad, unrestrained love. He kept about twenty horses in his stable and adored them all. He did not like France because there is not enough mist and snow there. In France people do not breathe the scented air from some villa, the way they do in Venice.

He was an atheist, yet he remained in churches all day long, rapt in silent contemplation and deep meditation.

When he was in England, he went out alone on horseback and enjoyed lathering his fine Arabian mare, while watching the smoke from his cigarette blown away by a gust of wind, mixed in with a December haze.

He frequented taverns, stables, and coach drivers. He was often seen there boxing with the grooms. He was adored by the people and hated by the nobility. On several occasions he came close to orating to the crowd.

Of an evening in Venice, he often hired a gondolier to take him several miles beyond the lagoon where he let himself be tossed about by the swells. When he returned home he took off his mourning clothes, and all night long he stared at the skull that was poised in the middle of his chimney mantelpiece. He loved Italy the way he would adore a mother or a sweetheart. He loved it because there you find hearts that love and hate, eyes that flash with love or passion. You always find a beautiful, unknown woman there, like a young man's golden dream. There you find either love or a dagger. There are always strains of guitar music and a sweet voice wafting over the moonlit water of a neighboring lake. You always find some theme for a drama or a novel.

Byron found nothing so beautiful as freedom, nothing so hideous as gold. Several times he faced danger out of pleasure or vanity. In Greece, he preferred to die rather than be bled. He went there to fight for the rebirth of a country that had been strangled by servitude. He went there to lift the chariot of freedom out of the mire where tyrants had plunged it. But that mire had an ennobling effect. It immortalized Byron, the son of the century.[2]

---

2. In a letter to Ernest Chevalier (August 24, 1835), Flaubert said of a Republican conspirator of April 1834: "One of those men of lofty concepts, Lagrange is the son of the century like Napoleon and Victor Hugo. He is the man of poetry, of reaction, the man of the century, that is to say, the object of hatred, malediction, and envy. An exile in this century, he will be a god in the next" (12:340).

A Fragrance to Smell; or, The Clowns

A Philosophical, Moral, or Immoral Tale, Just as You Wish

A FEW WORDS

These pages should be buried in the dust of your desk drawer, since they were written without connection, order, or style. If I dare to show them to a small circle of friends, it will testify to my trust, which I must explain to them.

An ugly, despised, toothless woman in a clown suit whose husband beats her will be joined under the same roof by a pretty clown crowned with flowers that are redolent of love. They will be torn by jealousy right up to the strange and bitter conclusion. After showing all this emotional scarring hidden by the clown's painted smile and festive outfit, after uncovering prostitution and deceit, the reader will be asked whose fault this is.

It's surely not the fault of anyone in this story.

Circumstances, bias, society, and our cruel mother nature are to blame.

Then I'll turn to the generous philanthropists who list railroads and primary schools as examples of intellectual progress, and I'll ask these contented sages what remedy they would propose for the social ills that my story lays before them. Probably none at all, unless they happen to cite *Anangke*, the Greek personification of *Necessity*.[1] This darkly mysterious

---

1. In a letter to Ernest Chevalier (July 23, 1835), Flaubert twice used the term *Anangke*, the motto of Hugo's *Notre Dame de Paris*, more to denote mischance than to imply the Greek concept of overriding fate (12:339).

divinity, coexisting with man yet outlasting him, has confronted empires in every century. Her terrible laughter greets the labored efforts of philosophers who deny her existence, squeezing them in her iron fist like a giant juggling dried skulls.

(February 1836)

ONE

As the parade was about to begin, a few musicians were tuning their oboes and screeching violins, groups were forming around the tents, and in their delight astonished country people focused on the huge red and black letters of a sign that read ACROBATIC TROUPE OF MASTER PEDRILLO.

Farther along there was a painted canvas backdrop with a naked figure of a primitive strong man hoisting a huge weight on his back. From his mouth there emerged a tricolor banner with the words I AM THE NORTHERN HERCULES.

You can imagine as well as I what the clown was shouting from the stage. In your childhood you must have stopped a few times in front of this grotesque scene and laughed like the others at the blows and kicks that constantly interrupted the speaker's commentary.

There was a different scene going on under the tent. Three children (the youngest was no more than seven years old) were either jumping on the inner railing of the staircase or practicing on the tightrope. Their weak, frail, and sallow features testified to the suffering of their misfortune. Beneath their pink blouses trimmed with silver piping, under their greasepaint and the sweet smiles they flashed, you would have seen thin arms, cheeks hollowed by hunger, and hidden tears.

"Say, Augustus," the biggest one said to another one who was getting up onto the tightrope with just a snap of the wrist, "listen," he repeated in a low voice, as though afraid of being overheard by a man with a sinister face who was walking around them, "it seems to me that mother has been gone for a long time."

"Oh, yes, for a long time," he replied, sighing deeply.

"Didn't I forbid you, Ernesto, to ever speak about that woman? As annoying as she was, she can go to the devil for all I care! But be quiet. The first time you bombard my ears with her name I'm going to thrash you."

And with that warning, the man went out into the street.

"He's always like that," the child resumed as soon as Pedrillo had left, "speaking only when he has harsh and hurtful things to say. He is such a mean person! At least our poor mother loved us!"

"Oh, yes! Mother! It upsets me so much," the youngest one said as he began to cry.

"The way he beat her so because he said she was ugly! That poor woman!"

"Come on, dry your tears. People are coming in now so you'll have to smile."

Each one took a seat in the grandstand, and soon the tent was filled. The parade had ended, and Pedrillo himself entered after announcing several times, "Gentlemen, gentlemen, you pay as you leave!"

First off, the youngest child began unsteadily to climb the ladder toward the tightrope. But then he briskly picked up his pace, encouraged by the predictable and steady chatter of Pedrillo, who studied the child's every movement as he climbed, "Courage, young man, courage! Good, good! Very nice! You'll get a lump of sugar this evening."

He came down.

Next, his other brother climbed up, venturing a few jumps before falling on his head. With fury in his eyes, Pedrillo picked him up. The child ran off in tears to hide.

Next came Ernesto's turn.

His entire body trembled with growing fear as he saw his father pick up a small, white wooden stick.

Surrounded by the audience and pressured by Pedrillo's stare, he had to move forward on the tightrope.

With his timid expression, the poor child studied the outline of the wand looming before him, like the bottom of a pit when you lean over the edge of a precipice.

Down below, the wand traced each movement of the dancer, now offering encouragement with its graceful swoop, now menacing as it bobbed furiously. It directed the dancer's steps and measured the tempo to be followed on the rope. In other words, it was his guardian angel and protector, or rather the Sword of Damocles poised above his head in anticipation of a false step.

For quite a while Ernesto's face was contorted by anguish, a whistle cut through the air, and the dancer's eyes welled up with large tears which were hard to swallow.

Still, he came down soon: there was blood on the rope.

The Northern Hercules (Pedrillo's stage name) was beginning his feats of strength when the man who guarded the entrance was heard arguing with someone outside.

"No, you're not coming in. I'm telling you, you're not coming in."

"But I want to."

"We don't let people like you in."

"I want to speak to Pedrillo. I want to talk to him, understand?"

"By heavens," the good sentinel repeated with growing irritation, "I'm telling you, we don't let people come in dressed the way you are. We don't let beggars come in."

This argument distracted the spectators.

Speaking to a miserable woman in tatters, Pedrillo said, "Ah, is that you, you old witch? I didn't expect to see you so soon. Where did you go? Oh, well, you can tell me all that later. Come in, Marguerite, the performance is going on now. Come and join in. You're going to do a few jumps, see? Do the best you can."

Even though his words invited no response, she tried to say, "Pedrillo, you know perfectly well that they'll make fun of me in my wretched clothes." She wanted to continue but thought better of it. "Come in, come on in!"

She had no choice, but as soon as the spectators saw her, a murmur arose, joined by derisive laughter, the kind of fierce laughter that greets a man who falls down, the way a proud man in his golden raiment disdainfully laughs at prostitution, or the way a child exhales his laughter at a butterfly whose wings he plucks.

Marguerite mounted the staircase with difficulty. She took no more than two steps before she fell heavily to the ground, causing her to utter a sharp cry. The wand was broken to pieces.

Soon most of the crowd filed out of the tent.

This last domestic scene scandalized most of them, including a disillusioned boy with plump pink cheeks who had wanted to be a tightrope dancer so that he could wear pink trousers and leather ankle boots.

TWO

When Marguerite was alone with Pedrillo and her children she asked, "Didn't I warn you?"

"What was the matter with you?"

"I'm sick and still hurting. Oh, I'm suffering a lot, Pedrillo. If only you loved me the way I love you!"

"Come on, Marguerite, are you going to start complaining again? You know how that gets on my nerves. Look, what's the matter with you?"

"You know perfectly well. Are you telling me that you don't remember the day when I fell, just like today? My leg was broken, I couldn't eat dinner, I cried too much, and from that point on I didn't want to tell you that I had become useless to you. I didn't want to go to the hospital, for fear of abandoning Ernesto and Garofa."

"Well, didn't you go to the hospital?"

"If I hadn't I would have died."

And the clowns withdrew beneath a canvas sheet, behind which a soup pot simmered over hot coals.

The night was cold and damp, and a November wind blew so hard it shook trees on the boulevard. From time to time it even penetrated the tent, causing the candle flame to cast its flickering light over the rope dancers who were gathered around. Encircling a huge steamer trunk, each one held his bowl in front of him while the vapor warmed his shivering hands.

As it knifed its way into the darkness, the blade of the candle flame shone on the huddle of faces and gave them a strange, eerie cast.

The group was waiting for someone to break the silence. It was Pedrillo. Looking at Marguerite, he repeated the question he had begun a half-hour before.

"Well, so that's where you went? Are you better now?"

Marguerite raised her head to look at her children for a moment. Then she lowered her head again in tears, before adding softly, "No, no, I'm still limping."

"What will I do with you, Marguerite? What will you be good for, after all?"

The poor woman leaned over toward her husband to whisper a few words into his ear.

Pedrillo continued: "Children, go to sleep, do you hear? Hurry up!"

Garofa found this confusing and asked sadly, "What about the sugar?"

Smiling bitterly, Pedrillo replied: "You poor child, you'll be lucky to have bread tomorrow."

His smile was forced. Turned bluish by the cold, his lips revealed both rows of white teeth, and the gaze of his large black eyes frightened the child. At that instant, the wind picked up so violently that it shook their shelter.

"But didn't you promise me some sugar?"

"I said for you to be quiet!"

"Oh, please, papa!"

He shoved him aside, causing the poor child to go off to bed in tears. Pedrillo was suffering just as much, with his teeth chattering from the cold.

Marguerite said, "How rough you were with him!"

"That's true."

He remained plunged in a deep revery, to the point of appearing asleep. A second gust of wind put out the candle. Inching toward him, Marguerite said, "I'm cold, really cold. Let me wear your coat."

"My coat? . . . But I sold it."

"Why?"

"For bread, Marguerite. Don't I have to give you some, too?"

"What did you want to tell me a while ago when you sent the children off?"

"What did I want to say? I don't know . . ."

"But I'm really cold!"

"What do you expect me to do, Marguerite, since I have absolutely nothing left?" Then he added, "Only a bullet . . ."

"Oh, for mercy's sake, Pedrillo!"

And she wrapped her thin red arms around him.

To see this ugly woman in rags showering affection on one who instinctively pushed her away at the sight of tenderness mixed with misery was at once hideous and sublime.

Pedrillo said, "So tomorrow you'll take my fiddle and the children to the public square, and you'll try to get us some bread."

Half an hour later, the performers were all asleep. The wind had died down. Freed from its surrounding clouds, the moon shone beautiful and clear through the crisp winter air. The canvas sign, which had been twisting and flapping around, was now silvery and as calm as the tent. Yet from time to time sighs and sobs were heard.

It was a woman crying.

THREE

The next morning Marguerite arose early, after a sleepless night. Her clammy hands were drenched with sweat in her continuing illness, her reddened feet were moist from fever, and her head was burning. She took Pedrillo's fiddle and an old Persian rug, and left with Ernesto and Garofa.

Now in the depth of winter have you ever encountered a beggar's face, hunched over by the portal of a church? In the evening, at the bend of a dark, narrow street, haven't you felt something grab your coat? You turned around and wasn't there a beggar in rags, some poor woman who told you through her bitter tears, "I'm hungry!" And then she sobbed when your fleeing shadow stopped at a theater door, amid carriages and smartly liveried servants.

Perhaps during the entr'acte you remembered those sad, pale faces outlined by the glow of a street light. And if you have a kind, generous soul, you went out to find them again to offer your help.

But it was too late. . . maybe the woman had entered a brothel to buy a scrap of bread through a life of prostitution, and the beggar was scrounging between the arches of the Pont Neuf, whereas the orchestra played on to enthusiastic applause.

As for me, nothing saddens me so much as misery hidden beneath the trappings of wealth, like a lackey braiding the bared tresses of poverty to embellish them, a song hiding a sob, a tear beneath a drop of honey. Out of sincere love, then, I pity mountebanks and prostitutes.

But if you had met Marguerite with her two children, Marguerite playing her fiddle as her children somersaulted on the carpet, if you had seen the indifference of that barbarous crowd which filed past wearing its stupid and ironic expression, your heart would have bled at the sight of such arrogance carried to its logical culmination.

It's true! Society has better things to do than to watch a mountebank and her brats! The State cares very little whether she has bread or not. To begin with, it has no money to give her. Doesn't it have to pay its eighty-six executioners?

Actually, on a raw November morning, I admit that no one is disposed to stop in the square to watch virtuoso acts. Whose interest did Marguerite draw?

Her red hair was held in place by a comb made from whitened horn, and she had a large, awkward figure. Her dress? It couldn't be seen because it was entwined by a piece of brown cloth down to her knees. As your eye continued to survey her from head to toe, it came across a large, lumpy calf wrapped in a pink stocking, then shapeless feet stuffed into thick, cracked leather buskins. She wore only a net head cover with pink ribbons and some faded flowers that fell on her pale cheeks and on her toothless jaw.[2]

Ernesto and Garofa had been wearing themselves out for nearly an hour, trying to draw the attention of the crowd. Stifled by tears, Marguerite's hoarse voice appealed several times to the generosity of passersby. Then a beautiful carriage drawn by two white horses passed near the dancers, splashing mud on their clothes. Marguerite's coat and pink hose were completely spattered. As her head bent low she shed a few tears, which ran from the neck of her fiddle, down inside the instrument. Her tears increased, and she hid her head under her coat. Then she succumbed to a bizarre and painful daydream. She saw herself surrounded by carriages that splashed mud on her, saw herself derided, despised, and dishonored. She saw her children die of hunger all around her, saw her husband go mad. Then all her memories flashed through her mind: she saw the hospital bed where she had slept and recalled the sister who cared for her; the pummeling that Pedrillo had given her on the preceding night, the greeting she was given when she first appeared . . . and all those memories flitted through her mind like appearing and disappearing shadows, erasing one another in turn. In her sleepless dream, her downcast eyes scattered warm tears over her hands.

For a while she stopped playing, but her children continued to dance. People stopped to watch them go through their paces, while their mother held her fiddle without playing a single note.

Soon she awoke from her revery with a start. Wearing an astonished expression, her large gray eyes suddenly opened to create a grotesque and laughable spectacle. Her strange apparel, her pink hose and tattered coat that rivaled the carpet spread on the pavement, her faded flowers and red hair all seemed ridiculous. A single word was heard, provoking laughter as people passed: "How ugly she is!" It was bitter cold. Marguerite no longer had any feeling in her fingers and didn't have the strength to move them. Her fiddle broke when she dropped it, scattering pieces on the carpet with a discordant sound.

With her arms folded, she gasped as she watched it rebound for a moment. What would Pedrillo say when he saw her return with no money?

---

2. On the origin of this description, and of the story itself, see Bruneau, *Débuts littéraires*, pp. 128–29.

Oh, did that thought torture Marguerite! It gripped her heart and tore at her pitilessly. As in a nightmare, her mind was beset by a thousand ridiculous stratagems for avoiding her husband's anger. Then they faded away, displaced by others even more bizarre.

At times she thought of running off with her children; but where? She didn't know, but at all costs she must flee the atrocity of Pedrillo's penetrating stare, escape from his mournful laugh, from these words: "What's going to happen to us, Marguerite?"

Once she thought about God, then invoked Satan and hoped to die . . . and she clung to life for her children. What would become of them without her?

Then, rolling up the old carpet to enclose the violin fragments, she left the square where she had been so insulted and had shed so many tears.

A pleasant idea came to mind, evoking the trace of a smile: by selling her coat or the rug, she could give Pedrillo some money and have his instrument repaired. But Pedrillo would ask what she did with her coat.

After making this objection to her own fantasy, she became sadder and charged the heavens with using reality to destroy a minute of hope, which lashed her martyred soul.

Around two or three o'clock in the afternoon the bright sun began to warm the whole city swarming with strollers, as it sometimes happens on winter Sundays. By six, the streets were still busy and some shops were open.

Marguerite stopped in front of a pastry shop where morsels that were fresh from the oven emitted a warm-scented lure, tempting the noses of passersby.

As she paused at the window, she looked in and saw a mother with two children about the same ages as Ernesto and Garofa. Both were well-mannered boys with blond hair and sparkling pink complexion. Their clothes were clean and well made, and their kerchiefs, reaching beyond their satin ties, were as white as sugarcoated candy.

The sight wounded Marguerite.

Wearing a hat and a green jacket belted with a gold-weave cinch, the mother was attended by a maid who held a small black spaniel in her arms.

When the children had eaten enough, they coaxed the dog to eat their scraps by lavishing hugs on him.

Marguerite had such hunger that she shook with anger. There she was, unable to satisfy her children's requests throughout the day for just *one* piece of bread! Fever burned her brow so much that she leaned it against the windowpane to cool it.

When the lady inside had paid for her delicacies, she went out with her children. The edge of her silk dress rustled as it brushed Marguerite's hands.

Overcome by a strange feeling that she could barely grasp, she remained for a long time with her face pressed against the panes. But in his annoyance, the pastry cook swore as he drove her away. What could she say?

Crossing the dark, crooked road, she saw a young woman reclining in bed while she sang obscene ditties. Then she thought about Pedrillo and about what was going to happen to her. For a long time she looked at the woman and listened to her songs.

"Oh, no, no! Who would want me?"

FOUR

Gold coins scattered across the tables. It was a gambling den, but not a legally authorized gaming house from around the Palais-Royal, frequented by finance ministers and bankers in their customary finery, with their impassive bearing indicating their practiced talent for this sort of dirty business. No, it was a gambling den earmarked by its hideous prostitution, one of those dives where one occasionally finds a mutilated corpse the next morning, amid broken shot glasses and bloodied scraps of clothing.

Surrounded by its low ceiling and smoky walls, men in dirty clothes hovered over tables. Behind them, rows of faces with clenched teeth clustered eagerly, eyes ablaze beneath shaggy eyebrows and knuckles white with anger. Despite their darkly brooding foreheads, you might have been able to discern crimes heaped together with their suffering. A few half-naked women strolled quietly around them, and off in a corner, standing over a young woman who lay bound on the floor, two armed men drew straws.

Dear reader: does this portrait of this half of society, the gambling den, make you shiver? The other half is the hospital, the guillotine. Well, my young friend, having been warped by a defective education, can you understand that you haven't yet plumbed the depth of misery? You haven't seen its wild and angry ravings, you haven't probed its wounds, you haven't understood its bitter pain, despair, and crimes! And you, young lady, there are places you know nothing about. Your ears have been spared the word "prostitution," which is the basis of our society.[3]

When the silence of waiting gave way to the grating noise of the croupier's rake, there arose the most abominable swearing and hideous curses, vengeance hit its mark as soon as the idea was born, and the glow of the lamp glinted off a knife blade as it was buried in a man's chest. Then the pit boss separated the two combatants by throwing a woman in their midst.

The door shook violently and suddenly jolted open. A man came in.

A clown's costume covered his large frame. His profuse, disheveled black hair hid the expression in his eyes, which must have been terrifying. His right fist was tightly clenched.

"There!" he said as he threw his money on the table, pausing to utter a convulsive laugh. "There's ten francs!"

Oh, pity that poor gambler of a clown, that man with such a lowly life, who doesn't love his children and beats his wife. Pity that poor wretch of a lowlife clown who beats his wife and doesn't love his children.

Misfortune has made him a clown. Hunger has so sharpened his appetite that it has driven him into a gambling den, and his upbringing has forced him into the gutter. His wife is ugly, a mass of red blotches and toothless. Oh, a mangy wife! And his children get on his nerves because they tell him "I'm hungry!" But that cry hurts him because he has nothing to give them.

Poor man! His wife returned a little while ago with the fiddle but without any bread.

By six o'clock in the evening it was cold and they were all famished. Should he just let his children die, his poor children with their hands folded in prayer as they groveled around his knees, smiling through their tears as they pleaded, "A piece of bread!"?

Kneeling in prayerful attitude before a clown! It's easy to see how misery can drag you down.

And then in his despair, he beat his wife, cursed his children, invoked Satan, and loaded his pistol, which then fell from his hand. With his head

---

3. Flaubert claimed that in prostitution "there is such a complex intersecting point of luxury, bitterness, the emptiness of human relations, muscular mania, and the clink of gold that your head swims and you learn so many things" (13:350). In *November*, the prostitute Marie explains to her lover that she has become an epitome of all the women her patrons have just left: "I'll be an entire harem" (11:655).

burning and everything spinning around him, he finally sold his gun. He found himself in a gambling den where his attention was painfully fixed on the dice bounding over the felt table . . . the dice that would determine his life and those of his wife and children.

And now, should he lose, he would become a robber or maybe a murderer. When they eventually lead him to the guillotine, mothers going by will point him out to their children as a hideous monster whose lone glance could bring evil. His head would roll on the damp planks, and the passing mob would continue to curse his body! There's a great criminal for you: a man who was hungry!

What about his wife? If she doesn't die of grief, she will die of misery or else will become as degraded as a prostitute, spat on by the crowd: "She's a murderer's wife, an ugly whore!"

As for her children, maybe they will be taken in by a charitable organization and raised with a holy fear of other men. Kept apart from society, they will be sheltered from the cold and given a piece of bread to ward off hunger . . . but who will dry the tears streaming down their faces in creases? Wealthy children passing by will occasionally throw them a shiny gold piece, with an ironic smile. When they grow up they will plot crimes against this society which cursed them for being children of the accursed! Those were the thoughts churning and violently twisting inside Pedrillo. His imagination made the ideas palpable to the point where he saw and felt them.

But he didn't even begin to understand why his family was unhappy. Paralyzed by his anger against heaven, he would have liked to destroy Creation and annihilated God.

His forced breathing occasionally turned into a sigh; he thought he would go mad. He clutched, caressed, and kissed the twenty francs in his pocket, but in a gesture of pride he threw them into the game.

The room rang with shouts. Whose money was that being raked in drifts across the table? It was Pedrillo's, who had just won ten thousand francs! He laughed and cried uncontrollably.

Happily enriched by that sum, the fool played them again. Ten thousand francs! Now a man of virtue, with his new wealth, can buy a suit, give his wife a dress, and give his children toys. With all that money in his pockets, as an "honest man" he can now throw his accumulated shame in the face of misery. Ten *thousand* francs! His enthusiasm began to wane, his laughter slackened, his expression became less animated, and his bearing sagged. Oh, now he had less than four hundred francs . . . he grips his chest . . . he still has fifty francs . . . he utters a brief cry of anguish . . . he is down to five francs . . . and now . . . nothing!

Misfortune did not seem to have crushed him, prompting the man next to him to ask why.

With the same laugh and accent he had shown when he bet his original ten francs, he said: "Look, just look!"

And he uncovered his bloody chest. His fingernails ran gory with human flesh.

FIVE

It was a dark and starry night, one of those frightening nights when you see ghosts and phantoms dancing on the moonlit wall of cemeteries. It was one of those nights when the wind makes you shiver with fright and your hair stands on end, when the plaintive howl of a prowling dog is heard around a hospital.

Pedrillo had left the gambling den. The cool night air soothed his forehead and made him soberly assess his situation. But little by little his imagination took over. As he walked along in a daze, everything around him took on gigantic proportions. Trees that were battered by the wind more than the preceding night seemed like hideous giants. All the houses were gambling dens. If he overheard the strains of an orchestra, it was music from hell. A woman who happened by became a courtesan, pivoting near a red curtain. The clink of glasses on a tray was an orgy. When snow soon began to fall, his clothes turned into a shroud.

He was plagued this way as he ran through the streets. Occasionally he stopped in the moonlight and sat down on a boundary stone to watch the clouds pass in front of the stars, taking on the most bizarre and grotesque shapes. There were grimacing monsters, then piles of gold, a woman with her children, a lion roaring in his cage, a corpse on the damp slab of a morgue. These were accompanied by the hiss of monsters and the clink of gold on gambling tables. He saw the tears of the woman and of her children, heard the lion's roar, and smelled the reeking cadaver, which was already turning green. He looked at it for a long time until it took another form. Fear made him begin to run without glancing backward until he reached his tent, panting, out of breath and visibly shaken.

Marguerite awaited him at the threshold.

She understood only too well how misfortune can tear at your soul, so she dared ask him nothing. She understood the sweat running down his face and the devouring anger in his eyes. Through the pallor of his brow she read his thoughts, and she knew why his teeth were chattering. They both stood speechless, without communicating their suffering or despair. Yet their eyes did all the talking, and shared sad and heart-rending thoughts.

When the children awoke the next morning, Pedrillo told them to pack, while he himself dismantled the tent and folded it up in their wagon. When the old nag was hitched up, the light cart began to move slowly over the paving stones. It had rained all night and now pelted the wagon's wooden frame. The regular rhythm of the rain, wind, and bridle eventually lulled the performers to sleep, jumbled together on their canvas sheeting and costumes.

With their eyes closed, their forms continued to flow with the bumps in the road, until Ernesto pulled up on the reins to allow the two wagons of a menagerie to pass. Peering through the misty window of one of the passing wagons, a showman recognized Pedrillo's head. Pedrillo was an old acquaintance of his. A crack of his whip woke the troupe, followed by a string of choice curses and swear words for his friend, concluding:

"The weather's thicker than soup today! The Eternal Father is emptying his bladder!"

An astonished Pedrillo raised his bluish face and stared at the man.

"What, is that you?" he said with astonishment as he opened his small window.

"Why, of course. Don't you recognize me, with your nose stuck up in the air? But judging from the looks of you, you don't seem too well off. I sure as hell bet you don't have an outfit like mine."

With that, he pointed to a cage and a young girl seated beside him.

At the first town they came to they pulled their wagons into a barn, and everyone got out to exchange greetings and hugs.

Pedrillo didn't hesitate to embrace Isabella, but Isambart held back.

"What's her name?" he asked his friend.

"Marguerite."

"She's sweet as a daisy,"[4] he added pursing his lips to place a delicate

---

4. Isambart makes two puns on Marguerite's various identities. Here he plays on the identity of her name and the marguerite. In the next section he will pun on the *mers* ("sea,"

kiss on her ruddy forehead, before continuing: "Well, will you just look at us together again! What do you say we throw in together and travel as one?"

"But . . . well, uh . . . if you want to."

Pedrillo realized that he couldn't let such a good chance slip, so he shook hands vigorously: "You've got a deal! You're a great guy!"

Isambart shuddered, but there was no getting out of it. He thought to himself, "Pedrillo's family will do their tightrope act while I show my animals. That way, everyone will profit. Afterward, he can take Isabella, for all I care."

They waited for the rain to pass, climbed aboard the wagons to head toward the nearest town where they would put on their show. When Isambart said this, he doffed his hat and added, "For the polite society there."

SIX

You have seen people like Isambart a hundred times. He's a short, stocky man with a ruddy complexion, a red nose, and gray eyes. He's the one in all acrobatic troupes who made you laugh as a child and weep as an adult.

With his red stockings, short trousers, slippers with large silver buckles, and the smooth gray hat of a Spanish grandee sporting a rooster feather, he's the one who always gets chalk dust in his face when he hits the rope and takes pratfalls, the one who falls from the top of the ladder when he climbs up to light the oil lamps. And with pretended dignity, he steps forward as the would-be stage manager with his hat tucked under his arm to announce the program.

Marguerite? You know her too. She collects the small coins that each spectator is supposed to pay as he leaves. She wears clogs, white hose

---

"mother") in the troupe. Both of these latter words derive from a common Sanskrit etymology (*ma*), which is also that of *matter*, as in "to be matter," the conclusion to the *Temptation of Saint Anthony*. Without making too much of Isambart's pun, one may observe that the symbolic association of woman and water has a long tradition in European folklore and recurs in many of Flaubert's writings. When we consider (a) Flaubert's respectful tenderness toward his mother, as well as his fear of offending her, (b) his repeated aphorisms ("Adolescents love other women because they more or less resemble the first one"; 8:26, 15:304), and then reconsider (c) his nightmares about his mother drowning and other visions of maternal drowning, we might wish to reread the epiphany of Maria, the love goddess who rose from the sea before his eyes, "this half-nude woman's body passed near me with its ocean scent" ("Diary of a Madman").

A Fragrance to Smell

tightly drawn around her calf, and an Indian kerchief on her head in the shape of a beret.

You have seen Pedrillo. He's a tall, slender man with a pocked face. He is the one who prances on the rope with a sprightly step and leaps without the aid of a balancing pole.

For two years now our combined troupes have gotten along well, and Pedrillo's family has had no reason to regret this association. Everyone's life was calm, happy, and carefree, dining on what they earned during the day. Only Marguerite was unhappy.

And yet her husband no longer beat her, and her children had bread. The reason was that twenty-year-old Isabella was pretty, with white teeth and beautiful eyes, black hair, a fine figure down to her delicate feet. On the other hand, the forty-year-old Marguerite was ugly, had gray eyes and red hair, and a large body with feet to match. One was a wife, the other a mistress; one issued complaints, whereas the other gave burning kisses. Isabella now had a boy as fine looking as she. He was Pedrillo's second love.

Isambart had looked on that scene philosophically and was satisfied to make bad jokes about it, saying that there was no need to fetch water to make soup, since the tent now had two *mers*. He repeated it to all comers, adding, "Aren't I a joker?" And he laughed for a half-hour.

What humiliated Marguerite all the more was this constant comparison with Isabellada,[5] which she had to undergo every minute of every day. Her every breath and gesture was derided. But what hurt the most was overhearing the nightly exchange of eager lovers' kisses or when she saw them wrap their arms lovingly around each other without a trace of shame or fear. Most intense was her brooding and bitter hatred toward Pedrillo's son.

One summer day all of the troupe except the children were dancing at a somewhat deserted crossroad. Isabellada and poor Marguerite were dancing.

Wearing a Chinese cap, Pedrillo the one-man band was thumping a kettledrum with his knee, playing an Arcadian flute, and beating on the

---

5. At this point in the story, Flaubert changed her name from "Isabella." In sec.9 the narrator informs us that Marguerite was annoyed by the euphony of the name "Isabellada." Flaubert paid special attention to names when he composed, pronouncing them aloud to savor their suggestive resonance.

large equipment trunk. In her white dress with a pink shawl around her neck, Isabellada whirled on the old Persian carpet.

Her bright eyes sparkled, her figure was trim and shapely, and her body dipped and rose like a swan's neck. Her dress was really just a light white petticoat with flowers embroidered around the hem, a filmy white underskirt that fell between her thighs onto pink hose, which clung voluptuously. Her waltzing and whirling were like the thoughts of love that cause a young poet's pulse to race. Her throat was whiter than the whitest marble. Her smooth and perfect bosom set off her head, eyes, and smile! When a woman is young and beautiful the aroma of her bosom is like a rose scent exuded from muslin. And in your dreams of love or on a sleepless night spent lamenting or cursing your mother, don't you cradle your hot, beating head on her breast? It's on her breast that you shuddered with love, as all the strands of your soul vibrated like a lyre plucked by a young girl's finger, stiffening with voluptuousness the way an athlete's muscles become gorged with blood. Didn't you plant lavish kisses between her breasts, and didn't you drink to the lees in the limpid pools of her eyes and cling to her smile? Weren't her delicate foot and well-turned leg in your bed in order to entwine yours?

And then the face surmounting her bosom, her woman's body, and the entire graceful, heavenly, and divine creation! There was something ineffable and unheard of, dreamy and pure in her look, in the movement of her eyes, in the rustle of her dress as it circled through the air, in the way her foot pivoted on the worn carpet. Spinning, jumping, and dancing like that, she was far less a woman than the idea of love itself. In the midst of that bitter and strange music, between Isambart and Marguerite, she was a diamond on a mud pile.

Isambart was still playing the insipid buffoon. He was wearing a three-quarters coat with blue and white stockings, and a half-red and half-black wig. He said a thousand funny and corny things under the guise of this grotesque outfit.

And what about Marguerite? She was suffering and crying in silence.

Yes, but suffering and crying aren't any concern of yours. I understand.

Well, each spectator who came to be charmed by the nymph glanced at the other woman who was standing nearby. What was she doing? Feats of strength.

Yes, that picture of youthful beauty stood in contrast to a ruddy woman with thick cheeks and badly shaped feet, whose clothes bespoke misfortune. She lumbered to the same music, and her feet touched the same carpet as Isabellada's. Yes, she was a clown just like Marguerite. But that woman leapt lightly, overwhelmed you with the fire in her eyes, and made your body tremble with a long, passionate shiver when her skirt feathered your thigh as she passed. She was paired off with that mass of severely contorted flesh who walked around with her head thrown all the way back to the level of her feet, with her long blue dress showing only her stomach where you would have expected to find her head, and her ugly breasts drooping heavily. Yes, and when she straightened up, her face was purple, her eyes were bloodshot, and her veins were swollen.

Despite this grotesque mélange, she had a certain coquettish and flirty manner about her. Her toothless mouth tried to smile but only grimaced. Her appearance was annoying and disturbing, but most irritating of all was the sharp squawk of her magpie voice.

"See for yourself how difficult that is, gents!"

The music played on while Isabellada danced, leapt, and whirled like thoughts of love in a young man's heart.

From time to time a clink was heard in the plate that lay on the rug.

"How generous," Isambart said as he removed his wig.

SEVEN

Perhaps you don't know about the four masks that one sees paraded around together in the theater district. There is a clown wearing an ox's head; he's a small, heavyset man with a rosy outlook who promises to "bust his hump for you," as he puts it. Next to him is a womanish figure in a black domino costume who shuffles around with her head bowed. Then comes a hardy Devil who is whispering to a pretty Swiss girl in a short petticoat, whose pride makes her disdain a mask.

A masked ball is truly special! I'm not talking about those boring ones at the Opera, which begin in January and die at Mardi Gras. I've never been to a masked ball at the Opera because, there again, you spy the banker's gold monocle beneath his mask, or the scented glove of the dandy beneath the monkey's paw. No, it was a stag dance for the common people in their rolled-up shirt sleeves, where for small change a guy can belly-laugh all night, where you find more intrigue than at the other kind, and where people get along fine. Running counter to the prejudices of the period, it was one of the balls that some big shots open to the public on Sundays when the weather is nice and if bread is not too expensive.

At such events you will find obscene dances that would make you blush, my poor little miss, and if you go there you just might not be a virgin the next day. And happy people have a good time—the men take theirs without shame and the fallen women have theirs without honor. You can be happy without virtues.

Didn't I say it was special? Didn't you imagine that you could be happy without virtues? Yet it's true. In that case, what good are they?

You have recognized these masqueraders: they are our clowns.

They used to go hungry and today they haunt the theaters, now that they are flush. Where did they get it? From Isabellada. Don't think for a minute that it comes from the animals of the grimacing Isambart, and they certainly don't owe their fortunes to Marguerite's antics. No, it comes from that beautiful child who is doing a wild, intoxicated Hungarian dance in the middle of the dance floor, to the applause, bouquets, and commotion of an entire audience stamping for joy.

Only one of the masqueraders sits sadly pensive on her bench. To her Isabellada's charm is a burden, and the cavernous applause brings tears to her eyes. There and elsewhere her mask hid the bitter jealousy, raging hatred, suffering, bloody injuries, and deep wounds. This is the black domino.

Isambart, on the other hand, danced clumsily, shouted and harangued the first person who happened by, and then sat down at the gambling table along with other clowns to cheat, belly-laugh, and make such a commotion as to draw a crowd around him. Then he started all over.

Marguerite had lost sight of him for quite a while when someone tapped on her shoulder. She turned around to see a clown with an ox's head.

She thought she identified him, but when he told her, "I recognize you, you masked beauty!" she realized from the sound of his voice that she had it all wrong. What could she possibly know for sure among all these people wearing the same costume! Animal heads were a popular costume at that time, and the mask disguised the voice. The clown said:

"I recognize you. Do you want me to tell you your name?"

"Yes."

"You're ugly Marguerite with her red splotches."

That shrill, tremulous voice, stupid bovine features with wide-flaring nostrils, and imbecilic laugh frightened Marguerite, who cowered and trembled in her corner.

"Hey," his voice continued through his perpetual smile, pointing at Isabellada, "just look at that girl leap. Do you recognize her? She's prettier than you. Do you see the charming way her breasts tremble, and did you notice her white hands and the way her outfit shows off her figure?"

Marguerite pawed the ground impatiently and bit her lips. The tears running down her black mask left two white traces.

Meanwhile, the ox head continued to laugh, flaring his nostrils. His lips parted with a somewhat ferocious stupidity, as his voice accelerated:

"After the last lights have gone out from tonight's ball and you rejoin your children in your tent, nearby you will hear the sound of amorous kisses."

"Oh, please, please don't!"

The ox head roared with laughter, and even began to throw his long sleeves around Marguerite's head and kiss her cheeks.

"That woman admired by everyone will belong to only one . . . your husband."

"Oh, please, Isambart, please stop!"

Sharing his laughter with those all around, he said: "Get a load of this one getting mad because I said her husband is sleeping with someone else."

He turned back to Marguerite and led her to a window enclosure where she couldn't get away from him. He could spit all his insults right in her face, rehearse all her sufferings for her, and remind her of her ugliness, especially compared with the young dancer, and finish off with the lavish details of Pedrillo's love for her. He could dramatize the heat of their passion in bed, their whisperings interspersed with sighs. And that's what he did.

"Tomorrow the gurglings of a happy baby will wake you . . . their baby!"

"Oh, Isambart, what have I done to hurt you?"

"Nothing, but still you disgust me. A while ago when I saw you running through your tricks, how I would like to have thrown mud on your blue dress, pulled your hair and pounded your breasts! Since you're better than most women, I know you've never done anything to me, except annoy me. I simply want to hurt you, that's all. For one thing, why do you cry all the time, mope around in that disgusting way of yours which irritates the life out of me? Always whining and complaining! Dammit, why don't you get the hell out of here? We feed you, but you're not the one who pays the bills. Your children? Well, the authorities will take good care of them. If I were you, I'd at least start to look alive. But then you're just too ugly! Oh brother, when I see your cat eyes through the holes of your mask, I think of your ugly face!"

He dropped his anger and left, howling with laughter.

An exhausted Isabellada asked Pedrillo if she could go. Leaving the dance, she leaned her head softly against his shoulder so as to reveal her cleavage and expose the heady scent of her back.

The applause rang out behind her.

EIGHT

Pedrillo left Marguerite alone and headed toward the menagerie. Isambart left the two of them alone before falling into an undisturbed sleep until one o'clock the next afternoon.

The black domino took off her stifling mask and sat down with her elbow propped on the table. She was rapt by the candle flame where, in her mind's eye, she relived the ball. Isambart's words came back to her, along with the laughter bursting from under his mask.

The memory of Isabellada's dancing hurt her the most. The other one got all the applause, her son got Pedrillo's love, whereas *she* was hooted. The ox head with its flared nostrils and wild laugh kept bursting into her imagination, for its stupid expression continued to frighten her.

I don't know whether you have studied all those grotesque faces as I have, but their creator must be an atheist or a misanthrope to have wedded the appearance of man and animal on the same sketch pad.

Isambart's groundless hatred made a vivid impression on her. His hatred was directed at her clumsy gait, red hair, and her love for her children. Her suffering was increased by that shameful remedy he had suggested for her pain, and by the callous insult of making her feel that she was a burden they sheltered out of pity. She had prayed only for Pedrillo as a loving husband who would understand her feelings and all the poetry sung by a clown's heart, by a woman who is cursed and derided by society.

When a proper lady wearing a hat passed by, Marguerite sighed, "Why can't I be like her?"

Then envy dug into her heart. When she saw Isabellada dance, she asked the heavens why nature had not made her that way, and she hated her husband's mistress. At those moments when she was cold and saw Pedrillo living happily and well, she became spiteful and no longer believed in God.

She was poor again! She sought love from a society that laughed in her face. As for humanity, she was directed to the hospital for the poor. And as for charity, well, Marguerite is a clown, and there's none of it for clowns, child abductors, or those who haunt back streets for a living!

Very well then, she vowed hatred and jealousy for that society which had denied her food, love, and sympathy. She was irreverent to the unresponsive God whom she had implored so many times, kneeling on paving stones with tears in her eyes. She scorned nature for having mistreated her.

Whenever she saw rich people who were happy, respected, and well cared for, she wished the greatest calamities on them. She laughed at the longing prayers of the poor and at their religious trinkets, which prompted her to spit on the thresholds of churches. When she saw public admiration for an elegant lady with a sweet smile, caressing eyes, jet black hair, and alabaster neck, she would say:

"What would it take to make her more like me? Different colored hair, smaller eyes, plus a less attractive shape, and she would be like Marguerite! If my husband hadn't loved her, had despised and beaten her, she would be disgustingly ugly like Marguerite!"

That's what was going on in her mind until she became drowsy. She fell asleep in the waning candlelight, propping her elbow on the table to support her chin.

NINE

The next morning she was wakened by the voice of Ernesto arguing with Isabellada. She eavesdropped.

"Why did you take it from me? Wasn't it mine? I want it back!"

Marguerite dressed quickly, hid behind the animal wagon, and watched in silence. She saw Isambart's daughter greedily holding a blanket belonging to one of Marguerite's sons.

She had plenty of reasons to hate that woman, without adding the apparent theft of the blanket. When she couldn't stand the sight any more, Marguerite leapt on her in one bound and yanked away the crib.

"*You* again, Isabellada!"

She pronounced the name in the harshest way she could because its euphony annoyed her. She then warmed to the occasion.

"Isn't it *enough* that you wedged yourself into our group in order to dominate and play the part of the queen? Aren't you satisfied to steal my husband from my bed and then install him in yours, you daughter of Satan? And to insult me with the beauty you pander to the first comer? Look: isn't that just about enough? As if it weren't enough for the rest of us to be civilization's outcasts without you happening along to rip the bandages from our festering wounds! Watch out, because that blood'll be on your head! And here all of those typical beauties get all the bouquets, applause, and money. Scorn, shame, and misery is what *we* get. Come on, Pedrillo, do I have it exactly right or not?"

"What's going on, Isabellada?"

"Her son wanted to take the blanket away from mine, and Marguerite claims it's hers."

"Marguerite, what do you have to say for yourself?"

"She's lying, Pedrillo! Don't listen to her!"

"No, *you're* the liar, Marguerite."

And he shoved her roughly into the tent. Inside, she tore at her hair and clothes, rolled around so much in the dirt that she bloodied her face. Then she got up. You might as well empty your glass to the bitter dregs!

"All right, Isabellada, give us an encore! Dance even better! Go on, Pedrillo, love her even more! And I'll hate you all the more."

Suddenly, she fell to her knees before Pedrillo, who had entered the tent at that moment.

"What are you doing here?"

"To get some money."

"Who for?"

"For her."

"Oh sure, always for *her*! Okay, Pedrillo, do you feel that strongly about her?"

"Yes."

"Oh, dear! Get her, her name, and her beauty out of here! I beg you to love me. What do I have to do to please you? Oh, please don't talk to me any more!"

At his feet, contorted by tears of anguish, was that woman with the bloody face and torn clothes, who touched his sympathies for just a moment.

"What's going on with you, sweetie?"

"Let's drop it for now, Pedrillo, but you can mark my words on this:

some day when her insults finally get me down . . . well, you know the way a Numidian lion roars in his cage and how eagerly he devours the meat they throw him in the evening? Well, one day I'm going to ask you for the same courtesy."

"What's the matter with you, Marguerite, come on back!"

"What's the matter with me? I'm jealous! I know, you don't know what that's like, do you? What's wrong with me? Maybe I'm crazy. All I know is that I hate her and love you!"

TEN

Rays from the boiling sun glance off the dusty road and sear the leaves of apple trees along the way. On those hot June days it's nice to let yourself be rocked by the movement of the carriage and surrender yourself to some poetic daydream, while your clothes become covered with dust from the breeze that blows a small cloud through the cracks of the closed blue fanlight curtains.[6]

That's true, but not everyone rides in a carriage, and our troupers were traveling in their light cart. Marguerite and Pedrillo were walking and conversing together. The silence of the countryside was broken only by the sound of their voices, by horses' hooves in the dust, and by a bee buzzing around the caged lion, who slept fitfully. Thoughts of the African sun and of the den he left so far behind in another realm filled his dreams too. He thought of the lioness lying behind him under the shade of a palm tree in his vast desert, and in his melancholy he gnawed the end of his claws. Let's leave him with his thought of lost happiness and his dreams of brutal joy; let's return to Marguerite's suffering.

"So, you love her," she snapped.

"Well, yes. Why are you always asking, Marguerite?"

"What do you like about her?"

"Everything. You're getting on my nerves, so what do you want?"

"Death!"

---

6. This surrender to the lull of poetic daydreams is shared by the narrator describing Djalioh in "Whatever You Want" ("It's a great feeling to surrender yourself to . . . the flow of revery that takes possession of your soul"; 11:324); by Mazza in "Passion and Virtue" (". . . to give herself completely over to a torrent . . . that somnolence when you feel yourself sliding into sleep . . . she was lulled by the motion of the carriage"; 11:339, 344); and by Charles Bovary ("he let himself be rocked by the gentle trot of his horse . . . he soon entered into a sort of drowsy state in which his recent sensations mingled with memories"; 1:61).

"Oh, you're crazy!"

"Maybe. You're too mean for me to ask you for love or sympathy, but I do want to know the source of your love and then seek my death."

"I don't know where it comes from," Pedrillo shot back angrily. "As for death, please, Marguerite: you know how a man can have fits of anger."

Marguerite laughed ironically: "And women can have fits of jealous hatred. I asked you why you love Isabellada. All right, now I'm going to explain my hatred for her and for you."

"Watch out, Marguerite!"

"No, here it is: she's beautiful and my ugliness makes me hate beauties; you love her and I hate all those you love; you're happy and I hate happy people; you're rich and I hate the rich. I'm unhappy, miserable, and unloved. Why did you throw me aside shamefully, Pedrillo? Oh, yes, it's because you were afraid of public ridicule. Well, then I hate you because I love whatever the polite world despises. I love clowns, prostitutes, and the dregs of society. And I hate your Isabellada. I'd crush her underfoot if I could and happily trample her body, breasts, head, and face. I'd eagerly devour her!"

Pedrillo flinched angrily.

"Be careful, Marguerite! The lion is pacing in his cage. Please, just drop it without another word."

"You must have been shamelessly rotten to scorn, deride, and slander me that way, to drag poor Marguerite through the mud when she loved you so. It was out of pure love that I threw myself into your arms, but you kicked me aside like a mangy dog who tries to lick his master's boot."

"Oh, Marguerite, Marguerite! You're going to play some awful trick on me!"

"And what's more, that woman's husband was pitiless toward her children. God watched over them to keep them from starving to death. The wild boar sometimes eats its own young, but it doesn't torture them with hunger. Well, okay, go ahead and throw me to that lion. I won't ask for your help or forgiveness, because if you have completed my misery I'll poison you with curses, insults, and accusations. Listen here, I have more to say and I repeat that I hate Isabellada. Yes, I hate her and would love to get my hands on her to crush her, rip her with my fingernails, slake my thirst with her blood and then drink deeply again!"

The lion roared in his cage, slapped his tail on the bars, stirred his mane, and opened his maw in anxious anticipation of the woman in Pedrillo's arms. He opened the cage door and threw her in.

The lion eagerly pounced on her, when suddenly Isambart came on the scene to learn the cause of the roars and plucked Marguerite away. Her chest was ripped and her hands showed claw marks.

ELEVEN

Who is that woman limping out of the hospital, with her large frame, red hair, and stupid look? Her head is covered by a dirty lace cap decorated with flowers, her clothes are torn, and her overall appearance cries out misery. By her eerie smile and halting speech, you can clearly tell she is a madwoman who moves about in fits and starts. Her hands and face are scarred. You could obviously tell it was Marguerite. Yes, it was she.

She wandered aimlessly for two days, not knowing where to turn, with nothing to eat, and coming away with nothing but the mud thrown on her by passersby. The street urchins who pursued her caused her to confront them with a grimace: "You must have no shame or feelings!" Her torn clothes and flowered cap provoked laughter, and she was beset by the hoots and jeers of the children.

Tired, harassed, and unable to continue, she nearly fainted on the grassy strip along a boulevard. Suddenly, she raised her head, looked all around her in a daze, and thundered:

"Where are my children? Augustus! Ernesto! Garofa!"

A small cab passed by. An elegant lady was comfortably ensconced in it. Her white cashmere wrap cascaded behind her, down to the footman's perch, and the black and white feathers of her hat bobbed gracefully. Her sweet smile, her slim figure, her diamonds, accessories, cashmere, and gold necklace all lent her the appearance of contentment.

Marguerite ran toward her, grabbed the wheel spokes, and shook with anger:

"I've had about enough squalid insults, without having you come along to rip the bandages from our wounds, Isabellada! Come on, I easily recognize you with your continual courtesan's preening and the way you flaunt your figure."

She was not mistaken. One day when Isabellada was dancing in the square, an aristocrat happened to see her, and since then she has been his consort.

The gentleman in the two-seater asked, "Who is that woman?"

"I don't know. Probably a madwoman."

"Oh, you think I'm mad? Perhaps."

"Drive her away, John."

The servant struck her in the face with his whip, but still she clung to the spokes.

"No, I won't go away! Wait, hear me out: if you crowned me with misery, I'll poison you with accusations and outrageous insults!"

The pursuing crowd exclaimed, "The madwoman, the madwoman!"

She stopped, struck by a sudden thought, and laughed out loud: "Death!"

And she scurried toward the Seine.

TWELVE

The woman's corpse that had just been fished out of the water was on display in the morgue. Her head was covered by the lace cap with its dirty flowers. You could see her emaciated limbs through her torn clothes. A few flies buzzed around to lick the coagulated blood at the corner of her gaping mouth. Her swollen arms had turned blue and began to show small black patches. The last rays of the setting sun filtered through the window bars and settled on her half-shut eyes to give them a strange cast.

As it lay on the damp slab, that swollen, greenish body was a hideous mass of scars—the wretched claw marks. The sickening smell rising from the ragged body repulsed those who happened on it but drew the interest of medical students. After one of them had silently scrutinized her for a while, he said:

"Well what do you know? She was in the hospital just the other day."

He was a true medical student in his threadbare, frayed green smock, red cap, and clay pipe, in which he smoked fine-cut Maryland tobacco.

"What do you say we buy her?"

"For what?"

A cab driver's voice resounded, "Watch out there!"

It was the same cab that had passed the other day, taking the young lady to the Opera.

The disciples of Aesculapius quickly moved aside, which made the smoker drop his pipe.

Giving it a kick, he exclaimed, "For the love of God, that's the third one I have broken today!"

MORAL

In his preface, that wise and judicious Gascon, Michel de Montaigne, wrote: "This is a book of good faith. I give these views not as true but as mine."[7]

I'd have to say that these pages were also written in good faith, and some were even composed in a mood of fiery enthusiasm. I wanted to rail against the prejudice of the times and perhaps draw fire for having been so bold.

As far as my title is concerned, "A Fragrance to Smell," I meant to imply that Marguerite was that fragrance. I could have added "a flower to see," because beauty was everything to Isabellada.

Now, lest the Holy Apostolic Roman Catholic Church strike me with a thunderbolt because of my odd subtitle, "a philosophical, moral, or immoral tale (just as you wish)," I'll explain myself when someone gives me a definition for separating morality from immorality.

WHATEVER YOU WANT

You may not know what a pleasure it is to write! Oh, writing! To write is to take full possession of the world, of its prejudices and virtues, and reduce it to a book. You feel the birth and growth of your idea, before it stands apart on its pedestal where it remains forever.

I've just finished this strange, bizarre, and incomprehensible book.[8] I wrote the first chapter in a day. Then I put my writing aside for a month,

---

7. Like Cabanis and Bichat (see note 2 to "Whatever You Want," below), Flaubert tends to cite Montaigne and Rabelais in tandem (cf. the end of "Rage and Impotence" and 12:346). His citation from Montaigne is an offhand recollection of the first sentence in the *Essais*, but the second sentence has no precise equivalent anywhere in Montaigne's writing. Even more telling than his reading of Byron is Flaubert's assertion that his initiation to Rabelais and then Montaigne marked the formal beginnings of his taste for grotesque laughter at the world and of his skepticism. The claim of some critics that Flaubert's *moralité* was influenced by Balzacian "realism" appears to invite a symbolic or allegorical reading. But the world of Flaubert's text is so artfully contrived that it requires the reader's participation to refashion or complete the story along allegorical lines. "Whatever you want" is a theme of common occurrence in Flaubert's early writing, as in the mature novels; see the subtitle of "A Fragrance to Smell" and note 1 to "Whatever You Want," below; cf. Rabelais's Abbey of Thélème in *Gargantua*. For the allusion to Rabelais in the next paragraph, see *Pantagruel*, "Prologue." (In "Whatever You Want," sec.2, I have bracketed the Rabelais attribution within the text.)

8. *Incompréhensible:* in a letter of Dec.16, 1838, he refers similarly to "Smarh" as being *inintelligible* (12:350).

after which I wrote five chapters in one week, and finished it in two days.

I won't analyze its philosophy. It is sad, bitter, dark and skeptical . . . hunt for it.

Now I'm tired and harried. I collapse on my chair in numbing fatigue, without enough strength to thank you if you have read me, or to deter you if you aren't familiar with the title of my original production.

Rage & Impotence

An Unwholesome Story for Sensitive Nerves and Devout Souls

God is only a word dreamed up to explain the world
—(Alphonse de Lamartine)[1]

Everything was calm and quiet in the town of Mussen. Of all the lights, which had gone out one after the other, only one continued to shine through the windows of Dr. Ohmlin, the physician for the area.

The little church clock had just struck midnight, rain was falling in torrents, and snow from the heights of Mount Pilatus was swirling wildly, driven by gusts from the avalanche. Hail beat down on the rooftops.

His solitary light lit a low-ceilinged room where a woman of some sixty years was seated with her knitting. She was stooped and covered with wrinkles. Fatigue often overcame her will power, forcing her to close her eyes and bow her head. If an unusually furious air current made the shutters creak, if the violence of the wind picked up, she would wake with a start from her drowsiness, turn her small hollow eyes toward the candle whose long wick still shed some light around her, shiver, draw her chair closer to the fireplace, and then cross herself. She was one of those kindly,

---

1. This epigraph from Lamartine is taken from a poem in the *Harmonies*, "Le Tombeau d'une mère" (A mother's tomb), line 14, which stems from the same ideas as those running through "Rage and Impotence" and, indeed, all of Flaubert's writing: "Rien n'est vrai, rien n'est faux; tout est songe et mensonge! / Illusion du coeur qu'un vain espoir prolonge" (Nothing is true, nothing is false; it's all a dream and a lie! / The heart's illusion, which false hope won't let die).

honest housemaids who serve their masters from birth to death, take care of children, and raise them. She had witnessed Dr. Ohmlin's birth, had been his wet nurse, and later became his servant. Thus, she trembled for her poor master, who had left that morning to go into the mountains and hadn't returned yet. She did not dare resume her work but remained seated near the foyer with her arms folded, her feet on the hearth, and her head cupped in her hands. She was terrified by the sound of the wind blowing through the keyhole and howling in the mountains. In her thoughtful sadness, she tried to recall one of those terrible and bloody legends they used to tell in her home when she was young. That was when the whole family gathered around the chimney to delight in a tale of murder or a ghost story set in the snow, torrents, and glaciers of the mountains on a very dark and cold winter night.

Her imagination wandered among these childhood memories. In that way, old Bertha went back over the uniformity of her entire life, which had been spent in a monotonous town but was nevertheless passionate, anguished, and painful within its narrow ambit.

But from a nearby square she soon heard the sinister and mournful barking of a dog and the irregular clop of a mule's hooves echoing off the pavement. She shuddered and got up from her chair, exclaiming, "It's him!" Then she ran toward the door and opened it. After a few moments a man entered the room. He was wrapped in a brown coat covered with snow, and water beaded on his clothes. He exhorted:

"Fire, Bertha, build a fire! I'm dying of cold!"

The old woman left and returned in a few minutes, carrying wood chips and kindling, which she lit with whichever whitened embers still gave off heat from the fireplace. As soon as a glowing fire began to crackle and light the room, Dr. Ohmlin took off his coat, revealing a man of ordinary height, somewhat slight but with a healthy complexion. His cheeks were hollow and pale, and when he removed his hat you could see his large white head and sparse black hair. His serious and reserved demeanor, accentuated by the sad, somber cast of his black beard, was tempered by the friendly smile that graced his lips.

He sat down, put his feet up on the andirons, and petted one of his beautiful Alpine dogs lying next to him. The animal sadly eyed its master and licked his wet hands, which were red from the cold. Bertha drew closer and asked:

"Well, how are you feeling? How are your teeth?"

"Bad, very bad! This cold mountain air makes me suffer. I've been kept awake four nights in a row. And I won't get any sleep tonight. Come here, Fox."[2]

That was the name of his favorite dog, which was stretched out at the doctor's feet. Fox began to make that unusual throaty noise Bertha had heard when he arrived with his master.

"Quiet, Fox, hush up!"

The poor animal began to whine like someone who is suffering or weeping.

"Be quiet, Fox, hush!" Bertha continued, shoving him aside with her foot.

"Why do you want him to be quiet? Can't you see he's in a bad mood because he's simply tired and hungry?" Dr. Ohmlin interrupted.

"Here boy!" Bertha said, throwing him a piece of bread she found in the cupboard next to the fireplace.

Fox looked at the bread with his dull, watery eyes and sadly turned his beautiful black head toward his master.

"You poor fellow," he said, "what's the matter with you?"

"That's a sign of disaster. May God and Saint Maurice keep us from it," she said.[3]

"You crazy old woman, he's sick."

"Are you hungry? Can I get you something?"

"Me? Oh, nothing. I'm going to sleep if I can. But if I can't, I have some sleeping pills I can try. Good night, Bertha. Put out the fire and sleep well, old girl. As for you, Fox, go to your kennel!"

He opened the door onto the courtyard. Fox refused to go and lay flat on his stomach, crawling over to the feet of Dr. Ohmlin, who arose im-

---

2. Fox is also the putative name of the dog in the first *Sentimental Education* (chap.26), where it is called "an illusion." Labeled elsewhere "a sign of disaster" (10:434; 11:633), intrusions of portentous dogs in Flaubert have inspired much critical commentary. They appear to indicate a category of creatures that the reader is presumed to recognize; in "A Fragrance to Smell" the dog belongs to "one of *those* nights . . . when the plaintive howl of a prowling dog is heard around a hospital," and in *Salammbô* the party in search of a guiding "human star" is seized by its own impotence, "like one of *those* dogs who bay at the moon" (2:174; emphasis added); cf. "Whatever You Want," sec.5.

3. Saint Maurice (1114–91) was revered in his native Carnoët (Brittany) for the many miracles he performed to forestall impending disasters.

patiently and quickly went up to his bedroom. He got in bed shivering with fever, swallowed his opium pill, and surrendered himself to heavenly dreams.

As for Bertha, she slept soundly and yet was awakened from time to time by the plaintive whining of poor Fox, who had stayed on the staircase. The snow let up, the sky cleared, and the moon began to peek from behind the summit of Mount Pilatus.

Around nine o'clock the next morning, old Bertha awoke, said her prayers, and went downstairs. She was surprised to see that Dr. Ohmlin's door was still shut:

"That poor man is sure having a good sleep. He'll probably be coming out soon." But soon Dr. Bernardo arrived, another doctor from the area, who asked:

"Where is he?"

"Up in his room, I think. Why don't you go see if he's still sleeping?"

He went up and entered without hesitation, bellowing, "Come on! Get up, it's late!"

Ohmlin didn't answer. His head was leaning out over the bed and his arms were dangling. Bernardo went over and gave him a good shake.

"Damn! He's sleeping like a log!"

But the body gave way with the impact of his hands and fell back in bed like a corpse. Bernardo went pale and took the cold hands. He bent over and found no breathing. He felt the chest, but there was no heartbeat! Stunned, he opened the eyelids, but the eyes just stared! He saw only the half-open eyes with their dull look of death.

Bernardo ran out of the doctor's room. Bertha asked him what was wrong, but the only signs were Bernardo's ashen look and white lips. A few hours later, a dozen sad doctors calmly surrounded their colleague's bed. The only sound that passed between their lips was "He's dead!"

Each one drew near the inanimate body, turned it in every direction, then drew back in horror and disgust, repeating, "He's dead!"

Only one of them dared to believe that he was just sleeping. But without any vital signs, he couldn't justify his conjecture and finally sided with the other doctors.

It was one of those sad and rainy winter days. While a watery mist swirled about, snow turned the village streets white. The whole town was sad that day! Its paternal benefactor was dead! The houses were closed up, people didn't speak, children no longer laughed in the public square, and people were deeply touched and wept.

The modest funeral procession headed toward the cemetery, resplendent despite all its grief. A few men in black carried the coffin, which was turning white from the falling snow, while blond-haired children followed behind in silent astonishment. The priests chanted in low voices, muffled by tears.

A friend followed the coffin all the way to the burial plot, his deep sadness more pronounced and pointed than that of anyone else. Was it a woman, a child, a mistress, or an acquaintance? No, it was a dog, poor old Fox, who walked with his head lowered, following his master with sad whining and tears as large as those of any man.

The cemetery was halfway up a hill, where the road was slippery and muddy. All you could hear were footsteps of the priests and the men whose hobnail boots stuck in the mud, and then the hymn for the dead, the falling snow, rain sloshing in the ruts, and the wind flapping the pall covering the coffin.

Finally, after some more dirt was dug out, the coffin was lowered to the accompaniment of a few prayers for eternity, the gravediggers threw in several spadefuls of dirt which resounded on the oaken coffin, giving it a hollow and empty sound. The group broke up, the iron grill creaked in its hinges, and the cemetery returned to its calm silence.

Of all the friends in the procession, only Fox remained. Lying on the ground, he sadly watched the swaying lamps disappear into the fog, and the long black outfits slowly descending like shadows into the misty valley.

A beautiful moonlit night quickly set in, descending on the tombs like doubt assailing a dying man.

Dr. Ohmlin was still slumbering a heavy, drugged sleep. He was dreaming splendid visions of voluptuous love and enchantment. He was dreaming of the Orient under its blazing sun and blue sky, with its gilded minarets and stone pagodas! The Orient, with its erotic poetry, redolent of incense! Perfumes, emeralds, flowers, and Oriental gardens with golden apples! The Orient, with its genii and caravans crossing sandy wastes! The Orient, with the distinctive delight of its harems! Like a madman he dreamed of the white wings of angels singing hymns from the Koran for the ears of the Prophet. He dreamed of the lips of pure, roseate women, of large black eyes with love for him alone. He dreamed of the distinctive brown and olive tones of the women of Asia, that satiny flesh which poets caress so often in their nocturnal dreams! He dreamed about all of that! But a somber, pitiless awakening would bring him back to reality!

He dreamed of funereal love, but dreams crumble and the tomb abides.

He opened his eyes, felt himself wrapped in long folds, and freed himself from them. With trembling hands he felt the wood all around him, above his head, at his sides, everywhere! He felt himself and realized he was naked. Oh, what a horrible dream, a hellish nightmare! Far from any thoughts about eternity, *he* wanted to cling to life! But eternity was the partner embracing him in his wedding bed and laughing behind his back with a devil's grimace.

He was gripped with fear of this hideous skeleton that seemed to rub its bones on his chest. Oh, no! That was impossible!

He wanted to go back to sleep and forget all that, to forget about reality, to erase from his thoughts that mass of lead weighing on his head, and to be lulled by other dreams. No, he had dreamed too much! Were there other dreams now? Dream about eternity, if you wish. The Orient? All right, now dream about the Orient in the tomb, in voluptuous thought and golden dreams! No, no! These are hellish dreams and agony that tears out your hair, writhes in despair, invokes Satan and curses God!

Yet his initial terror was calm and quiet, a strange and stupid astonishment—an idiot's stupor. As he felt all around him, he tried to deceive himself.

"Oh, no, no! To die that way of despair and hunger in a tomb would be terrible! I must be going crazy or I'm dreaming! This wood must be from my bed. And this wrapping material? My bed covers . . . but it's a hell, a tomb, a shroud!" And he uttered a bitter laugh that would have resounded if it hadn't burst forth in a tomb.

Then he became cold. The dampness from the tomb felt wet on his bare skin. He was trembling, his teeth were chattering, and fever was flowing through his veins. Something pricked his finger, but when he raised it to examine it, he could see nothing in the thick darkness! He had snagged his finger on a coffin nail and smelled blood on his finger.

"To *die* this way, pitilessly and hopelessly! Oh, no! I'll get out of this hell and leave this tomb. That's unheard of; it'll drive me mad before I die of despair . . . yes, I'm going to die . . . to *die*! Never again to witness life on earth or see nature, fields, the sky, the mountains, to leave all that behind me forever!" And he writhed in his tomb like a snake clutched by a tiger's claws.

He wept with rage, pulled out his hair, and cried out for life, since he was brimming with strength and health. He covered his eyes in his tomb and wept unrestrained tears. In his anger, he beat continually on the lid of his coffin, ripped his shroud with his nails, and tore it apart with his teeth. He needed to smash something and destroy it with his hands because he felt himself so mercilessly crushed by the hand of fate. Then his despair subsided; he lay back on his plank, closed his eyes, and thought of God.

A ray of hope began to shine in his tomb, and his thoughts once again turned to the doubtful state of his soul. He believed in the God whom he had cursed a while ago, and he longed for the life about which he had earlier despaired.

He cocked his ear to listen for a faint, imperceptible sound of scratching in the dirt above his head. The more he listened, the louder the sound got. He smiled with happiness and joined his hands in a prayer to God: "Oh, thank you, thank you! You have given me back my life! Are you really returning it to me? So I won't die after all in this cold and hideous tomb? I'll die, but only much later, years from now! I'm going to live, *my* life with all its pleasures and delight," and he wept for joy, cursing his worldly skepticism and impious prejudices: "Thank you, God, for returning all of that!"

He distinctly heard men's feet over his head. Oh, they were going to free him for certain! Some charitable soul must have taken pity on his misfortune. They must have suspected that a man and not a corpse lay in this tomb, and they were simply coming to disinter him. There was no question about it. Oh, bless that man who was going to give him life, bless him! His heart beat wildly and he laughed joyously. Had he been able to, he would have jumped for joy.

The steps came closer, then drew back. Everything became calm again. It was the gravedigger who had come looking for the pickaxe he had forgotten. He was afraid it might rust in the rain.

A fine young fellow, that gravedigger who smoked a small German pipe, wore a straw mountaineer's hat, and liked Rhine wines. He had a charitable soul, for when he saw a dirty, mud-covered dog playing around by digging in holy ground, he just pushed it away with his foot instead of killing it, as others would have done in the same situation.

Dr. Ohmlin listened for a very long time, but nothing! He listened again: not a sound! Oh, that was the end! He was going to die! To die the cruel and horrible death he had anticipated earlier, the one that happens every minute, kills you slowly, and savors its meal! When would death come? When will this agonizing suffering end, the death rattle that goes on for centuries? And he began to laugh out of pity for his former beliefs. Since heaven didn't want to save him, he called on hell. Hell came to his aid, giving him atheism, despair, and blasphemy.

At first he doubted the existence of God, and then denied it before mocking and insulting it. With a forced laugh, he said to himself, "Bah! Where is he, that creator of misery! Where is he? If he exists, let him come and deliver me! . . . I denounce you as a word invented by the fortunate! I denounce you for being only a fatal and stupid power, like an incinerating lightning bolt."

And he ripped out his hair and shredded his face with his nails. "Do you think I'm going to pray for you at the hour of my death? I'm too proud and too wretched for that. I won't implore you, because I abhor you! Eternity? I deny it! Your paradise? An illusion! Your hell? I'll dare it! Eternity? A death's head that will be found right here in a few months."

Laughter was written on his face and tears stifled his voice. "Me, bless the hand that strikes me? To kiss your torturer! Oh, if you can assume human form, come join me in the tomb so I can take you straight to the eternity that will devour you one day and give you over to the emptiness that gives you your name! Come! Come on, so that I can smash you, crush you between me and my tomb, and eat your flesh! Make yourself flesh so that I can laugh at you and tear you apart!"

His teeth chattered like those of the Devil when Christ defeated him. In his fury, he jerked and writhed in his tomb, cursing God with screams in his mouth and despair in his soul. "Where are you? God in heaven, come to me if you exist! Why don't you deliver me? If you exist, why have you made me so unhappy? What pleasure do you get from seeing me suffer? If I didn't believe in you, it was because I was miserable. I'll love you if you give me back my life . . . if that doesn't depend on you, well, do it because you are all-powerful. Do it, return my faith to me! . . . Why don't you want me to believe in you? You see me suffering and crying. Shorten my suffering and dry my tears."

Then he stopped, fearful of his blasphemy and trembling with fright.

What was he afraid of? The earth could disappear, revolutions could shake the dust from the globe, and what did it matter to him? In his warm, humid tomb with its cadaverous odor, he would still have fetid air to breath, enough even for a few minutes.

But he was afraid of the eternity he was braving, dreaded that word he laughingly mocked as he lay there hunched up with his face toward heaven, which for him was reduced to a coffin lid. He still feared for his fate and was certain of absolutely nothing.

Don't believe those people who call themselves atheists. They are only skeptical, and that's because of their vanity. When your doubt is born from suffering, you want to do away with all probabilities and have reality plain and simple. But doubt increases and eats at your soul.

All he heard was the barking of his dog, who was crying over his death and intuiting his misfortune. "My poor friend," he said, shedding his only tear out of a comforting tenderness.

He was tired, his arms were injured, and he hungered for something to eat. Finally, he turned over on his back and curled into a ball in an effort to smash his coffin, crying out furiously, "I'll get out of here in spite of you. I'll live despite your will!" And turning over on his stomach, he tried with successive jolts to bend the iron-hard plank that covered him. He managed to break it with one final effort of rage and despair.

Seeing the tomb open slightly, or rather feeling his arched back crack open the lid, he gave out a triumphant laugh and felt the onset of freedom. But six feet of dirt blocked him and would crush him if he made the slightest movement. The dirt, which had been supported by the lid, wouldn't stay in its original position. The slightest change in the position of the covering plank would make it fall.

Dr. Ohmlin went pale and nearly fainted when he realized this. He remained still, not daring to make the slightest motion. Finally, he decided to try one final effort that would kill or save him. The freshly moved dirt offered little resistance, so he tried to raise up quickly and smash through with his head. Despair drove him mad. He jerked upward but the lid came falling down.

The most patient people get bored with everything.[4] That proverb is old

---

4. Cf. Jean de La Bruyère, *Les Caractères*, "On Strong Minds," no.32, in *Oeuvres de La Bruyère* (Paris: Hachette, 1865), 2:249–50; and La Rochefoucauld, *Oeuvres complètes* (Paris: Gallimard, 1950), pp.296 (no.352), 327 (no.532), and 330 (no.555).

but true, because our worthy gravedigger, tired of the barking of the melancholy dog we mentioned, decided to find out what interested him so much. He dug into the dirt hoping to find something, maybe buried treasure. Who knows? He was greatly astonished to see the coffin lid broken.

"What the devil! That's really strange! Something is going on in there."

He lifted the lid. This is what he saw and what he told about later when he tried to build himself up.

"The corpse had turned over on its stomach, its winding sheet was all torn, and its head and arm were under its chest. When I turned it over with my shovel, I noticed that its left hand was clutching a bunch of hair and that it had eaten its forearm. A grimace covered its face, which frightened me with good reason. Its wide-open eyes were bulging out of its head, the nerves in its neck were stiff and stretched, and its white teeth shone like ivory because the open lips were turned up at the corners of its mouth, showing its gums as though he had died laughing."[5]

As for Fox, he left the cemetery, ran up into the mountains, and one day was killed by a hunter who hadn't bagged anything and fired off a shot just for something to do.

And Bertha no longer sat at her place by the hearth, and from that point on the children in the village referred to her as "Mad Bertha." When the moon shone bright, the wind howled in the mountains, and snow covered the ground, people could see an old woman running through the cemetery in tears. One day she threw herself into the river at the foot of the hill where cypresses rise above the tombstones.

A CYNICAL MORAL TO INDICATE THE CONDUCT ONE SHOULD TAKE AT HIS FINAL HOUR

Michel de Montaigne, a decent, upright, and easygoing fellow, often wondered "What do I really know?" in his writings. And the happy skeptic Master François Rabelais, doctor of medicine, the priest of Meudon from Chinon in Touraine, who knew how to live it up, help himself to good wine, and rub the ladies the wrong way, even more often qualified his own writing with "Perhaps!"

Well, gentle and brave reader, and you too, my benevolent and tireless

---

5. Bruneau cites numerous contemporary variations on the theme of burial alive (*Débuts littéraires*, pp. 171–72), to which the most germane example of Balzac's "Le colonel Chabert" (1832) could be added.

lady reader, what do you think our hero would have answered from his tomb if some clumsy person had asked his opinion about God's goodness? Would he have replied, "Maybe," "Does it exist?" or "What do I know?" As far as I'm concerned, he might as well have said, "I doubt it" or "I deny it."

And if the same crude person continued asking his dumb questions, alleging the goodness of this same merciful God, the man in the tomb would have told the bumpkin to go to hell with the same "Crap!" that Pantagruel exclaimed when the arrival of Panurge disturbed his meal. And our hero would have done well, because when you kick off that way and your soul is skinned raw, you might as well swear at the one who skins you.

Now, here is my provisional conclusion from all this: you had better make sure you don't disturb the dying in their agony or the dead in their sleep, lovers in bed, wine tasters with their demijohns, and the Eternal Father in his stupidities.

And here's the moral of my silly little story. Having approved of the right and proper conduct of the above-mentioned doctor, I invite all brats to throw their cookies at the baker's head if they're not sweet, winos to chuck their wine if it's bad, the dying to shuck their souls when they croak, and men to throw their existence in God's face when it's bitter.

A Lecture on Natural History— Genus: *Clerk*

From Aristotle to Cuvier, from Pliny to Blainville, natural science has made great strides.[1] Each scientist has brought his aggregate of observations and studies to this field. Intrepid explorers have traveled the world over and have made important discoveries, but for the most part they have brought back only small black, yellow, or multicolored furs. It was helpful to learn that bears eat honey and have a weakness for cream tarts.

I admit that those are very great discoveries. But no one has yet thought about discussing the *Clerk*, the most interesting animal of our era. No one has specialized narrowly enough, or meditated, observed, and traveled sufficiently to be in a position to speak with reasonable authority on the Clerk.

Another obstacle arose: how should one classify this animal? For a long time people were undecided among the sloth, the howling monkey, and the jackal.

---

1. This opening sentence exemplifies the sort of ambiguous irony that shades *Bouvard et Pécuchet* throughout. The stature of Aristotle and Pliny as Greek and Roman natural scientists matches the Classical balance of the sentence, but not that of Cuvier and Blainville. Renowned for his *Lessons in Comparative Anatomy* and *Animal Kingdom*, Baron Georges Cuvier (1769–1832), became councillor of state under Napoleon until his death, five years before the composition of this text. His prize student, Henri Blainville (1777–1850), was a zoologist who lectured on mollusks and worms at the Museum of Natural History, and replaced Cuvier as chair of comparative anatomy at the Academy of Sciences, after publicly debunking some of his tutor's basic principles. The ideas of Blainville appear in the penultimate paragraph of this treatise.

In short, the question remained undecided. The solution to this problem was left to the future, along with discovering the origin of the genus: *dog*.

Indeed, it was difficult to classify an animal so illogical in its makeup. Its otter hat would make your judgment lean toward an aquatic life, just like its shaggy brown frock coat, whereas its thick wool vest proved indisputably that this animal originated in the northern countries. Its curved nails would lead you to take it for a carnivore, if it had teeth to match. Finally, the Academy of Science stipulated that it was digitigrade. Unfortunately, people soon realized that it had an ironwood cane and that it occasionally paid visits on New Year's Day in a hackney coach and went to dine in the country in a one-horse chaise.[2]

My long experience has placed me in a position to instruct humankind. I can speak with the modest confidence of a zoologist. My frequent trips to various offices have left me enough impressions to describe the anatomy and customs of the animals that inhabit them. I have seen all species of Clerks, from tax collectors to record keepers. Those trips have completely ruined me, and I ask my readers to sign the appropriate approval forms for a man who has devoted himself to science, in the process has worn out two umbrellas and a dozen hats (including their oilcloth rain protectors), and has had his boots resoled six times.

The Clerk is between thirty-six and sixty years old. It is short and pudgy with a ruddy complexion. It has a snuffbox called a "rat tail," a red wig, silver glasses for the office, and a cotton-print handkerchief.

It often spits, and when you sneeze it says, "God bless you!" It has its fur groomed differently, according to the season.

In the summer it wears a straw hat and light cotton pants over which it spreads a handkerchief to keep from getting ink spots on them. Its shoes are made of beaver and its vest is twill. Invariably it wears a detachable velvet collar. In winter it wears blue trousers with an enormous frock coat for protection against the cold. The coat is the element of clerks, as water is to fish.

Originating in Eurasia via Africa, it is unfortunately very widespread in these climes. It is mild-mannered but defends itself when attacked. It usually remains unmarried, so it leads a bachelor's life. The bachelor's life! In other words, when it goes to a cafe, it addresses the lady at the cashier's

---

2. The name used for the one-horse chaise (*coucou*) indicates that the Clerk is up to date in his post-1830 tastes.

desk as "Miss," takes along the remaining sugar cubes on its saucer, and sometimes allows itself a cheap, slender cigar. Oh, but then the Clerk can be a hellion! The day it smokes its cigar, it is quarrelsome, cuts itself four pens before finding one suitable, is gruff with the office boy, drops its glasses, and smears ink on its ledger, which greatly upsets it.

In other instances, the Clerk is married. Then it is a peaceful and proper citizen, no longer a youthful hothead. It takes its turn standing guard, goes to bed at nine o'clock, and never goes out without an umbrella. On Sunday mornings it takes its coffee with milk, reads the *Constitutional*, the *Echo*, the *Parliamentary Register*, or some other paper of similar persuasion.[3]

It is a strong partisan of the Charter of 1830 and of the freedoms of the July Revolution. It respects the laws of its country, shouts "Long live the King!" with fireworks in the background, and cleans its sword belt every Saturday evening.

The Clerk supports the National Guard. Its heart is stirred when a drum roll summons it to the parade ground, tightly buckled up and choked by its collar as it hums the tune "Oh, what a joy a soldier's life is!"

As for its mate, she stays home to darn socks, makes him cloth oversleeves, reads melodramas from the Ambigu Theater, and—as her speciality—dunks bread in her soup.

Although it is chaste, the Clerk nevertheless has a licentious and playful mind, for it says "my pretty child" to young ladies entering its office. Moreover, it is a confirmed reader of Paul de Kock, especially sitting near the stove in the evening, wearing its slippers and its black silk cap.[4]

You ought to see this interesting biped in the office, copying its register.

---

3. The *Parliamentary Register* approximates the American *Congressional Record*; the other newspapers testify to the political volatility and dread of revolution that were belied and yet explained by bourgeois conservatism following the Hundred Days (as Napoleon's return from Elba is called). The *Constitutionnel*, for instance, was a child of that period (cf. sec. 11 of "Whatever You Want"), founded by former revolutionaries. Like Jacques Arnoux's *Art industriel* in *L'Education sentimentale*, the paper changed its name according to shifting political currents, to *L'Indépendant*, *L'Echo du Soir*, and back to *Le Constitutionnel* shortly after the restoration of the Bourbon family (June 28, 1815). Attacks on the government led to its decline, after which it became eminently bourgeois and conservative, as would befit the Clerk. His support of the July Revolution (next paragraph) places him in the camp of Louis-Philippe (the so-called Orleanist, bourgeois, or July monarchy), in the golden age of the European middle class.

4. Paul de Kock (1793–1871) was a popular novelist who turned successfully to comic opera. The Théâtre de l'Ambigu-comique (Boulevard du Temple) mentioned in the preceding paragraph was newly inaugurated in 1828, primarily as a puppet theater.

A Lecture on Natural History

It has removed its coat and collar, working in shirtsleeves and wearing its wool vest.

It is hunched over the desk, with its quill tucked above its left ear. It writes slowly, savors the smell of ink, and enjoys watching it cover a huge sheet of paper. It repeats to itself what it writes, with its mumbling giving off a constant nasal sound. But when it is in a hurry, it hastily scatters periods, commas, dashes, "The Ends," and paragraphs. That is the height of talent. With its colleagues, it often discusses the return of snails after the frost, the repaving of the port, the iron bridge, and the use of natural gas. If it peers through the curtains that keep out the light and notices that the weather is rainy, it suddenly exclaims, "Damn, gonna be thick as pea soup!" Then it turns back to its work.

The Clerk has a mania for staying warm and lives in a perpetual oven. Its greatest pleasure is to get the stove near the cashier's desk red hot. Then its laughter echoes contentment. Steadily panting, it takes its handkerchief and joyfully wipes the sweat streaming down its face. But soon it is so stifled by the weight of its happiness that it cannot keep from exclaiming, "It's so nice here!" And when it rises to this bliss, it begins to copy with renewed vigor. Its pen goes faster than usual, its eyes sparkle, it forgets to put the lid back on its snuffbox, and rapt with heady joy, it suddenly gets up from its seat and hurries to the sanctuary to bring back an enormous log. It approaches the stove, backs away several times, opens the door by reaching out with a ruler, and then throws in the piece of wood, announcing, "One more match!" It just stands there for a few moments with its mouth open, listening to the flame rumble in the flue with a muffled and pleasing sound.

If you unfortunately leave the door open when you enter its office, the Clerk becomes furious, extends its nails, scratches its hair piece, stamps its foot, swears, and from the midst of the columns, the copies, and the numerous ledgers with their credits and debits, you can hear a voice yelping, "Close the door, fer Chrisake! Can't you read? Look at the sign on the cashier's desk! The heat's going to escape, dammit!"

Do not consider hailing it as "Clerk!" Instead, address it as "Mr. Employee."

The Employee has long nails because one of its favorite pastimes is filing them. In the morning it brings its small loaf of bread in its pocket, opens its desk, takes out its broad green visor, and waits for the office boy to bring it a breakfast of salted butter or its daily cheese.

When the day draws to a close, the Employee is thoroughly tickled to see the cashier's door crack open so that the person lighting the oil-burning lamps can be seen. For the Argand lamp furnishes the bureaucrat with a wondrous subject of conversation that inspires much debate among all the employees. As soon as the lamp is lit, it is scrutinized to see whether the wick is good or whether it has slipped out. If the knob gets turned too high or if a half-dozen lamp glasses get broken, it complains bitterly and repeats with the deepest sadness that the light hurts its eyes. That is why it wears the enormous visor that casts a shadow over its neighbor's sheet of paper. The neighbor declares that it cannot possibly write without any light and asks that the visor be removed. But the sly Clerk pulls the visor down more tightly over its ears and even fastens the chin strap.

At the theater every Sunday it sits in the loges or in the orchestra section. It whistles for the curtain to go up and applauds the vaudeville acts. In its youth it engages in a match of dominoes between acts. Whenever it loses, it goes home and breaks a couple of dishes, no longer refers affectionately to its mate as "my bride," neglects its dog Azor, gobbles down the boiled beef reheated from the previous evening, furiously salts its green beans, and then falls asleep to dream about columns of numbers, the weather, civic improvements, and its daily sums.

I believe that just about covers everything in general about the Clerk, or at least I am beginning to feel that the reader's patience is running short.

I still have numerous observations in my notes on the different species of this genus, such as the Clerk of the tax collector, the Clerk of the dry goods merchant, the Clerk of the customs official (who sometimes rises to supervisor, dabbles in literature, and writes billboard copy and serialized stories), the traveling salesman, the Employee of the mayor's office, and a thousand others.

Those are the uncompensated fruits of my studious nights. But if times get better and if the turbulent political climate improves, well, I might appear on the scene again and publish the conclusion to these zoology lectures as a huge slice of society extending from the Tax Clerk to the stockbroker's Cashier.

Dream of Hell

A Fantastic Tale

You often hold a very false opinion of someone else's mind when you don't feed it with nonsense.
—JEAN DE LA BRUYÈRE

ONE

A lethargic sleep covered the earth, making practically no sound at all over its surface. The only noise was the battering of the ocean as it foamed over the rocks. The sea gull's cry rang through the cypresses, the slobbering lizard crawled over the tombs, and vultures pounced on rotting bones from the battlefield.

A torrent of rain blotted out the dim light from the moon, across the face of which passed an endless succession of gray clouds. The stormy wind agitated the waves and made the forest leaves tremble. Its whistle diminished and then picked up, the way a sharp cry suddenly blots out low murmurs.

A lone voice came from the ground, saying:

"End the world! Let today be its final hour!"

"No, no, all the hours must be struck."

The first voice rejoined, "Hasten them. Exterminate mankind with ultimate chaos and don't create any other worlds."

"There's still another one that is superior to this one."

"You mean more miserable," the earth answered. "End it for the well-being of your creatures. Since you have botched all your works up to the present time, at least don't make anything more from now on."

The voice from heaven replied, "Yes, yes, the other men have complained of their weakness and their passions. The next one will be strong and emotionless. As for its soul . . ."

Here the earthly voice burst out laughing, filling the expanse with its immense disdain.

TWO

Duke Arthur Alamaroës was an alchemist, or at least passed himself off as one, although his valets would have pointed out that he rarely worked at it, that his furnaces were always filled with cold ashes instead of hot coals, and that the pages of his half-open books never turned. Nonetheless, he remained for days, nights, and entire months without leaving his laboratory, plunged in deep thought like a man working and meditating. People believed that he was in search of gold, an elixir of long life, or the philosopher's stone. He was a man with a forbidding exterior and deceptive appearance. His lips neither smiled nor screamed with anguish. He never experienced any of those nights of burning fever like men who dream ambitious thoughts. Seeing his serious and cold aspect, you would have said he was a robot who thought like a man.

People mentioned his name everywhere as the most powerful of the powerful and the holiest of holies, two seemingly incompatible traits, except for God himself: saintliness and power. They were persuaded that he was a sorcerer, a devil, or Satan incarnate. *He* was the one whose laughter could be heard in the evening around the cemetery, the one who slowly trudged along the cliffs screeching like an owl. He was the one they saw dancing in the fields with will-o'-the-wisps, the one they saw on winter nights with his darkly somber face looking down from the old feudal castle, like an old legend about blood on the ruins of a tomb.

When the peasants sat by their front doors in the evening, resting from the day's work, they often sang some old regional song, a national air the old-timers had learned in their youth from their grandfathers and sang up in the mountains where they took their goats to graze, and then transmitted in turn to their children. During these restful evenings when the moon begins to appear, and bats flit and dart around the belfry, when the crow dives down to the strand as the last pale rays of the sun disappear, it was then that one occasionally saw Duke Arthur appear.

People hushed when they heard his footfalls, children gathered around their mothers, and men looked at one another with astonishment. They were frightened by that leaden stare, cold smile, and pallid face. Anyone who happened to brush his hands found them like a reptile's skin.

These country people fell silent as he quickly approached, passed through their midst, and just as quickly disappeared from view. He was as swift as a gazelle, as finely spun as a fantastic dream—a shadow. The sound of his footsteps in the dust gradually diminished, leaving not a single trace of his passing, except for fear and terror, like the eeriness after a storm.

If someone had been bold enough to follow him in his winged flight, to notice the direction he took, he would have seen him reenter the ruins of the old castle, which no one dared approach in the evening. For you could hear strange sounds that rose through the arrow slits of the towers. At night the battlements were slowly paced by a large black ghost, trailing behind him the clink of chains and a death rattle, who stretched his arms out wide toward the heavens and with his bony hands made the rocks of the fortress tremble.

Well, that satanic terror appeared to be a scion of hell, a demon's fancy, the work of a cursed alchemist, whose cracked lips seemed to respond only to the touch of fresh blood, and whose white teeth gave off the odor of human flesh. That infernal creature, that deadly vampire was but a pure, inviolate spirit, cold and perfect, infinite and regular. He was like a powerful, thinking, acting, and self-willed marble statue with a soul, whose blood coursed frigidly through his veins, who understood without feeling, whose gestures lacked forethought, eyes lacked passion, and heart held no love.

Forget about life's daily needs and material reality! Everything was thought and ecstasy, but more like a vague and undefinable ecstasy that bathes in clouds, sees its reflection in the moon, and derives from will and instinct the way scent does from a flower.

His head and his expression were beautiful, as was his long hair which, when he leaned over, cascaded marvelously over his shoulders in long blue waves and folded over his back in elongated masses. Light reflecting off the snow gave a silvery tint to his skin, which was as soft as satin and as white as the moon.

Other creatures before him had had passions, body and soul, and they had all acted somewhat randomly in a kind of whirlwind, trampling, jostling, and pushing one another. Some had risen in status, while others lost all prominence. All other men had hurried, huddled, and shoved in this immense chaos, in this long cry of anguish, in this prodigious mire called life.

But *he,* this heavenly spirit cast down to earth like the last word of Creation, this strange, unusual being arrived in the midst of mankind without passing through humanity himself. He could assume their shape at will, their speech and expression, but in a superior way and with a nobler heart that needed only passion to sustain itself. Instinctively seeking these passions the world over but finding only men, why had he come? He was shrunken, worn out, and irritated by our customs and instincts.

Having only a fleshly appearance, would he have understood our carnal pleasures, the warm kisses of a woman, her arms moist with perspiration, with her tears of love and her bare breasts? With his heart an abyss of knowledge, an immense world, would all those pleasures have made his pulse race one fine morning?

Our pitiful delights, our pathetic poetry, our incense, and all the joy and splendor on earth—what would that have meant to him, who had something angelic about him? He was bored with this earth, then, but with the kind of ennui which eats away like a cancer, which burns, tears, and drives men to suicide. But *he*? Suicide? How many times had people come across him at the peak of a cliff, bitterly laughing right in the face of death and defying it by pointing to the empty expanse that refused to engulf him! How many times did he gaze fixedly into the barrel of a pistol, then throw it uselessly aside in anger, since he was condemned to live! How often did he spend whole nights walking in the woods, listening to the waves on the beach, smelling the seaweed that blackened the rocks! How many nights did he spend leaning against a rock or letting his thought ramble endlessly and fly up to the clouds!

But all that nature, sea, woods, and sky was small and unworthy: flowers had no smell, a woman's nakedness held no beauty, song had no melody, the sea held no terror. There was not enough air for his lungs, not enough light for his eyes, and no love for his heart.

Ambition? Empire? Glory? He gave them no thought. Knowledge and history? But he knew the future, and in that future he found only one thing that made him smile from time to time, as he passed by a cemetery.

Would he have feared God when he felt himself to be nearly his equal, knowing that the day would come when the void would carry away this God, just as God would carry him off? Would he have loved him, having spent so many centuries cursing him?

Poor heart! How you suffered, inconvenienced, displaced from your normal sphere, and shrunken into the world like the soul in a body.

A self-mocking instinct often lifted a goblet of wine to his lips and feathered them, without leaving the trace of a smile. Then he noticed that his gesture had been pointless and useless. He picked up a rose but quickly drew back as if it were a thorn. One day he decided to become a musician. Men might not have understood such a sublime, strange, and fantastic idea, but Mozart's genius would have been condemned for such a thought, an infernal idea that would sicken, irritate, and kill. When he began, the bewildered crowd applauded and shouted its enthusiasm, then with silent trembling it bowed down to the ground and listened. Pure and plaintive sounds swelled the nave sublimely and became lost in the upper ribs and vaults. It was merely a prelude. He would have continued had he not broken the organ with his hands.

From that point on there was nothing for him! Everything was empty and hollow. There was nothing but an immensely weary dissatisfaction, a terrible solitude, with still more centuries to live and curse existence, yet he had neither needs nor passions and desires! But he did have despair!

THREE

He became resigned, and his superior nature gave him the means to live apart and alone in a German village, far from the burdensome presence of men.

Situated high on a hill, a castle in ruins seemed suitable for his thoughts, and that evening he took up residence.

He lived alone that way, with no retinue, no trappings, and hardly any servants, limiting his social contacts to the confines of his own mind. Thus, each day his name took on a more and more problematic existence. The sound of his voice was unfamiliar to his own valets, who knew his face only for his dull stare between half-closed eyelids, which made them tremble when he turned his cold glance their way. Moreover, they were completely free in that their master reproached them for nothing and gave them hardly any orders.

Over the course of time, the castle where the count lived took on some of the sadness of its inhabitants. The blackened walls, stones without mortar, the brambles surrounding it, and the silence that bore down on its towers all had something wondrously strange about them. It was even worse inside: long dark corridors, doors that banged violently at night and trembled in their frames, high narrow windows, smoky wainscoting; and here and there in the galleries were a random antique ornament, a suit of armor of a former baron, a full-length portrait of a princess, a mounted rack of antlers, a hunting sword and a rusted dagger, rubbish in several dim recesses, and plaster that had fallen from the ceiling of the old salon on winter evenings when the sustained roar of the wind howled more furiously than usual through the long galleries.

The old caretaker, who was more decrepit than the castle itself, made his daily rounds every afternoon. He began by slowly climbing the big stone staircase whose banister had been removed for sale by the previous tenant in order to buy an acre of land. When he got to the main gallery, he opened all the shabby bedrooms, each of which had long ago served its purpose but still bore its former number despite being empty. Next, he came to the sitting room and then to the chapel. Finally, he came to the old salon, an immense, square apartment where you could still see some shreds of crimson velvet as the remnants of its sumptuously beautiful appointments from the previous century. His progress was impeded by about a hundred hay bales that had been stored there for some twenty years, now rotting from the rainwater that the evening wind had driven across the flagstone. The rest of the salon was occupied by old armchairs, worn out harnesses, some worm-eaten saddles, and a great quantity of kindling and dry wood. The caretaker never opened it except to shove in something else that was broken or dilapidated; he negligently piled it up on an old painting, a statue from the garden, or a chair whose stuffing was coming out. Once back in the corridor, he resumed his slow, weary pace, the nails in his boots scratching over the broad flagstone and leaving their mark. Then he retraced his steps, watching the swallows extend their mud nests in the upper reaches of the castle, as though it were their realm; they flew at will in and out of windows whose broken panes were strewn over the floor, while their twisted lead casings held nothing.

The castle was bordered by large poplars with bark seared by the salt air. They often swayed with the ocean breeze, mixing the rustle of their leaves with the slap of the waves. A gap had been cut in their foliage so that from the highest windows the immense and terrible ocean could be seen stretching out in front of the sinister castle, which seemed merely to be its mournful accompaniment.

Over there you could see the drawbridge leading to a terrace; over here were crenelated battlements so dilapidated that you dared not touch them for fear of dislodging stones. Higher up was the dungeon where the caretaker never dared to venture because, like the uppermost floors, it had long ago been given over to the bats and owls that circled the roofs, punctuating the night air with their shrill cries and the prolonged beating of their wings. The castle's cracked walls were covered with moss. Their gummy, humid touch made shivers run down your back, like the sticky path of a reptile.

That's where he lived. He loved the extensive vaults where you could hear the night birds and the sea breeze; he loved the craggy ruins bound together by ivy, those dark halls, and any appearance of death and destruction. Having fallen so far from so high a position, he loved anything that had also fallen from a great height. Disillusioned, he wished for ruins, longed for destruction, and found emptiness in eternity. He was alone in the midst of mankind! He wanted to withdraw completely and live that life which at least resembled his dreams, what he should have been.

FOUR

Duke Arthur was seated in a large easy chair of black morocco, with his elbow resting on the table and his head in his hands. The room he lived in was large and spacious, with a ceiling blackened by soot. Its paneling was hidden by a great quantity of earthen pots, retorts, vases, measuring devices, and notebooks.

In one corner were an oven and a crucible for magical procedures. Then, here and there above ashes that were still warm, were half-open books with slightly torn pages which seemed to have been touched by feverish hands and pored through avidly by eyes that had read nothing at all.

The room was dark except for the glow emitted by a few dying coals in the furnace, which outlined luminous, unsteady circles on the ceiling.

The alchemist remained motionless for a long time, then rose and went to study the crucible at length. The red glow from the coals suddenly lit his face with a fantastic tint. He had one of those washed-out faces of infernal alchemists: vacant red eyes, drawn white skin, long thin hands, altogether suggesting the many sleepless nights, ardent dreams, and thoughts of a genius.

And does that smile strike you as a hint of vanity? Do you think that those hollow cheeks were thinned by prolonged study, that his complexion was faded by heat from the coals, that the tears of rage were those of a man who sought fame and immortality? Do you believe that those books thrown aside in anger, those torn pages, that fist clenched so tightly as to draw blood . . . do you consider that he is wracked with despair because he has not found a single nugget of gold, a poison to prolong life?

He was going to return to his workbench when he glanced at the blackened wall and noticed that brilliant lines had cast sharp outlines and soon formed an unusually hideous monster, similar to the famished gargoyles one sees above the portal of a cathedral, with hollowed sides, a dog's head, pendulous breasts, red skin, flaming eyes, and cockspurs.

He quickly turned from the wall and rushed to the furnace. You could hear his fine, slender fingers scratch over the stones that heated the crucible.

Arthur asked the monstrous form, "What do you want with me?"[1]

"Me? Nothing!"

"But aren't you the cursed spirit who damns men and tortures their soul?"

"Well, yes," answered the monster with a joyous cry, "yes, I'm Satan."

"What do you want with me? Why have you come here?"

"To help you."

"To do what?"

"To find what you are looking for, gold, the elixir of life."

"Oh, really! Don't you know that I can live entire worlds, that a single one of my thoughts can bring gold tumbling to my feet? No, Satan, if that's all the power you have, then you can leave now because you can't help me."

"No, no, I'll stay, I'll remain," Satan said with a curious smile, and thinking to himself, "Vanity is my eldest daughter. She gives me the souls of all of those who possess her, and I'll have yours!"

---

1. I have corrected Flaubert's attribution "dit-il à Arthur," following "What do you want with me?" Obviously, as the following dialogue confirms, it is Arthur who poses the question, not Satan.

At this moment the coals that had gone out flared up slightly to illumine Arthur's face. Satan found it more beautiful and more terrible than those of even the most beautiful of the damned.

Arthur said to him, "Let's get out of here. The wind is whipping the trees, the ocean is growling, and the shore is torn up. Come on! We can discuss eternity and nothingness better against the background of the storm and the anger of the sea." So they left.

The path leading to the shore was rocky and shaded by the large black trees surrounding the castle. It was cold, the ground was dry and hard. The overcast sky blocked out all starlight and moonbeams. Arthur slowly walked along bareheaded and without a scarf to protect his face. He enjoyed feeling his silky blue hair brush his face. He loved the sound of the wind and the sinister groan of the trees when they bent violently. In back of him, Satan was howling and deftly bounding among the rocks with his head lowered.

When they finally arrived at the beach, the fresh sand was damp and covered with shells and kelp, which the ebb tide drew back into the sea along with some pebbles. They both stopped.

Arthur laughed wildly at the sound of the waves, saying:

"This is what I love, or rather what I hate the least, but that anger isn't brutal or heavenly enough. Why does the wave stop rising and end there? If the sea extended beyond the shore and the rocks, how far it would run and how high it would leap! It would be enjoyable to see, but that . . ."

"Is it death you want, then, the death of everything?"

"I crave nothingness."

"Why? Don't you believe that nothing exists after the death of the body, that your eye no longer sees when you close it, that the cold, pallid head is completely without thought?"

"Yes, I believe that, at any rate for me."

"What do you want? What is it that you desire?"

"Happiness!"

"Happiness? Do you really think about *happiness*? You can find it in knowledge, fame, and love."

"Oh, nowhere! I've been searching for it for a long time, but I've never found it. That kind of knowledge is too limited, that fame is too narrow, that love is too petty."

"Do you mean that you consider yourself superior to other men, that your soul . . ."

"Oh, my soul! . . . My soul! . . ."

"Don't you *have* one? Don't you believe in anything . . . not even God? Oh, you'll give in, my weak and arrogant friend, you'll die because you refused my offers. You will succumb like the first man. How proud he was, how insolent and confident he was about his happiness when, strolling in Eden one day, he contemplated my tearful defeat with open-mouthed astonishment! And I beheld his fall as well, groveling at my feet, crying, cursing and blaspheming as I did! Our cries of despair mixed together, and from that point on we were companions in torture and suffering. Oh yes, you will fall as he did, for you will love something."

"Does that mean that you take me for a man, Satan? One of those vulgar and common beings who wallows wherever the insane wind of misfortune happens to blow me and where I'll die for lack of air to breathe and something to feel, understand, and love? Do you believe that this mouth eats, that these teeth chew, that I rely on life the way a face needs its mask to hide it? If I were to remove the skin covering me, Satan, you would see that I too am one of the accursed like you, that I am your equal and perhaps your master. Can you stop a wave, Satan? Can you smash a rock in your hand?"

"Yes."

"Satan, if I wanted to, I could crush you in my hands, too. What do you have that makes you superior to everything? What? Is it your body? If you put your head down by my knee and my foot, I'll grind you into the ground. What do your glory and pride come from—pride, the essence of superior minds? Well, what do you have? Answer me!"

"My soul."

"And in all of eternity, how many minutes of happiness has this soul given you?"

"Yet when I see human souls suffer as mine does, my pain is consoled and my despair is comforted. But what's so heavenly about you? Your soul?"

"No! It's because I don't have one."

"No soul? Well, now! Do you mean you're a robot driven by the spark of genius?"

"What a ridiculous and pathetic idea! I have *genius*?"

"No soul? Who told you that?"

"Who told me? I guessed it . . . Listen and you'll see. When I came to this earth, it was on a cold and terrible night like this one. I remember that I was borne by the waves onto the sand . . . I got up and walked. I felt happy then and breathed the air of freedom. There was something unblemished and pure inside me that made me dream confused, vague, and indeterminate ideas. I had a distant recollection of somewhere else, of a calmer and more pleasant condition. When I closed my eyes and listened to the sea, it seemed to me that I was heading back to those superior regions where everything was poetry, silence, and love, and I believed that I was sleeping continuously. It was a heavy, stupefying sleep, but how sweet and deep it was! Indeed, I remember that there was a moment when everything disappeared behind me and dissolved like a dream. I returned from that happy intoxication with life and with ennui. Those dreams that I thought I would find on earth disappeared little by little like this revery. My heart shriveled, and nature struck me as abortive, aged and worn out, like a humpback child disguised by an old man's wrinkles. I tried to imitate men and have their passions, their interest, to act the way they do, but it was pointless, like an eagle trying to sit in a woodpecker's nest. Then everything seemed to darken, covered over by a black veil. Existence became an extended agony, the earth a tomb where people were buried alive. After many centuries and ages, after seeing races of men and empires pass before me, I felt nothing stir in me. When everything was dead and paralyzed in my mind, I said to myself: "You're mad to wish for happiness when you have no soul! When you understand that everything is oblivion, you're out of your mind to let your spirit soar and to lift your heart too high, you who love nothing and believe that the body brings satisfaction, that matter gives happiness! It is true: that mind was lofty, that body was beautiful, that matter sublime; but there was no soul, belief, or hope!"

Dragging his breasts over the sand and stretching to his full height, Satan responded: "And you pity yourself! Oh fortunate man, you should instead bless heaven because you will die! You don't wish for anything, Arthur, you love nothing, you live happily because you resemble a stone, you resemble nonbeing. What are you complaining about? Who is bothering you and upsetting you?"

"I'm weary and bored."

"Yet can't your body bring you human pleasure?"

"Earthly delights, do you mean? The showy kisses of humankind and their indifferent embrace? I've never enjoyed them, and in fact I despise them."

"But a woman?"

"A woman? Why, I'd smother her in my arms, pulverize her with my kisses, and kill her with my breath. You're correct to say that I want, crave, and love nothing . . . And you, Satan, you'd like my body, wouldn't you?"

"A body? Oh, yes, something solid, sentient, and visible, for I have only a form, a puff of breath, an appearance. If I were a man with a broad chest and strong thighs . . . it makes me envious, hateful and jealous . . . but all I have is a soul—that withering and sterile wisp which devours itself and rips itself apart. The soul! But I can't do anything except skim the surface of kisses. I can observe but I can't touch or possess. I have nothing at all except for my soul. Oh, how many times have I gone out to drag myself over the corpses of girls that were still warm! How often have I come back depressed, with blasphemy in my heart! Why can't I be a brute, a reptile, which at least has its joys and family happiness? An animal's desires are fulfilled and his passions are assuaged. Do you want a soul, Arthur? A soul! But have you considered that carefully? Do you wish to be like men, to cry over the death of a woman or the loss of a fortune? Do you want to wither away in hopelessness, to fall from illusion into reality? A soul! But do you long for cries of mindless despair, madness, idiocy? A soul! Do you want to believe and lower yourself to the level of hope? A soul! So you wish to be a man, a little more than a tree but slightly less than a dog?"

"Not at all, no! I don't want anything," Arthur said before wading silently into the surf. Soon Satan watched him run over the waves with a light and rapid gait, and the whitecaps sparkled beneath his feet. In his jealous hatred, Satan said, "You happy man, you are wearied by life on earth, but later you will sleep, and *I* will be in despair for eternity, and when I contemplate your corpse . . ."

"My corpse? Who told you that I'll die? Didn't I tell you? I don't wish for anything, not even death."

"The most terrible means . . ."

"Try it," said Arthur who had stopped for a moment on a gently swaying wave as if he were standing on a board.

Satan thought about the alchemist in prolonged silence, saying to himself: "I have fooled him. He doesn't believe in his soul. Oh, he'll love a woman, all right. I'll endow her with so much charm, beauty, and love that he'll love her . . . for he's a man, despite his pride and knowledge." Then he said:

"Listen, Arthur, tomorrow you'll see a girl from up in your mountains, and you will love her."

Arthur began to smile, saying, "You poor fool, I'd like to try. Or rather, try to kill me if you dare!"

"No, my power extends only to souls," Satan said as he was leaving.

Arthur remained on the rocks. When the moon began to appear, he opened his huge green wings, spread out his snow-white body, and flew toward the clouds.

FIVE

In the evening the red streaks of the dying sun barely touched the valley and mountains. It was the hour when you see women in the fields with white gossamer strands clinging to their hair, and to their lacy clothing and silken material. From the grass and from under the wheat stalks comes the sharp chirping of the crickets. That is the moment when mysterious voices and strange concerts rise from the fields. Far away, a small bell wanes and dies, signaling the passage of cows going down the mountain. That is when the keeper of the goats and cows hastens her step without glancing backward; every now and then the approaching night makes her stop, trembling and out of breath, for it's the time when young and older men come up the path in her direction, this poor, frightened sixteen-year-old child.

Julietta gathered her cows and headed toward a scattering of houses near the village. However, on that day she was sad and didn't run along the way to pick flowers for her hair. No more childlike jumps at the sight of a beautiful daisy that her foot almost crushed, no more joyful song on that day, no more pearly tones or long roulades! No more heady delight, nor did you see her pretty white neck jauntily thrown back. No longer did she dance to a light music, bathed in harmony. Rather, in her distraction the melancholy girl was all repeated sobs, dreamy appearance, and tearful eyes. She trudged on her dreamy walks in the high grass, with no worry that her feet were soaked by the dew or that her cows had disappeared.

How many times that day did she run after her flock, and then sit to regain her breath and collect her distracted thoughts . . . or to think of nothing at all! In her depression, her heart burned with the desire for something vague and indeterminate. It abandoned its whims as soon as it embraced them, and harbored boredom, desire, and uncertainty at the same time. Lassitude, nostalgia for the past, and a dream of the future all flitted through her childlike head, lying in the grass and looking at the sky as she grasped her forehead. She was afraid of being alone in the middle of the field, and yet she had passed her childhood there, playing in the woods and running through the harvested grain. The noise of the rustling leaves made her tremble so that she did not dare to go back. She always seemed to see a demon's face behind her, grimacing with a horrible laugh.

For a long time she watched the reddish rays of the sun gradually diminish, here and there outlining luminous circles which grew until they disappeared, only to return. She waited for the church clock to stop ringing, and when its last vibrations disappeared in the distance she painfully arose, ran after the herd, and began walking back toward her father's house.

Suddenly, she saw about twenty small flames rising from the ground some fifty paces away. The flames disappeared but after a few minutes Julietta saw them again. They slowly approached and then one disappeared, then another and yet one more, until the last one jumped, stretched out, and danced with an eerie liveliness. The cows stopped suddenly, as though a natural instinct forbade them to go any further. Their plaintive, monotone lowing droned on for a long time but slowly faded. The flames increased, and you could distinctly hear peals of laughter and children's voices. Julietta's face lost its color; dumb struck with fright, she leaned for support on the horn of a heifer. She heard steps behind her, felt her cheeks brushed by hot breath, and then a man stepped right in front of her.

His rich clothing was made of black silk and his gloved hand shone with diamonds. Small silver bells tinkled at his slightest movement, sounding as if they were blended with the clink of gold coins. His red mustache and hollow cheeks complemented his ugly face, but his eyes shone like red coals and gleamed beneath thick, bushy eyebrows that looked like a handful of hair. His face was wrinkled, pale and bony, and the upper part was carefully hidden by a red velvet cap. You would have thought that he feared to show his head.

"My child, you beautiful child!" he said to Julietta, drawing her toward him with a powerful hand and a smile that seemed horrible, even as he tried to soften it. "Are you in love with someone?"

"Oh, leave me alone," she said, "Your arms are killing me! You're crushing me!"

The gentleman continued: "What! No one? You'll love someone, because *I* am powerful enough to give both hate and love. Here, let's sit down on the back of your white cow."

The cow lay down on its side to offer her flank. The stranger sat on its neck, took one of its horns in one hand and Julietta's waist in the other.

The will-o'-the-wisps had stopped; the sun had set, leaving the dim, weak moon to struggle in the darkening evening against the dying day.

Julietta looked in terror at the stranger's fierce expression.

"Leave me alone! In the name of God, leave me alone!" she pleaded.

"God?" he rejoined bitterly and began to laugh, before continuing: "Julietta, do you know Duke Arthur Almaroës?"

"I've seen him a few times, but he's just like you, and I'm afraid of him . . . oh, leave me! Leave me alone! I must go . . . my father! Oh, if he knew . . ."

"Your father! Well?"

"I'm telling you that if he knew that you are holding me this way, so late in the evening . . . I'm telling you he would kill you!"

"You're free to go, Julietta, so leave!"

And he dropped the hand that had gripped her so firmly. She couldn't get up because something held her to the stomach of the animal, which moaned sadly and licked the ground with its slobbery tongue. It bellowed and moved its head all around on the ground as if it were dying of pain.

"Well, Julietta, leave! Who's stopping you?"

She tried again, but nothing could make her budge. Her iron will was breaking before the fascination and magic power of this man.

"What *are* you?" she asked. "What harm have I done to you?"

"None . . . but let's speak of Duke Arthur of Almaroës. Isn't he rich and handsome?"

At that point he became silent and clutched his forehead with both hands: "Well, let him come. Let him come, then."

Both of them remained that way for a very long time. With his eyes steadily fixed on the trembling girl, he contemplated her eagerly.

"Are you happy?" he asked her.

"Happy? Oh, no!"

"What do you require?"

"I don't know, but nothing pleases me at all. I'm especially sad today, and again this evening . . . your evil appearance . . . it'll drive me mad!"

"Wouldn't you like to be a queen, Julietta?"

"No!"

"Don't you love the church, with its incense, its high nave, blackened walls, and mysterious song?"

"No."

"Don't you like the sea, shells on the beach, the moon above, and dream-filled nights?"

"Oh, yes! I love all of that."

"What are your dreams like at night, Julietta?"

She became submerged in thought.

"Don't you hope for another life, with distant travels? Wouldn't you like to be a rose petal blowing through the air, to be a bird flying around, the dying strains of a song, a rising cry? Isn't Duke Arthur handsome, rich, and powerful? He too loves dreams and sublime ecstasy. Oh, have him come," he added, whispering to himself, "just let him come, so that she can love him warmly, passionately, totally. They'll lead one another to destruction."

The moon rolled along beneath the clouds, shedding its glow on the mountains and valley, turning the silhouette of the old gothic castle into a ghost on a cemetery wall.

"Let's get up and walk," the stranger said.

He had Julietta follow in his footsteps. Her cows were frisking and galloping in the field, chasing madly after one another, and then returned to gather around Julietta, still capering excitedly. The only sounds were the noise of their hooves and the voice of the gentleman with the golden spurs who spoke continuously in an odd voice that intoned like an organ. They walked for a long time on an easy road, then moved quickly over new grass which was as slippery as a polished mirror. Julietta's tired legs gave out.

"When will I get there?" she often wondered.

And her melancholy gaze shifted to the deep darkness of the horizon. After a long while she recognized her father's cottage. The stranger by her side no longer spoke, but his face beamed with contentment. He muttered a few words of an unknown language, and then with his mouth agape he listened with silent concentration. Once again he asked,

"Do you love Duke Arthur?"

"I hardly know him, but what does it matter to you?"

"Well, there he is!"

Indeed, a bare-chested man passed in front of them. His body was as white as snow, his hair was blue, and his eyes shown with a heavenly luster.

The stranger immediately disappeared. Julietta began to run until she came to a wooden door surrounded by a hedge. She grasped the iron knocker and beat it vigorously. An old man opened the door. It was her father.

"My poor child, where have you been? Come in!"

The young girl ran into the house where her family had been awaiting her for several anxious hours. Each one cried out with joy, hugged and kissed her, and questioned her. Then they sat at the table, gathering around a huge iron kettle that gave off a thick steam. Her mother asked:

"Did you bring your cows home?"

When Julietta nodded "yes," her mother told her to go milk them. She left and returned in a few minutes with a large tin pail, which she struggled to lift onto the table . . . but it was blood.

"Oh, heavens! Blood!" Julietta cried. She blanched and dropped down on her mother's knees. "It's him!"

"Who?"

"Him! The one who stopped me!"

"What's going on?"

"I don't know!"

"It is I!" cried a voice from a corner of the room, followed by a piercing laugh.

The stranger and Duke Arthur pressed up against the wall. The old man bounded over to his rifle hanging by the fireplace and took aim at them.

"Have mercy on him!" Julietta cried, as she forcefully threw her arms around his neck. But the rifle had already fired, silence returned, and the two phantoms disappeared. After a few moments a window shattered and a rifle bullet ricocheted off the floor.

Satan had returned fire.

SIX

All of that was unnatural, suggesting the hidden sorcery of a magic trap. And then that milk changed to blood, that bizarre apparition, Julietta's delay, her bewildered look, her tremulous voice, that bullet which skipped around them, and that sinister laughter which seemed to emanate from the wall—it all made the family grow pale and tremble. They immediately huddled together in silence. Julietta rested her head in her left hand, braced her elbow on the table, untied her ribbon to let her hair fall down over her shoulders, and then opening her lips she began to sing very low to herself. Balancing lightly on her chair, she whistled a bitter and monotonous old refrain, seemingly trying to fall asleep. Her empty expression and half-closed eyes gave her an indifferent and dreamy bearing.

Her astonished family listened to the same sharp and muted sound, to the same buzzing she was making. Little by little these weak and reedy sounds diminished until they faded away.

The long, sad night was spent this way, for none of them dared to move, speak, or glance behind them. The old man dozed soundly in his wooden chair, her mother soon closed her eyes in fear and weariness, while for a long time their two sons rested their heads on their hands in a futile effort to sleep. When sleep came, it was troubled by ominous dreams.

Those drowsy and exhausted heads made quite a sight, gathered around a dying light that bathed their worried brows in a faded and dreary glow. With his mouth slightly open and his skinny hands resting on his thighs, the father's face appeared grave beneath his abundant gray hair. From time to time the old woman seated directly in front of him turned her head from side to side, showing the remarkable expression of bitter misfortune written on her face. Julietta's long blond hair whisked across the table when her calm, whitened face nodded, still whistling the monotonous song through her teeth with a sweet, rapt expression.

Instead of sleeping, she spent the night hours listening to the mournful lowing of the white cow in the stable. The poor animal was still suffering and was probably writhing in agony on its bed dampened with sweat. In fact, when the morning came and Julietta went to put it out to graze, you could still see the trace of a scratch mark on its neck.

She went out, quickly climbed the hill, and sat down when she reached the summit. In her crazed but drowsy condition, the hem of her clothes rustled against her feet in the dewy grass. She ran but then suddenly stopped, braced her forehead with her hand, and scanned around to see if he was coming.

For the poor child loved him! She was in love with a great, rich, and powerful nobleman, a handsome gentleman with proud eyes and a haughty smile. She loved a strange, unknown man, a devil incarnate. She found him to be a cultured and highly poetic creature.

No, nothing of the kind, for she was in love with Duke Arthur Almaroës!

At other times, she fell back into her daydreaming with a bitter smile, as though she distrusted the future. When her thoughts strayed back to him, she saw him there in her mind's eye, sitting on the pearly grass next to her. There he was, whispering sweet words and holding her with his powerful gaze. His soft and pure voice trembled with love, like an entirely new and sublime love. She remained that way for a long time, with her eyes fixed on the unchanging horizon which struck her as being dreary, meaningless, and stupid.

When evening finally arrived after the sun had set on that day of anguish, which was just as long as the previous night, Julietta was still there. Then she slowly headed back down the mountain, stopping at each step to listen for sounds behind her. The only sounds were the crickets chirping in the grass and the sparrow hawk flying back to its nest at top speed.

Tired and hopeless, she went on her way with her head lowered to her breast, which was swollen by her sighs. In her left hand she held the damp rope around the neck of her poor white cow, limping to favor its left shoulder, the one that Satan had sat on.

When she arrived at the spot where the stranger had left her the night before, and where Arthur had appeared to her, she stopped instinctively and held her struggling heifer strongly in check so that it would not keep pulling her off the path. When Arthur suddenly presented himself, she let go of the rope, and the cow went bounding off at a gallop toward the stable.

Julietta looked at him with love, envy, and jealousy. When he passed by, he eyed her the same way he would scan the woods, the sky, or the fields.

She called him by name but he was as deaf to her shout as he would be to the bleat of a sheep, the song of a bird, or the barking of a dog.

"Arthur," she cried in desperation, "Arthur, oh, Arthur! Listen!"

She ran after him, clung to his clothes, and stammered in sobs. Her heart beat violently, and she wept with love and anger. There was so much passion in her wail, in her tears, in that chest heaving tumultuously, in that weak and fragile creature dragging her knees across the ground. Her lament was so far removed from the distress of a woman lamenting over a piece of broken porcelain, the bleating of a sheep, the cry of a bird, or the barking of a dog that Arthur stopped to examine her for a moment . . . before continuing on his way.

"Oh, Arthur, please listen to me for a minute because I love you, I love you! Ah, come with me and we will live together by the sea, far from here. Or else, we'll make a lovers' suicide pact."

Arthur continued walking.

"Listen, Arthur! Just look at me! Am I that hideous, so ugly? You're not a man at all, since your heart is as cold as marble, as hard as stone!"

She fell to her knees at his feet, rolling over on her back as if she were going to die. She really was dying of exhaustion and fatigue, writhing in despair, and trying to tear out her hair. Then with a forced laugh, she sobbed choking tears. Her bloody knees were torn from being dragged over stones. She loved with a full, wounding, and satanic love. It was a furious, surging, and exalting love, even as it devoured her. From those deranged cries and that fire consuming her soul, it was clear that her heart was being ravaged with a love inspired by hell. That turbulent and induced satanic passion was so unparalleled that it seemed bizarre, strong enough to lead to madness.

"Until we meet again tomorrow, then, Arthur? Please be merciful, and afterward I'll give you everything, my blood, my life, my soul, and eternity if it were mine to give! You can kill me, if you wish, but until tomorrow! Tomorrow on the cliff in the moonlight? . . . A night of love, against the background of waves crashing on the rocks. Until tomorrow, Arthur . . . all right?"

And from his disdainful lips he nonchalantly let two words fall:

"Until tomorrow!"

SEVEN

Until tomorrow! Tomorrow! Like a woman possessed, she ran to the cliff. She was no longer seen in the village. She left the region.

Satan had taken her away.

EIGHT

The solitary moon shone pure and white on a cloudless night. Its light streamed through the open window of Arthur's study. He leaned over the banister to smell the deliciously fresh night air. When he heard the same light noise of small paws on the bricks of his oven, he turned around. It was Satan, but this time he was even more hideous and sallow. His sides were hollowed and his open mouth showed greenish teeth like moss-covered tombstones. Arthur spoke:

"Well, Satan, is it true that I now love someone? Do you believe that I have been touched by her pleading sobs, her tears, and those strained convulsions?"

"Really, you are absolutely insensitive! And you let her die?" the demon replied, trembling on all fours.

"She's dead?" Arthur asked with a cold stare.

"No, but she's waiting for you."

"She's waiting for me?"

"Yes, on the cliff. Didn't you promise her? She's been there for a long time, and she is waiting for you."

"All right, I'll go."

"You'll go? Well then, Arthur, I ask only for this last favor. Afterward, you can do what you want with me. I belong to you."

"What do you want me to do? Do you think I want your soul?"

"You'll love it, I tell you . . . Arthur, didn't you tell me that you wanted to have passions, a strong, burning love, unlike other loves? Well, you'll have that love . . . but then . . . look: you know you're going to give me yours in exchange, don't you?"

"I don't have one."

"That's what you think, but you've got one. You're human because you're in love."

Satan was so used to seeing so much pride and vanity that he believed that's all there was. Misery sees only vice, and the starving feel only hunger.

Spreading his green wings and showing his blue tresses, Arthur answered: "A man? Say, Satan, have you seen any of those men who stretch themselves clear up to the clouds? Have you ever seen hair like this? Have you seen any of them with a body as white as snow, Satan, or with a hand this powerful," he added, strongly gripping his skin with his nails, "and have any of them ever dared to insult you this way? Since you want my soul, kill me right now, crush my head with your teeth, rip me with your claws, try to find out if I'm a man."

Frothing with anger, Satan bounded onto the flagstone. He leapt about with such agitation that he nearly hit the ceiling with his back. Arthur remained unmoved as he spoke:

"Satan, you're indeed strong, you're powerful. I think you could annihilate me with one swipe. Go ahead, try it. Please, kill me! . . . Yes, I have a soul. Take it, it's yours. Kill me, that's easy. I'm only a man."

The devil leapt at his throat with a hellish scream that arose from his bowels. He tried to overcome him, but the skin slipped away from under his teeth. Arthur pulled his neck loose. Satan made a mad leap with his claws extended. He fell in a heap without ever touching the perfectly polished skin. With eyes aflame, he stamped and jumped frenetically, emitting a coarse bark from his bloody lips. Arthur lay down and spread his wings. Satan slipped on them, and began to crawl and grovel; he opened his mouth to gash Arthur, but his claws began to wear down as if he were scraping them against rock. As he turned red with rage, he slobbered and gasped over the fact of his first defeat. And the other, the other was softly laughing, yet the prolonged resonance of this relaxed laugh rang like a heavily struck tuning fork. The gruff hiss of his breath revolted Satan, the way the steady ring of a tocsin sounding in the nave of a church can vibrate the pillars until they collapse and the vault falls in.

You had to see these two incredible creatures going at each other, each one an unparalleled creation. One was entirely spirit, the other incarnate in divine matter. You would have witnessed soul against body, and this soul, this pure, ethereal spirit, was stamping with frustrated outrage against the lofty arrogance of raw, stupid matter.

Those two monsters of Creation were thrust together in hateful combat. It was total war, a fight to the death, . . . which would necessarily lead to a wearying doubt . . . just as with mankind.

These two incoherent principles were locked in hand-to-hand struggle. Faced with the body's patience, the tired spirit fell from exhaustion.

Oh, how sublime and gigantic those two were together; those two opposites, if they were wedded, would constitute a God, the spirit of evil and the force of power! How terrible and mighty that struggle was, with hellish cries mixed with wild laughter, and then the rocks of the entire building in ruins shook underfoot as in a dream!

After Satan had jumped around and fallen to the ground a number of times, he was left panting in exhaustion, with hollow eyes and broken claws, and covered with icy sweat. Arthur considered him at length, worn out from wild anger and groveling sadly at his feet. For a long time he savored the death rattle emanating from his chest and counted the heartbreaking sighs of agony that could no longer be contained. When Satan finally recovered from his cruel defeat, he lifted his feeble head toward his conqueror but still found the cold and impassive expression of that automaton, which seemed to laugh disdainfully. Arthur spoke:

"And you also let yourself be beaten like a man . . . by pride again! Now do you think I spoke the truth?"

"Maybe you aren't a man, but you do have a soul."

"Very well, Satan, tomorrow I'll go out to the cliff."

And when the caretaker made his rounds through the halls the next morning, he found that the squares of flagstone had been disturbed and ruined here and there, as though by an iron claw. It drove the old man mad.

NINE

For four years Julietta scanned the rocks and tearfully awaited the duke night and day. The years pass quickly in a tale, as in the mind. Memory speeds them up, but hope makes them limp along slowly.

During the day she walked along the beach, listened to the sea, and looked all around to see if he was coming. When the sun warmed the rocks, fatigue made her fall asleep on the sand. Then she got up to go pick some fruit and hunt for the bread that a few kind souls had left in a depression in the rocks.

At night she paced the cliffs, wandering there in her long white clothes with her hair disheveled and whimpering painfully. For hours on end she sat amid the jagged rocks, watching the waves break in the moonlight and run their fingers up onto the beach, frothing with white foam between the large rocks and small stones.

"Poor madwoman!" people said of her, "so young and beautiful, and bereft of hope when she is scarcely twenty years old! . . . Such a shame, but it's also her fault for falling madly in love with a prince. Pride has undone her for surrendering herself to Satan."

Yes, she was surely mad for loving Duke Arthur instead of stifling her love or killing herself. But her belief in God kept her from suicide.

It is true that she often contemplated the hundred-foot drop from the cliff to the water. And when she began to smile to herself, her grimace frightened the children. She was completely insane to believe in God, to respect him, suffer for his pleasure, and weep for his delight. "Belief in God, Julietta, brings happiness; but you believe in God and suffer for it. You are certainly mad!" That's what people will tell you.

No, sadness gave way to despondency, and tears replaced wild laments. Instead of outbursts or deep sighs, she restrained her imperceptible moans, as though venting them would kill her. Misfortune had aged her and turned her hair white. Like time, it passes swiftly but weighs heavily and hits hard. Even more, despair needs fewer tears to emaciate a man than a storm needs drops of water to hollow out a tombstone. Hair can turn white in a single night.[2]

Her hair was white and her clothes were ripped, but her feet had become toughened from walking barefoot and from being torn by the brambles and thorns. Her hands were cracked and furrowed by the cold, bitter salt air, which chaps and burns like a northern frost. She was haggard and thin, but her lifeless, empty eyes were still livened by a ray of love and lit by an infernal spark. Her half-open mouth contracted from an involuntary and convulsive movement. But she was still bronzed from exposure to the sun, and her strangely attractive expression was still seductive. She was still that sublimely passionate soul which Satan had chosen in order to tempt dormant matter, the body stripped of its senses, and the flesh without its voluptuousness. When she saw a man, she ran toward him, fell at his feet, called him Arthur, and then she returned with her hopes dashed, saying, "That's someone else. He's not coming!"

People said, "Oh, the poor madwoman, so young and beautiful . . . disconsolate when she's only twenty!"

Brilliant white stars radiating from the deep blue of the beautiful night sky accentuated the soft calm of the silent sea as it lapped gently against the rocks beneath the cliffs. Julietta was still there in her solitary revery. And then Arthur emerged, as though from some kind of dream! Arthur! But he was still cold and self-possessed: "I'm waiting for you, Julietta. I've been at our rendezvous a long time!"

Her voice trembled when she said, "Sit down with me on this rock, dear Arthur. What more do you need? The moon is beautiful, the stars are shining, the sea is calm, and it's beautiful here, Arthur . . . sit down and let's chat."

---

2. The phenomenon of hair turning white as an affective index of hardship is consistent in Flaubert's writing: cf. note 2 to "Whatever You Want," below; "Passion and Virtue," sec.4 (11:345); and "Smarh," esp. "My white hair shows how pain has aged me" (11:542), and "Being a poet means to have your hair turn white before its time" (11:575). When Madame Arnoux said good-bye to Frédéric at the close of *Sentimental Education*, she removed her hat near a lamp which "lit up her white hair. It was like a blow to his heart" (3:393); cf. Flaubert's correspondence: "One's hair falls away like one's feelings" (13:177).

He stretched out next to her.

"What do you want from me, Julietta? Why are you more forlorn than the other women? Why did you ask me to come here?"

"Why? . . . But Arthur . . . I love you!"

"What do you mean?"

"What! When I look at you like this, here, with this smile . . . ," and she put her arm around his waist, ". . . when you feel my breath, when I caress your mouth with my hair, well, don't you feel something right here in your chest, something pulsating and breathing?"

"No, not at all! Yes, I understand that you are a woman with a soul. But I don't have one." He looked at her proudly and asked, "What is the soul, Julietta?"

"I don't know . . . but I love you! Oh, love, Arthur, love turns your hair white like mine!"

She gazed at him as she dragged herself along on her chest; she plied him with her kisses and caresses, whereas he remained impassive beneath that shower of affection, cold to the touch of her kisses.

You had to see that woman spent from her emotion, offering all her passion, love, poetry, and consuming, intimate ardor in attempting to bring Arthur's lethargic body to life. But he felt nothing from her burning lips and tremulous arms, like the touch of a lizard to a beast. Julietta was as brimming with love as Satan was consumed with angry rage.

She spent many hours embracing Arthur as he looked at the sky. He himself was rapt by sublime dreams of love, with no thought that there before him was a heavenly reality, an exceptional love, both vivid and exalted.

Julietta! He let her fall exhausted, but she made one last effort. She ran to the highest rocks and leapt. There was silence for a few seconds before Arthur heard the sound of a body falling heavily into the water. The gently soothing night was as beautiful and calm as the waves of the sea softly dying on the beach. The waves rolled and broke, bringing with them shells, kelp, flotsam and jetsam. One wave in particular rolled in from far out, came well up on the strand, and left something bulky in its wake.

It was a woman's body.

"Well?" said Arthur as he looked at Satan.

And when Satan saw that his brow was still pale and unwrinkled, that no tears wet his eye, he said:

"No, no! You don't have a soul! I was wrong," he added, looking at him with envy, "but I'll have hers."

And he plunged his cloven hoof into the throat of the corpse.

TEN

Several centuries passed by. In its lethargic sleep, the earth was untroubled by any sounds except for the foamy crash of the ocean's waves. When they rose twisting furiously in the air, the shore reverberated from the shock as though shaken by the hands of a giant. A fine but steady rain hid the moon's dusky light, and wind smashed through the forest and billowed the skies above, the way a breeze bends a reed by the edge of a lake.

The air was filled with an extraordinary mixture of tears and sobs, as if the earth were emitting its death rattle.

Rising from the earth, a voice said, "Enough, enough! I have suffered and bent my back for too long. Oh, please don't create any other worlds!"

And like the voice of an angel, a sweet, pure, and melodious voice descended to the earth and said:

"No, no! It's for eternity. There will be no more worlds!"

March 21, 1837

Whatever You Want[1]

Psychological Studies

ONE

Come to me, my insomniac thoughts! Bring on the dreams of this poor madman! All of you come, you friendly little devils with broad wings and trailing beards, who hop onto my feet when I'm in bed and run up my windows onto the ceiling. Purple, green, yellow, black, and white, you shake the door jam of my bedroom and rattle the hinges. The breath from your greenish lips makes the candle flame tremble and falter.

I often see you enter quietly on pale winter evenings, wearing your brown greatcoats that plow through the snowy rooftops. Your little bony skulls slip through my keyhole, and then you go over to the grating of my fireplace to warm your long nails before the embers die.

Come one and all, my brainchildren, and lend me one of your follies and

---

1. The titular theme of this tale has clear implications for the problem of assigning meaning to the uncommitted conclusions of Flaubert's early writing. So far as I am aware, the origin of the title has never been pointed out. It derives from Martial 1.105.4: "As new wine that is born in Nomentian fields increases in age, Ovid, it changes both name and nature; when it is mature, you may call the jar that contains it whatever you wish." New Nomentian wine is undrinkable; when properly aged, it is highly prized. Within the context of old wine in new bottles, see the list of literary antecedents and the discussion of scientific interest in breeding monsters cited by Bruneau (*Débuts littéraires*, pp.129–30), and Leyla Peronne-Moisés, "*Quidquid volueris*: The Scriptural Education," in *Flaubert and Postmodernism* (Lincoln: University of Nebraska Press, 1984), pp.155–57. On monstrosities as alternative creations with their self-sufficient logic, see 10:68–69 and 12:358.

fits of strange laughter. That way you'll spare me the trouble of composing a modern preface coupled with a Classical invocation to the Muse.

TWO

"Tell us about your trip to Brazil, my friend. Adele will enjoy it." Those were the words that Madam de Lansac spoke to her nephew Paul one beautiful autumn evening. Adele was the pretty blond who casually hung on his arm when they strolled down the gravel paths in the park. Paul replied:

"But auntie, I assure you I had an excellent trip."

"You already told me."

"Oh, yes . . . ," he said, trailing off into silence.

The surrounding silence continued unbroken, with each one lost in private thoughts. At odd moments, one plucked petals from a rose, another shuffled the gravel underfoot, while the third watched the moon through the giant elms, standing out clearly and serenely between the interconnecting branches.

The moon again! Still, it is practically a required prop for any ominous scene, just as you come to expect chattering teeth and hair standing on end. But the fact is that on that night there *was* a moon. Why do you want to take my poor moon away from me? Oh, moon, I love you so! You shine on the castle's steep roof, you change the lake into a silver ribbon. In your pale aura every single raindrop suspended from the tip of a rose petal is like a pearl poised on a woman's lovely breast. That's such a cliché that we ought to break off right there and return to our sheep, as [Rabelais's] Panurge put it.

Yet there was a languid quality in the studied ease and dreamy abandon of that young woman who leaned easily on her cousin's arm. There was something seductive about the way her smile featured her sparkling teeth, the way her blond curls framed her fresh and winning features. The scene was redolent of the sort of love that thrills your very soul.

She wasn't a hot Latin beauty, a daughter of Mediterranean climes whose eyes flash like a volcano and blaze with burning passion. Her eyes weren't black and her skin wasn't as downy soft as that of Andalusian types. Her misty appearance was as mysterious as those snowy-necked Scandinavian sprites who walk barefoot through mountain snows and, airy and evanescent, emerge from river banks on starry nights to greet the poet as he sings his love.

From her watery blue eyes and wan complexion, you would have thought her one of those children who had suffered from colic, who drink water, bang out some Liszt on the piano, love poetry and melancholy thoughts, and have stomach trouble.

Who was her love? Was it her swans gliding across the pond, the monkeys fussing over the nuts she slipped between the bars of their cage? Then there were the birds and squirrels, the flowered park, her handsome giltedged books, and her childhood friend, her cousin Paul. He had long black sideburns, was big and strong, and in two weeks he would be her husband.

Rest assured that she'll find happiness with such a husband! I see him as an eminently level-headed sort who hates poetry, who has a solid constitution and a dry heart, qualities needed to make your fortune and to live to be a hundred years old. The practical man is the one who can get by without paying his debts, who knows how to sip a glass of fine wine, who uses a woman's love like an occasional article of clothing and then tosses it aside among other old clothes, like discardable feelings that are no longer in style.

Indeed, he'll ask you what love really is: "If it's foolish, I'll take advantage of it. What about tenderness? Rationalists find it silly, and besides: I don't have any. Poetry? It can't prove anything, so I stay away from it. What about stuff and nonsense like religion, patriotism, or art? As for the soul, Cabanis and Bichat long ago proved that the heart is made up of veins, and that's all."[2]

Now there goes a man with common sense, well respected and honored. He supports the public militia, dresses like everybody else, talks morality

---

2. Pierre Cabanis (1757–1808) and Xavier Bichat (1771–1802) were two of the most famous French physicians of the period. Cabanis largely studied the influence of climate and surroundings on temperament, and the relationship between inborn and acquired traits. Bichat's great *Anatomie générale* (Paris: Brosson & Gabon, 1801) was based on observation and experimentation, and propounded the influential principle of "vital properties" for determining physical and psychological causes as derived from the structure of any organism; Bichat held that hair is the seat of affections (see pp.427, 451, 550–57; cf. "Dream of Hell," sec.9). His book exerted a great influence on Flaubert's father. In a letter to George Sand in 1871, Flaubert wrote, "Do you know what I am reading to pass the time now? Bichat and Cabanis, whom I enjoy enormously. They really knew how to write books back then. Oh, how far the doctors of today are from those men!" (15:60).

and philanthropy, and votes for railroads and for the abolition of gaming houses. He lives in a nice manor house with his wife, his son who is studying to become a notary, and a daughter who is going to marry a chemist. If you chance to meet him at the Opera, you'll see him with gold-rimmed glasses, a black suit, and cane, sucking on menthol lozenges to hide his cigar breath (he can't stand pipes because they're way out of style).

Paul hadn't married yet but soon would, for the obvious convenience that it would double his fortune. As it was, he was only a little short of having an income of fifty thousand pounds. In school he had excelled at mathematics, but he always found literature to be stupid.

The silent contemplation of their walk continued for a long time, enhanced by the beautiful night sky that blanketed the trees, thickets, and pond with a blue aura created by moonlight shining through the misty veil surrounding them.

They didn't reenter the salon until nearly eleven o'clock. In the sputtering candlelight, you could see some roses which had fallen from the mahogany flower stand to be strewn all over the waxed parquet by careless foot traffic. So what! There were a lot more!

Adele felt the dew dampen her satin slippers. With one hand dragging on the floor, she was sleeping on the sofa to get rid of her headache. Madam de Lansac had gone to lock up the house and make a few preparations for the next day. That left only Paul and Djalioh.[3]

Paul looked at the gilded candelabra, at the bronze pendulum clock that struck midnight with its crystalline chime, the grand piano, paintings, arm-chairs, white marble table, and patterned sofa. Turning to the window, he looked toward the most forested part of the park:

"Rabbits will come out around four o'clock in the morning."

Djalioh was watching the girl as she slept. He wished to say something, but his shy and modulated speech was mistaken for a sigh.

It doesn't matter whether it was a comment or a sigh, since he put his entire soul into it!

THREE

When a warm sun rose the next morning, then, the hunter set out with his favorite retriever, two basset hounds, and his warden, who carried his big

---

3. For commentary on the way Flaubert often fashioned names from an assortment of other names and words, see Peronne-Moisés, "*Quidquid volueris*," p.148.

game bag, powder and shot, assorted hunting gear, and a huge duck pâté that Paul himself had ordered two days prior. On command, the horn was sounded and they began to stride into the field, preceded by assistants who were to flush out the game.

Right away, one of the window shutters on the third floor opened wide enough for a head swathed in long blond hair to peek out amid the riot of jasmine that decorated the large manor's expanse of red and white brick wall. By the way her hair flowed loose over her bare shoulders and relaxed form, you might have thought she was wearing a short-sleeved negligee. Occasionally, her muslin-trimmed blouse would gape open. When she suddenly pushed open the window to watch Paul's departure, she inadvertently scraped her plump, white arm against the wall. She waved and blew him a kiss. Paul turned around and for a long time fixed his attention on that fresh and innocent young head framed by jasmine flowers. He mused on the flowers, girl, and love that soon would be all his, concluding, "How nice she is!" Then a white hand reached out to close the shutter, just as the clock struck four. The cock began to crow, while a shaft of sunlight pierced the mantle of foliage to dance over the slate roof. A silent calm was restored.

Paul had not returned by ten. Lunch was announced and served. The cavernous room's decor was Louis Quinze. Above the fireplace a dusty frame held a dim pastoral scene in which an elegantly powdered shepherdess, sporting various beauty spots, was decked out with wicker baskets and attended by a flock of snowy white sheep; while a cupid hovered above, her cute little pug dog lay at her feet on a rug embroidered with a picture of a bouquet of roses tied by a gold strand. White pigeon eggs with green speckles projected from the molding, linked like beads on a strand. Here and there the faded white wainscoting was decorated with family portraits and vivid landscapes from Norway or Russia, or else with snowy mountains and harvest scenes; and in the distance you could dimly make out engravings in black frames. Over here one saw a full-length portrait of some illustrious politician, swathed in ermine and crowned by his wig of office. Farther off a German knight wheeled his steed, whose long bushy tail twisted and undulated like the bands of a snake. The smoke-filled tavern scenes of several Flemish paintings were marked by beer-guzzling worthies, crude humor, large bare breasts, raucous laughter emanating from fleshy lips, and an unabashed materialism extending from the curly-haired child gulping his wine to the fleshy Virgin serenely ensconced in her dingy, grimy niche. Through the high, wide windows sunlight danced around the room to grace the worn furniture with a youthful sparkle. A black and white tile floor extended between the marble fountains at each end of the room.

But the most sensually memorable piece of furniture was the spacious old sofa, remarkable for its inviting softness. Against a background of elegant white satin the material was richly splashed with bold yellow and green birds of paradise and bouquets of flowers. After the servants had cleared the dinner dishes, the mistress of the manor customarily seated herself amid its silk cushions to await the return of the gentleman hunter who might chance to pass that particular way, so as not to disturb anyone, in an effort to find a thirst-quenching drink. In all likelihood, quite a few pretty marchionesses with pink skin tones and fine hands, or important countesses with short petticoats and svelte figures, had taken in the pleasant musings that many a priest or atheist slipped into a conversation about the needs of a sensitive soul. Yes, the walls had overheard plenty of subtle sighs, furtive kisses, and tears.

All of that was gone! The pleasantries of marquises, abbots, and gentlemen, the provocative red high-heeled slippers, had all vanished to leave only memories of kisses, loves, tender effusiveness. The sofa was still resting there on its mahogany legs, but its gilded moldings were tarnished, and its gold embroidery was ragged.

Djalioh was seated next to Adele. She was pouting when she sat down, pushed back her chair, blushed, and quickly poured herself a glass of wine. There was nothing really disagreeable about her companion, who had not spoken a word in the month that he had spent at the manor. Some said he was whimsical, others thought him melancholy, while the most authoritative found him stupid, mad, and a deaf mute. All those who saw him regarded him as Paul's odd friend.

He was small and frail. His hands with their short blunt fingers and large hooked fingernails were his only sign of strength. The rest of his body was feeble, and his complexion was so pathetic as to make you shudder that such a young man seemed destined for the grave, like those broken and leafless trees that continue to survive. His black clothes only emphasized the livid, coppery yellow color of his skin. Large white teeth showed between thick lips like a Negro's or a monkey's. His narrow head was compressed in front but in back was prodigiously developed, which was all the more emphasized by the wrinkled scalp that showed through his sparse hair. There was a strangely wild and animalistic aspect about him, which made him look less human than strangely bestial. His large round eyes had a dull and lifeless coloration, but when he cast a gentle glance your way, you felt the impact of its strange fascination, although his features had nothing harsh or threatening. He met all looks with a smile, but his laugh was stupid and cold. If he had opened his shirt, you would have seen his thick black skin and the hair of his broad athletic chest, which rose and fell visibly because of his enormous lungs.

Ah, but his heart was as vast as the sea and as immense and empty as the desert! In the forest, atop mountains, or at sea, his wrinkled brow suddenly smoothed out, his nostrils flared forcefully, and his entire soul opened to nature like a rose opening to the sun. An inner voluptuousness made him tremble all over, causing him to grip his bowed head in the throes of a lethargic melancholy. At those moments his soul shone through his physical features the way a beautiful woman's eyes shine through a black veil. For his exceptionally ugly and hideous features, his sickly pall, his shrunken skull and rickety limbs all took on such an air of elated enthusiasm, and his wretched monkey eyes blazed with such poetry, that he seemed violently shaken by some sort of galvanic action in his soul. His passion was like madness, and his love was frenzied. His heartstrings were more sonorously responsive than other people's; his pain turned to convulsive spasms, and his pleasures became unheard-of voluptuousness.

Even though at seventeen years of age he was in the bloom of youth, he seemed so old and broken, so worn out and battered by the storms in his soul, that he seemed more like sixty, one hundred, or even centuries old. Ask the old man of the sea how wrinkled his forehead is and how many waves there are in a storm!

He had lived for a very long time, but not the life of the mind. His life had not been occupied for a single moment by dreams or philosophical reflection. But his soul had lived so expansively that his heart was already old. Yet his feelings were directed to no one in particular, since he was a tangle of the strangest feelings. Logic had given way to poetry, and passion had taken the place of knowledge. At times he seemed to hear voices emanating from a patch of roses and melodies from out of the blue. Nature in all its forms lay at the heart of his strength, the delights of his soul, his violent passions and gluttonous appetites. He epitomized great mental and physical weakness, coupled with the vehemence of a fragile heart that shattered whenever it met any obstacle, the way a senseless lightning bolt smashes castles, burns crowns to a crisp, and flattens cottages before it is harmlessly extinguished in a puddle of water.

That's the kind of natural monster who was befriended by Paul, who was himself a marvelous monster of civilization outfitted with all its symbols, great intelligence, and shriveled soul. Just as he loved effusiveness of the soul and sweet nothings of the heart, Djalioh loved nocturnal revery and dreamy thoughts.[4] His heart took to what was beautiful and sublime the way ivy takes to ruins, the way flowers go with springtime, corpses with tombs, and the way misfortune clings to men until the day they die. Wherever intelligence left off, the vast and infinite empire of the heart took over, for its love took in the entire world.

He loved Adele the way he loved all of nature with a tender and universal sympathy. This love steadily increased as his love for all other beings waned. Indeed, all of us are born with a certain wealth of tenderness and love which we happily invest in the first things that come along—horses, property, honors, kingdoms, women, pleasures—which are scattered to the winds and borne off in floods. But if we collect it all, we will have a treasure. Throw tons of gold on the desert floor, and soon the sands will engulf all of it; yet if you heap them in a single pile, you will form pyramids.

Well, he soon focused his entire soul on one single thought, and he lived on that thought.

FOUR

A lengthy two-week wait for the girl slipped by, suggesting a cold indifference toward her fiancé. In marriage she envisioned a husband, cashmere,

---

4. This passage has attracted a spectrum of critical readings, ranging from Bruneau's concern for what he sees as flawed rhetorical alignment (*Débuts littéraires*, pp.346–47) to Jean-Paul Sartre's enormous disquisition on the way this awkward comparison reflects Flaubert's, and Sartre's, major theme of "loser wins"; see *The Family Idiot*, trans. Carol Cosman (Chicago: University of Chicago Press, 1981), pp.208–9. On the same point, Sartre (p.228) says that "Gustave's ever-flowing pen assigns to the same term two functions which are hardly compatible."

a loge at the Opera, horse races in the Bois de Boulogne, dances all winter long—in short, all her heart's desires! These were the stuff of a seventeen-year-old girl's gilded dreams in the privacy of her room.

On the other hand, her future husband foresaw a wife, bills to pay for cashmeres, a small doll to clothe, and then again everything that a poor husband dreams about when he takes his wife to the ball. He was conceited enough to think that all women were in love with him. That's what he always asked himself when he studied himself in a mirror and when he curried his black sideburns. He married because he was bored with living alone, and he didn't want another mistress since learning that his manservant had one too. Besides, marriage would make him stay home, which would be all to the good. And he would no longer have to be bored by hunting outings. Best of all, he would find domestic love, blissful devotion, tranquillity, children . . . no, better than tranquillity would be love, happiness, an income of fifty thousand pounds from productive farms, and solid banknotes that he could invest in Spanish securities.

In Paris he bought a seat on the stock exchange for ten thousand francs, gave a ball for one hundred twenty guests, and returned to his mother-in-law's chateau, all within a week. What remarkable energy!

The wedding took place on a cold and damp Sunday in September. A heavy mist covered the valley, and sand from the garden clung to the ladies' new slippers. Few attended ten o'clock mass. Borne along by the flow of the crowd, Djalioh entered the small old church with cramped, whitewashed walls, where he was surrounded by the warm and fragrant atmosphere emanating from the incense on the altar. The stained glass was intact, thanks to the attention of the caretaker. The choir loft was surrounded by invited guests, the mayor, the city attorney, friends, the notary, a doctor, and a robed chorus. The calm scene was spotted with white gloves everywhere, digging five-franc pieces from their purses. The clink in the collection plate interrupted the monotony of the ecclesiastical chants. The bell sounded.

Djalioh recalled that once before he had heard the bell intoning over a coffin. He had also seen people dressed in black praying over a corpse. Then, turning toward the fiancée in white, bent over the altar with flowers at her brow and a pearl necklace on her undulating cleavage, a horrible thought struck him. He stumbled toward the security of an altar niche, which was empty except for . . . a horrible and frighteningly grotesque woman.

Right next to the bride was her beloved, the object of her affection, whose large black eyebrows and blue eyes were like two diamonds set in ebony. Lolling in his crimson velvet armchair, he scanned the women all around him with his lorgnette made of gold-encrusted shell.

Djalioh stood motionless and silent. No one noticed his drained face or the bitterness of his smile, since people assumed that he was as cold and indifferent as the grimacing gargoyle right above his head. Yet a storm raged in his soul and anger smoldered in his heart, like snowcapped Icelandic volcanoes. Far from a mad, brutal outburst, it was more like a silent, effortless implosion without weeping, wailing, or cursing. His leaden eyes gave no more sign than the lips of his stupid face.

Beautiful young women live a long time with a fresh, soft complexion. But then their white, satiny cast begins to fade as the glow in their eyes diminishes, weakens, and finally dies. And that lithe, attractive woman who flitted among salons with flowers in her hair and had such white hands that gave off the scent of musk mixed with rose? Well, one fine day a doctor friend of hers will inform you that a cancer two inches below her ample cleavage is killing her. Now her springlike complexion is cadaverous. That's the story of all intimate passions and all frozen smiles.

The laughter of malediction is horrible, worse than the most intense suffering. After that, you needn't place your faith in smiles, joy, or gaiety. What can you believe in, then? Believe in the inviolable sanctuary and deep sleep of the tomb.

What an immense chasm the word "eternity" opens up! Let's pause for a moment to consider those words: life, death, despair, joy, happiness. Some day when you are weeping over a loved one and find yourself tossing and turning in bed, ask yourself why we live and die. Why do the winds of misfortune and despair blow us about in torrents, like grains of sand? What kind of Hydra slakes its thirst on our tears and rejoices in our anguished sobs? Why? And then we feel ourselves sucked into the swirl of a bottomless pit, which resonates with the laughter of the damned. Your soul is imbued with powers and shaded by thoughts that impel you toward satanic depths, as though your head were made of iron which a magnet pulled down toward your misfortune.

Ah, yes, the hollowed eyes and fixed stare of a skull! Does reality come down to its yellowish pall and chipped jaw? Is that what reality is? Does everything end in oblivion?

Djalioh sank into a bottomless abyss of the most burning doubt and most bitter suffering. As he looked over the smiling faces in that festive atmosphere, he thought about his love for Adele, about his life, about her charms and soft glances, and he wondered why they couldn't be his. He was like a man condemned to starve and be tortured by a few iron bars that separate him from food placed only inches beyond his reach. He didn't know why that feeling was different from any others, because when he was living in the South American tropics, he welcomed strangers to the shade of his palm trees and to the fruit of his garden. Now he wondered why his love for her was so exclusive and complete. It's because love is a whole, indivisible world.

And then he bowed his head on his chest and for a long time whimpered like a baby. Only once did he utter a shrill cry like an owl, but this squawk was drowned by the organ's soft and melodious voice, as it sang a *Te Deum* ["We praise thee, O Lord"]. Its pure, full-bodied tones resounded as they swelled their way through clouds of incense up into the nave.

He then noticed that the entire audience began to stir, scraping their chairs as they left. A shaft of sunlight shone through the stained glass. It played over the golden comb of the bride-to-be, and for a few moments it sparkled across the gilded bars of the cemetery, the only separation between the city hall and the church. The well-kept grass in the cemetery stands so tall and plush that the guests got their feet and white stockings wet and muddied their pumps. They cursed the dead.

The mayor was standing at his place at the head of a square table covered by a green cloth. When it was time to pronounce the fatal "I do," Paul smiled, Adele blanched, and Madame de Lansac took out her smelling salts.

A pensive Adele couldn't get over her astonishment: just a while ago she was alternately madcap and thoughtful, she ran through the fields and read novels, poetry, and short stories, she galloped her horse down bridal paths in the woods, she loved to hear the leaves rustle and the brook murmur. And she became a young lady before she knew it, strolling down the street, unattended except for her large shawl! She would wake from her dream, and this vague expectation, these intimate stirrings of the heart, and this need for poetry and sensations as catalysts for turning her mind to the future and thinking about herself would all be dispelled!

Too bad for all those young innocent hearts and minds! They are doomed from the cradle to a life of domestic chores and lavishing kisses on a crabby old stick of a husband who is hobbled by the corns on his feet!

When the crowd parted for the cortege, Adele felt an iron claw scratch her hand. It was Djalioh who scraped her with his fingernail when he went by. Her glove turned red with blood, so she had to wrap it with her sheer linen handkerchief. As she turned to step up into her carriage, she saw Djalioh leaning on the runningboard. She shuddered and then disappeared into the cab.

He was as ashen as the bridal gown. His thick, pimply lips were cracked from fever and became animated as though he were mimicking rapid speech. His eyelashes fluttered and his eyeballs rolled in their sockets like those of an idiot.

FIVE

That evening, there was a ball at the chateau, which was festooned with Chinese lanterns at every window.[5] There was a parade of coaches, horses, and valets. From time to time a light shone in the near distance between the elms. Through the maze of carriage paths it was seen to change directions as it approached, until its carriage and lathered horses arrived at the front porch. The carriage door opened and a woman alighted. She could have been young or old, beautiful or ugly, dressed in pink or white, as you wish. Before entering, she carefully retouched her coiffure with a few quick,

---

5. Scholars have shown how this description of the chateau and its natural setting arose from a visit Flaubert made at Michaelmas (Sept.29) in 1837 to the Château du Heron on the invitation of the Marquis de Pomereu. Some have observed not only how the account transforms the walk taken by Flaubert as a fifteen-year-old schoolboy along the bay of Trouville with Elisa Schlésinger but also how the portrayal parallels the initial manuscript description of Emma Bovary as she strolled the grounds at the Château de la Vaubyessard (see Shanks, *Flaubert's Youth*, p.37; Bruneau, *Débuts littéraires*, p.129; 10:490–91; and cf. "Whatever You Want," sec.3, and "Diary of a Madman," sec.9). Bruneau (p.495) states that the episode profoundly affected the young Flaubert, but the deepest connections with the dreamlike anticipation and disappointment of the chateau's initiatory social rituals may lie elsewhere. Charles Bovary's entry at Michaelmas into the world's confusing codes of language is "like the initiation to the world, the access to forbidden pleasures," where crescendo introduces a resounding crash (1:57); he proposed marriage at Michaelmas, one full year before Emma waltzed at Vaubyessard; her first seduction occurred around Michaelmas, with the apparent blessing of nature; Flaubert supposedly lost his virginity on Michaelmas (13:534).

deft strokes of her hand in the glow of the exterior oil lamps. Against the background of trees and the wall carpeted in flowery green, she shed her coat, gave her boa to the servants, and entered through the double doors. There was a clatter of chairs and boots as people rose to acknowledge her. A thousand casual conversations began to buzz heatedly, while the guests exchanged airy pleasantries and flitted from one end of the hall to the other, like wisps of moisture in a greenhouse.

The dance began at ten o'clock, accompanying the melody with sounds of slippers shuffling on the parquet and the rustle of dresses. Outside, one could hear the whisper of leaves, the noise of distant coaches on the muddy trails, swans beating their wings on the ponds, a dog from the village baying at the music rising from the chateau, and the unaffected chatter of the country people who joked as they stared into the windows of the salon.

Off in one corner were Paul's former friends from his bachelor days, sporting blue or yellow gloves, lorgnettes, and swallowtail frock coats and looking like figures from another time with beards such as neither Rembrandt nor the entire Flemish school had even dreamed of. One of them, a member of the Jockey Club, asked:

"Would you mind telling me who that is over there behind the woman talking to your wife, the one who is frowning and wrinkled like an old woman?"

"Who, that? That's Djalioh."

"Who on earth is Djalioh?"

"Oh, that's a whole story in itself."

"Well, why don't you regale us," asked a nearsighted young man with his hair slicked back over his ears, "since we have nothing to amuse us?"

A tall, pale gentleman with a slight build and prominent cheekbones wittily rejoined:

"Why not just have some grog punch, then?"

"I don't want any, and for a good reason: it's too strong."

"How about some cigars?" asked the member of the Jockey Club.

"Forget about the cigars, Ernest. Don't you realize there are ladies present?"

"I have ten mistresses who smoke like dragons, and two of them have commandeered all my pipes."

"I've got one who drinks kirsch as if it's going out of style."

"Let's drink up!" said one of his friends who didn't like cigars, punch, dancing, or music.

"No, let Paul tell his story!"

"My friends, it's not long, so here is the whole story. I made a wager with a Mr. Petterwell, a friend of mine who is a Brazilian planter. I bet—a pack of Virginia tobacco against a slave of his named Mirsa—that a person could raise, yes, a monkey. In other words, he dared me to pass off a monkey as a man."

"Well, are you saying that Djalioh is a monkey?"

"Not that way, you idiot!"

"But you just . . ."

"I should explain that on my trip to Brazil I especially enjoyed myself. Petterwell had a black slave who had just arrived from the Bahamas straits, damned if I can remember her name! Anyway, since she was pretty and unmarried, there wouldn't be anything to keep me from buying her. That crazy woman wanted no part of me, and probably found me uglier than a savage."

Their laughter made Paul blush.

"Well, one day when I was bored, a Negro sold me the finest orangutan you ever saw. For a long time the Academy of Science had been trying to solve this problem: can you crossbreed a monkey with a man? Now, I had my score to settle with that little Negress, and one day as I returned from hunting I learned that my monkey, whom I had locked in the room with my slave, had escaped, leaving the slave bloodied by his claw marks. A few weeks later she felt abdominal pains and heart pangs. And then five months after that she vomited for days on end. I was pretty sure I had things pegged right. She once suffered from nerves so frightfully that I had to have all her limbs bled for fear she might die. The point is that one fine day she gave birth on a manure pile. She died a few hours later but the kid was doing great, and, by golly, I was very happy that the matter had been settled. I tendered the official report to the Institute, and on the minister's recommendation I was awarded the Legion of Honor."

"Too bad, old sport. That's nothing to brag about."

"Maybe sophomoric, but women like it and smile at it when you talk to them. I raised the child and loved him like a father."

A jovial man inquired, "Really! Why didn't you bring him back to France on one of your earlier trips?"

"I thought it best to leave him in his native country until I left for good. Besides, sixteen was the age determined by our wager, and it was made within my first year in Rio. In short, I won Mirsa, was decorated at twenty, and on top of that I produced a child through a unique procedure."

"How infernal, Dantesque!" a pasty friend volunteered.

Another with large, flushed cheeks added, "How funny! Ridiculous!"

A dandy chimed in with "Nice going!"

Over on a love seat, a slightly built man with a flat forehead shuddered with pleasure: "I'm laughing so much I could die!" He wiggled and twisted like a carp jumping in the air. He had small eyes, blunt nose, and thin lips; he was as round as an apple, with the complexion of a cantaloupe: "That's a classic master stroke! No ordinary man could have pulled that off."

"What does Djalioh do? I'll bet he likes cigars!" said the smoker, extending two handfuls and letting them purposely drop on a lady's knees.

"Not at all. He hates them."

"Does he like to hunt?"

"Even less. Gunshots frighten him."

"Surely he must work, read, and write all day long?"

"First he would have to learn to read and write."

A convalescent asked if he liked horses.

"Not at all."

"In other words, he's an inert and unthinking animal. What about the fair sex?"

"One day I took him to a brothel, but he ran away carrying a rose in one hand and a mirror in the other."

Everyone agreed that he sounded like a complete idiot. The group broke up to continue their socializing. The men showed off their manners for the women, who preened and glittered during the intermission. What with all the dancing and social niceties, the hour was getting late, yet the music played on, echoing across the carpet. In the midst of lively dancing, the clock struck midnight.

Djalioh had been seated near the musicians since the opening festivities, occasionally shifting his position. Many a happy and carefree celebrant became steeped in confusion, aglow with wine, and intoxicated by that chain of charming women with bared bosoms and smiling lips. But each turned sad and pale at the sight of Djalioh, which is why the mere presence of this phantom or devil was so annoying.

When the tired dancers sat down to enjoy the calm, refreshments were passed, and only the clink of glasses on trays interrupted the steady buzzing of everyone talking at once. A violin and bow sat atop the open piano.

Djalioh picked up the instrument, turned it around like a child playing with a toy, and bent the bow to the point of nearly breaking it several times. After he tucked his chin into position, people began to howl with laughter at the strange, discordant, and incoherent strains. He looked at the wide-eyed men and women lolling in their easy chairs and stretched out on benches and sofas. Not understanding all that laughter and sudden joy, he continued to play.

At first the sounds were slow and subdued, as the bow feathered its way from the bridge to the tuning pegs, while hardly emitting a note. Slowly his head began to bob and bend over the instrument, while his brow wrinkled, his eyes closed, and the bow jumped over the strings like a quickly bounding rubber ball. His jerky playing produced many sharp and grating sounds. That extremely oppressive music weighed on your chest like a lead weight. He attempted bold arpeggios as he rose through the octaves, with masses of notes climbing steadily like the spire of a Gothic tower, changing chords in rapid leaps. All of these separate sounds and whistling, chorded notes without measure or tune, rhythm or melody! These vague and flighty phrases succeeded one another like devils singing a round, a steady whirlwind of fleeting dreams that displace and pursue one another.

As he gripped the neck of the violin, Djalioh occasionally lifted one of his fingers while his nail picked the string to make it sing just before it died. Whenever the frightening music made him stop, he would smile stupidly before continuing to pursue his revery even more lovingly. And when he was overcome with fatigue, he would stop and listen attentively to see if all of that would return. Nothing. The last vibration of the final note had died from exhaustion. Everyone looked at his neighbor in stunned amazement at having allowed that weird racket to go on so long.

Dancing began again . . . a cotillion, since it was three in the morning. The older women had already departed, along with husbands and the infirm, leaving only the younger women. For more spacious waltzing, they opened in succession the doors of the salon, the billiard room, and finally the dining room. Each waltzer claimed his partner, they listened for the snap of the bow striking the music stand, and then they began.

Djalioh was leaning against one of the doors as the spinning waltzers came by, brimming with joyful laughter. Adele would periodically emerge only to disappear before his eyes. Each time he saw her she had her hand poised on the arm of her partner, who was turning with his hand around her waist. And every time, he felt a demonic shudder inside and a wild instinct roaring within him, like a caged lion. On the same baton stroke, at the same measure, same note, and the end of the same period, for the full twenty minutes of the dance, the hem of a white, flowered dress and two open satin slippers passed before his eyes. When the dancing stopped, Adele was so sated from the festivities that she was nearly overcome and had to daub her forehead. Then off she went again with a bound, more gaily, prettier and fresher than ever.

Djalioh suffered the agonies of the damned. Imagine having all the passion necessary for love and having your soul consumed by flame, by the volcano where you are imprisoned! There you are, tied to a dry rock with your mouth athirst. Like Prometheus, you see your innards being devoured by a vulture which, in your frustrated anger, you would like to strangle with your bare hands. While the dance ran gaily on, captivated by the lilting strains of its own magic, Djalioh sat with his head bowed in bitter suffering, wondering: "Oh why can't I dance happily like all of them? Why am I so ugly when those ladies are so beautiful? Why do they turn away when I smile? Why do I suffer this way, annoy and despise myself? If only I could seize her, rip away all of her clothes, and shred the veils that hide her. I'd take her in my arms and steal her far away, through fields and forests, across the sea. We would finally take shelter under a palm tree, and there we would feast our eyes on one another until she took me in her bare arms, and then . . . oh!" He continued to weep with anger.

The lamps were being extinguished. The clock struck five. You could hear carriages pulling up as the dancers collected their wraps and departed. The servants closed the shutters and then left.

Djalioh hadn't moved. When he raised his head everything had vanished—the women, the dancing, the music. The last lamp flickered away its life in the remaining few drops of oil.

At that moment, dawn appeared on the horizon behind the linden trees.

SIX

He took a candle and went up to his room. After taking off his coat and shoes, he fell onto his bed and laid his head on the pillow, but sleep was impossible! His head rang with a prolonged buzzing, a complete din of strange music. Fever coursed through his arteries, the veins in his forehead were green and swollen, and the excessive warmth of blood flowing to his brain nearly asphyxiated him. He rushed to the window to calm his senses with the fresh morning air. Clouds joined the moon in flight from the dawn's first rays. He spent a long time rapt by the thousands of fantastic forms that nocturnal clouds outlined, and then he turned his gaze toward the candle flame and the glow it cast on the green silk curtains. An hour later, he left.

There were still traces of night, and dew hung from every leaf on the trees. It had rained for a long time. Carriage paths rutted by coaches had become thick with mud. Djalioh plunged down the darkest, twistiest path and walked for a long time. He trudged through the first leaves of autumn, blown along in yellow gusts. Walking on the wet grass, through the arbor, against the background sound of wind rushing through the trees, he heard the distant murmur of nature awakening.

How nice it is to dream that way! It is enthralling to hear the sound of feet treading on dry leaves, of chipping away an occasional piece of dead wood. It's a great feeling to surrender yourself to uncharted paths, like the flow of revery that takes possession of your soul. But then you are gripped for a long time by a sad, poignant thought as you watch the leaves fall from those moaning trees. All of nature greets the dawn with a dirge, as though rising from its tomb. Then the cherished face of a mother or a loved one, robed in white, emerges from the shadows before moving gravely along the length of darkened wall. The specter of the entire past returns, bringing along its troubles and agonies, its tears and a few laughs. At a certain point the hazy, ill-defined figures of the future appear, wrapped in gauze netting like nymphs rising from a bush amid a flight of birds. It's a joy listening to the gale whipping the lofty trees, making them intone like a procession of the dead. Gusts muss your hair and cool your burning brow.

Djalioh was lost in more terrible thoughts. A dreamy melancholy, spurred on by the imagination, can stem from the dull ache of a wound. But you can actually feel despair. It was reality that was crushing him. Ah, yes: reality! It's an oppressive phantom like a nightmare, and yet, like the mind, is only a stretch of time!

What did the vanished past mean to him, any more than the future, which could be summed up in one measly word: death? No, it was the present, the very instant that obsessed him, because it was the present moment that he wanted to destroy, to kick apart and strangle with his bare hands. When he thought about his poverty, his despair, and about his empty arms . . . and then thought about the gay whirl of the ball, about those women and Adele, about her bare breasts, shoulder, white hand . . . when he thought about all that, he broke out in a wild laugh that resounded in his mouth like a tiger dying of hunger. In his mind's eye he saw Paul's laugh, his wife's kisses, he saw both of them stretched out on a silky couch, entwining in one another's arms with sighs and moans of delight. He saw everything there, even the drapes where they were tangled by their embraces, the flowers, furniture, and carpet. And when he applied these images to himself as he walked alone on the grass and over broken branches, when he scanned the trees surrounding him, he began to tremble. He understood the huge distance that separated him from them. When he finally began to wonder why everything was the way it was, an insurmountable obstacle seemed to block his path, and a black veil clouded his vision.

Why wasn't Adele his? Oh, if only she were, he would delightedly take her into his arms, rest his head on her breast, and cover her with burning kisses! And he sobbed. If only he were like other men in realizing that when life obsesses you, it can be dispatched with the squeeze of a trigger; if only he had known that men can be happy with just a few coins in their pockets, and that the river swallows up many corpses! . . . Oh no, misfortune is part of nature's plan. It has laden us with a prolonged feeling of existence.

He came to the edge of a pond where swans were gliding on the crystal surface. They were playing with their young, their wings open and their necks craned over on their backs. The largest male and female pair were swimming together in the rapid current of the stream that cut through the pond. From time to time they turned their white necks toward one another and held each other's gaze as they swam. Then they turned around, dipped their bodies, and agitated the water with their play by beating their wings and thrusting out their breasts like the bows of twin ships.

Djalioh studied their graceful movements and beautiful forms. He wondered why he was not as beautiful as these animals. Everyone fled him like an outcast when he approached them. Why didn't he have their fine features? Why hadn't heaven made him a swan, a songbird, something light, airy, and lovely? Or else, why couldn't he disappear? As he kicked at a rock, he wondered, "Why am I not like that stone? I kick it, it flies along, but it doesn't suffer!" Then he hopped into a boat, cast off, took up the oars, and began to row toward the fields on the far side where animals are scattered about.

After a few moments he headed back to the chateau. The servants had opened the windows, rearranged the furniture in the salon, and set the table, since it was nearly nine o'clock. All this had taken place during his long, slow walk. Joy and tears both make time pass quickly, and Father Time gallops along without breaking stride. Run along quickly without pausing, you old white-haired creature, mow them down! Run without stopping, you who are condemned to live and to bring misery in your wake. Rush us into the common grave, where you heap all the obstacles that block your path!

SEVEN

After lunch it was time for a walk, since the sun had begun to break through the clouds. The ladies wanted to take a boat ride to refresh themselves from the night's revel.

There were three groups among the guests. Paul, Djalioh, and Adele formed one band. She seemed pale and drawn, but in her blue muslin dress with white flowers, she was prettier than ever. Adele felt it would be proper to accompany her husband, which Djalioh didn't understand. For as much as his soul was drawn instinctively to love, his mind resisted everything we consider refined, customary, honorable, proper, and seemly. He sat in the bow and rowed.

In the middle of the pond there was an islet designed as a refuge for the swans. The curved branches of its rosebushes could be seen reflected in the water, including a few faded roses. The young lady broke a piece of bread to scatter crumbs in the water for the swans. They glided toward the boat, stretching their necks to seize the crumbs before the stream carried them away. Each time she leaned over and stretched out her hand, Djalioh felt her breath on his hair and her cheek brush his feverish head. The water was clear and calm, but a storm raged in his heart. Several times he thought he would go crazy. He buried his head in his hands like a delirious man who thinks he is dreaming.

He rowed quickly yet trailed the other boats, since all his movements were jerky and convulsive. From time to time his dull gray eyes turned slowly in Adele's direction and then focused on Paul. Although Djalioh seemed self-possessed, it was the calm of ashes covering hot coals. The occasional words exchanged by the husband and wife were interrupted only by the splash of the oars in the water, which in turn gently slapped the sides of the boat. They looked at one another and laughed while the swans swam swiftly by. The breeze blew a few leaves on the boaters. Farther ahead, the sun shone on the green fields where the river snaked along, carrying the boat quickly and silently along in its course.

At one point, Djalioh slowed down and wiped away the warm tears from his eyes. When he picked up the oars his tears rolled off his hands into the water. And when Paul saw that they were getting away from the other groups, he took Adele's hand and caressed her satiny glove with a long kiss, which resounded in Djalioh's ears.

EIGHT

Like other older women, Madame de Lansac had a passion for the large number of monkeys she kept because, like dogs, they did not reject her affection. This is not to malign older women, and if it were, it would be to please younger people who hate them intensely. Lord Byron claimed he could not stand to watch a pretty woman eat. Perhaps he never thought about the company of that woman forty years later, which would be reduced to her lapdog and monkey. You know all those young and perky women you see? Well, if they reach sixty years of age some day, they will be wilder about their dogs than about men and cohabit with a monkey instead of a lover.

It's so sad but true. After losing their fresh complexion over the course of a dozen years and shriveling up like old parchment, they eat their dinner by the fireplace with a novel in hand. Accompanied by her cat and her maid, this angel of beauty will die and become a cadaver, a stinking corpse before turning into dust, into nothing except the fetid air trapped in a tomb.

I constantly see skeletal people whose yellowish skin seems to take on the coloration of the earth that will contain them.

I don't take to monkeys very much, and yet they do seem to imitate human behavior perfectly. When I see one of those animals (I'm not talking about men here), I seem to see myself in a magnifying mirror: the same feelings, same brutal appetites, a little less arrogance—and that's all. Djalioh felt himself drawn to them by a strange sympathy. He often watched them for hours on end, plunged into a deep meditation or minutely scrutinizing them.

Adele drew near their common cage (for it sometimes seems that young women love monkeys as symbols of their husbands) and threw them hazelnuts and sweets. They pounced on them right away, squabbling as they tore off pieces, grubbing like politicians over crumbs that fall from the minister's desk and crying out like lawyers. One in particular snatched a large sweet, ate it quickly, took the best nut, broke it open with his nails, peeled away the shell fragments and showed his largesse by throwing them to his companions. He had a crown of bristles scattered over his shrunken head, making him slightly resemble a king. Another was seated humbly in a corner, lowering his eyes with the modesty of a priest and sneaking whatever he could not steal boldly. A third was a flabby female with long hair and puffed eyes, who paced everywhere with obscene gestures that made the young ladies blush, biting and pinching the males while she whispered in their ears. She resembled many prostitutes I have known.

Everyone laughed at their riotously funny habits and manners. Djalioh hunkered down on the ground with his knees up around his head, arms on his thighs, and his half-dead eyes fixed on a single spot. He was the only one who wasn't laughing.

They left for Paris in the afternoon. Djalioh was still seated in front of Adele, as though fate took continual joy in laughing at his suffering. In their fatigue, each was lulled to sleep by the gentle rocking of the coach and the noise of its wheels in the ruts hollowed out by the rain. The fetlocks of the horses glistened with mud. The carriage window behind Djalioh ventilated the coach, while the breeze played over his shoulders and neck.

Everyone's drowsy head bobbed around in time with the carriage's movement. Djalioh alone did not sleep but kept his head lowered on his chest.

NINE

I think it was around seven in the morning, toward the beginning of May, when the sun rose in all its splendor to illumine Paris and awake it to a beautiful spring day.

Before her bath, breakfast, and morning walk, Madame Paul de Monville rose early and retired to the salon to finish a novel by Balzac.

The newlyweds lived on a deserted street in the aristocratic quarter of

Saint-Germain. Shadows from the broad walls entirely covered the wide street, the large town houses, the sprawling gardens with their acacias, the linden trees whose thick and trembling tufts reached over the walls where blades of grass grew out of the stones. Silence dominated the scene, except for a rare carriage rolling over the paving stones, drawn by two white horses, or for youthful shouts signaling the return from nightly orgies or from a performance featuring a few bawds with naked breasts, reddened eyes, and torn clothes.

Djalioh, lived with Paul and his wife in one of those town houses, and for almost two years his soul had been very troubled. A stream of tears had deeply furrowed it.

One morning (that's the day I'm speaking about) he got up and went out into the garden where a one-year-old child slept, swaddled in muslin, netting, embroideries, and colored shawls, there in his boat-shaped cradle with its bowsprit graced by the sun's golden rays.

His nurse was away. Djalioh looked all around before drawing right up to the cradle. Quickly he removed the blanket and then stood there contemplating that poor, drowsily sleeping creature with dimpled hands, rounded shape, white neck, and small nails. He picked him up, flipped him upside down, and threw him with all his might onto the grass with a thud. The child uttered a cry, and his brain spurted ten feet away near a gillyflower.

Djalioh opened his pale lips and gave a forced laugh, cold and terrible like the laughter of the dead. Quickly he headed back to the house, climbed the stairs, opened the door to the dining room and then shut and locked it; he took the key as well as the one to the hall, and when he got to the salon vestibule, he threw them all out the window into the street. Then he slowly tiptoed into the salon, where he locked the door a double turn. The venetian blinds had been so carefully closed that the room was nearly dark.

When Djalioh stopped, the only sounds he heard were Adele's white hand turning the pages of a book, as she lay sprawled on a red velvet sofa; and through the blinds came the chirping of birds in the cage out on the terrace and the sound of their wings beating on the iron grating. Off in the corner of the salon next to the hearth was a mahogany flower box, redolent with fully leaved pink, white, and blue flowers, standing tall on their polished green stems; they were shown in full view by the large mirror behind them.

He approached her and sat down beside her. With a slight jump, she fixed her startled blue eyes on him. Her dressing gown of flowing white muslin was open in front, and beneath the material her two crossed legs traced the outline of her thighs. She was wreathed in an intoxicating perfume. Her white gloves were thrown onto the chair along with her belt, handkerchief, and small shawl, all of which exuded such an especially fine scent that Djalioh flared his nostrils to savor it deeply. The close presence of one's beloved emits such a heady scent!

"What do you want with me?" she asked in fright as soon as she recognized him.

A long silence followed. Without answering, he fastened a devouring look on her and drew closer. He grasped her by the waist and planted a burning kiss on her neck, which struck Adele like a snakebite. He saw her skin blush and palpitate. In her fright, she exclaimed, "Oh! I'm going to call for help! Help!" And when she looked at him, she added: "Oh, the monster!"

Djalioh didn't reply except to stammer and strike his head in anger as if to ask, "What, do you mean I can't even say one word to her or detail all my torture and suffering, with nothing to offer her except the tears of an animal and the sighs of a monster! And then to be repulsed like a reptile! To be hated by what one loves and confronted by the impossibility of saying anything at all! To be cursed yet unable to blaspheme!"

"Leave me alone, please! Leave me! Can't you see that you horrify and disgust me? I'll call Paul, who will kill you!"

Djalioh showed her the key in his hand and stood still. The clock chimed eight o'clock, while the birds chirped in their cage. For a moment the rumbling of a cart was heard.

"Well, are you going to leave? In heaven's name, go away!"

She tried to get up, but Djalioh held her by the back of her gown, which his nails ripped.

"I have to go outside, I must go outside . . . I have to check my child! Please let me see my baby!"

A horrible idea made her tremble all over and turn pale, made her add: "Yes, my child! I have to see him . . . immediately, right now!"

She turned to see a devil's face grimacing in front of her. In a single burst, he let out such a loud, prolonged laugh that Adele fell on her knees at his feet, petrified with fear.

Djalioh went down to his knees, picked her up and sat her upright on her knees. He began ripping her clothes with both hands, and tore away the sheer fabric that veiled her. When he saw her in tears and shaking like a leaf, naked to the waist with her arms crossed over her bare breasts, with red cheeks and bluish lips, he felt a strange oppression weigh down on him. Then he collected the flowers that were strewn all over the floor, closed the red silk curtains, and proceeded to take off his clothes.

When Adele saw him undressed, she shook with horror and turned her head. Djalioh drew near and clutched her to his chest for a long time. Against her warm, smooth skin she felt the cold, hairy hide of the monster. He leapt on the couch, threw aside the pillows, leaned over the back and balanced himself for a long time in a seesaw motion, thanks to his flexible spine. From time to time he uttered a guttural sound and smiled to himself.

What else could he hope for? A woman in front of him, flowers at his feet, a new dawn with its pale pink rays, and the noise from the cage for music!

He soon stopped his exercises, ran to Adele, dug his claws into her flesh, and stripped her. Seeing herself in the mirror completely nude in Djalioh's arms, she cried out in horror and prayed to God. She wanted to call for help, but she couldn't utter a single word.

When Djalioh saw her naked with her hair disheveled down over her shoulders, he was frozen speechless like the first man to look upon a woman. He spared her for a while, tore out some of her blond hair and put it in his mouth, chewed on it, and then kissed it.[6] Next, he rolled around the floor on the flowers, between the cushions, and on Adele's clothes. He was happy, out of his mind, and drunk with love.

Adele was crying. A trickle of blood ran down her white breasts.

His unrestrained brutality knew no limits. He jumped on her in a single bound, spread her hands apart, stretched her out on the floor, and pushed her around wildly. He uttered frequent ferocious cries and, stupefied and motionless, held out his arms. Then he gurgled with voluptuousness, like a man who is . . .

---

6. This same image recurs in the central scene of sexual ecstasy in *November* (11:645; cf. "Passion and Virtue," sec.5. The Goncourt brothers report that a bemused young Flaubert would fall into deep revery, "while twisting a lock of hair in his fingers and biting his tongue": *Journal de Goncourt* (Monaco: L'Imprimerie Nationale de Monaco, 1966), 6.8.

Suddenly he felt Adele's convulsions beneath him, feeling her muscles stiffen like iron. She cried out with plaintive sighs, which were stifled by kisses. Then he felt her go cold; her eyes closed, and she turned over with her mouth open.

After feeling her motionless and stone cold, he got up, rolled her all around, kissed her feet, her hands, her mouth, and then ran about, bouncing off the walls. He repeated this several times. But finally he ran head first into the marble fireplace and fell motionless and bloody on Adele's body.

TEN

When they came looking for Adele, she had large, deep scratch marks on her body. Djalioh's head was badly shattered. It was thought that the young woman had defended her honor by killing him with a knife. It was in all the newspapers, enough to provoke a week's worth of oohs! and ahs!

The next day the dead were buried. The funeral cortege was wonderful, with the coffins of the mother and child draped in crepe trappings, candles, chanting priests, a large crowd, and men dressed in black with white gloves.

ELEVEN

"How awful!" was the comment a few days later made by an entire family of grocers gathered formally around an enormous leg of mutton, which gave off an inviting aroma.

The grocer's wife opined, "The poor child! To kill a child like that! What harm did he ever do?"

"What! And to go out 'n kill dat po' li'l woman! Dat's turrible!" Such was the retort of her eminently moral husband whose virtue was offended. He had been decorated with the Legion of Honor for having served with distinction in the National Guard, and he subscribed to the *Constitutionnel*.

"But I also think that's the result of passion," added a large, chubby boy who was the scion of the family. At seventeen years of age he had just completed his fourth level in school because his father held the view that youth should be "edjicated."

"People must really lack discipline," said the young grocer, while asking for the third time to have someone pass him the green beans.

A bell tinkled to indicate that a customer had entered the store, so he got up to go sell a couple of candles.

TWELVE

You probably insist on a conclusion, don't you? And you think I'm a long way from providing one. Well then, here it is.

Adele was buried, all right. But after two years her beauty had disappeared, for her body was exhumed for reburial in the Père-Lachaise cemetery, and it stank so badly that one of the gravediggers got sick.

What about Djalioh? Ah, he's just fine under his polished varnish and is wonderfully cared for. You know, of course, that the ministry of zoology claimed the body to make it into a magnificent skeleton.

And Paul? What do you know: I almost forgot about him! He remarried. I saw him a while ago in the Bois de Boulogne, and this evening you'll see him at the theater.

Passion & Virtue

A Philosophical Tale

> Can you speak of what you do not feel at all?
> —SHAKESPEARE, *Romeo and Juliet*, ACT 3, SCENE 5 [1]

ONE

She had already seen him twice, I believe. The first time was at a ball at the Minister's house, and the second was at the Théâtre-Français.[2] And although he had neither superior attributes nor good looks, she frequently thought of him in the evenings after extinguishing her lamp. She often lingered for a few thoughtful moments with her hair scattered over her naked breasts and her head turned toward the window where the night cast a dull light, with her arms hanging out of her bed and her soul floating between vague and hideous emotions—like those confused sounds that rise in the fields on autumn evenings.

Far from being the kind of exceptional soul one finds in books and plays, he was dispassionate, equitable, and above all a chemist. But he was

---

1. In fiction and nonfiction throughout his career, Flaubert played freely with remembered texts. In his letters to a wide variety of correspondents, he often cited himself and other writers as a continual exercise in the kind of phrasemaking that he derided in the "copybook" to *Bouvard and Pécuchet*. To his youthful writing he frequently appliquéd Classical writers he had studied in school and many of his earlier enthusiasms, especially Chateaubriand. In this epigraph he wrongly cites *Romeo and Juliet* 3.5 (instead of 3.3) and transforms Shakespeare's statement ("Thou canst not speak of that thou canst not feel") into a question, which he then poses to his own story (cf. "Diary of a Madman," sec. 5).

2. "Théâtre-Français" is the name adopted by the Comédie Française when it was reopened on May 30, 1799.

also a master of the theory, principles, and rules of seduction. To use the true but crude expression, he had the knack of a skillful man for getting what he wanted.

We're not talking about a pastoral method in the style of Louis XIV, where the first lesson begins with sighs, the second with love notes, and it continues that way until the conclusion. That's the technique outlined so well by Faublas, by second-rate comedies, and by the *Moral Tales* of Marmontel.³ But nowadays a man approaches a woman, eyes her with his lorgnette, finds her acceptable, and makes a bet with his friends. If she's married, the farce will be all the better.

Then he gets his foot in her door, lends her books, takes her to the theater, and makes sure to do something remarkable and ridiculous to catch her attention. Day after day he takes greater liberties in going to her house. He becomes a friend of the family, of her husband, her children, and her servants. Finally, she notices the trap and wants to drive him away like a lackey. But in response he becomes indignant, threatens to publish a brief letter that he interprets in a scandalous way, no matter for whom it was intended. To her husband, he will repeat a random word that was perhaps uttered in a moment of vanity, flirting, or desire. That's the cruelty of an anatomist, but science progresses, and there are people who dissect a heart the way they do a cadaver.

Then that poor, distracted woman cries and begs. But there is no pardon for her, for her children, husband, or mother. Being a man, he is unbending and can expend his strength and violence; he can bruit it about that she is his mistress and can publish it in the newspapers, detail it in a memoir, and prove it, if need be.

Half dead, she surrenders to him. Then he can even parade her in front of his lackeys, who sneer among themselves behind their elegant trappings when they see her return to their master's house in the early morning. And when he has abased and broken her, leaving her to her regrets and thoughts about the past and her deceit, abandoned to her misfortune, he goes away and scarcely recognizes her. At times he even hates her, but he did win his bet, and he is a lucky man.

3. Louvet de Couvroy's *Amours du chevalier de Faublas* (1787–89) is an adventurous serial novel portraying frivolity and scandal in the eighteenth century. Jean-François Marmontel (1723–99) wrote historical novels, plays, and moral tales for children that were published in 1761 by *Mercure* and translated into many languages.

So he is no Lovelace, as he would have been called sixty years ago, but rather a Don Juan, which is more attractive.

The man who possesses such knowledge in depth, who knows the hidden ins and outs,[4] is not rare these days. Indeed, when you have no soul or sympathy in your heart, it's so easy to seduce a woman who loves you and then leave her there with all the other ones! There are so many ways to get them to love you, either through jealousy, vanity, merit, talents, pride, horror, and even fear or else through your fatuous manners, the stylish casualness of wearing your tie, the pretense of being in despair, sometimes through the cut of your clothes or the elegance of your boots! After all, how many people have owed their conquests only to the competence of their tailor or bootmaker?

Ernest had noticed that Mazza returned his glances with a smile. He pursued her everywhere. For instance, she got bored if he didn't attend the ball. And don't believe that he was such a novice as to praise the whiteness of her hand or the beauty of her rings, as a schoolboy might have done to practice his rhetoric. In her presence he tore down all the other women who were dancing since he knew the strangest and most unheard-of adventures about each one of them. All of that made her laugh and secretly flattered her when she thought that there were no stories to tell about her. Standing right at the brink of the precipice, she firmly resolved to abandon him and never see him again—but a smile on a lover's mouth makes virtue evaporate quickly.

He had noticed that she loved poetry, the sea, the theater, Byron; summing up all these observations into a single one, he said, "She's foolish and I'll have her." When she watched him leave and the door of the salon closed quickly on his departure, she too often said, "Oh, how I love you!"

In addition, consider that Ernest made her believe in phrenology and magnetism,[5] that Mazza was thirty years old, and that her purity had always kept her completely faithful to her husband, turning away from all the desires that arose each day in her soul only to die the next day; con-

---

4. This phrase, "les détours et les replis cachés," adapts a verse from Jean Racine's *Bajazet*, 4.7.1424: "Nourri dans le sérail, j'en connais les détours," which Flaubert modified repeatedly over the years (cf.15:584).

5. At several stages, Bouvard and Pécuchet become fascinated with animal magnetism, galvinism, phrenology, and the experiments of Franz Mesmer and Armand Puységur (see 5:192, 249; cf. "Whatever You Want," sec.3).

sider that she was married to a banker and that, in the arms of this man, passion was nothing less than a duty for her, like watching over her staff and dressing her children.

TWO

She was content for a long time with that state of amorous and half-mystical duty. She enjoyed the novelty of gratification, and for a long time played with that love, longer than with the others, and finally became quite smitten, at first by habit and then by need. Laughing and playing with your heart is dangerous, for passion is a firearm that can go off and kill you when you don't believe yourself at risk.

One day Ernest arrived early at Madame Willer's. Since her husband was at the Stock Exchange and her children had gone out, he found himself alone with her. He stayed at her house all day, and when he left around five o'clock in the afternoon, Mazza became so dreamy and sad that she didn't sleep all night.

They conversed for many hours, declaring their love, speaking of poetry, rehearsing the sort of strong and expansive love one reads about in Byron, and then complaining about the social constraints that drew them together and kept them apart for life. They had voiced the trials of their hearts, of life and death, of nature, and of the ocean, which roared nightly. Understanding the world and their passion, their expressions had spoken even more than their lips, which touched often.

It was on one of those long, dreary, and morose March days that imbue your soul with a vague bitterness. Their words had been sad, and Mazza's especially had a harmonious melancholy. Each time Ernest was about to say that he loved her for life, each time he smiled at her, looked at her, or protested his love, Mazza didn't answer. With her mouth open and her brow pale, her large black eyes stared at him in silence.

On that day she felt oppressed, as if an invisible hand were weighing on her chest. She was afraid without knowing why, content to remain in that fear mixed with a strange sensation of love, revery, and mysticism. Once she drew her chair back, frightened by the wild and fearful bestiality of Ernest's smile. But he moved closer to her, took her hands and brought them to his lips. She blushed and said in a tone of affected calm;

"Would you like to court me?"

"To court you, Mazza! You?"

That answer said it all.

"Do you mean that you love me?"

He smiled at her.

"Ernest, you would be wrong."

"Why?"

"My husband! Do you think about him?"

"So what! What does that mean?"

"I'm supposed to love him."

"That's easier said than done. In other words, the law tells you 'You will love him,' and your heart responds like a regiment on maneuvers or an iron bar that you bend with your hands, and if I love you . . ."

"Be quiet, Ernest. Think about what you owe to a woman like me who receives you alone in the morning when her husband is out, subject to your charms."

"Yes, if I love you in turn, it must be because I'm no longer *supposed to*, and nothing more. But is that reasonable and proper?"

"Ah, your logic is marvelous, my dear friend," Mazza said, leaning her head over on her left shoulder and turning her ivory needle case between her fingers. A lock of her hair came undone and fell on her cheeks. She swept it back with a quick but graceful movement of her head. Ernest got up several times, took his hat as if he were going to leave, but then sat down and resumed his conversation.

They often interrupted one another or else looked at each other in silence, barely breathing, heady and satisfied with their glances and sighs. Then they would smile.

Once when Mazza saw Ernest at her feet, sunk down on the carpet of her bedroom, when she saw his head resting on her knees, his hair pulled back, and his eyes drawn close to her breast with his unlined white forehead in front of her mouth, she thought that she was going to take his head into her arms, press it to her heart, and cover it with kisses.

"I'll write you tomorrow," Ernest told her.

"Farewell!"

And he left.

Mazza's mind alternated indecisively from a strange breathlessness to vague foreboding to ineffable daydreams. She awoke at night. Like the eye of a condemned man looking at you, her lamp cast intersecting reflections of trembling circles on the ceiling. She remained that way until daybreak, hearing the hours sound on all the clocks, listening to all the nighttime sounds, the rain falling against the walls, the wind blowing and spinning in the shadows, the windowpanes trembling, the wooden bed groaning with each movement she made when she turned on her mattress, haunted by torturing thoughts and terrible images that completely covered her as she squirmed in her bed sheets.

In such hours of delirious fever, who has not felt those intimate movements of the heart? Who hasn't heard those convulsions of a tormented soul, endlessly twisting under the weight of undefinable thoughts full of both torment and voluptuousness, at first vague and as ill defined as a phantom? Soon that wavering thought stops and comes together, takes on a bodily shape, and becomes an image that makes you weep and tremble. On warm, steamy nights when your skin is seared and insomnia eats at you as you sit at the foot of your bed, who hasn't seen an ashen, dreamy face looking at you sadly? Or else it appears in its gala clothes, if you have seen it dance at a ball, or else wrapped in black veils and crying. And you recall its words, the sound of its voice, the languidness of its eyes.

Poor Mazza! For the first time she felt that she was in love, a love that was going to become a need, then a sentimental delirium and mania. But in her naiveté and ignorance she quickly foresaw a happy future, a tranquil existence where passion would give her joy, and delight would give happiness.

Actually, couldn't she live happily in the arms of the one who loved her and at the same time deceive her husband? "What is all that compared to love?" she wondered. Yet she suffered from that sentimental delirium and sank into it deeper and deeper, like those who get drunk out of pleasure, only to become ravaged by drink. It is true that those palpitations of the heart are poignant and bitter, the anguish of a soul torn between an evanescent world of virtue and a future of real love.

The next day Mazza received a letter written on glazed paper, redolent of roses and musk. It was signed with an E, surrounded by a flourish. I don't know what was in it, but Mazza reread it several times, examining both sheets and their folds, intoxicated by their scent. Then she rolled it into a small wad and threw it in the fire. Consumed by the fire, the letter fluttered, wafted, and then came to rest softly on the andirons like a pleated white veil.

Ernest loves her! He told her so! Oh, how happy she is. The first step has been taken, and the others won't be difficult. Now she will be able to look at him without blushing, and she won't need so many stratagems and the engaging facial expressions women use to make themselves attractive. He comes by himself, gives himself to her, her modesty is controlled, and it's that reserve which women always keep and maintain even in the depths of the most passionate love and most ardent sensuality, like a final sanctuary of love and passion which they use as a veil to hide everything brutal and delicate in them.

A few days later, a veiled woman crossed the Pont des Arts at a fast clip. It was seven o'clock in the morning.

After walking for a long time, she stopped at the service entrance and asked for Ernest. He hadn't gone out, so she went up. The staircase seemed endless to her, and when she got to the third floor she rested on the banister for fear she might faint. She felt everything spinning around her and low muted voices whispering in her ear. Finally, she rang the doorbell with a trembling hand. When she heard its repeated, piercing sound, an echo resounded in her heart, like a galvanic repercussion.

Finally the door opened. It was Ernest himself.

"Oh, is that you, Mazza?"

Drained of color and drenched in sweat, she couldn't answer. Ernest looked at her coldly, twirling the silk cord of his dressing gown. He was afraid of compromising himself.

"Come in," he finally said.

He took her arm and sat her down in an armchair. After a moment of silence, she told him: "Ernest, I have come to tell you something. This is the last time I will speak to you. I must leave you and not see you again."

"Because . . . ?"

"Because you are a burden to me, you overwhelm me, and will be the end of me!"

"I? How is that, Mazza?"

He got up, pulled the curtains, and closed the door.

"What are you doing?" she cried out in horror.

"What am I doing?"

"Yes."

"You are here, Mazza, you came to my apartment. Come on, don't deny it," he said smiling, "I know women."

"Continue," she added angrily.

"Well, Mazza, that's enough."

"And you are so insolent as to tell me that to my face, to a woman you claim to love?"

"Excuse me! Oh, forgive me!"

He knelt and looked at her for a long time.

"Oh, yes, I too love you more than my life. Here, I am giving myself to you."

And right there between the four walls, under the silk curtains, on an arm-chair, there were more than enough love and kisses, intoxicating embraces, and burning delight to drive you mad or kill you. And after he had sapped, worn out, and thoroughly exhausted her with his embraces, after leaving her spent, broken and gasping, after pressing his chest against hers many times and seeing her faint in his arms, he got up and left her alone.

That evening he had an excellent dinner at Véfour's, where plentiful iced champagne made the rounds and you could hear him raising his voice over dessert, "My good friends, I got another one!"

That other one went home with her soul deeply saddened and her eyes full of tears—not because of her lost honor, for that particular idea did not torture her in the slightest. Having initially asked herself what honor was and finding it to be only a word, she went beyond that. But she thought of the sensations she had experienced and, on reflection, found them only bitter deception, saying to herself, "That's not what I dreamed about!"

For when she left her lover's arms, it seemed to her that something was rumpled within her, just as her clothes had been, something tired and downcast like her eyes. She felt she had fallen far, that love wasn't limited to that. Finally, she wondered if there wasn't a greater voluptuousness beyond the one she had experienced, if there wasn't a greater enjoyment after gratification, for she had an unquenchable thirst for infinite love and unlimited passions. But then she saw that love was only a kiss, a moment of ecstasy where lover and mistress punctuate their caresses with groans, locked in their embrace. And when she realized that it all ends with him getting up, with her leaving, that their convulsive passion needs a bit of flesh for its heady satisfaction, her soul was overcome with a deep weariness, like those starving people whom nothing can nourish.

But she soon gave up her thoughts of the past so as to think only of the smiling present. She closed her eyes to what no longer existed, shook off the fantasy of her former boundless dreams, her vague, ill-defined breathlessness, in order to give herself completely over to a torrent that swept her away. Soon she reached a state of inactivity and nonchalance, of that somnolence when you feel yourself sliding into sleep and intoxication, feel the world slipping far away from you, whereas you remain alone on the skiff that the wave coddles and the ocean sweeps away. She thought no longer of her husband and children, and even less of her reputation, which other women eagerly ripped apart in the salons, while Ernest's young friends sullied and vilified her at will in their cafes and coffeehouses.

But suddenly she heard a melody in nature and in her soul which had remained unknown to her until then. She discovered new worlds in both, immense spaces and limitless horizons. It seemed that everything was born for love, that men were creatures of a superior order, susceptible to passions and feelings, that they were good only for that, and that they should live only for the heart. As for her husband, she still loved him and valued him even more highly. Her children seemed agreeable, but she loved them the way one loves another person's children.

Each day, however, she felt that she loved more than the night before, that her love was becoming needful and necessary for her existence. But that passion which she had initially played with laughingly became serious and terrible. Once it entered her heart, it became a violent love and then mad frenzy. Her passion had so much fiery heat, so many immense desires, such a hunger for ravishment and pleasure coursing through her veins, under her skin, right down to her fingernails, that she became mad and drunkenly disoriented and would have wanted to carry her love beyond the limits of nature. It seemed to her that offering voluptuous caresses, dissipating her life in nights given over to feverish passion, wallowing in everything sublime and wild that passion offers would open up to her a continuous round of ravenous pleasure.

Often, in her raptures she exclaimed that life was only passion, that love was everything for her. With eyes ablaze, hair disheveled, and chest heaving with sobs, she asked her lover if he did not share her desire to live together for centuries in the solitude of a mountain retreat, high atop a rocky pinnacle with waves smashing below. Didn't he also want the two of them to merge with nature and heaven, to blend their sighs with the roar of the storm? And then she looked at him for a long time, asking him again for new kisses and new embraces—and then she fainted silently into his arms.

And when her husband returned in the evening, his inner tranquillity was reflected by his calm exterior as he told her about the day's profits, the good speculation he had made in the morning, how he had bought a farm, sold stock, and that he could add one more servant to their staff and buy two horses for his stable. After these words and these thoughts, he started to kiss her and call her "his love and his life." But fury gripped her soul; she cursed him, and in horror she repelled his caresses and kisses, which were as cold and frightful as those of a monkey.

His love held bitter pain for her, like the dregs of wine, which make it more acidic and harsh.

And when she left her house, family, and staff and found herself seated alone by Ernest's side, she told him that she would like to die by his hand and feel herself smothered in his arms. Then she added that she no longer loved anything, that she despised everything and loved only him. Next she said she had abandoned and sacrificed her love of God for him, was leaving her husband to suffer his humiliation, and was abandoning her children as well. She spit on all of that quite willingly. She ground virtue and religion under her heel, sold her reputation for caresses, and with the greatest delight she made a burnt offering of all that, just to please him. For a single glance or a kiss, she destroyed all her beliefs, illusions, and virtue—in short, everything she loved. And it seemed to her that she would be even more beautiful for having just left his arms and his endless kisses, as faded violets exude the sweetest scent.

Oh, who could possibly know how much sensual frenzy there is beneath the two palpitating breasts of a woman!

Ernest, however, was beginning to love her a bit more than a dancer or an available working girl. He even presented her with poetry he had written for her. Moreover, one day I saw him with reddened eyes, from which you might conclude that he had been crying . . . or had slept badly.

THREE

One morning he was thinking of Mazza, seated in a large, comfortable easy chair with his feet propped up on the andirons and his nose buried in the folds of his nightshirt. As he stared at the crackling flames lapping up against the fireplace grill, he was suddenly struck by a surprising thought. He became frightened.

Remembering that he was loved by a woman like Mazza who so lavishly sacrificed her beauty and love, he trembled fearfully at the spectacle of that woman's passion—like children who run far away from the ocean, saying that it is too big. A moral idea came to mind, for that was a habit he had begun to cultivate since he started contributing to the *Journal of Useful Knowledge* and the *Family Gallery*.[6] As I say, he thought it was immoral to seduce a married woman that way and turn her aside from her conjugal duties and maternal love, and that it was wrong to receive all these burnt offerings placed at his feet like a sacrifice. Finally, he was bored and wearied by that woman who took pleasure seriously and could conceive only of a complete and exclusive love, but who could not discuss novels, styles, or the opera.

At first, he wanted to break it off, to leave her there rejected in the middle of society along with other women who had also been used up. Mazza noticed his cool indifference, attributing it to refinement, and loved him all the more. Ernest often avoided and fled from her, but she crossed his path everywhere: at the ball, strolling in public gardens, in museums. She knew how to pick him out of crowds, whisper in his ear, and make him blush in front of all those people who were looking at her.

At other times, it was he who came to her house. He entered with a serious expression and a severe attitude. His young, naive mistress threw her arms around his neck and covered him with kisses. But he coldly repulsed her, saying that they should not make love any more, that it was over between them now that the moment of mad delirium had passed, and that she must respect her husband, adore her children and attend to her family. He added that he had witnessed and studied a great deal, moreover, that Providence was just, that nature was a masterpiece and society an admirable creation, and that, after all, philanthropy was beautiful and one should love mankind.

At that point she cried tears of rage, pride, and love. With a smile on her lips and bitterness in her heart, she asked him if she was no longer beautiful and what she must do to please him. And then she smiled at

---

6. The *Journal des Connaissances Utiles* was founded in 1831 by Emile de Girardin, who appreciably lowered its price by increasing distribution, thus making it an important instrument for informing citizens about politics, commerce, and agriculture and esp. for explaining postrevolutionary laws. The *Musée des Familles*, founded in 1833, was an illustrated monthly journal with wide appeal; it contained short stories, poetry, and brief critical articles (see 12:382). Both were typical of the popular publications that sprang up after the July Monarchy.

him, displaying her fair complexion for him, her black hair, her throat and shoulders, and her naked breasts. Ernest was unmoved by such seductiveness because he didn't love her any longer, and he left her house with the sort of emotion people feel when they see madmen. And if a trace of passion, or if a slim ray of love kindled his heart, he quickly extinguished it with a bit of logical argument.

How fortunate those people are who can use words to fight against their hearts and use morality to destroy the passion rooted in their souls—a morality that you find pasted only on books, like a bookseller's glaze and the engraver's frontispiece!

One day when she was carried away by delirious rage, Mazza bit his chest and dug her nails into his throat. Seeing blood flow from their lovemaking, Ernest understood that this woman's passion was terribly ferocious, that she was surrounded by a poisoned atmosphere that would choke him and in the end would kill him, that this love was a volcano which always needed something to devour and smash in its convulsions, and that her voluptuous sensuality was a molten lava searing her heart. Therefore, he had to go away and leave her forever—or else throw himself along with her into that whirlwind which pulls you along like vertigo in the immense path of passion, which begins with a smile and ends only at the tomb.

He preferred to leave.

At ten o'clock one night, Mazza received a letter in which she read these words:

"Farewell, Mazza! I will not see you again. The Minister of the Interior has assigned me to a scientific enterprise charged with analyzing the mineral deposits of Mexico. Good-bye! I am leaving from Le Havre. If you wish to be happy, stop loving me. Instead, love virtue and your duties. That's my last advice. Again, adieu! Kisses. *Ernest*."

She reread it several times, stricken by that word "adieu." She sat still with her eyes fixed on that letter which contained all her misfortune and despair, where she saw all the happiness of her life slip away. She shed no tears and did not cry out. She rang for a servant and told him to order some post-horses and to prepare her post-chaise. Her husband was traveling in Germany, so no one could restrain her will.

She left at midnight, making the horses run at full gallop. She stopped in a town to order a glass of water and resumed her chase, believing that she would see the sea appear at the next turn, over the next hill, at every bend in the road. The ocean was the goal of her desires and her jealousy, since it was going to take away someone dear to her heart. She finally arrived in Le Havre around three o'clock in the afternoon.

As soon as she dismounted, she ran to the end of the jetty and looked out over the sea . . . a white sail was disappearing over the horizon.

FOUR

He had left! Gone forever! And when she raised her head and peered through her tears, she saw nothing more . . . except the immensity of the ocean.

It was one of those scorching summer days when the earth exhales warm vapors, like the burning air of a furnace. When Mazza got to the end of the jetty, the fresh salt air revived her a bit, for a southerly breeze was swelling the waves, which softly died on the strand and gave their last gasp on the pebbles. To the left, thick black clouds were massing near the setting sun, which shone red on the sea. The clouds seemed on the point of bursting into tears. As it gathered its strength, the ocean struggled against itself, seeming to moan a dirge. When it smashed against the rocks of the jetty, the waves leapt in the air and fell in a silvery dust.

There was a kind of savage harmony in it all. For a long time Mazza listened to it, fascinated by its power. The noise of the waves spoke a special language to her. The sea was as sad and thoroughly anguished as she was. Like her, its waves died as they smashed on the rocks, leaving on the wet sand only a trace of their passage. A patch of grass that grew out of a slit in the rocks bowed its head under the weight of the heavy spray. Each new wave tried to rip it out by the roots, and each time it was detached just a little more. Finally, it disappeared under a whitecap, never again to be seen. And yet it was young and bore flowers! Mazza smiled bitterly. Like her, the flower was borne away by the wave in the freshness of its springtime.

Sailors were returning, lolling in their fishing boats, trailing their nets behind them. Their voices echoed in the distance, along with the cries of night birds who soared and beat their wings above Mazza's head before pouncing all together on debris strewn over the sand by the backwash. She heard a voice calling to her from the depths of an abyss, and leaning her head toward the chasm, she estimated how many minutes and seconds it would take for her agony to end in death. All of nature shared her sadness, and it seemed to her that the waves were sighing and the sea weeping.

I don't know, however, what miserable feeling of existence told her to live. It told her that there was still happiness and love on earth, and one had only to wait and hope in order to eventually discover them. But when night came, the moon appeared in the midst of its dear friends like a sultana appearing in a harem among the women, and you could see only the foaming swells, which shone on the waves like lather on the mouth of a steed—whereas the noise of the town began to recede into the fog. That was the time for Mazza to depart.

Around two o'clock in the morning she opened the coach window and peered outside. They were on an open plain going along a road lined with trees. Moonlight filtering between their branches made their forms resemble gigantic ghosts running in front of Mazza. As they swayed in the gusts of wind, breezes ruffled their foliage like disheveled hair. At one point, the coach stopped in the middle of a field to repair one of its broken harness traces. In the dead of night, all you could hear were the sound of the trees, the breath of the gasping, lathered horses, and the sobs of a lone woman.

Near morning she saw people going toward the nearest city, on their way to market, carrying fruit that was still on the stem and covered with moss to keep it fresh. They were also singing; since the climbing path slowed their steps, she listened to them at length. "At least some people are happy!" she said.

By now it was broad daylight on a Sunday. In a village several hours from Paris, at the time when everybody was filing out of the church into the square, a bright sun was shining on the church's weathervane and making its modest rose window translucent. From inside her coach Mazza could look through the open doors to glimpse the interior of the nave and the candles illuminating the shadowy altar. She examined the blue paint on the wooden vault and the bare old pillars made of whitened stone. Suddenly she saw the benches where the entire population was assembled, dressed in variegated colors. She heard the organ intoning, followed by a swelling mass of people who were stirring about and leaving. Several of them carried bouquets of artificial flowers and wore white stockings. It was a wedding scene, punctuated by rifle volleys in the square to announce the exit of the newlyweds.

The smiling bride wore a white cap and was looking at the tab ends of her sash of embroidered lace. The bridegroom kept pace with her, radiating his happiness as he scanned the crowd while he shook hands with various well-wishers. One was the mayor (and hosteler) of the region who that day was giving his daughter's hand to his deputy mayor, the school's headmaster.

A group of women and children stopped in front of Mazza to admire the beautiful open carriage and the red cape hanging from the door latch. They were all smiles and talking in loud voices. After changing horses and starting on her way, she came across the procession as it was entering the town hall. A smile crossed her lips when she saw the lather from the mouths of her horses spray on the newlyweds, as the dust from the hooves covered their white clothes. She leaned forward and gave them a pitiful, envious glance because she had turned from her wretchedness to become spitefully jealous. Then the people showed their hatred for the wealthy. They responded with curses and insults, throwing stones at the luggage compartments of her carriage.

As she continued her long trip, she was lulled by the motion of the carriage suspension and the jingle of the small bells on the harnesses. While a dusty mist discolored her black hair, her thoughts turned to the village wedding and the fiddler at the head of the wedding cortege, the organ sounds, the voices of the children who had stood all around her—all of that beset her ears like the buzzing of a bee or the hiss of a snake.

She was tired from the oppressive heat that penetrated the leather covering of her carriage. The sun struck her in the eyes, causing her to lower her head on the white cushions and fall asleep. She woke up when they arrived at the old gates of Paris.

When you trade the open fields of the country for city streets, daylight recedes into dreariness, as in those theaters at country fairs which are drab and poorly lit. Mazza eagerly plunged into the most tortuous streets, intoxicated by the sounds and rumbling noises that withdrew her from private thoughts and thrust her into the world. Like the shifting projections cast by Chinese lanterns, heads shot past her carriage door. They all seemed cold, impassive, and colorless. For the first time, she was shocked by the misery of those going barefoot along the quays, sporting smiles to hide the hatred in their hearts and the holes in their ragged clothes. She saw the crowds swallowed up by the theaters and cafes, the entire populace of servants and lords that was spread out like a colored cape on parade day.

It all seemed like an immense drama, a vast theater with its stone palaces and brightly lit stores, its elegant outfits, its ridiculous apparel, pasteboard scepters, and queens for a day. Over here the carriage of a ballerina jostles the crowd, while over there a man dies of hunger as he looks at a pile of gold on the other side of a store window. Everywhere there are laughter and tears, wealth and misery, and vice insulting virtue by spitting in its face, like the worn-out shawl of a prostitute brushing against a priest's black cassock as he passes her. Ah, yes! In the heart of a city you find a corrupt, poisonous atmosphere that overcomes you with headiness—something heavy and unhealthy, like those gloomy evening fogs that hover over rooftops.

Mazza filled her lungs with that air of corruption, tasted its aroma, and for the first time she understood the breadth and depth of vice, the sensual voluptuousness of crime.

When she returned home, the great amount of suffering she had undergone in the short span of her intensified life made it seem as if she had been away for a very long time. All night long she wept as she thought of her departure and return. In her mind's eye she saw all the towns she had passed through and the entire road she had traveled. She still seemed to be standing on the jetty, watching the sea and the sail as it disappeared. The wedding with its festive regalia and smiles of happiness also flooded her memory. She recalled the noise of her coach rolling over the paving stones and heard the muffled roar of the waves as they leapt up beneath her. Then she became frightened by the length of time, believing that she had lived for centuries, that she had become old and gray—so much does pain wear you down and misfortune gnaw at you, for certain days age you as if they were years, and some thoughts bring on an abundance of wrinkles.

Smiling with regret, she also remembered her days of happiness, her relaxed vacations on the banks of the Loire when she ran down the shady promenades in the woods, playing with the flowers and crying as she saw beggars pass by. She recalled her first dances, when she waltzed so well and loved the gracious smiles and pleasant chatter. Again she remembered her hours of feverish delight in the arms of her lover, her moments of anger and rapture when she would like each glance to have lasted for centuries, a kiss for eternity. She wondered if all of that was gone and erased forever, like dust along the road or the wake of a ship on the high seas.

FIVE

She finally returned, but alone! She had no one to sustain her and nothing more to love. What was she to do? Which way could she turn? Well, of course: death and the tomb a hundred times over! Despite the difficulties she had undergone on her trip, she had held little hope in her heart.

What was she waiting for?

She didn't know herself, except that she still had faith in life. She still believed that Ernest loved her, until one day when she received a letter from him. But it was one more disillusionment.

The letter was long, well written, and replete with rich metaphors and impressive words. Ernest told her that she mustn't love him anymore and that she must think of her obligations and of God. In addition, he gave her excellent advice on the family and maternal love, concluding like Monsieur de Bouilly or Madame Cottin with a bit of fine sentiment.[7]

Poor Mazza! So much love, affection, and tenderness offered to such cold and calculating indifference! She declined into lethargy and a feeling of disgust, telling herself one day, "I thought a person could die from a broken heart!" From disgust she fell further into bitterness and envy.

That was when the world's symphony sounded discordant and infernal, when nature seemed like one of God's cruel jokes. She didn't love anything and harbored animosity for everything. As each tender feeling was squeezed from her heart, hatred replaced it so thoroughly that she no longer loved anything on earth, except for one man. Whenever she saw mothers playing with their children in public gardens, smiling at their caresses, and women with their husbands, lovers with mistresses, she both envied and cursed them all for sharing happiness, for smiling and loving life. She wished that she could have crushed them all underfoot. Her lips curled into an ironic smile of pride as she muttered a few scornful words when she passed them in the street.

At other times, despite her raging soul, she smiled when people told her she must be happy in life because of her wealth and position, her good health and sparkling complexion, her apparent contentment, and her every need fulfilled. She exclaimed to herself, "Oh, those imbeciles who see only

---

7. The best known comedies of Jean Nicolas Bouilly (1763–1842) were *L'Abbé de l'épée* and *Deux Journées*, both presented in 1800. Marie Cottin (1770–1807), called Sophie Risteau, wrote popular adventure novels and maxims.

happiness written in the calm of your face and don't know that torture extracts your laughter."

From that point on, life was a continuous cry of agony. When she saw women adorned with their virtue, others with their love, when she saw happy people who were confident about their faith in God, she tormented them with sneering sarcasm. She made passing priests blush when she gave them a lusty glance and laughed in their ears. As for young virgins, she made them aghast by the love stories and passionate tales she related. People wondered who that haggard woman was, that wandering ghost with the fiery eyes who wore the expression of the damned. If you wanted to come to know her, you would find only a single pain in the depth of her existence, only tears in her actions.

Oh, women, women! It was especially the young and beautiful that she hated from the bottom of her heart. She hated them when they were bathed in candlelight at a ball or in the radiance of chandeliers at the theater, displaying their undulating bosoms and decked in lace and diamonds, with men crowding around to return smile for smile. And when those men flattered and praised them, she wanted to rumple their clothes and their embroidered veils, to spit in those pretty faces, and drag those coldly impassive and haughty faces through the mud. She believed in nothing but misfortune and death.

For her, virtue was only a word, religion an illusion, reputation an impostor's mask like a veil hiding wrinkles. Then she discovered the satisfaction of arrogance, the pleasure of disdain, and she spit on the stoop of churches when she passed by.

When she thought about Ernest, about his voice, his words, his arms, which had held her so long in trembling surrender to love and which she remembered especially when her husband was kissing her, she was contorted with anguished pain as she struggled against herself, like a man in the midst of his death rattle who cries out a name or weeps for a particular memory. She had children by this man, children who resembled their father, a three-year-old girl and a boy of five, whose playful laughter reached her ears. In the mornings, they came up laughing to kiss away the fresh tears on her cheeks, whereas *she,* their mother, had not any relief all night from her outlandish torments.

When her thoughts turned to Ernest wandering the high seas, perhaps buffeted by a storm that threatened him alone and made him cling to life, and when her mind's eye saw a corpse bobbing in the waves as vulture's prey, her revery was interrupted by joyful cries, the voices of children as they came running up to show her a tree in bloom or the sun making the frost shimmer on the grass. For her, it was like the pain of a man who falls down in the street, only to see the crowd laugh and applaud.

And what was Ernest thinking, so far from her? Sometimes he actually missed her when he had nothing to do, in moments of leisure and idleness, thinking of her, of her wild passion, of her ripe buttocks, her white breasts and long black hair. But he quickly ran for the arms of a slave girl to quench the fire that was kindled in the strongest and most consecrated of loves. Moreover, he made little work of consoling himself for that loss by thinking he had done a good turn as a proper citizen, and that Ben Franklin or Lafayette wouldn't have done better—for at that moment he was standing on the national home ground of patriotism, of slavery, coffee, and temperance: America.

He was one of those people in whom judgment and reason occupy such a large place that they have devoured the heart, like an unwelcome neighbor. An entire world separated them, for on the other hand Mazza was entirely distracted and anguished. While her lover wallowed as much as he wanted to in the arms of Negresses and mulattoes, she was dying of boredom, believing that Ernest too lived only for her and was undergoing an agony that he actually derided with his wild, brutish laugh. He was devoting his efforts to another woman. While that poor woman was crying and cursing God—calling on Hell to aid her and writhing as she wondered why Satan was so long in coming—she passionately kissed a lock of his hair. And perhaps at that same moment, Ernest was strolling across a public square in some city in the United States, attired like a plantation owner in white pants and jacket, on his way to a slave market to trade some gold for a pair of strong and well-muscled black arms, pendulous breasts, and the promise of pleasure.

Besides, he was going about his scientific experiments. He had filled two huge boxes of notes about flint deposits and mineralogical analyses. In addition, the climate suited him very well, and he was thriving in that atmosphere, energized by its scientific academies, railroads, steamboats, sugar cane, and indigo.

What air did Mazza breathe? She lived in a more restricted circle, but it was a world apart which revolved around tears and hopelessness, and which was to become engulfed in the abyss of a crime.

SIX

A black cloth hung over the manor's carriage entrance. Its two attached ends looped up to a central point to form a kind of broken ogival arch that allowed you to peer through and see a coffin flanked by two candles. Gusts of wind passing over the black crepe, studded with silver tears, made the flames tremble like the voiced shudder of a dying person. From time to time, the two sextons in charge of the proceedings stood to the side in order to make way for guests who were arriving one after another, all dressed in black with white ties, pressed ascots, and hair freshly done. They doffed their hats when they passed the coffin, and dipped a black-gloved finger in the holy water font.

It was snowing. After the procession left, a young woman in a black cloak came down to the courtyard and walked on tiptoe across the blanket of snow covering the flagstone. Through the slit in her black veil you could see her pallid face as she strained to watch the hearse roll out of sight. Then she extinguished the candles, went back up, undid her coat, warmed her white slippers near the fireplace, and turned her head to look again. But she saw only the black coat of the last funeral employee as he turned the corner.

When she couldn't hear the monotonous clatter of the iron-rimmed wheels of the hearse on the cobblestones, when it was all over—the priests' chants, the funeral cortege—she threw herself on the death bed, twisting her body this way and that, and exclaiming in fits of convulsive joy, "Come, now! It's yours, it's all yours! I am waiting for you, so come on! The pleasures of the nuptial bed are all yours, beloved, yours and yours alone! We'll have a world of love and ecstasy! Come here so that I can stretch out beneath your caresses and feast on your kisses." On the commode she saw a small rosewood box that Ernest had given her one winter day just like this one. When he had arrived, he was wrapped in his coat with snow sprinkled on his hat, which added to the rose scent of his kisses. In the middle of the scented box the initials M and E were entwined. She breathed its fragrance deeply and for a long time remained in dreamy contemplation.

Soon her children were brought to her. They were crying and asking for their father. They sought consolation in Mazza's kisses. She sent them away without so much as a word or a smile.

She was thinking about him, far away from her and never to return.

SEVEN

She lived that way for several months, as time rolled along, feeling happier and freer each day, while her heart emptied out to make way for love. All the passions, feelings, and sentiments that fill one's heart had fled, like the concerns of childhood. At first there was modesty, followed by religion and virtue, and then their residue, like the fragments of a broken glass. Except for love she no longer had any feminine traits, but it was a terrible, consuming love that inflicted tortures on itself and on others, like Vesuvius ripping itself apart and spilling its molten lava over the flowers in the valley.

She had her children, but they died like their father. Each day they grew increasingly pale and scrawny, awakening each night in a paroxysm of fever, shivering on their bed of agony and saying that a snake was eating away at their chests, for something was incessantly burning and devouring them. Mazza studied their agony, smiling out of anger and vengeance.

Both of them died on the same day. She shed no tears when she watched their coffins being nailed, nor did her heart sigh. Her eyes were cold and dry when she watched them being wrapped in their shrouds. When she was alone at last, her night was happy and sanguine, her soul was calm, and joy filled her heart. She had no regrets or anguished cries, because she was planning to leave France on the following day, after avenging a profaned love and the terrible fate that destiny had given her; after deriding God, men, life, and the fate that had toyed with her for a while; after amusing herself with life and death, tears and grief; and after trading her suffering to heaven in exchange for crimes.

Farewell to European soil, with its mists and glaciers, where souls are as cool as the climate, where love is as slack and soft as its gray clouds. I'll take America and its fiery climes, its hot sun and limpid sky, its beautiful nights in the palm and plain tree groves! Good-bye to the world, and thanks! I'm going on board and leaving. Go, beautiful clipper, run swiftly before your billowing sails! Let your bow split the waves, outrace the storm, ride the bounding main, and should you founder, cast me along with your flotsam on the shore where he breathes!

The night was spent in wild excitement, but it was the frenzy of joyful anticipation. When she thought about him, about kissing and living together forever, she smiled and cried with happiness.

The cemetery ground where her children lay was still freshly damp with holy water.

EIGHT

The next day she received a letter, mailed seven months earlier. It was from Ernest. She trembled as she broke the seal and eagerly read through it. When she finished, she tried to reread it but was too drained from fright. This is what the letter said:

"Why are your letters so dishonest, madame? Especially the last one. I burned it out of embarrassment that someone else might read it. Couldn't you restrain your passion just a little? Why do you keep after me with your memories, disturbing my work and distracting me from doing my job? What have I done to make you love me so much?

"Once again, madame, I think love should be reasonable. Now that I have left France, you should love your husband and forget me as I have forgotten you. Happiness is found on the beaten path. The paths toward the rocky peaks are strewn with rocks and brambles that soon cut and exhaust you.

"I am now living happily in a small, charming house on a river bank. The river cuts through a field where I hunt for insects and flora. When I return home my Negro servant greets me with a sweeping bow, kissing my feet when he wishes a particular favor. I have shaped a happy, calm, and agreeable existence in the heart of nature and science. Why don't you do as much? Who is stopping you? Where there's a will, there's a way.

"For you and for your very happiness, I advise you to not think of me any more and to stop writing me. What is the point of such an exchange? What good will it do for you to tell me a hundred times that you love me and go on to write as many times in the margins, 'I love you'?

"You must forget all that, madame, and think no more about what we were to each other. Didn't we both get what we wanted?

"I am becoming well established. I am the principal director of the commission on assaying ore, the daughter of the managing director is a charming seventeen-year-old, her father has an income of sixty thousand pounds, and as his only daughter, she is sweet, good, very reasonable, and will have no trouble at all in raising a family and overseeing a household.

"I'm getting married one month from now. You should be pleased if you love me as you always claim, since I am doing it for my happiness.

"Adieu, Madame Willer. Stop thinking about a man who has enough tact to stop loving you, and if you wish to do me one last favor, please send me a pint bottle of prussic acid as soon as possible. The Secretary of the Academy of Sciences is a very competent chemist who will give it to you on my recommendation.

"Farewell. I am counting on you to not forget my acid. *Ernest Vaumont.*"

When Mazza finished the letter she uttered an inarticulate wail, as if someone had burned her with red-hot tongs.

She remained for a long time in a state of surprised consternation. "Oh, that coward!" she finally said. "He seduced and abandoned me for another woman! After giving him everything and having nothing left to give! After throwing everything overboard except for a solitary plank that slips out of your hands while you slip under the waves!"

That poor woman loved him so much! She had sacrificed her virtue for him and offered him all her love. She had renounced God and—far worse!—her husband and children whom she had watched agonize and die, while she smilingly thought of him. What was she going to do? What would become of her? He was telling another woman that he loved her, while he kissed her eyes and breasts, and told her that she was his life and his passion. Another woman! And what about her? Had she had others before him? Hadn't she turned away from her husband in their marriage bed, thinking of him? Hadn't she deceived him with her adulterous lips? Hadn't she poisoned him with her tears of joy?

As her God and her life, he had abandoned her after using her, enjoying her while taking everything from her. And now he is discarding her, throwing her into the bottomless pit of crime and despair!

At other times she couldn't believe her own eyes, as she reread that fateful letter and covered it with her tears.

When her dejection turned to furious anger, she said to herself, "What! What do you mean saying that you're leaving me alone in the world, without any family or relatives? I sacrificed them for you. I am alone, since I sacrificed my honor as a burnt offering to you. I am bereft of reputation because I sacrificed it along with my kisses, in full view of all those who called me your mistress. Your mistress! And now that embarrasses you, coward!

"Where are those who have died?

"Where am I to turn? I had only one thing in my heart, one single idea, and now it's gone. Should I search for you when you send me away like a slave? If I seek out other women, they will abandon me to their laughter, proudly pointing their fingers at me, for they have never loved anyone and don't really know what tears are. So there! Since I still crave love, passion, and life, they will tell me to go wherever pleasure and caresses are sold for a certain price. And in my evenings spent with my companions in luxury, I'll hail passersby from my window. When they come up, I'll have to make sure they get all the pleasure they want, so that when the transaction is completed they will leave satisfied. I won't have any complaints about that good bargain, and I'll laugh at anyone who comes along, for I'll have deserved my fate!

"And just what did I do? I loved you more than any other. Oh, have mercy, Ernest! If you could hear my lament, you might take pity on me, on me who had none for the others. Now I curse myself. I wallow in anguish here, and my clothes are soaked by my tears."

And she ran around madly before falling to the ground and rolling about, as she cursed God, mankind, life itself, everything on earth that lived and thought; she ripped out handfuls of her hair, and her nails were bloody.

"Oh, to be unable to put up with life! To be reduced to throwing myself into the arms of death, as into a mother's arms! And to wonder right up to the last minute whether the tomb holds further suffering, whether oblivion promises more pain! To have no more faith in anything, not even love, the first religion of the heart, and to be unable to rid myself of this continual malaise, like a drunken man who is forced to drink more!

"Why did you invade my solitude to tear me away from my happiness? I was so tranquil and pure, until you came along to love me and I to love you!

"Men are so handsome when they look at you! You offered me the love that you now refuse me, and I nourished it with crimes. And now it kills me too! I was virtuous when you first saw me, and now I am ferociously cruel. I'd like to have something to crush, tear, despoil, and then toss aside, just as was done to me. Ah, I hate everything: men, God, and I hate you too. And yet I still feel that I would give my life for you in return!

"I loved you more and more all the time, like those who drink sea water to quench a thirst that it only increases. And now I am going to die . . . death! The end of everything! Shadows, a tomb, and then . . . the immensity of complete emptiness. Oh, but I still feel that I would like to live and suffer, as I have suffered! Ah, happiness! Where is it? It's just a dream. And virtue? Disappointment. The tomb? What do I know?

"But I will know."

NINE

She got up, dried her tears, and tried to still the heaving sobs that were stifling her lungs. She looked in a mirror to see if her eyes were still red from crying so much, fixed her hair, and went out to accomplish Ernest's last request.

Mazza went to the chemist's home and asked to see him. She was asked to wait in a small sitting room on the second floor, appointed with red and green upholstered furniture, a round mahogany table in the middle, lithographs of Napoleonic battles on the paneled walls, while on the gray marble mantelpiece there was a gold clock with a cupid clinging to the dial as he reclined on his arrows with his other hand. When it chimed two o'clock, the door opened and the chemist entered. He was a small, thin man, with formal manners. He had thin lips, glasses and beady eyes. When Mazza explained the reason for her visit, he began to praise Ernest Vaumont, his traits, character, and attitude. Finally, he produced the vial of acid, led her by the hand to the bottom of the stairs, and even got his shoes damp in the courtyard when he guided her back to the door giving onto the street.

Mazza's head was burning so much she could hardly walk. Several times she thought the blood would burst through the pores of her flushed cheeks. She walked through streets where wretchedness clung to the houses the way fingers of color streak whitened walls. Seeing all that misery, she addressed it, saying, "I'm going to cure myself of your misfortune." Holding the poison with both hands, she passed by the palace of kings and said, "Farewell, existence. I'm going to rid myself of all your cares." When she got home, she glanced backward before closing her door, bidding adieu to the populace she was leaving, and to the city bursting with noise, with commotion and lively voices.

TEN

She opened her writing desk, sealed the bottle of acid, addressed the package, and wrote another note to the main superintendent of police. She rang for a servant and gave it to him.

On a third piece of paper she wrote, "I loved a man. I killed my husband for him, and I killed my children for him. I die without remorse, without hope, but with a few regrets." She placed it on the mantle.

"Just another half-hour," she said. "Soon he'll come to take me to the cemetery."

She took off her clothes, examined her lovely naked body for a few minutes, thinking of all the voluptuousness it had given and the great pleasure she had bestowed on her lover.

The love of that kind of woman is such a treasure!

After more tears, she thought about the time that had slipped away from her, about her happiness, dreams, youthful frolics, and then thought about him again for a long time. She wondered what death was like, losing herself in that empty gulf of thought which gnaws and tears at itself out of powerless rage. Then she suddenly arose, as if roused from a dream, poured a few drops of poison in a silver-gilt cup, drank it eagerly, and lay down for the last time on the sofa where she had surrendered so often to the raptures of love in Ernest's arms.

ELEVEN

When the commissioner entered, Mazza was still in the throes of agony. She writhed on the ground for a while and twisted a few times. All her limbs stiffened, and she uttered a piercing cry.

When he approached her she was dead.[8]

---

8. On the origin of this story in a newspaper account of the trial called "The Modern Brinvilliers," which appeared in the *Journal de Rouen* (Oct.4, 1837), see René Herval, *Les Véritables Origines de Madame Bovary* (Paris: Nizet, 1957), p.139.

Dance of the Dead

So many words for so little.—[1] UNIVERSAL EPIGRAPH

Death brings everyone to judgment.—DEATH DANCE

ONE RECOLLECTION

Let the dead join the dance! Begin dancing when midnight sounds and the entire nave rocks with the strains of its mournful harmony. Black clouds fill the sky, owls fly above the ruins, the universe becomes filled with ghosts and demons, and funereal voices, moans, and sighs are heard. Then the tombs open a crack, skeletons with earth still clinging to their bones cast off their shrouds. They stand up, walk, and dance. Let the dead begin dancing! Leave your tombs, now that the hour has struck. Listen to the droning ring of the bells as they murmur, "Don't stop!" Dance, now that you're dead, now that life and misfortune have left your flesh! Have at it! There will be no tomorrow to your celebrations, for they will be as eternal as death, so dance! Rejoice in your oblivion. You'll have no more cares or labors, since you no longer exist. No more misery for you in your nonbeing. Ah, my dead ones, dance!

Dance! Join hands in a huge circle and celebrate joyfully! Dance until daylight, and then return to your stone beds. Choose your ladies, and may their hair be white and their long teeth polished. Their flesh is cold; in

---

1. Bruneau (*Débuts littéraires*, p.197) located the source of the first epigraph in the *Musée de la caricature en France*, ed. E. Jaime (Paris: Delloye, 1838).

fact, it's very cold, isn't it? And don't their eyes stare at you? Make them leap and be carried away by the dance! What delight! In their nakedness, they show you their hearts, the place where their soul was, where so many nice things stirred. They are beautiful and shapely, they have long, white polished nails, and their hair floats down over their shoulders. Dance, my dead ones! Kiss in toothless embrace, now that your mouths are pure. The orgies of red wine, luxury, lies, and blasphemy are over. The passing worm has carried off their lips.

Do it! What prettier chandelier could you ask for than the moon above? It shines through its clouds, as though through a blue curtain, which in turn reflect on you. The immense plain where you dance is the earth itself, as you dance on through the centuries. And if you meet a pleasing woman with a few teeth left, who is more beautiful than the angels, whose shroud is silkier, longer, softer, less yellow, and if she loves you too, sit down together and kiss while thinking of the joys you left back on earth. You will both bed down on the grass by the tombs, and your heads will touch as you kiss.

For love renews. And when you are no longer anything at all, like the ground you dance on, a soft summer breeze redolent of delightful perfume may blow the dust of your bones onto a bed of roses.

Dance, my dead friends! The night belongs to you alone.

But what do you do on long winter days when snow covers you and people tread above your heads? You weep in your shrouds and turn over in your graves. And then the worms begin to climb over you and sometimes wake you.

Don't you think that girls think about their loves, kings about their crowns, and madmen about their glory, which rots just as they do? Or else you are waiting for the hour that doesn't come, and you tremble from discomfort, the wood annoys you, the earth smothers you, and it's cold and dark.

Oh, no! we are sleeping.

TWO

On that particular day some sort of gust of virtue, a wind of philanthropy, had blown across the face of the earth, but Satan was annoyed. All alone in the heavens, he was lurking around the gates of paradise at the spot where people tend to situate God and which philosophers place beyond the frontier of empty space.

When Jesus Christ came by, he heard laughter at his feet. It sounded like a death rattle, but it stemmed from pride.

Seeing the cursed face of the monster who had risen like a comet a few hundred feet below, he said, "You again, accursed one!"

For a long time, his soft voice resonated through the expanse with a heavenly harmony.

"You again, my master. You know that I am eternal, that I am God. It was granted to me by the scriptures, and the most impious people place their faith in me."

"You are very prideful and bitter. But enough from you, spirit of darkness. Silence!"

"Are you powerful enough to make me be quiet?"

"Quiet! It is written: 'Thou shalt not tempt the Son of man.'"

"And once again, that's false. You experienced it yourself when you were so terribly hungry in the desert. Your stomach came very close to winning out over grace."

"But I beat you, serpent! On the day I died, a shudder of joy ran through heaven, and the earth pulsated down to its core with happiness. Hope had come."

"It has flown off since then. The preceding night you had a strange fever on the Mount of Olives."

"That was indeed a terrible night. How many temptations! Love alone supported me then."

"But not as well as the cross where you died."

"What about the archangel? Will you deny your defeat?"

"What does that prove, since I win every day?"

"That vanity again!"

"Ah, that vanity is an admirable thing and has come in very handy. I use it to create the genius of poets and women's virtue."

"Do you really triumph?"

"Ask your father. If you really knew, you would weep over your past trials. Your father likes the way I have ruled all religions, all castes, all empires. Come down to earth with me and you'll see."

"Isn't the Holy Spirit there any more?"

"No, it died a few centuries ago from pneumonia."

"Nevertheless! . . . But . . ."

"What can you do to me? Annihilate me? I'll thank you for it. Alleviate my suffering? I'm too proud for that. Make me happy? You can't. Come with me, and if the living aren't enough, I'll show you the dead. Then you'll see which one of us will be beaten."

THREE

"Let's go down there, and you will see that I'm the master, that everything bows before me out of respect, that I am showered with a king's praise. My throne is more imposing than any king's, my ministers are shown deference, and people lay down their lives for me in adoration. The constant petitions and pleas I hear are music to my ears, my voluptuous nights match the orgies that fill my days, while crime runs rampant. Ah, yes, crime! The dagger brings forth streams of blood, while people grovel over piles of money. The women I create are more beautiful than your angels, since devils make better lovers than saints."

"That sounds just like you, you spirit of hell with your body draped in luxury, blasphemy in your mouth, and pride in your soul."

"Pride? You don't know how delicious it is. Why, that ambrosia burns all the way down, but it is intoxicating."

"What about blasphemy, the refuge of the damned?"

"It's the only comfort for those who no longer take comfort."

"And luxury, which you know how to use so skillfully to abase my father's creature when you make him resemble an animal?"

"Just consider that beautiful creature, heaven's reflection, the mightiest of men: Alexander the Great. He wallowed like a drunken mule skinner or a mangy dog in the arms of a whore. Go on, I laugh heartily (if I do have a heart) when I see philosophers burn their books, when I see saints smash your image, and when poets throw aside their poetry in order to throw themselves into the arms of a woman whom I'll admire two days from now for her putrefaction."

"Are you saying that your greatest delight is mankind's suffering, and that your joy stems from someone else's tears?"

"Yes, I feed on them as my only pleasure. To suffer alone like a cenobite would be unworthy of Satan. I do my job quite well. When the Eternal One threw me out of heaven, my beaten hands clutched the earth and still tear at it."

"You never show any compassion?"

"I have more than you and your whole family put together. The days of those who love me are filled with sweet and pleasant impiety. Their drunken sleep will see them comfortably through endless nights."

"Have some pity! Do you think that your pathetic joys are the only ones there are, momentary pleasures as fleeting as a smile? Have you never seen saints, the sublime transports of hearts brimming with love and faith, lives of devotion, the beautiful things that arise from the soul? No, because you are denied the purest delights. You have never heard the voices of angels, and you've never even heard the grace notes from their golden harps, which reach the earth only as a faint echo."

"No, never."

"Never has your heart felt bliss, saintly ecstasy, divine ravishment. That's because you have never seen the home of the blessed where eternity is nothing but joyful delight."

"And as for you, *your* hands have never run over the breasts of concubines, amid gleaming red streams of wine and smashed goblets, with luxurious trappings spread over the red tablecloth. After a flurry of festivity the last drop is poured, the flesh falters, and only dead bodies remain, whereas the royal diadem is borne off just as winds blow away a scrap of cloth. Glory becomes tarnished, virtue falls asleep, and voices become hoarse from preaching. And I seize all of that in my hands, break open graves so that the dead can dance, returning every night when I summon them. That's beautiful, master. You should see the ghost procession array itself on the greenish wall when the moon illuminates the tombs and night birds beat their wings on the yellowed skulls. My domain extends to that death which the blessed curse. That old toothless hag is always there, shadowing us and embracing everyone. You pay her before you can lie down in the bed she provides for you. You have to strip and give her your clothes, your loves, treasures, empires, for she wants it all. But I wake them at night so that they'll dance right here."

"What about their souls?"

"Yes, I bring them to life because they have loved and cursed. There's still some passion left in their skeletal breasts."

"So then, your persecution reaches beyond the tomb?"

"And yours?"

"Do you continue to persecute corpses?"

"They occasionally complain, but they have to get up and dance. I happen to enjoy the nightly spectacle of seeing them repeat what I had them do in life, so if there are any mistakes I can correct them. It's an exercise."

"Those poor people! When will you find shelter in my bosom from damnation?"

"Oh, do you mean at the end of the world? When that comes, I'll cross my arms and get back to my dirty work."

"For your own solitary damnation?"

"Before that I'll complete my masterpiece: the Antichrist. I've sketched him out quite a few times, but if I really put my mind to it I'll strike gold. You'll see, master. If you happen to visit the Pope, why not drop by to see me on the way? Look, there's a falling star. I'm already on my way, so let's get going!"

FOUR

The blue expanse reached everywhere: above, below, to the right, to the left, on all sides. It went on forever, reaching past unknown worlds. The storm drove the planets headlong, trailing their starry dresses behind them. You might have thought them to be madly distracted queens running over a blue velvet carpet.

Everywhere the vault sparkled with a thousand specks of light. Mounted on their diamond setting, the stars sparkled against the pure blue backdrop. Yet the entire scene was slowly revolving along its immense, gigantic, infinite course. Far below, where nothing shines in space, where clouds glide and merge, you could see a black pinpoint full of shadows. It was the earth, a slippery sphere, unpleasant and dark, as cold as an empty glass.

Souls mounted to heaven on white wings. As they rose toward the realm of the saints, their singing sounded like a distant hymn to love, with gentle breezes streaming in their ethereal wake and trailing behind them a perfume that arose from the heart.

SOULS RISING TO THE SKY
I

"Courage, sisters! We've been flying for a long time, yet I haven't seen anything so far, nothing but the moon bathing in its azure waves, nothing but its blue aura reflecting on us. We've heard nothing except confused voices from the abyss.

"And aren't we happy to be free to leave without restraint, like sighs escaping or song rising. We're happy because nothing holds us back. We were poor flowers clustered under the earth, but now our scent is emanating."

II

'We're getting tired. When will we see the Eternal One, his Son and the saints? I have to rest on that cushioned cloud covered with gold cloth fringed in blue."

III

"We've been flying for a long time. Where is heaven? Could it be paradise, floating around in a vacuum?"

IV

"I was a poet when I was a girl, a free spirit but a lost soul when I fell to earth, like a flower thrown into the mud. When I left this prison of flesh where I was buried, it was sighing its last. Birds were singing as I was leaving. I wanted to rest on a bed of roses, but they had faded.

"Near the woods, beside a brook babbling over mossy stones, I found a shady spot on some grass that shone silver beneath the morning dew. But the water became turbulent, the flower faded, and I wandered a long time. Now that I've found all of you, here we are rising into the heavens, traveling through an expanse as large and deep as my thought, with no fear of constraints, of being imprisoned behind a wall of flesh like a condemned prisoner held back by his chains.

"Let my body perish now! Get thee behind me, abject clay that soiled me and covered me with slime so many times! I am a soul rising to heaven."

V

"Oh, heaven! I dreamed of it at length when I was a child, praying to the Virgin, covering my feet with leaves picked in the fields, breathing smoking incense as its clouds curled upward toward the dome of the cupola. I have dreamed of it while lying in a bed of daisies, shielding my eyes while through the slits between my fingers I watched the sun gild the clouds and set them ablaze; while the herd was lowing on its return home in the evening, set against a reddening horizon; while insects buzzed in the grass and gossamer caught in my hair.

"Even when I was in love, I dreamed of heaven."

VI

"It seems to me that I'm going to be sated with pleasure and incense. When harmony fills my soul, I will hear angels praying and voices singing instead of my beating heart."

VII

"Yes, yes! All of that is heaven! I see it far off, like a sun that is bigger than the other one. Do you see it, sisters?"

"Alas, no!"

"I guess the poet sees heaven beyond the stars and sees happiness beyond the vast expanse. Do you hear the sacred chorus singing?"

CHORUS OF THE ELECT

"Hosanna! Glory to God! What sweetness, my brothers! Since we left the earth, doesn't it seem that we have lived in continuous harmony, that we have been nourished by aromatics, by thoughts of love and delicious things, and by voluptuous ecstasy? Haven't we been covered by a precious veil, a light netting covered with roses that lulls us to sleep with feelings of love? And oh, how our souls pulsate freely in these endlessly open reaches, freed from the body's constraints. Hosanna! Glory to God!"

"Let's go a little farther, master," Satan suggested. "You know I don't like that monotonous screeching music that people call hymns. Gracious! I hate hymn singing on earth and in heaven. I give the earthly singers stomachaches during the divine service and voices that would make the saints jump out of their stone sculpture. I heartily detest heavenly choruses and find thunder more melodious, all the more because some people think that's the father grumbling in anger, while others believe it to be my laughter."

Jesus tilted his head. His long blond hair hung down his back, over the blue tunic that covered him down to his feet. As he descended, he looked at the worlds revolving all around him in space.

Riding a sphere, Satan scrutinized the bottomless gulf below him, but his soul was larger than the chasm and his distress was deeper.

When Satan lowered his head, his nostrils flared right up to the middle of his livid face. His half-open eyes emitted only a red flame, as devouring as fire. His horns cut through the clouds floating above the earth like a blue carpet being billowed by children at play.

Passing through mountain gorges, Christ's halo glistened on the snow like the sun.

In the middle of the shadows, they heard a voice rising toward the sky like the crash of waves. The immense voice was confusing, like an angry mute stammering and frothing with rage. It was the earth speaking.

"Ah, it's a curse. I'm home," Satan said.

FIVE

They stopped one summer night in the countryside at a village cemetery and sat down on a broken stone covered with velvety green moss.

It was halfway up a hill near the woods, where leaves trembled whenever a bird returned to its nest with a piece of meat in its mouth, which it had dug up in the field. Beneath the beautiful moon that stood out sharply against a starry backdrop, the leaves seemed silvery when they shivered, as though a mouth were whispering words of love. All around, the wind made the flowers bend down to the aromatic bouquet of the dewy grass. Zephyrs swirled like soft sighs blown into the wind, making the shadows of the cypresses vibrate and whisper through their foliage to the tombs laid out at the foot of their trunks. Something as tender as a loving glance and as fragrant as a kiss ran through the woods, settled on the grass, moved about the branches of the trees, and rose in the air. You might have thought it a soul making the earth its bed.

Not even a murmur disturbed the silence. There was nothing on earth, except for the dead who were sleeping beneath the flowers.

The tall grass was thick; the warm, verdant earth was blanketed by a savory scent, by shadows and silent calm. The dead slept under their sweet-smelling winding sheets.

"How beautiful that silent summer night was, decorated with its stars, white moon, green carpet, and yellow flowers whose essence wafted like perfumed breath! That is where the dead rested in their tombs! Emptiness and flowers."

Christ said, "Oh, how I love you, sweet and full of harmony, resting in your sleep like a baby. That's the way I saw you from Calvary before my final sigh, smiling through my agony as I contemplated the way my father endowed you with luster."

"Lend an ear, Son of God, listen and tell me what you hear. Listen, do you hear the horses neighing as they champ at their foamy bits, chewing as they stamp their hooves? They will be leaving for a race that has been going on for six thousand years: war. Do you hear empires crumbling, beliefs falling like empires and crashing into ruin like temples? Do you hear the shouts and curses, the scythe harvesting men with each swipe? The blades of grass cry out beneath the blade of steel, but still it cuts. Look and tell me what you see. In the distance there is a field covered with bleached bones—five thousand cities razed! Watch the flames rise as I ignite the globe. Behold those horses parading over the heads of four million men, whose bodies are piled in drifts clear up to the breast-piece of the harnesses! Look over there at your churches filled with dancing, singing, and drinking. The altar serves as a banquet table and the Communion chalice as a goblet for shimmering wine. There is the sybaritic Orient, intoxicated by its own aroma and sleeping like a drunken sultana; Africa dying of hunger in its deserts; the youthful but enslaved America, baked by its sun, stooped like an old man; and Europe, like a madwoman running her machines and saying how much she despises you."

"Oh, father, father!"

"I am a powerful emperor, aren't I? Moreover, I have invented pleasures a hundred times more voluptuous than any you ever created. When they kill you, they leave a smile on your lips. My ally is emaciated ambition, with the wan complexion and sunken cheeks, stationed at palace doors as the soldier who devours empires. That black crow over there is pride, taking shelter in men's hearts and speaking through all mouths, as empty as the desert, as powerful as the ocean, and as big as you are; then there are the thousand cries of envy and anger which smash the world with their fists; and there is laughing, naked luxury, hiding in caves where it can wallow in private on its satin cushions, summoning young and old alike, imperious and stupid, brutish and sovereign. I also have shining gold, which creates more than heaven does—gold that provides everything: virtue, thrones, and glory. Gold shimmers on crowns, on titles and positions; it circulates, speaks, applauds, and makes you strong and powerful. The ragged miser in his garret eagerly smiles at it, because he alone has all the delights and pleasures of the whole world in his sacks. With his treasure he can buy everything: virtue, glory, the mightiest empires, the most beautiful women, and the most unheard of sensual delights."

When Satan ran out of breath, he looked at Christ, whose eyes were ablaze just as his heart was depressed. Because it was all so beautiful, as beautiful as the storm and as vast as oblivion.

CHRIST

"What! Is there never any rest? Will battlefields always steam with blood! Will there always be shouting, always be assaults by the swirling storm! Under your control, the world must be tired of its moans and convulsions, dizzy from its blasphemies and cries of pain."

"Don't you see that its life now is only a prolonged death rattle it has been trying to utter for a thousand years? And don't you see that when I am astride the earth, I make it bend its back the way a knight pushes his tired horse? Tripping over its own legs and foaming at the mouth, its exhausting race won't be finished until the same fall throws both of us into the capacious bosom of eternal death."

"What! Do you mean that there was no point in assuaging the world's pain by sowing my suffering and tears? Did those seeds of God lying in the furrows of faith dry up from the hot breath you blew over the face of the earth? What! Did the angels shed tears in my paradise, seeing their brethren reach out their arms to them in vain? After striding, running, faltering, and falling into ruin like a madman, poor world, won't you be able to rest as a faded flower sleeps in its calyx or the tired day sleeps at night? And you, Humanity, won't you find an oasis to slake your thirst by washing down the dust of empires that has parched your throat? Having wandered so long on your trek through the desert of life, as the empty horizon always stretched out before you on the endless trip, won't you be able to close your eyes to the searing sun?"

Turning his mouth downward, Christ with his heavenly breath revitalized the earth. The trees softly swayed while breezes made their leaves tremble in the moonlight, the way a heart replete with love softly pulsates in the evening and murmurs the lilting words of a mysterious language, taught by one's lodestar of desire. But soon the pair stop dead in their tracks, as an exhalation of death sweeps over the land. The pure white and blue sky seems illuminated by the glow of an infernal blaze. Tombs open a crack and lift their lids to reveal the dead sleeping in their death shrouds, with their heads on their chests and their arms crossed. At first they gently stir like an infant leaving his dreams to awake with a smile. These cold bodies partially elevate themselves, slowly unwind their shrouds, and solemnly lift their skulls, which the balmy scented night air has gently warmed.

Why do they awake? Who summoned them? They slept so soundly! Nothing remains under the ground except for an occasional worm that climbs up to their chest before heading back down. Everyone of them knows Satan. Oh, yes, when his grimacing face appeared at the head of their sepulchral beds, they closed their frightened eyes and surrendered to him. And now he conjures them because this voluptuous emperor loves to witness the dance of his dead sultanas, while Death joyfully accompanies their jerky steps with his fiddle.

CHORUS OF YOUNG WOMEN
I

"It's so stifling hot in that bed! The heavy sleep makes you groggy. How long have we been sleeping? It has been a long time, hasn't it? These boards have made my arms and legs stiff.

"Where are the flowers that surrounded our coffins while we slept? I thought people were singing and throwing flowers.

"Where is my bird calling from under the branches of the orchard? Where is the moonlit lake with its calming sounds, where are the dying strains of guitar music wafting over the silver surface of the water?

"Where are the yellow, red, and blue circles radiated by the sunset in the corner of the garden, against the shady backdrop of a dark green mass provided by the thick trees?

"Where are our party dresses? The earth has made them a soiled mess. Let's shake them off so we can dance. To the dance, sisters! I hear violin music keeping time to the sound of glasses being smashed. Let's dance."

II

"And yet I would like to sit on this grass, to soak in the dew, because my skin is burning hot. Actually, since my flesh is now gone, all I have are my earrings and necklaces rattling on my chest when I walk. My sisters, where is the one who was smiling at us? Have you seen him? Is he sleeping like us?

"Where are our loves, our flowers, our perfumes, our evening sighs?

"Where is the jasmine bower where he kissed me?
"Where is the gay ball, with its waves of light and shimmer of gold?
"Where is life?
"But the dance is beginning.
"Let's dance!"

III

"No, leave me alone. I'd like to know how long I slept without waking.

"It seems to me that someone sat down on me and cried. Were they tears or drops of water from the storm? They're coming to get us. Let's dance!"

And the pair wandered along that way for a long time.

Who could have actually measured the length of their journey, undertaken by a god and a devil! When they were well past the seas, they stopped.

In the sweet mournfulness of his soul, the Son of God suffered continually from a pain as vast as his heart. The tears falling from his limpid blue eyes spread a heavenly scent, the way a summer rain steeps the earth in a redolence that makes it exhale gusts of flowers.

Satan lowered his glance for a moment, but when he raised it up, Christ felt that he was intent on burning some souls. You could hear something beating inside his hollow chest, but it was only the desert wind passing through his body and whistling out between his blackened teeth in a death rattle.

A voice rose to the clouds like the softly beating wings of a dove, like a zephyr caressing the blue waters of the southern seas, like the whisper of green leaves, the stream over its mossy bed, the wind gently bending flowers in the moonlight. The voice climbed to the vault of heaven and left behind only a wake of harmony that resonated a long time and died slowly like the gilded sun setting behind the waves.

IV

"Oh, my seraphim, my blue-winged angels with white cheeks, oh come to me my saints! Oh, my paradise, so pungent from all the love it exudes, like an incense burner!

"Oh, sing tirelessly on your harps of gold, and may you endow the earth with your divine melody in order to rejuvenate faith that has withered like a flower past its prime. Let ravishing love pour from your lips! May your heart proffer an ambrosial essence to embalm souls for their loving sleep!"

A wail immediately rose from the demon's chest, vibrating like thunder. It was like the hiss of a striking snake, like the roaring, raging storm, like the hurricane tearing away mountains and throwing them aside, like the desert wind skipping over its fiery bed.

And that endless shout had no echo. It was a perpetually agitated ocean, unchecked by any shoreline and beyond measurable dimension, yet bursting with angry sobs. It churned in all directions to the point of self-destruction, like a God who has gone mad.

In its wild course, the shout smashed against dry rocks, transforming the sounds into an angry froth that sprayed high into the sky.

Satan was speaking.

V

"All mine! The world, life and death, emperors and their peoples, empires and nations are all mine! People, remove your shrouds! Empires, lift up your ruins! Emperors, lift your embalmed and rotten coffin lids! Come and tell us what life is, what a people is worth, the value of a crown, how many worms and centuries it takes to eat this person, how many minutes to pulverize that one. You lived your life and now you are dead!

"People, where are your names, now that the windblown sand has erased them like so many before them?

"Kings, where are your crowns, now that they have been blown away by the breath of death?

"Come to me, you worldly men, and tell me what has become of your passions and virtues. They have passed away like your flowers, your palaces, your glory, and your ashes!

"And you, ladies! Where are your hearts, bursting with love? Your hearts have rotted even before the lace on your clothes.

"When you are all assembled here, you'll tell me right away what death is, what you have been thinking for so many centuries, asleep under a world that throbs above your heads like a victim still shaking in his agony.

"Each of you will tell me where your soul has gone, and whether it occasionally comes to revisit the mud that enclosed it."

DANCE OF DEATH

In an immense, red-hot desert, Death sits alone with its head propped on its knees and its jaw resting on its bony hands. Like a harvester at evening time, Death was singing to itself. At first, a huge sigh escaped its lips, and it said:

DEATH'S SONG

I

"When the snow slowly falls on a winter night, like white tears from heaven, that's my song you hear on the wind, shaking the cypresses as it passes through their foliage.

"With black birds darting beside me, I pause along my way to sit on a cold tomb and look with dazzled eyes at the black clouds forming and then stretching across the horizon, like shrouds for covering dead giants. Meanwhile, the dead are asleep, the trees sway, and everything else sheds tears or slumbers.

"How many nights, centuries, and years have been spent that way!

"I have seen the birth of everything, and I have witnessed its death.

"I can hardly tally the nicks in my scythe caused by each new generation. I am eternal like God. I play nursemaid to the whole world as it sleeps each night in its cherished bed. It's the same old round of revelry and work. I leave each morning and return in the evening, using my shroud as an apron for gathering my harvest, and then I seed it to all the winds."

II

"When the waves rise, the wind howls, the vault of heaven bursts into sobs, and the ocean is worked into a madman's fury, when everything is caught in a roaring swirl, that's when I stretch out on the whitecaps to let the storm gently rock me, like a queen in regal repose. For several days the water refreshes my feet, which were scorched by the tears of past generations who grasped at my legs in their attempt to stop me.

"Then when I want everything to stop, when this anger begins to make me drowse the way monotone music does, I simply signal for quiet with a nod, and the huge, arrogant storm dies out, just like the men, armadas, and armies that it shook on its breast."

III

"I have walked from north to south, east to west, I have traversed India and the Germanic countries, seas, rivers, forests, and deserts. I have cut down everything; I have smashed and destroyed thrones, peoples, emperors, pyramids, and kingdoms. Just cite me a single wave in the ocean, a mere word of hate or love, a shout, a glance, the flight of a solitary bird, an empire, people, fame, a crown—all such passing vanities, blossoming only to fade within a day, have been erased wherever I have passed.[2] The seeds of life contained within the earth are the first fruits of death."

IV

"Everything has sought me out. Some got here early, others a bit later. Many others have summoned me and then come running after me.

"How many things have been dashed against my chest! How many loves have nestled there, and how much happiness has blossomed there! How many curses have resounded against it!

"How I tramped and then ran, enough to make me dizzy and out of breath!

"What, then, have I loved in everything I have witnessed: thrones, peoples, love, glory, grief, crime, and virtue? Nothing but the death shroud covering me!"

V

"And my horse, my horse! Oh, how much I love you too!

"How you gallop over the face of the earth, striking and smashing an occasional head with your iron shoe, oh my horse!

"Your eyes blaze, your mane is straight and full, but it flows over your neck when the wind lifts us up and away on our endless trajectory. You never tire, for there is never any rest or sleep for either of us.

"Your whinny is the rumor of war, your steaming nostrils are the plague that sets in like fog.

"Your course is as true as my arrows! With your breastplate you smash pyramids and empires, and your hoof breaks crowns with a single kick.

"How you are admired and respected!

---

2. This sentence was taken from "The Woman of the World," which Flaubert dated June 1–2, 1836: "Just cite me a single wave in the ocean, a mere word of hate or love, a gust of wind, a flight in the sky, a smile on one's lips, which has not been erased" (11:262).

"On trembling knees, popes offer their tiaras to request a favor, kings give their scepters, people present their misfortune, poets give up their fame. And you gallop, leap, and prance on their bowed heads.

"Each day we both resume the same route and we both enter the same arena.

"We always speed over the same road, while everything bends a knee as we pass. Leaning into your mane when your gait makes you stretch out your neck, I hear the wind whistle in my ears, vibrate my scythe until it sings, rustle the feathers of my arrows hanging by your rump, and the cries rising toward us from the ground, and the regular thud of the steel on your hooves.

"Oh, my horse! You are my only gift from heaven when it saw me aging. Your hocks are made of iron, your head is of bronze; you can run for centuries as though you had eagles at your fetlocks. When you get hungry every millennium, you eat flesh and drink tears.

"Oh, my horse! I love you as only Death can love!"

VI

"I have often seen children playing with flowers, lovers surrender to the arms of their mistresses, kings unctuous with pride beneath their royal mantles, self-satisfied eras that take pride in their immense corruption, and I seized it all at once. Flowers, children, loves, kings, thrones—all of that is gone, faded, blown away like the dust on the road I travel.

"Whenever I see freshness, youth, a young flower, another girl to despoil, I make both the flower and the girl wither. Dead roses provide me with the sweetest fragrance.

"When the battle rages and blood flows, all the bloody melees are mine. Mine are the cursed peoples who drag along their green-tinged carcasses, half-eaten by the plague that covers and devours them. The joys of agony are mine, for I take voluptuous delight in the bane of existence.

"I have witnessed the birth and death of generations. I have heard crowns and thrones come tumbling down, I have listened to waves of angry people rising and falling, and I have heard maledictory shouts, sighs, and curses. All that combines to form a vast harmony called the world, of which the last note sings my name."

VII

"I have lived a long time! I've seen everything. How much I know, and how many mysteries and worlds I contain!

"Sometimes when I have harvested well, galloped on my horse and wreaked hardship in all directions, weariness brings me to a halt.

"But I have to start all over and resume my infinite course across worlds and through space. I am the one who collects beliefs and glory, loves and crimes, *everything*. I have ripped up my own shroud. A terrible hunger tortures me endlessly, like an eternal serpent devouring my vital organs.

"I cast my eyes around me and see a smoking conflagration, darkness at noon, life's death agony. I see the tombs I have built and the plains of past ages completely reduced to rubble.

"That's when I sit down to relax my tired legs and back, my weary head droops from the need for sleep, and my worn-out feet need relief. I scan the boundless immensity of the endless red horizon that opens up forever. I shall devour it like all the rest.

"When will it be my turn to sleep, O God? When will you stop creating? When will I be able to sleep on my tombs like a gravedigger? To rest on the world when it gives its last gasp like the death rattle of nature?

"Then I'll be able to throw aside my arrows and my shroud. I'll set my horse free to graze around the pyramids and sleep in the palaces of emperors, to drink the last drop of the ocean, and to breathe the last scent of blood.

"For centuries he will be able to wander day and night wherever he wishes, to leap from the Atlas Mountains to the Himalayas, to run at his own proud pace from heaven to earth, to enjoy stirring the dust of fallen empires, to rove the plains of the dried ocean beds, to leap over the ashes of great cities, to fill his lungs with oblivion, to parade and leap at will.

"And when you also tire, looking for a gulf to swallow you up, you will come here panting for breath and will collapse from your mad dash through the oceanic expanse. With the corners of your mouth lathered, your neck extended, and your muzzle toward the horizon, you will beg as I did for an eternal sleep where your flaming hooves can rest, and for a bed of green leaves where your burning eyes can close. In motionless anticipation on the desert wastes of existence, you will plead for something stronger than you to crush you beneath its heel. You will ask to rejoin the calmed tempest, the faded flower, and the rotten corpse. You will seek sleep, because eternity is torture and oblivion consumes itself.

"Why have we come to this point? What storm has thrust us into the abyss? What storm will blast us back to the unknown worlds whence we came?

"But before that, O my steed, you can run again, you can flatter your pride with the sounds of your destruction. Take heart, because your voyage is long! We have ridden together for a long time; an even longer time will pass, and the two of us will not age. The stars will fade, the mountains will sink, the earth's diamond axes will wear out, and we alone are immortal. Nothingness will live forever.

"Today you can sleep at my feet and polish your teeth on moss from the tombstones because Satan commands and an unnamed power links me to his will. The dead are going to waken. It's God's design, which will recall my youth, my yesterday and my tomorrow."

VIII

"I love you, Satan! Perhaps you alone understand my joys and delirium. But one fine day when the world no longer exists, you too will be able to rest and sleep in the void.

"And I who have lived and worked so much, who have had only chaste and austere thoughts, I will have to endure. Mankind has the tomb, glory has oblivion, and day reposes in the bosom of night, but *I* . . .

"And I am alone on this road strewn with bones and bordered by ruins!

"Angels have their brothers, and demons have their infernal companions. Yet I have but the sound of my scythe when it harvests, my whistling arrows, my galloping horse. Always the sound of the same wave eating away at the world."

SATAN: "You pity yourself, yet you are the happiest creature in heaven, the only one who is as big, beautiful, immutable, and eternal as God, the only one who can equal him. One day you will beat him down when you have beaten down the universe under your horse's hoof!

"How delightful it will be for you when God is finished and the universe dissipates everywhere, when the stars wander aimlessly, when souls leave their resting place to wander in the immensity to jostle and smash one another with sighs and sobs.

"You'll establish your eternal hegemony over heaven and hell so you can knock down entire worlds of stars and planets, all the heavens, all the worlds. You'll be able to let your horse roam fields laden with emeralds and diamonds, to give him a stable bed made of wings torn from angels, and to cover him with Christ's blue mantle. You'll be able to embroider his saddle with all the stars from the sky, and then you will kill him. And when the total destruction you wreak leaves only a void, after you tear up your shroud and break your arrows, you'll make yourself a crown of rocks from the highest mountain and will leap into the abyss. Even if you fall for a million centuries, you will die for (aside from myself) the world must end. I will be more eternal than God and should live to form the chaos of other worlds."

DEATH: "You don't have to endure my glacial emptiness."

SATAN: "No, but I have a relentless fever, a lava that burns others and devours me.

"At least you only have to destroy. But I initiate and sustain life, direct the course of empires, and dominate affairs of state and of the heart.

"Do you see that virtuous man over there whose generosity, calm bearing, and modesty are well known? That's because one morning when he awoke with indigestion, Vanity came to greet him in his bed, and he resolved to lead a life of sobriety.

"Another man lusts after a woman, carries her off, violates her, and then abandons her. In that case, I was assisted first by Love and then by Modesty.

"Here you have a self-possessed woman, but her heart is arid and her mind is limited.

"There's a poet, a great man who recites his verse into the morning mists and gets a cold. The poor fool! I gave him genius and he kills himself.

"And then I have to be everywhere. After putting aside the gown of a duchess, sparkling with glittering gems, I take up the modest outfit of a peasant girl who is seduced by a great lord. I make money clink, diamonds glitter, and titles resound. I whisper words of love, glory, and ambition into the ears of women, poets, and ministers. I frequent both Messalina and Ninon de Lenclos; I visit Babylon and Paris at the same time.[3] If someone discovers an island, I am the first to plant the flag. If it's a Godforsaken

---

3. Ninon de Lenclos (1620–1705) was a beautiful Parisian whose salon was famous for its banter and free thinking. Messalina was the scandalous wife of the Emperor Claudius (see *Bouvard et Pécuchet*, 5:178). The linking of Paris with Babylon recurs in *Madame Bovary* (cf. 4:106; 15:25); on one of Emma's assignations with Léon in Rouen, the "city spread out before her eyes like an immense metropolis, a Babylon into which she was entering" (1:284).

rock lost in the ocean, I establish a toehold ahead of the two men who are at each other's throat to dispute ownership. I stretch out on the worn-out couch of the courtesan as on the perfumed litter chair of emperors.

"Hatred, envy, pride, and anger all drip from my lips. I work day and night. While people burn Christians, I luxuriate voluptuously in rose-water baths, drive headlong in chariots, despair in misery, and roar with pride.

"I have finally ended up by believing that I was the world and that everything I saw was taking place in me.

"Sometimes I get tired, go crazy, lose my common sense, and do foolish things to make the last of the demons laugh pitifully.

"No one loves me either, neither my father in heaven nor my subjects in hell nor the earth for whom I am God. There are always disturbances, convulsions, rage, blood, frenzy. My eyes never sleep any more and my soul never rests.

"At least you can rest your head on the coolness of tombs, but I am faced with the warm sparkle of palaces, the dark malediction of hunger, and crimes that stink to high heavens.

"And oh, how I am punished by the God whom I hate! But I feel that my soul is more spacious than his anger, that just one of my sighs could make the entire earth breathe, inhaling it so that it too could feel my burning anger.

"When will your trumpet sound, O Lord?

"It seems to me that a capacious harmony will cover the hills and oceans then, for I will suffer with the whole world. The shouts and sobs will soften my own sounds."

When Satan stopped talking, Death rose on its yellowish legs, with its mouth agape, to address these last words. A shroud fell in large folds behind its back but didn't cover all of its livid, dull flesh. Its bald head was decorated behind with a single lock of red hair;[4] its eyes were intense and voracious, its forehead shone like copper, and its voice was softly weary. You would have thought it an old mother preparing to summon her children. It opened its mouth and gasped a hideous sigh, like a yawning tomb before it closes. It painfully extended its scrawny arms, lowered its head

---

4. Fortune is traditionally represented with a long forelock, while the back of her head is bald; to prevail on her before she escapes, one must seize the forelock. Cf. note 1 to "A Fragrance to Smell," above.

on its bony chest where the skin was so thin that you could see something palpitating inside, like a writhing snake.

Satan was as motionless as a statue of despair, surveying the plain in the direction of the fiery horizon, and bloated with a dreary and terrible anger.

The Son of God also leaned his head over his blue gown. His golden locks hung over his white shoulders, his eyes were filled with silver tears, probably thinking of his paradise, his saints and virgins, the rays of his infinite love extending to all souls, his father supported by golden clouds, and his mother imbued with divinity, poetry, and grace, whence all heavenly things flow.

Filled with a sublime melancholy, bursting with melody and with psalms from the soul, he became quiet.

In that limitless red desert, in that atmosphere which seemed like the fiery breath of hell, the sighs you could hear escaping from these three chests made it sound as if the world were going to burst into tears, seized with an immense, vague desire to die.

But suddenly the vast expanse became peopled with ghosts, while smoky forms began to take shape in the bottomless pits.

You could see hideous skeletons rising from the midst of the earth, frightened at having been wakened.

At first they slowly lifted their heads and raised up by themselves, then they got up and walked. They wandered around in blind astonishment. Some of them had torn strips of velvet trailing behind them; others shored themselves up with their rotting scepters; still others felt their heads to locate their crowns, finding instead only a bare, cold skull.

"Those are the kings," Death said.

One of them began to speak:

THE KING: "I have slept a long time, but I awaken with the sun gilding my tent. My sentries have been relieved three times since dawn, my white horses prance on their silver horseshoes, they neigh impatiently, deeply breathe in the smoke from the campfires and battlefields. For a long while a dozen Ionian slave girls with enameled breasts, ivory arms, and rosy fingers have been tending incense burners to watch over the essences of Asia which three flotillas brought back to me from the banks of the Ganges. The flanks of my war horse were long ago outfitted with a saddle blanket of tiger skin.

"I hear the sound of trumpets reverberating in back of the mountain, as if a God were shouting from hill to hill: 'To war! To war!' Yes, let us rise and get going. Today I want to trample bodies, and I want my mare to be covered in blood up to her breastplate. This evening I want to build myself a stack of skulls as an announcement to future centuries, 'He passed this way!'

"But where are my swarthy Numidians, my dozen Persians to steady my stirrup, my thirty Syrian eunuchs who plied me with perfume when I passed by and who bowed so low you would have thought them a black carpet?

"What! I no longer see any tents, men, or silk pennants. Since the plain is empty, does that mean that it's all over and I am the victor?"

The skeleton wobbled, turned in all directions, and said:

"I have conquered India of the blistering sun, cut through Africa like a storm at sea, and gone from the icy north to the tropical oceans where the water boils like lava. I will be master of the world after one more battle. When I win everything, I will chisel a throne in the Alps, where I will rule the world."

DEATH: "Hurry, hurry!"

THE KING: "Who are you, phantom?"

DEATH: "I am not a phantom; it's you who are the ghost which my breath will wither."

THE KING: "Is it the image of a conqueror who has come to find me on my throne?"

DEATH: "Your throne? I'll use it to make the planking for my tomb."

THE KING: "Get away, you hideous specter! Let me sleep on my bed of roses, let me rock in my hammock made from women's hair, while everything else merely forms a concert to sing the praises for the world's master."

DEATH: "You get away from me, you grub worm or I'll crush you underfoot, you, your crown, and your empires! I am Death."

The skeleton dragged along on his knees, weeping bitter tears while his hollow chest shook with great trembling.

"Help! Mercy! I haven't lived enough. I will spread my empire over the world; I will make the earth an empty plain where I alone will drink from the streams, gather flowers, sleep under the trees. Have pity on me!"

"You are trembling," said Death, taking him by the hair and dragging him on his knees across the sand and rocks. "I'll sit at your table, kiss your concubines, and break your diamond chalices with your scepter."

"Life, life!" he repeated.

"Well, then, die!" Death said, pushing him away with a thunderous laugh.

The livid skin lifted at the corners of his mouth, revealing a sharp, slicing jaw.

A group of skeletons mounted on chariots were rapidly advancing with triumphal cries of joy. Behind them hung their shattered armor and laurel crowns whose dried, yellow leaves were quickly blown away by the dusty wind.

"Well, there goes Eternal Rome in triumph," Satan said. "Its Colosseum and Capitoline are two grains of sand that served as its pedestal, but Death hewed them at the base and the statue fell. Listen! Nero is in the lead, that son so dear to my heart, the greatest poet the world has ever known."

Nero was racing in a chariot pulled by a dozen skeletons of horses, striking their bony rumps with the scepter in his hand. His shroud fluttered and floated in great billows. He turned his fiery eyes from side to side, shouting as he went.

"Faster, faster still! I want your hooves to scorch the sand, I want your nostrils to froth and stream foam down your breastplates. What! The wheels aren't smoking yet! Do you hear the fanfares resounding as far as Ostia, do you hear the people applauding and shouting with joy? Look, they are showering me with handfuls of saffron. And look at the sand drenched in perfume! My chariot is rolling along so smoothly, as your necks stretch out beneath the golden reins! Come on, faster! The dust is blowing, my coat is billowing, and the voice of the wind says, 'Triumph, victory!' Come on, quicker! Faster! People are applauding, stamping, rushing about. It's Jupiter ascending to heaven. Faster! Go even faster!"

And his chariot seemed to be pulled by demons, as a black mist and bloody dust swirled together in the air. In his wild course he smashed tombs, and the wakened corpses bent double under the chariot wheels. He climbed down.

"While six hundred of my slave women perform silent Greek dances, I bathe in rose water in my marble bath. Afterward, all of them will come with me, every one of them. I want them naked, stripped of diamonds, perfume, and veils. I want them to join hands and dance in a circle, so that their alabaster buttocks can be viewed from all sides, softly swaying like reeds in India bending to and fro of an evening in the loving water of a scented sea.

"I will give the hegemony of the seas, the Senate, Olympus, and the Capitoline to the one who loves me most, whose heart I will feel beating under mine, who will be most adept at letting me grasp and play with her hair, who will smile as she wraps her arms around me, who will best put me to sleep with her love song, and then wake me and overwhelm me with passionate rapture and voluptuous biting. I want Rome to remain silent on that night, without any boats disturbing the Tiber's waters, so that I can enjoy the moon reflecting in the swells and the resonance of the women's voices. When daylight hits my curtains, I want them to allow scented breezes to penetrate. Ah, I want to die intoxicated with love and delight! And while I dine on morsels intended for me alone, accompanied by singing, young women naked down to their belts will serve me from golden plates and lean over to look at me at the same time that someone's throat is being slit; as one of God's pleasures, I love to mix the aroma of blood with the scent of delicacies. And those voices of death will lull me to sleep at the table. On that day I will burn Rome. It will light up the sky, and the river will run red with blood."

The skeleton was silent for a long time; then it raised its head, clacked its teeth, and said:

"Later I want to cover the Italian sea with a wooden floor made of aloe wood, so that all of Rome can come there under purple sail to sing. My bed will be made of eagle feathers, and in full view I will hold the most beautiful woman in the Empire, as the entire crowd applauds the pleasures of a God. Then the storm will roar against me to no avail as I restrain its anger underfoot, and the sounds of my kisses will calm the waves."

The skeleton was silent for an even longer time. Death drew closer.

"What now? Vindex is revolting and my legions are abandoning me.[5] My women are fleeing down the corridors. All weep silent tears. Only the voice of thunder is heard. Am I going to die?"

DEATH: "Right now!"

---

5. Caius Julius Vindex was a Roman general of Gallic origin during the reign of Nero, against whose cruelties he encouraged the Gauls to revolt. He committed suicide after his defeat.

NERO: "I'll have to abandon my voluptuous nights and my days replete with feasts, delights, performances, my triumphs, my crowd!"

DEATH: "All! Everything!"

SATAN: "Hurry, master of the world! They are coming, coming to slaughter you! Let the Emperor learn how to die!"

NERO: "To die? I have barely lived! Oh, what great things I would accomplish to make Olympus tremble! I would even fill in the ocean and parade over it in my triumphal chariot. I still want to live, I still need to see the sun, the Tiber, the fields, and the amber sand of the Circus Maximus! Oh, yes! I want to live!"

DEATH: "I will give you a cloth for your tomb, an eternal bed that will be softer and calmer than the cushions of an Emperor."

NERO: "Yes, I am very slow to die."

DEATH: "Well, die!"

And Death bore him off in the folds of its shroud, which floated over the earth.

SATAN: "Look, farther over there. Those are philosophers who are dying for the pleasure of being applauded at the last moment, like that wretched skeleton positioned so as to draw the glances of the crowd. It's a prostitute or a gladiator.

"Farther off, look at the Church, that hideous body under its gold cope.

"The Pope is drawing near, worn out by age, corrupted by debauchery, with his back hunched and his head bent down heavily. He is going to die and is praying to Death on bended knees, throwing his blessings, desires, regrets, tears, and prayers at his feet. He drags his whitened hair in the dust. See how his voice trembles! The old saint is frightened!"

DEATH: "No, no! Remove your papal trappings and your diamond-studded tiara. Get down from your sovereign throne and come to my arms. I have been calling you for a long time. You have been clinging to the bars of faith, but I'll tear you away. Come on!

"Say good-bye to your lofty Church, which my horse's hoof will knock down some day when it happens to pass over it. Farewell forever to your Vatican, to your holy celebrations, your incense, your subjects kneeling in the streets, the voices whispering their lies.

"Everything showed you obeisance and bowed before your face. The pilgrim came from the heart of his country to kiss the leather of your sandals, but I too am a pilgrim come from afar to embrace you with a devouring love."

With an expression more atrocious than its words, Death was happy to hold this living symbol of eternity in its arms.

Christ said, "No one thinks of me, and yet I have suffered for them, and have shed tears of blood! And I died for them, full of faith and the love I poured out like refreshing dew on suffering hearts! All of these have damned themselves by their greatness and their arrogance. Since faith abides with the lowly, it is the beggars I love."

DEATH: "The one who drags himself on his belly up to that other one stretched out in his velvet shroud and tries to bite him on his chest, that's the pauper whose life is made up of suffering, his virtue is made of pride and his heart of envy."

THE PAUPER: "Oh, how long my life is! My arms are tired from working; I have no clothes to cover my body, no pleasures for my soul. I am alone with my misery and envy. I have to resist all temptations, all tortures of the body and soul. What have I done, for goodness' sake!"

SATAN: "You were virtuous? Can you pray to the God who makes you suffer?"

THE PAUPER: "Oh, death, death! I have called on it for a long time, and it will come."

SATAN: "Renounce your virtue and your rags, since the world finds both of them shameful. Walk! You are poor but you can become rich, a millionaire rolling in gold."

DEATH: "Here I am, you wretch! You called me and I came. You will close your eyes tonight, your arms will rest, your trials and suffering will all stop. I am Death, the gate through which waves of life plunge into oblivion."

THE PAUPER: "Death! So soon! Leave me alone! I might be able to become rich and live happily. Leave me one minute of happiness."

DEATH: "But you'll have it for all eternity."

THE PAUPER: "It's not sleep I want but life, a life full of pleasure, riches, and celebrations."

DEATH: "Vanity of vanities!"

THE PAUPER: "Take my future, but just leave me a few days! Leave me my life! What do you want with me? I don't have a crown, a palace, wealth, or fancy clothes. I have only a beggar's bowl, a stick, and some rags.

"Let me warm myself in the sun, walk in the fields, look at the dew on the tip of each blade of grass, at the flower on each tree. Let me hear the bird on the branch, the murmuring stream, the river flowing, the sea smashing, the leaves trembling, the insect chirping in the wheat field. In the morning let me survey the flowers, woods, daisies, and emeralds in the misty valley that seems like a smoking censer on an altar garnished with diamonds. Leave me nature. That's all a pauper has, but he loves it like his mother.

"For mercy's sake! I love life, however bitter it may be. The sun is so beautiful, the moon so white! Each tree speaks to me and each breeze is a sigh which mixes with mine.

"I have cursed eternity, so leave me life! I have abandoned God, so leave me the realm of Satan. I can always get a crust of bread in the street to relieve my hunger and a ray of sunlight to warm my body."

DEATH: "What do you cry for when you say farewell to the world? Is it for the dog you leave behind, for the God who is deaf to your anguished pleas, and for the soul you lose? Go join all the others in the dance. Take the Pope's hand, and mix with the round dance I have formed to amuse its creator."

The dead were dancing. The long line of skeletons was twisting and turning in an immense spiral that rose up to the highest heaven and descended into the deepest abyss. There the king gave his hand to the beggar, the priest to the torturer, the priestess to the courtesan, because everything blended in the sovereign equality of nothingness. All skeletons look alike. Beggars and monarchs, young and old, beauty and ugliness were all represented in the ebb and flux of the joyful crowd entering the long dance.

In the meantime, others kept rising continually out of the earth, like a stream of conjured shadows. Some appeared saddened by being awakened, in the mistaken belief that they were being recalled to earth. They were lamenting like those who grieved for them. The devil's daughters were among the saddest, palest, and most woefully disheveled.

Rising from their tombs, they said, "Alas, we are living again! Must we rise before daylight to prepare ourselves at dawn to welcome lewdness, to enter a portal of shame all day long?

"Alas, our eyes are dazzled by sleepless nights, wine, and the sparkle of brilliant chandeliers. Oh, let us sleep! Alas, we come here every day. In winter, we are cold from leaving our breasts bare so that drunkenness can slink over and plant its heavy kisses. In the summer we have to surround ourselves with fresh flowers, fragrant roses which are fresher than we are and which the fiery sun does not fade so quickly.

"It's true that we fell in love at first, then we had our doubts, then great pleasure, followed by disgust. Corruption gradually set in after that, the way it first strikes the extremities of a corpse before proceeding to the heart, where everything dies.

"We are called madwomen, the joyful ones! Yes, when the grog burns going down but warms us up, when luxury excites us, when the orgy is in full swing, we laugh, too. But when we recover from our stupor, we tremble with cold, for our souls are empty and bare, unwarmed by a single ray of life or love.

"When our lips are fiery, our hearts are frozen.

"Sometimes we have hours of bitterness and gripping misery. We remain seated all day and every night with smiles pasted on our faces and hunger in our bellies. We laugh, although crying would be sheer delight to our souls, which are sealed and more withdrawn each day from the attentions of the mob. Childhood, youth, and old age all visit us to spit scornfully in our faces while paying us. We lose our childhood in order to use our youth.

"Alas, how many times have we reached our exhausted arms toward heaven! How many times have we tried to rise from the mire that was choking us, and how many times were we pulled back in by greed's silver hook, by gem-studded pride parading around in its finery, and by hunger, the mother of crime!

"Ah, let's sleep, let us sleep!

"Curse the Lord who made us lead an existence of hatred and misery, who wanted our lives to be made up of tears hidden by a smile! Curse the one who made our days and nights so long, so full of bitter delight and corrosive loves!"

SATAN: "Son of God, do you hear those hymns wafting up from the earth?"

CHRIST: "Alas, alas!"

DEATH: "No! May peace be with you, daughters of misfortune and infamy. No! You will sleep forever, forever! Only for today your long line is to pass in review, disheveled, sad, and pale!"

THE PROSTITUTES: "Why? Why, since our sleep was so sweet and our dreams so beautiful! In our deep sleep we dreamed of loving someone young, pure, and passionate. We dreamed we were loved in return with a heavenly love as fresh as the dew, as brilliant as the sun, and as vast as God. This dreamed love was a perfume that steeped our souls in tenderness and affection. How we loved oblivion!"

DEATH: "Sleep, sleep for centuries. Oblivion is happiness!"

And then two lone skeletons came into view, walking apart from all the others and looking at one another often while rolling their hollow eyes skyward, toward the ground, and then once again toward each other to say:

"We are in love, the sky was made for our eyes, the woods to veil our kisses, and the night for our sighs.

"How intoxicating! To melt delightfully day and night in voluptuous ecstasy, to pour one's soul into a kiss, all of one's love into a glance! To feel your beloved's heart beating for you next to your chest, to be roused by the shape of that breast, to run your hands through her hair, to feel that warm breath penetrate your heart, and finally to understand that she would give all she has and even more just to have the winds bring her a sigh, a tear, a word, or a kiss."

When those two remnants of life kissed, their yellow skulls rattled with voluptuous delight.

"We will live for centuries," they said, "for entire centuries at the edge of a stream, with our heads bent down to our knees; we will shower our hair with flower petals, and our words will be like pearls flowing endlessly from a stream of love."

DEATH: "You are truly pitiful idiots, with your empty words, your thoughtless heads, and your hearts full of a wine that I drink."

THE LOVERS: "No, no! You will carry off both of us with our lips stuck together and our souls united for our voyage to heaven."

DEATH: "My arms are long and strong enough to smash both of you with a single blow."

THE LOVERS: "Mercy! Have mercy! Let us live, and when our kisses have sated our heart's desire, when our evening sighs have infused the charms of the night, the perfume of the flowers, and all of nature, then you can come. If you knew what love is, you would retrace your steps. Oh, leave us, for goodness' sake! Let us love each other forever."

DEATH: "You are young, beautiful, and happy. Beauty and youth are mine!"

THE DAMNED: "We have used up all pleasure in life, all voluptuousness and crimes, we have emptied the wine cups, the love from our hearts. For us the ground is barren; the sky is no longer pure, nor is the stream clear. Our heart is a mire that rises in our gorge and suffocates us. When will death come to put us to rest forever, far from the banquets, tepid embraces, and everything that has a price?"

DEATH: "I am coming."

THE DAMNED: "We welcome you among us, like a calm and eternal night after a stormy sky."

The dead were dancing in lively unison. The Pope, kings, beggars, love, hate, ugliness, all rotated together before being engulfed in a limitless whirlwind. Some looked for their missing crowns, others for their golden miters—everything they loved was lost, as they were, to nothingness.

The poet was alone, resting on his own feeble body, often stretching his hands to his yellow head, as if he wanted to tear out a bunch of hair along with his thoughts.

"O, poetry, daughter of God, come to me! But why do you need words in order to speak? You breathe in nature, you cry in man, you sing in love.

"Come, for I'll write no more poetry, because of its limitations.

"I'll lose myself in the wandering course of the world.

"I'll wander in the mists of mysterious reveries.

"Like a sailor, I'll give myself over to a vast ocean of despair and I too will request that death be deferred.

"I took the flower of my soul and one by one I plucked every fragrant petal. It only remains for me to shed tears at sunset, seeing the sun grow pale and autumn return to its wintry tomb.

"I don't have a wife who loves me, and I have neither a mother nor a family. The poet is an orphan.

"He is a world unto himself and takes everything to the tomb with him.

"But my soul—where will you go? Come, Death, and rid me of this gripping pain. My soul, I feel you and would like to deny you, but you take up too much space and smother me."

The poet became silent, lowered his head, and seemed to be sleeping.

DEATH: "Time is fleeting, master Satan, day is going to break. Just now I should have smashed an empire, a century, glory, and an ant that lived one day too long.

"I could still make you live for years to come so that you could witness the years rolling past and dying like corpses.

"But look, there is History. Ask what she knows."

HISTORY: "Nothing, Satan, for you occupy me completely. I always feel your two claws leaning on my shoulders and strewing my path with blood."

DEATH: "Is that all?"

HISTORY: "Everything!"

DEATH: "And what do you want?"

HISTORY: "I want you, or rather I want the world that you take away each evening . . . while I remain. When will I be able to join the funereal caravan, I who am its leader and master?"

Death whistled to its horse and leapt on with a bound when it came running up. And then Christ wept, surrounding himself with a white cloud, and went to find his father in whose bosom he was already sleeping.

And Satan laughed more horribly than Death, a laugh of joy and arrogance. He plummeted to earth, covering it with his bat wings, which enveloped him like a black death shroud.

Diary of a Madman

THESE PAGES ARE DEDICATED AND GIVEN TO YOU, DEAR ALFRED[1]

They enclose an entire soul. Is it mine? Is it another's? At first I had wanted to write a personal novel where skepticism would be pushed beyond the final limits of despair. But while writing, the personal impression emerged from the tale little by little; my soul stirred the pen and crushed it.

So I prefer to leave that in the mystery of conjectures; as for you, you will do no such thing.

Only you will perhaps believe, in many places, that the expression is forced and the tableau willingly obscured; remember that it's a madman who has written these pages, and, if the word often seems to surpass the feeling that it expresses, it's because, elsewhere, it has bent under the weight of my heart.

Farewell, think of me and for me.

ONE

Why write these pages? What good are they?—What do I know, myself? It's rather foolish, in my view, to go around asking men the motive of

---

1. Flaubert's senior by five years, Alfred Le Poittevin shared much of the world outlook and literary tastes of young Gustave and was an essential influence on him—the only man, besides his father, whom Flaubert claimed to love. This dedication was written on January 4, 1839; the third version of the *Temptation* (1874) was also dedicated to Le Poittevin. The "group of friends" in sec. 15 may include Alfred, Guy de Maupassant, and Ernest Chevalier.

their actions and of their writing.—Do you yourself know why you have opened the miserable pages that a madman's hand is going to trace?

A madman! That's horrifying. What are *you*, reader? In which category do you align yourself, with fools or with madmen? If you were given a choice, your vanity would still prefer the latter condition. Yes, once again, I truly ask what good is a book that is neither instructive nor amusing, neither chimerical nor philosophical, neither agricultural nor elegiac, a book that gives no formula either for sheep or for lice, which speaks about neither railroads nor the Stock Exchange, about neither the private folds of the heart nor medieval dress, about neither God nor the devil, but speaks of a madman—that is to say, the world, this great idiot which has been turning for so many centuries in space without taking a step and which howls, slobbers, and rips itself apart.

I don't know any more than you what you are going to say, for this is not at all a novel or a drama with a fixed plan, or a single premeditated idea, with landmarks to make thought meander along perfectly straight paths.

Only I'm going to put on paper everything that comes into my mind, my ideas with my memories, my impressions, my dreams, my caprices, everything that passes through thought or the soul; laughter and tears, white and black, sobs initiated by the heart and spread like paste in sonorous phrases, and tears diluted in romantic metaphors. It weighs on me, however, that I'm going to crush the tip of a bunch of quills, that I'm going to waste a bottle of ink, that I'm going to bore the reader and bore myself; I'm so used to laughter and skepticism that from beginning to end you will find a perpetual joke, and the people who like to laugh will at the end be able to laugh at the author and themselves.

They will see how you must believe in the plan of the universe, in the moral duties of man, in virtue, and in philanthropy—an opinion that I want to inscribe on my boots, when I get some, so that everyone will read it and learn it by heart, even the lowest views, the smallest bodies, the most groveling, the closest to the gutter.

They would be wrong to see in this anything but the recreation of a poor madman. A madman!

And you, reader, perhaps you have just gotten married or paid your debts?

TWO

So I'm going to write the story of my life. What a life! But have I lived? I'm young, my face has no wrinkles and my heart no passion. Oh! how calm it was, how sweet and happy it seems, tranquil and pure! Oh! yes, peaceful and silent, like a tomb whose soul would be the cadaver.

I have scarcely lived: I have not known the world; that is to say, I have no mistress, no flatterers, no servants, no carriage; I haven't entered society (as they say), for to me it always seemed false and hollow, covered with tinsel, boring, and stiff.

Now my life is not actions: it is my thought.

What, then, is this thought that leads me—at the age when everyone is smiling and happy, when people marry, when they love; at the age when so many others are drunk with their loves and with all the glory, whereas so many lights shine and festive glasses brim—to find myself alone and naked, cold to all inspiration, to all poetry, feeling myself die and laughing cruelly at my slow agony . . . like that Epicurean who had his veins opened, bathed in a perfumed bath, and died laughing, like a drunk leaving an orgy that has spent him?

Oh, how long this thought was! Like a Hydra, it devoured me beneath all of its faces. A thought of mourning and bitterness, a thought of a weeping clown, a thought of a philosopher who meditates . . .

Oh, yes! How many long and monotonous hours of my life have slipped away in thinking, in doubting! How many winter days, with my head bowed before the whitened ashes in the pale glow of the setting sun; how many summer evenings, moving through the fields at dusk, watching the clouds float away and unfold, the wheat bend in the breeze, hearing the woods rustle, and listening to nature sigh in the night.

Oh! how dreamy my childhood was! What a poor fool I was, without preconceived notions, with positive opinions! I watched the water flow between clumps of trees that incline their tresses of leaves and drop flowers. From my cradle I watched the moon against its blue background, which lit my room and outlined strange forms on the wall. I was ecstatic in the face of a beautiful sun or a spring morning with its white haze, its flowering trees, its daisies in flower.

I also loved to look at the sea—and it's one of my tenderest and most delicious memories—to watch the waves foam against one another, the whitecap break into spray before it spreads out on the beach and cries out as it ebbs over pebbles and shells.

I ran on the rocks, I let sand from the ocean slip away in the wind between my hands, I moistened seaweed, I deeply inhaled this fresh salt air from the ocean, which penetrates your soul with so much energy, with sweeping poetic thoughts; I scanned the immensity, space, infinity, and my soul sank before this boundless horizon.

Oh, but that's not the boundless horizon, the immense pit! Oh, no, a wider and deeper abyss opened before me. That gulf has no tempest; if there were a storm, it would be full—and it's empty!

I was happy and smiling, loving life and my mother. Poor mother!

I still remember my small joys in seeing the horses run on the path, seeing the steam of their breath, the sweat overrun their harnesses; I loved the monotonous and cadenced gait that makes the tops of surrounding buildings appear to wobble; and when you stopped, everything was silent in the fields. The steam escaped their nostrils, the shaken carriage stabilized on its springs, the wind blew against the windows; and that was all . . .

Oh, how my eyes also opened wide at the crowd dressed in festive clothes, joyful, tumultuous, shouting, a stormy sea of men, angrier than the storm and more foolish than its fury.

I loved the carts, horses, armies, military uniforms, drum rolls, noise, powder, and the cannons rolling over the paving stones of towns.

As a child, I loved what I saw; as an adolescent, what I felt; as a man, I no longer love anything.

And yet how many things do I hold in my soul, how many intimate powers, how many oceans of anger and love jostle and break in this heart that is so weak, so feeble, so fallen, so tired, so spent!

People tell me to renew my life, to mix with the crowd! . . . But how can a broken branch bear fruit? How can the leaf revive, once it is torn away by the wind and dragged through the dust? And why so much bitterness for one so young? What do *I* know? It was perhaps my destiny to live this way, tired even before bearing the load, breathless before having run . . .

I have read, I have traveled with heated enthusiasm, I have written. Oh, how happy I was then, how high my delirious thought flew, to those regions unknown to men, where there are neither worlds nor planets nor suns! I had a more immense infinity than God's, if that's possible, where poetry was cradled and spread its wings in an atmosphere of love and ecstasy; and then it was necessary to descend again from those sublime regions toward words. And how can speech shape that harmony which rises in the poet's heart or gigantic thoughts which crumple sentences the way a strong and beefy hand tears the glove that covers it?

There again was deception; for we touch the earth, this frozen earth where all fire dies, where all energy wanes! Through what ranks do we descend from the infinite to the concrete? Through what calibration does poetry lower itself without breaking? How can you shrink this giant who embraces the infinite?

Then I had moments of sadness and despair; I felt my strength break me, and this weakness shamed me because speech is only a distant and weakened echo of thought. I cursed my most cherished dreams and my silent hours spent on the limits of creation. I felt something empty and insatiable devouring me.

Weary of poetry, I threw myself into the field of meditation.

I was first of all taken by this imposing study which proposes man as its goal and which intends to explain him, which goes so far as to dissect hypotheses, discuss the most abstract propositions, and geometrically weigh the emptiest words.

Man is a grain of sand thrown into the infinite by an unknown hand, a poor insect with weak legs that tries to poise itself on all the branches at the edge of the abyss, clasps virtue, love, egoism, ambition, and makes virtues from all that in order to sustain itself, clings to God, and always weakens, releases its grip and falls . . .

Man wishes to understand what doesn't exist and to make nothingness into a science; he is a soul made in God's image, whose sublime genius stops at a blade of grass and can't surmount the problem posed by a speck of dust!

Weariness overcame me; I came to doubt everything. As a young man I was old; my heart was wrinkled, and in seeing old men still alive, full of enthusiasm and belief, I laughed bitterly to myself, so young, so jaded by life, by love, by glory, by God, by all that is and by all that can be.

Still, I had a natural horror prior to embracing this faith in nothingness; at the edge of the abyss I closed my eyes—I fell.

I was content; I no longer needed to fall. I was as cold and calm as a tombstone. I believed I had found happiness in doubt; how senseless I was! There you roll along in an incommensurable void. That void is immense and makes your hair stand on end when you approach the edge.

From doubting God I came to doubt virtue, a fragile idea that each century has erected as well as it could on the still shakier structure of laws.

Later I will tell you all the phases of this dreary and meditative life, spent beside the fireplace, crossing my arms while yawning from eternal boredom, alone for a whole day, from time to time shifting my gaze to the snow on the neighboring roofs, to the setting sun with its sprays of pale light, to the floor of my room, to the yellow, toothless skull grimacing endlessly on my mantle, a symbol of life and, like it, cold and mocking.

Later perhaps you will read all the anguish of this heart that is so beaten, so devoured by bitterness. You will learn the adventures of this life that is so calm and banal, so filled with feelings, so empty of deeds.

And then you will tell me if everything is not mockery and a foul joke, if everything that is preached in school, all that's spun out in books, everything that's been felt, spoken, if everything that exists . . .

I have so much bitterness in saying it that I can't finish. Very well, then, all that is just a piteous illusion, so much smoke, nothing.

THREE

I was in school from the age of ten, and there I soon contracted a deep aversion toward men. This society of children is as cruel for its victims as the other small society, that of men.

The same injustice of the crowd, the same tyranny of prejudice and power, the same egoism, no matter what people say about the disinterestedness and fidelity of youth. Youth, the age of madness and dreams, of poetry and stupidity, synonyms in the mouth of people who judge the world *sanely*! I was assailed for all my tastes: in class, for my ideas; at play, for being a loner. From then on, I was a madman.

Thus, I lived alone and bored, pestered by my teachers and abused by my acquaintances. My character was critical and independent, and my biting and cynical irony no more spared the caprice of a single one than the despotism of them all.

I still see myself seated on the benches in class, absorbed in my dreams of the future, thinking of things the imagination of a child can dream sublimely, while the teacher made fun of my Latin verse, and my mates looked at me derisively. Imbeciles! *They* laugh at *me*! They who are so weak, so ordinary, so narrow-minded; I, whose mind was drowning at the edge of creation, who was lost in all the worlds of poetry, who felt myself bigger than all of them put together, who received infinite pleasure and who felt celestial ecstasy in the presence of all the intimate revelations of my soul!

Feeling as big as the world itself, a single one of my thoughts, as fiery as lightning, could have reduced it to dust, poor fool!

I imagined myself at twenty, young and surrounded by glory; I dreamed of distant travel to southern countries; I saw the Orient and its immense dunes, its palaces trampled by camels with their small brass bells; I saw mares leap toward the horizon reddened by the sun; I saw blue waves, a pure sky, silver sand; I smelled the fragrance of those warm seas of Mediterranean climes; and then beside me, under a tent in the shade of a broad-leafed aloe, some brown-skinned woman with fiery glance who wrapped me in her arms and spoke the tongue of the houris.

The sun sank into the sand, the she-camels and the mares slept, insects buzzed at their teats, and the evening wind passed near us.

And when night came, when that silver moon cast its pale glance on the desert, when the stars shone against the blue sky, then in the silence of that warm and balmy night I dreamed of infinite joys, of heavenly voluptuousness.

And it was still glory, with its applause and fanfares to the heavens, its laurels, golden dust thrown to the winds; it was brilliant theater with adorned women, lit diamonds, a heavy atmosphere, panting breasts; then a religious contemplation, words that devour like a firestorm, tears, laughter, gasps, the headiness of glory, cries of enthusiasm, the stamping crowd—vanity, noise, nothingness.

As a child I dreamed of love; as a young man, of glory; as a man, of the tomb—this final love of those who no longer have any.

I also saw the ancient period of centuries that are no more, and races recumbent beneath the grass; I saw the band of pilgrims and warriors marching toward Calvary, stopping in the desert, dying of thirst, imploring this God whom they sought and, tired of its blasphemies, marching always toward the boundless horizon; then, spent and breathless, arriving finally at journey's end, despairing and old, to kiss a few barren rocks, the whole world's homage.

I saw knights in armor riding on horses covered with iron; I saw jousting in tournaments, and the wooden bridge lowering to receive the liege lord as he returns with his sword bloodied and captives on the crupper of his horses; again at night in the somber cathedral, the whole nave decorated with a garland of people who seemed to rise toward the vault, chanting from the galleries, the stained glass resplendent with light; and on Christmas night, all of the old town with its pointed roofs covered with snow, illuminated and singing.

But it was Rome that I loved, Imperial Rome, that beautiful queen wallowing in orgies, dirtying her noble robes with wine and debauchery, prouder of her vices than of her virtues. Nero! Nero with his diamond chariots flying through the arena, his thousand carriages, his tigerish loves and gigantic feasts!

Far from the Classics lessons, Rome, I headed toward your immense pleasures, your bloody illuminations, your burning pastimes.

And lulled by these vague reveries, these dreams of the future, rapt and borne away by this adventurous thought like a runaway mare that crosses torrents, climbs mountains, and flies in space, I remained for hours with my head between my hands, staring at the floor of my study or at a spider spinning its web on our teacher's chair. And when I awoke and my eyes popped open, they laughed at me, the laziest of all who would never have a positive idea, who would show no acumen for any profession, who would be useless in this world where each one has to take his piece of the cake, and who finally would never be good for anything—at best, would play the fool, exhibit animals, hack out books.

(Although in excellent health, I was perpetually irritated by the existence I led and by contact with others. My cast of mind had created a nervous irritation that made me vehement and carried me away like a bull maddened by insect bites. I had dreams, frightful nightmares.)

Oh, the sad and sullen era! I still see myself wandering alone in the long, whitened corridors of my school, watching owls and crows fly from the top of the chapel; I see myself abed in the dreary dormitory, lit by the lamp whose oil was coagulating. At night I listened at length to the wind blowing lugubriously in the empty apartments and whispering through the keyholes, making the panes shudder in their casing; I heard the steps of the watchman walking slowly with his lantern, and when he came near me I pretended to be asleep, and I actually did fall asleep, half in dream and half in tears.

FOUR

They were frightening visions, enough to drive you mad with terror.

I was in bed at my father's house; all the furniture was preserved, yet everything that surrounded me was tinged with black. It was a winter night, and the snow cast a white clarity in my room. Suddenly, the snow melted and the grass and trees took on a burnt red cast, as if a fire had illuminated my windows; I heard footfalls, someone mounting the stairs, warm air; a fetid mist reached me. My door opened by itself and someone entered. They were numerous, maybe seven or eight. I didn't have time to count them. They were small and large, covered with black, scraggly beards, unarmed but all bearing a steel blade in their teeth, and as they circled my bed their teeth began to clack, and it was horrible.

They drew back my white curtains, and each finger left a trace of blood. They looked at me with large and steady lidless eyes. I looked at them too; I couldn't move at all and wanted to cry out.

It seemed to me as if the house rose from its foundation, as if a lever had lifted it.

They looked at me for a long time, then withdrew, and I saw that each was missing the skin from half of his slowly bleeding face. They picked up all my clothes, and all were bloody. They began to eat, and the bread they broke dripped drops of blood; and they began to laugh with the rattle of the dying.

Then when they were gone, everything they had touched—paneling, staircase, floor—was covered in blood.

I had the taste of bitterness in my heart. It seemed to me as if I had eaten flesh, and I heard a prolonged cry that was sharp and hoarse. The windows and doors opened slowly, and the wind slammed and groaned, like a bizarre song whose every whisper tore at my chest with a thin dagger.

Elsewhere, there was a green field studded with flowers alongside a river—I was with my mother, who was walking by the bank; she fell. I saw the water swirl in widening circles that suddenly disappeared. The water resumed its course, and then I heard only the noise of the water passing between the rushes and bending the reeds.

Suddenly my mother called: "Help! . . . help! Oh, my poor child, help me!"

I lay flat on the grass to watch and saw nothing; the cries continued.

An invincible force bound me to the ground, and I heard the cries: "I'm drowning! I'm drowning! Help me!"

The water flowed, flowed clear, and the voice heard at the bottom of the river undid me with despair and rage . . .

FIVE

That's how I was, an uncaring dreamer with an independent and caustic temper, shaping a destiny and dreaming of all the poetry of an existence full of love, and also living on whatever memories a sixteen-year-old can have.

I had an antipathy toward school. It would be interesting to study this deep disgust of noble and elevated souls, caused by the irritating contact with men. I have never liked an ordered life governed by regular hours, punctuated by the clock, where each thought stops when the hour is struck, where everything is predetermined for centuries and generations. This regularity may suit the multitude, but for the poor child who feeds on poetry, dreams, and chimeras, who thinks of love and all the nonsense, it awakens him endlessly to this sublime dream, denies him a moment's rest, stifles him by bringing him back into our atmosphere of materialism and common sense, which horrifies and disgusts him.

I continued apart, with a book of verse, a novel, poetry, something that makes a young man's heart quiver, virginal to sensations but wanting them.

I remember with what joy I devoured the pages of Byron and *Werther*; with what transport I read *Hamlet*, *Romeo*, and the most ardent works of our time, all the works that melt a soul in delight and burn it with enthusiasm.

I fed myself then on that bitter poetry from the north, from Byron, which resounds so like the waves of the sea. On the first reading I often retained whole fragments, and I repeated them to myself like a song whose melody charms you and follows you forever.

How many times have I repeated the beginning of *Giaour*: "Not a breath of air"; or else in *Childe Harold*: "Whilome in Albion's isle" and "I have loved thee, Ocean!"[2] The platitude of French translation disappeared in the face of thoughts alone, as if they had their own wordless style.

This temper of burning passion linked to the deepest irony must have strongly affected an ardent and virginal nature. All these echoes unknown by the sumptuous dignity of classical literature held a scent of newness for me, an attraction that ceaselessly drew me toward this gigantic poetry

---

2. It is peculiar that these verses from *Childe Harold* come from the very beginning and end of the poem (vv. 10 and 1648), as if to imply a reading of the entire poem; but in a letter of Oct. 11, 1838, Flaubert says, "I am learning English. I am working at it and I am assured that in two or three months I will be able to read Shakespeare and, at the end of a year, Byron, the hardest things there are to read in English" (12:347). Max Milner, *Le Diable dans la littérature française* (Paris: Corti, 1960), 1:219–20, shows numerous parallel passages between "Diary of a Madman" and Byron's *Cain*.

which gives you vertigo and makes you fall into the bottomless abyss of infinity.

I had thus falsified my taste and my heart, as the professors say, and among so many beings with such ignoble tendencies, my independence of mind had made me value the most depraved of all; I was dropped to the lowest rank by superiority itself. They barely conceded me my imagination: that is to say, according to them, an exaltation of mind approximating madness.

SIX

If they slandered my mind and my principles, they didn't attack my heart, since I was good then, and the misery of others would wring tears from me.

While still a child, I remember that I loved to empty my pockets to the poor. What smiles greeted me as I passed, and what pleasure I had in doing good for them!

It's a pleasure that has been unknown to me for a long time, because my heart and tears are now dry. But curse those who corrupted and hardened me, as good and pure as I was! Curse the barrenness of civilization which withers my heart and saps every bit of poetry that sees the light of day! This old, corrupt society which has seduced and used up everything, this greedy old Jew will die of emaciation and exhaustion on a pile of manure that he calls his treasures, without a poet to sing his death, without a priest to close his eyes, without gold for his mausoleum, for he will have used up everything for his vices.

SEVEN

So when will this society end, bastardized by all its debauchery, debauches of mind, body, and soul?

Then, there will no doubt be joy on earth over the death of this hypocritical liar called civilization; the royal mantle, scepter, diamonds, crumbling palace, the collapsing city will all be abandoned so that men will enter the woods to die.

The earth will be parched by the fires that burned it and full of the dust of combat; the breath of desolation that passed over men will pass over it, and the earth will give only bitter fruit and thorny roses, and races will die in the cradle, like plants beaten by winds that wither before flowering.

For everything must end and the earth must be consumed by trampling; for the immensity must be weary of this speck of dust that makes so much noise and bothers the majesty of nothingness. Gold will exhaust itself from circulating and corrupting, this steaming blood must dissolve, the palace crumble under the weight of the riches it holds, the orgy end, and then one must waken.

Then there will be immense laughter of despair when men see this emptiness, when life gives way to death, to ever hungry death. And everything will crack and dissolve into nothing, and virtuous man will curse his virtue, and vice will clap its hands.

A few men still wandering on the barren earth will hail one another; they will approach and withdraw in horror, frightened by themselves, and they will die. What will man be then, he who is already more ferocious than wild animals and more vile than reptiles? Good bye for ever, dazzling carriages, fanfares, and fame; good-bye to the world, to these palaces, mausoleums, pleasures of crime, joys of corruption! The stone will suddenly fall, crushed by itself, and grass will overgrow it. And the palaces, temples, pyramids, columns, kingly mausoleums, pauper's shroud, dog's carcass will all be reduced to the same level under the earth's green mantle.

Then the unfettered sea will peacefully beat the shore and make its waves flow over the still-smoking cinders of cities; trees will grow and blossom without a hand to break them; the rivers will flow in the fields dotted with flowers, nature will be free from human constraint, and this race will be extinguished, because it was cursed from the time of its childhood.

What a sad and strange era we live in. Toward what ocean does this torrent of iniquities flow? Where are we heading in such a deep night? Those who wish to feel this sick world will quickly draw back, frightened by the corruption that stirs in its entrails.

When Rome felt its agony, it at least had a hope; it glimpsed the radiant Cross behind the shroud, shining on eternity. This religion has lasted two thousand years and now it is running out, no longer sufficient, derided; churches are falling, cemeteries are heaped and overrun with the dead.

And what religion will *we* have? To be our age and still walk the desert like the Hebrews who fled Egypt.

Where will the promised land be?

We have tried everything and we renounce everything without hope; and then a strange greed has gripped our soul and humanity. There is an immense unease gnawing at us. There is a void among our number, and we feel the chill of the sepulcher.

Humanity has been caught up in mechanization, and seeing the gold that flows from it, humanity has cried out: "This is God!" And humanity devours that God! There is wine to drink before dying, because everything is finished, adieu! Adieu! Each person rushes where his instinct pushes him. The world swarms like insects on a corpse. Poets pass without having the time to sculpt their thoughts; as soon as they throw them onto the pages, the pages blow away. Everything shines and echoes in this masquerade, this ephemeral kingdom with its cardboard scepters. Gold and wine flow, cold debauchery lifts its gown and stirs . . . horror! Horror!

And then there is over all a veil of which each one seizes a part and hides himself as well as he can.

Derision! Horror! Horror!

EIGHT

And there are days when I have an immense weariness. A somber ennui envelops me like a shroud wherever I go; these folds weigh me down and disturb me. Life weighs on me like remorse. So young and so tired of everything, when there are those who are old and still filled with enthusiasm! And *I* am so fallen, so disenchanted! What can I do? Watch the moon cast its trembling clarity on my paneling like broad foliage, and the sun gilding the neighboring roofs? Is that living? No, it is death, minus the repose of the sepulcher.

And I have small joys for myself alone, childhood reminiscences which still warm me in my isolation, like rays of the setting sun that stream through prison bars: a trifle, the least circumstance, a rainy day, a mighty sun, a flower, an old piece of furniture, remind me of a series of memories that pass in confusion, erased like shadows. Children's games on the grass in the midst of a field of daisies, behind a flowering hedge, along a vineyard with its gilded bunches of grapes, on the brown-green moss, under broad leaves, fresh shade; like a memory of the first age, calm and smiling memories pass me by like faded roses.

Youth, its impetuous raptures, its instincts confused by the world and the heart, its throbs of love, its tears, its cries! A young man's loves, ironies of adulthood. Oh! you, return often with your somber and dull colors, driven away by one another as passing shadows run across walls on winter nights. And I often fall into ecstasy before the memory of some good day from long ago, a mad and joyous day with outbursts and laughter that still echo in my ears, still palpitate with gaiety and make me smile bitterly. It might be a race on a bounding and lathered horse, some dreamy walk under a broad promenade covered in shadow, watching the water flow over the stones; or contemplation of a beautiful and resplendent sun, with its fiery shafts and red halos. And I still hear the horse's gallop, its nostrils steaming; I hear the water slip by, the leaf tremble, the wind rush over an ocean of wheat.

Others are gloomy and cold like rainy days; bitter and cruel memories return; hours on Calvary spent crying hopelessly, and then necessarily laughing in order to chase the tears hiding my eyes, the sobs covering my voice.

For many days, many years, I sat thinking about nothing or about everything, swallowed by the infinite which I wanted to embrace and which devoured me.

I heard the rain fall in the gutter, the bells resound tearfully; I saw the sun set slowly and the night come, the drowsy night that calms you, and then day reappeared, always the same, with its troubles, its same number of hours to live, and I joyfully saw it die.

I dreamed of the sea, distant travels, love, triumph, all aborted things in my existence—a corpse before having lived.

Alas! So all of that wasn't made for me? I don't envy others, for each person complains of the burden that fate imposes; some cast it off before death, others carry it to the end. And will *I* bear it?

I had hardly seen the light of day, when an immense disgust entered my soul; I tasted all the fruit, it seemed bitter to me, I pushed it away, and here I am dying of hunger. To die so young, without hope, in the tomb, without being sure of sleeping there, without knowing if its peace is inviolate! To throw yourself in the arms of nothingness and to doubt whether it will receive you!

Yes, I am dying, for is it living to see your past emptied into the ocean like water, the present like a cage, the future like a shroud?

NINE

Some insignificant things that have deeply affected me I will always retain like the brand of a hot iron, although they may be banal and foolish.

I will always remember a kind of chateau not far from my town, which we used to see often.[3] One of those old women of the last century lived in it. Everything there retained a pastoral memory; I still see the dusty portraits, the sky-blue clothes of the men, and the roses and carnations molded on the paneling with shepherdesses and their flocks. Everything had an old and somber aspect; the furniture, almost all embroidered with silk, was spacious and soft; the house was old; former moats (at that time planted with apple trees) surrounded it, and the stones that dislodged from time to time from the former battlements rolled to the bottom.

The park planted with great trees was nearby, with somber walks, stone benches covered with moss and half broken, amid the boughs and brambles. A goat passed by, and when the iron gate opened it ran off into the foliage.

On nice days shafts of sunlight pierced the branches and gilded the moss here and there.

It was sad; the wind blew hard in those broad brick fireplaces and frightened me when, especially in the evening, owls cried out in vast lofts.

We often prolonged our visits rather late in the evening, gathered around the old chatelaine in a great hall that was covered with white flagstone, before a vast marble fireplace. I still see her gold snuffbox full of the best Spanish tobacco, her shaggy white pug, and her dainty foot covered by a pretty, high-heeled slipper decorated with a black rose.

How long ago all that was! The chatelaine is dead, as well as her pugs; her snuffbox is in the notary's pocket; the castle is used as a factory, and the poor slipper has been thrown into the river.

AFTER A THREE-WEEK PAUSE

I am so weary that I have a profound disgust at the thought of continuing, having reread what precedes.

Can the work of a bored man please the public?

Still, I am going to try to amuse both of them some more.

Here the Diary really begins . . .

TEN

Here my memories are at once the tenderest and most painful, and I approach them with an entirely religious emotion. They are alive to my

---

3. A thinly veiled allusion to the Château de Mauny, near Rouen.

memory and still almost warm to my soul, so much has this passion made it bleed. It is a broad scar on my heart which will last forever, but at the moment of relating this page of my life, my heart beats as if I were going to rake through cherished ruins.

These ruins are already old; walking through life, the horizon opened beyond, and how many things have happened since then! For the days seem long, back to back from morning until evening. But forgetfulness reduces the framework that contains the past, so much that it seems brief.

For me, everything still seems alive. I hear and see the trembling of leaves, I see the slightest fold of her dress; I hear the timbre of her voice, as if an angel were singing near me—a sweet and pure voice that elates you and makes you die from love, a voice that embodies beauty and seduces, as if there were a charm to its words.

It would be impossible to tell you the precise year; but then I was very young—fifteen, I believe; that year we went to the seaside resort of X, a town in Picardy,[4] utterly charming with its chockablock houses, black, gray, red, white, turned in all directions, without alignment or symmetry, like a pile of shells and pebbles that waves have driven onto the shore.

A few years ago no one went there, despite its having more than a mile of splendid beach and its charming location; but recently it has come back in vogue. The last time I was there I saw a quantity of yellow gloves and livery; there was even talk of building a theater.

Everything was simple and wild then; there was hardly anyone except artists and people from the area. The shore was deserted, and at low tide you saw silver-gray sand shimmering in the sun, still damp from the waves. To the left there were rocks where on somnolent days the sea lazily slapped the breakwater, blackened by seaweed; then in the distance you could see the blue ocean under a burning sun, bellowing indistinctly like a weeping giant.

And when you returned to the town there was the warmest and most picturesque scene. Black nets that had deteriorated from the water were spread out on the doors; everywhere half-naked children were walking on

---

4. This is probably a reference to Trouville. See B. F. Bart, *Flaubert* (Syracuse, N.Y.: Syracuse University Press, 1967), pp.23–28, 66–68; cf.11:671.

gray pebbles, which were the only pavement of the area; there were sailors in red and blue clothes; and all of that was simple and robust in its grace. Everything was imbued with a vigorous and energetic character.

I often went alone to walk on the strand. One day chance led me toward the place where people went swimming. It was a place not far from the last houses of the town, frequented mainly for this use; men and women swam together; they undressed on the bank or in their houses, and they left their robes on the sand.

That day a charming fur-lined red coat with black stripes had been left on the beach. The tide rose, the beach was dappled with foam; a stronger wave had soaked the fringe of this coat. I picked it up to place it farther away; the material was soft and light; it was a woman's coat.

Evidently I had been seen. Since everyone was having lunch that day in the same room at the inn where we were staying, I heard someone say to me:

"Thank you for your gallantry, sir."

I turned around; it was a young woman seated with her husband at the next table.

"What?" I asked her in my preoccupation.

"For having picked up my coat; wasn't that you?"

"Yes, madam," I replied with embarrassment.

She looked at me.

I lowered my eyes and blushed. What a gaze! How beautiful that woman was! I still see those fiery eyes beneath black eyebrows staring at me like the sun.

She was tall, dark-complexioned, with magnificent black hair curling down to her shoulders; she had a Greek nose, burning eyes, high eyebrows that were admirably arched, her skin glistened like burnished gold; she was slender and delicate, and you saw bluish serpentine veins on that crimson-brown throat. Add to that a subtle down shading her upper lip and giving her face a masculine and vibrant expression that made blond beauties pale by comparison. One might have taken exception to her plumpness, or rather her artistic casualness. So, women generally found her badly mannered. She spoke slowly; in a modulated, musical, and sweet voice . . .

She had a delicate dress of white muslin which suggested the soft contours of her arm.

When she rose to leave she put on a white hooded coat with a single pink bow; she tied it with a fine, plump hand, one of those hands you dream about for a long time and you would love to sear with kisses.

Each morning I went to see her swim; I contemplated her from afar under the water; I envied the soft, calm wave that slapped her side and covered that panting breast with sea foam; I saw the contour of her limbs under the soaked clothes covering her, I saw her heart beat, her breast swell; mechanically I contemplated her foot stepping on the sand, and my gaze remained fixed on her footprints, and I would almost cry to see the wave slowly efface them.

And then when she returned and passed near me, when I heard the water drip from her clothes and the rustle of her pace, my heart beat violently; I lowered my eyes, the blood rose to my head, I choked. I felt this half-nude woman's body pass near me with its ocean scent. Deaf and blind, I would have guessed her presence, for there was something intimate and soft in me which was drowning in ecstasy and in graceful thoughts when she passed that way.

I believe I still see the spot where I was transfixed on the beach; I see the waves approaching from all sides, breaking, spreading out; I see the beach dappled with foam, I hear the indistinct sound of the bathers' voices speaking with one another, I hear the sound of her steps, I hear her breath when she passed near me.

I was bemused, as if Venus had descended from her pedestal and begun to walk. That's when I felt my heart for the first time, I felt something mystical and strange like a new sense. I was bathed in infinite, tender feelings; I was lulled with hazy, vague images; I was at once taller and prouder.

I was in love.

To love, to feel young and full of love, to feel nature and its harmonies palpitate in you, to need this revery, this emotional experience and to feel happy from it! Oh, man's first heartbeats, his first palpitations of love! How sweet and strange they are! And later, how silly and ridiculously foolish they seem! How bizarre! There is some torment and joy at the same time in this insomnia. Is it still from vanity? Ah, could love just be pride? Is it necessary to deny what the most impious people respect? Should the heart be laughed at? Alas, alas! The wave erased Maria's steps.

At first it was a unique state of surprise and admiration, in some sense an entirely mystical sensation, quite apart from any notion of sensual pleasure. It was only later that I felt this frenetic and somber ardor of body and soul devouring each other.

I felt the astonishment of a heart that feels itself beat for the first time. I was like the first man when he realized all his faculties.

It would be quite impossible to say what I dreamed about; I felt new and alien to myself; a voice had come into my heart. A trifle, a fold of a dress, a smile, her foot, the most insignificant word, all impressed me like supernatural things, and I dreamed of them all day long. I followed her footstep at the corner of a long wall, and the rustle of her clothes made me palpitate happily. When I heard her steps, on the nights when she strolled or approached me . . . no, I couldn't tell you the amount of sweet sensation, sentimental giddiness, beatitude, and madness there is in love.

And now, so scornful of everything, so bitterly persuaded about the grotesqueness of existence, I still feel love, that love as I dreamed it in school without having it and felt later, which made me cry and about which I laughed so much, how I still believe that it would be both the greatest sublimity and the most comical of stupidities!

Two beings thrust on earth by chance or something, and who meet and fall in love because one is a woman and the other a man! There they are, panting for one another, strolling together at night and getting soaked by the morning dew, looking at the moonlight and finding it diaphanous, admiring the stars, and saying with every possible intonation: "I love you, you love me, he loves me, we love one another," and repeating that with sighs and kisses; and then they go back in, both driven by an unparalleled ardor, for these two souls have their vital faculties violently heated, and there they are, soon grotesquely coupled with groans and sighs, both anxious to produce one more imbecile on earth, some unfortunate who will imitate them! Consider them, more stupid at that moment than dogs and flies, fainting and carefully hiding their private pleasure from the eyes of others—perhaps thinking that happiness is a crime and voluptuousness is shame.

I think I will be excused for not speaking of Platonic love, this exalted love, like that for a statue or a cathedral, which drives off any idea of jealousy or possession and which should be found equally among mankind but which I have rarely had the chance to observe. A sublime love if it existed, but only a dream, like everything beautiful in this world.

I stop here, for the mockery of an old man shouldn't tarnish the virginal feelings of a young man; I would be as indignant as you, dear reader, if someone had used such cruel language with me. I believed that a woman was an angel . . . oh, how right was Molière to compare her to a soup!⁵

ELEVEN

Maria had a child, a girl. She was loved, embraced, bored with caresses and kisses. How I would have received a single one of those kisses, cast profusely like pearls, like those placed on the head of that child in her sweater!

Maria nursed her herself, and one day I saw her uncover her bosom and offer her breast.

It was a plump, round bosom with brown skin and blue veins that appeared under that lustrous skin. At the time I had never seen a naked woman. Oh, the special ecstasy in which the sight of that breast plunged me! How I devoured it with my eyes, how I would like to have just touched that chest! It seemed to me that if I had placed my lips there, my teeth would have passionately bitten it; and my heart melted in pleasure, thinking of the voluptuousness that this kiss would give.

Oh, how I recalled that palpitating bosom for a long time, that graceful neck and that head with its black hair in curlpapers. She tilted her head toward that nursing infant, which she slowly rocked on her knees while humming an Italian tune!

TWELVE

We soon got to know one another better: I say *we*, because I personally would not have ventured to address a word to her, given the state in which the sight of her had plunged me.

Her husband was something between an artist and a traveling salesman; he wore a mustache, smoked intrepidly, and was a lively, nice friendly sort; he was no stranger to the dinner table, and once I saw him walk several miles to look for a melon in the nearest town; he had come in his post-chaise with his dog, his wife, his child, and twenty-five bottles of Rhine wine.

---

5. The allusion is to Molière's *L'Ecole des femmes*, 2.3. In a letter to Ernest Chevalier written around the time he was completing this story, Flaubert exclaimed, "Oh, how right Molière was to compare woman to a soup, dear Ernest. Many men wish to eat some of it, get burned by it, and then are replaced by others" (12:347; cf.13:350, 475). And in the first *Sentimental Education*, Emilie is compared to a "strange ragout."

At seaside resorts, in the country, or traveling, people converse more easily and wish to meet others. A trifle suffices for conversation: rain and good weather enter in much more than elsewhere; people protest the inconvenience of lodgings with their detestable food. The latter characteristic is especially appropriate: "How dirty the linen is! Too much pepper, too spicy! Oh, horrible, my dear."

If you go walking together, the game is to see who can fall into greater ecstasy over the beauty of the countryside. How beautiful! How blue the sea is! Add to that a few poetic and turgid words, two or three philosophic reflections larded with sighs and rather heavy breathing; if you can sketch, take out your morocco-bound album or, better yet, push your cap down over your eyes, cross your arms, and sleep in order to give the impression of thinking.

There are women whom I could spot as intellectual sorts a half-mile away, merely by the way they looked at the surf.

You'll have to complain about mankind, eat little, and wax ecstatic over a rock, admire a field, and die of love for the sea. Ah, then you will be found delightful; people will say, "What a charming young man! What an attractive smock he has on! How nice his boots are! What elegance! What sensitivity!" It's a need to talk, this instinct of going with the pack where the boldest walk ahead; it formed societies at the beginning, and in our day it creates social gatherings.

It was no doubt a similar reason that led us to converse for the first time. It was a warm afternoon and the sun's rays pierced the room, despite the slatted transom. Maria, her husband, and I had remained artfully stretched out in our chairs, smoking while drinking toddies.

Maria was smoking or, at least, if a remnant of feminine foolishness kept her from it, she enjoyed the smell of tobacco (monstrosity!); she even gave me some cigarettes! We talked about literature, an inexhaustible subject with women; I entered in and spoke passionately at length; Maria and I shared the same views on art. I have never heard anyone feel it with more naturalness and less pretense; she used simple, expressive words that stood out sharply; and she especially used them with such matter-of-fact grace, such disregard and nonchalance, that you would have said she sang them.

One evening her husband suggested a boat ride. Since the weather was so grand, we accepted.

THIRTEEN

How can words capture those things for which there is no speech, those impressions of the heart, those deep mysteries that the soul itself doesn't know? How will I tell you everything I felt, everything I thought, all those things I enjoyed that evening?

It was a beautiful summer night; around nine o'clock we boarded the launch, the oars were readied, and we left. The weather was calm, the moonlight reflected on the smooth surface of the water, and the boat's wake made the image shimmer on the swells. The tide rose and we felt the first waves slowly rock the launch. There was silence until Maria began to speak. I don't know what she said; I let myself be charmed by the sound of her words as by the rocking of the sea. She was near me; I felt the slope of her shoulder and the touch of her dress; she raised her eyes toward the pure, starry heavens, resplendent with diamonds and reflected in the blue waves. She was an angel, seeing her that way with her head raised and with that heavenly expression.

I was intoxicated with love; I listened to the twin oars rise in even cadence, the swells slapping the sides of the boat;[6] I let myself be moved by all that, and I listened to Maria's voice, soft and vibrant.

Can I ever tell you about all the melodies of her voice, all the charm of her smile, all the beauty of her gaze? Will I ever tell you how it was something to make you die for love, when the night was redolent of the ocean's scent, with its transparent waves, its sand made silvery by the moon, that calm and beautiful sea, that resplendent sky, and then that woman near me! All the joy in the world, all its voluptuousness, the sweetest and most intoxicating that there can be! It had all the charm of a dream with all the pleasure of reality. I let myself be swept away by all these emotions; I plunged ahead with an insatiable joy, became intoxicated with delight over that voluptuous calm, that woman's gaze, that voice. I plumbed my heart and found infinite pleasure. How happy I was in the twilight of hap-

---

6. This section is shot through with literary reminiscences and with images that Flaubert continued to use in his later writing. Cf. the boat ride of Djalioh ("Whatever You Want," sec.7) and Lamartine's "Le Lac": "Que le bruit des rameurs qui frappaient en cadence" (Just the sound of the oars keeping time all at once). Sec.13 closes by recalling a famous tableau of Chateaubriand's *René*: "I felt a stream of boiling lava flowing in my soul," which Flaubert recasts in *November* as "filled with boiling lava which flowed in my soul." The closural image of the dripping candle (symbolizing a schoolboy's sexual fantasies) is used comparably in *November*; for the halo reflections, see my Introduction.

piness, which recedes with the night, a happiness that slips away like a crested wave over the strand . . .

We returned. We disembarked, and I accompanied Maria to her house; in my timidity, I didn't say a word; I followed her, dreamed about her, about her footfalls, and when she went inside I stared at the wall of her house bathed in the moonlight; I saw its light shining through the windowpanes, and I looked at it from time to time as I returned by the beach; then, when that light disappeared, I told myself: "She's asleep." And then, suddenly, a thought struck me, a thought of jealous passion: "Oh, no, she's not sleeping"—and I was plagued by all the tortures of the damned.

I thought about her husband, that vulgar and jovial man, and the most hideous thoughts appeared to my mind's eye. I was like those prisoners who are starved to death, surrounded by the most enticing viands.

I was alone on the beach. Alone. She wasn't thinking of me. Looking at the solitary expanse and at that other, even more terrible solitude, I began to cry like a child, for a few steps away . . . there she was, behind those walls that I devoured with my gaze; she was there in her naked beauty, with all the sensuous pleasure of the night, all the charms of love, all the chasteness of marriage. That man had only to open his arms, and effortlessly she came to him without delay, and they exchanged lovers' kisses. All the joy and delight were *his;* my love was ground underfoot; she was entirely his, her head, bosom, breasts, her body and soul, her smiles, her soft arms around him, her words of love; he had it all and I had nothing.

I began to laugh, for jealousy filled me with obscene and grotesque thoughts. Then I defiled both of them; I heaped the most bitter ridicule on them, and I tried to laugh out of pity at those images which had made me weep with envy.

The tide was beginning to fall, and now and again you could see large depressions full of water made silvery by the moonlight, sections of wet sand covered by seaweed, here and there a few rocks at water level which appeared black and white as they rose above; splayed nets that were ripped by the sea, roaring as it receded.

I was stifling from the warm weather. I went back to my room in the inn and tried to sleep. I still heard the swells against the sides of the skiff, I heard the oar fall, I heard Maria's voice when she spoke. I had fire in my veins as those scenes passed before my mind's eye, both the evening walk and the one at night on the strand; I saw Maria in bed and I stopped there, for the rest made me tremble. My soul boiled with lava, I was beset by all of that, and lying on my back I watched my candle burn, its halo reflected on the ceiling; in a senseless stupor I saw the melted wax flow around the brass candlestick and the blackened wick lengthen in the flame.

When day finally began to break, I fell asleep.

FOURTEEN

We had to leave; we parted without being able to say goodbye. She left the spa the same day we did. It was Sunday. She left in the morning, we left in the evening.

She left, and I didn't see her again. Goodbye forever! She went like the dust that blew away behind us on the road. How I've thought about it since then! How many hours, bemused by the memory of her expression or the intonation of her words!

Snug in the carriage, my heart was projected farther ahead on our route, and my mind returned to a past that would return no more; I thought of the sea, its waves, its beach, everything I had just seen, all I had felt; spoken words, gestures, actions, the least thing, all of that came alive. Chaos, an immense murmur, madness raged in my heart.

Everything had slipped by like a dream. Goodbye forever to all those beautiful flowers of youth which fade so quickly and to which you return later with bitterness and pleasure at the same time! Finally I saw the houses of my town, I returned home, and everything seemed deserted and lugubrious in its hollow emptiness; my routine continued: eating, drinking, sleeping.

Winter came and I returned to school.

FIFTEEN

If I told you that I loved other women, I would be lying like a rat. Still, I believed it; I tried to bind my heart to other passions, but it slid over them like ice.

As a child, you read so many things about love, you find that word so melodious, you dream about it so much, you hope so much to have the feeling that makes your pulse race when you read novels and dramas, that each time you see a woman you say to yourself, "Isn't this love?" You try to love in order to become a man.

I was no more exempt from this childish weakness than anyone else; I sighed like an elegiac poet, and after much effort I was astonished to find that several weeks would elapse without my thinking of the one whom I had chosen to dream about. Maria's image made all that childish vanity disappear.

But I should go back in time. I pledged to tell everything; the fragment you are going to read was partially written last December before I had the notion of writing the *Diary of a Madman*. Since it was supposed to be separate, I had put it in the following framework.

Here is the way it was:

Among all the dreams of the past, old memories and youthful recollections, I have kept a small number to entertain myself during hours of boredom. All the characters return at the mention of a name, with their dress and speech, to play their role as they did in real life, and I see them stir before me, like a God who would entertain himself by watching the world he created. Especially the first love, which was never excessively passionate, eroded since then by other desires, but which still remains at the bottom of my heart like an ancient Roman road that has been crossed over by the unworthy modern railroad car;[7] it's the tale of those first heart palpitations, of the onset of vague and ill-defined voluptuousness, of all those hazy things that occur in a child's soul at the sight of a woman's breasts, her eyes, at the lilt of her voice; this is the medley of feeling and revery that I had to lay out like a cadaver before a group of friends who would come by of a cold December day to warm themselves and calmly chat before the fireplace, while smoking their pipes and allaying the bitterness by sprinkling in some sort of liquid.

After everyone had arrived and each had taken a seat, after pipes were stuffed and glasses filled, after we had gathered around the fire, and one had taken up the firetongs while another worked the bellows and yet another stirred the ashes with his cane, each busied with some chore, I began:

"Dear friends," I said, "you are supposed to watch for something, some improper turn of phrase that may have slipped into this account."

(All nodded their heads and signaled me to begin.)

"I remember that it was a Thursday around November two years ago—

---

7. Cf. the same image in sec.22 below and in *November*, 11:661.

I was in the second year of the 'second cycle' at school. The first time I saw her she was having lunch at her mother's.[8] I entered at a fast pace like a schoolboy who all week long had anticipated Thursday's meal. She turned away; I barely greeted her, for I was so foolish then and so callow that I couldn't see a woman—at least among those who didn't call me 'a child' as the married ladies did, or 'a friend' as the granddaughters did—without blushing or rather without remaining still and silent.

"But thank goodness, since then I have made up in vanity and effrontery what I lost in innocence and candor.

"The two girls were sisters, friends of my sister, poor English girls who had been taken from their boardinghouse and removed to the fresh air of the countryside, to be taken for rides, to play in the garden and be entertained away from the watchful eye of a governess who would impose a sober decorum on children's play. The older one was fifteen, the second was barely twelve. The younger one was small and thin, with larger and more beautiful, sparkling eyes than those of her older sister, who, however, had such an elegant head, a fresh pink complexion, short white teeth beneath pink lips, and all that so well framed by a coronet of beautiful chestnut hair that you could not help preferring her. She was small and maybe a bit stout, her most visible flaw; but what I found most charming about her was a childlike grace without pretense, a scent of youth that added fragrance to her surroundings. There was so much innocence and frankness that even the most impious could not stem their admiration.

"I still seem to see her through the window of my room, playing in the garden with her friends; I still see their rustling silk dresses quickly ripple against their heels, and the high step of their running on the sandy paths of the garden, their stopping breathlessly as they held one another's waist, strolling with measured steps as they discussed (as I imagine) parties, dances, fun, and love—poor girls!

"Soon we established a close bond; after four months I kissed her like my sister, and we addressed each other in the familiar way. I enjoyed talking with her so much! Her foreign accent contained a delicate elegance that made her voice as fresh as her cheeks.

"Moreover, English manners have a natural openness and a disregard

---

8. On the identity of the young English girl, see Lucien Andrieu, "Un Amour inconnu de Flaubert: Caroline Anne Heuland, l'anglaise probable de *Mémoires d'un fou*," *Les Amis de Flaubert* 23 (Dec.1963):27–29. She would have been fourteen years old at the time.

of all our conventions, which you could mistake for refined flirtation but which is simply a ceaselessly fleeting attraction like a will-o'-the-wisp. We often took family walks, and I remember that one winter day we went to see an old lady who lived on a hill overlooking the town.

"To get to her house we had to cross apple orchards where the grass was tall and wet; fog shrouded the town, and from the top of our hill we saw the tight jumble of snow-covered rooftops; and then came the silence of the countryside and in the distance the faraway sound of a cow's or horse's hoofs treading in a furrow.

"While passing a white fence, she caught her shawl on the thorns of a hedge; I went to free it, and she thanked me with such casual ease that I dreamed of it all day long.

"Then they began to run, and their coats, billowing behind them in the wind, undulated like crested waves. They paused breathlessly. I still recall their panting as it resounded in my ears, escaping in jets of steam through their white teeth. The poor girl! She was so good and kissed me with such naiveté!

"Easter vacation arrived, and we spent it in the countryside. I remember a day . . . it was hot, her sash had come loose from her shapeless dress. We took a walk together, trampling the dewy grass and the April flowers. She had a book in her hand; I think it was poetry; she dropped it. We went on.

"She ran, I kissed her neck, my lips remained fixed on that satiny skin, drenched by a scented perspiration.

"I don't know what we spoke about . . . the first things that came to mind."

"You're going to become idiotic," interrupted one of the others.

"That's right, my friend, the heart is stupid.

"In the afternoon my heart was filled with a tender and vague joy; I dreamed delightfully, thinking about the curlpapers that framed her alert eyes and about her already mature bosom, which I always kissed as far down as her formal attire would allow. I hiked in the fields, I haunted the woods, I sat in a ditch, and I thought of her.

"I lay face down, I pulled out shoots of grass, spring daisies, and when I raised my head the dull blue and white sky patches formed an azure dome reaching to the horizon beyond the green fields; I happened to have paper and pencil, and I wrote some verses . . ."

(Everyone began to laugh.)

"... the only ones I have ever written; maybe thirty verses; I hardly spent a half-hour, since I had always had an admirable facility for improvising stupidities of all kinds; but for the most part these verses were as empty as lover's assurances, as enfeebled as goodness itself. I remember there was:

> worn out by the seesaw's play.
> ... At the close of day

"I wracked my brains to depict a warmth that I had never read in books; then, for no particular reason, I switched to a brooding melancholy worthy of Mark Antony, although in reality my soul was imbued with ingenuousness and a tender feeling mixed with nonsense, sweet memories steeped in sentiment, and out of the blue I said:

> My pain is galling, my sadness profound,
> And it shrouds me so, like a corpse in the ground.

"The verse wasn't even poetry, but I had the sense to burn it, a madness that must torture most poets.

"I returned home and found her playing on the circular lawn. The girls' bedroom was next to mine; I heard them laughing and talking for a long time, whereas I . . . I went to sleep as soon as they did, despite all my effort to stay awake as long as possible. For at fifteen you were probably the way I was, and you once thought you were in love with that burning and frenzied love you read about in books, whereas you had only lightly scratched the surface of your heart with that iron claw of passion, and with all the strength of your imagination you blew on this small fire that was scarcely burning.

"A man's life has so many loves! At four years of age, the love for horses, the sun, flowers, shiny weapons, a soldier's uniform; at ten, the love of the young girl who plays with you; at thirteen, the love of a full-breasted mature woman, because I recall that what adolescents adore to distraction is a woman's bosom, white and lusterless, as Marot says [in his "Epigramme du beau tétin"]:

> Bosom, white as an egg is its mound
> Bosom, satiny white, freshly found.[9]

---

9. "Tétin refect, plus blanc qu'un oeuf, / Tétin de satin blanc tout neuf." See *Clément Marot: Les Epigrammes*, ed. C. A. Mayer (London: Athlone Press, 1970), p.156.

"I nearly took sick the first time I saw a woman's two breasts completely naked. Finally, at fourteen or fifteen the love of a hometown girl, a little more than a sister, less than a lover; then at sixteen the love for another woman until you're twenty-five; then you perhaps love the woman you will marry.

"Five years later, you love the dancer who makes her gauze dress billow over her plump thighs; next, at thirty-six, there is the desire for a deputyship, speculations, honors; at fifty, the desire to have dinner with the minister or the mayor; at sixty, the love for the prostitute who hails you through her window, as you return an impotent glance drawn from your sad past. Isn't all of that true? . . . for I have undergone all those loves; but yet not all, since I have not lived out my span of years, and each year in the estates of a man is marked by a new passion, for women, gambling, horses, well-turned boots, canes, spectacles, carriages, status. How much madness there is in a man! Oh, a harlequin's patchwork outfit has without question no more nuances than the human mind in its folly! And both end up wearing themselves to a frazzle and occasionally provoke laughter: the public chasing after money, the philosopher after knowledge."

"Get back to your story!" pleaded one of my listeners, who had remained impassive until then, smoking his pipe throughout, except to comment on my digressions—which were also dissolving in smoke—by spitting.

I hardly knew what to say next because there was a gap in the story, one less verse to my elegy. A few interludes occurred that way. In May, the girls' mother came to France to bring their brother. He was a nice boy, as blond as they, brimming with a child's pranks and English pride.

Their mother was a pale, thin, nonchalant woman. She was dressed in black. It's true that her bearing, speech, and clothes seemed casual to the point of slackness, yet they resembled the classic Italian idler. But the entire effect was bathed in good taste, with a patina of aristocratic luster. She stayed in France for a month.

Then she returned, and we carried on as though we were all family, always taking walks, vacations, and respites together. We were brothers and sisters.

There was so much refinement, spontaneity, intimacy, and freedom in our daily encounters that for her it may all have degenerated into love, and I had plenty of reason to think so.

Here I can assign myself the role of the moral man because I had no passion. I really wish I had.

She would often approach me and put her arm around me. She looked at me and conversed. What a charming girl! She borrowed books—plays, which she rarely returned. She showed me her room and it flustered me a little. Could I presume so much boldness from a woman, or was this complete naiveté on her part? One day she fell asleep on a couch in a very suggestive position. I was seated silently beside her.

It was clearly a critical moment, which I let slip by without exploiting it.

At other times she embraced me in tears. I couldn't believe that she really loved me. Ernest was persuaded of it and pointed it out to me as though I were an imbecile—whereas I was actually both timid and nonchalant.

There was something childlike and sweet about it, which was in no way spoiled by the idea of possession but which by that very fact lacked energy. But it was too immature to be Platonic.

A year later their mother came to live in France; a month after that she returned to England. Her daughters had been taken out of the boarding-house and resided with their mother on a second floor in an empty street.

During her trip I often saw them at the windows. One day as I was passing, Caroline called to me and I went up to see her. She was alone, she threw herself into my arms and kissed me passionately; that was the last time; she has recently married.

Her drawing tutor had visited her frequently. They planned to get married, but the knot was tied and untied a hundred times. Her mother returned from England with her husband, who had never been mentioned. Caroline was married in January. One day I came across her with her husband. She hardly greeted me.

Her mother has changed both attitude and apartments. Now she receives apprentice tailors and students in her flat; she goes to masked balls and takes her daughter along.

We haven't seen them for eighteen months.

That's the way the affair ended. It promised an emotion that might come with time, but it unraveled by itself.

Is there any need to add that it had been no more comparable to love than twilight is to broad daylight, and that Maria's glance withered the memory of this pale child?

A mere flicker: no more than cold ashes.

SIXTEEN

This page is short; I wish it were shorter. This is what happened.

Vanity pushed me into love; no, into voluptuousness; not even that . . . into the flesh.

I was teased about my chastity, and I blushed over it. It made me ashamed and weighed on me as though it were a corruption.

A woman offered herself; I took her. And I left her embrace, filled with disgust and bitterness. But then I could play the part of a Lovelace in the tavern, cursing as much as anyone else standing around the grog punch. *Then* I was a man; as if out of duty I set about committing vice and bragged about it. I was fifteen and spoke about women and mistresses.

I began to hate that woman. She would come to me, and I would leave her. She lavished smiles on me that disgusted me like hideous grimaces.

I had regrets, as if the love for Maria were a religion that I had profaned.

SEVENTEEN

I wondered if those were the pleasures I had dreamed about, those fiery raptures I had imagined in the virginity of this tender and childlike heart.

Is that all? Must it follow that after this cold pleasure-taking there should be no other that would be more sublime and expansive, something rapturously divine? Oh, no! Everything was finished. I had come to desecrate the love that your glance had kindled; I had wasted it whimsically on the first woman who came along, without love or desire, urged on by a child's vanity, by calculating pride, so that I wouldn't be made to blush any more by licentiousness and would retain my composure at an orgy. Poor Maria!

I was spent. A deep disgust seized my soul, and I pitied those momentary joys and those convulsions of the flesh. I really must have been miserable, *I* who was so proud of this lofty love and sublime passion, who considered that my heart was wider and more beautiful than other men's. *I* carry on like *them*? Oh, no. Probably not a single one of them did it for the same reasons. Almost all of them were impelled by their senses. Like dogs, they instinctively obeyed nature. But it was far more degrading to calculate the whole thing, to get excited by corruption, to throw yourself into a woman's arms, to work her flesh, to wallow in the gutter, just to pick yourself up and display your stains.

And then I was ashamed of them, as of a cowardly profanation. I would like to have hidden my vaunted shame from my own eyes.

I addressed my mind to the period when the flesh held no shame for me, and when desire directed me toward the vague and voluptuous forms that my heart fabricated. *Never* can you explain all the mysteries of a virginal heart, everything it feels, all the worlds it spawns. How delightful its dreams are! How evanescent and tender its thoughts are, how bitter and cruel its disappointment! . . . To have loved, dreamed of the sky, seen the soul's purity, all the body's languor! To have dreamed of the sky and fallen into the mud!

Who can now give me back all I have lost, my virginity and dreams, my illusions, all those faded things—poor flowers killed by the frost before opening up.

EIGHTEEN

I owe any moments of enthusiasm to art, and yet what vanity art is! Trying to depict a man in a block of stone or his soul with words, feelings through sounds, and nature on a lacquered canvas . . .

I don't know what magical power it is that music has; I spent entire weeks dreaming of the cadenced rhythm of a tune or the sweep of a majestic chorus. Certain sounds penetrate my soul, and there are voices that melt me with ecstasy. I loved the booming orchestra with its waves of harmony, its sonorous vibrations, and that immense energy which seemed muscled yet died on the end of a violin bow. My heart followed the melody as it spread its wings toward infinity, rising in pure, slow spirals like a fragrance drifting heavenward. I loved the sounds, diamonds sparkling under the light, all those gloved ladies' hands casting bouquets. I watched the lively ballet, the swirling pink outfits; I heard the steps landing in cadence; I watched knees softly set off by the light as the dancers bent at the waist.

At other times, rapt by works of genius and enchained by its powers, at the murmur of these voices, at the seductive onset, at this purring enticement, I lived the fate of those strong men who manipulate the crowd like lead, who make it weep, groan, and stir with enthusiasm. Those persons who invite people into their hearts must have plenty of room, whereas everything has aborted in my nature. Convinced of my impotence and sterility, I was seized by a jealous hatred; and I told myself that was nothing, that chance alone, had dictated these words. I threw mud on the exalted things to which I aspired.

I had mocked God, and I could certainly laugh at men.

Art! Art! What a beautiful thing this vanity was!

If there is an adored belief amid the world's nothingness, if there is something sacred, pure, sublime, something that approaches this immoderate desire for the infinite and the vagueness we call the soul, it is art. And what a reduction! A stone, a word, a sound, the arrangement of everything we call the sublime. I would like something that doesn't require expression or form, something pure like a scent, strong like a rock, inaccessible as a song, whether it be all or none of those things. Everything seems limited to me, shrunk, stillborn in nature.

With his genius and art, man is only a miserable aper of something loftier.

I sought beauty in the infinite and found only doubt.

NINETEEN

Oh, infinity! The infinite is an immense gulf rising from the abyss to the highest regions of the unknown, an old idea in which all of us spin, gripped by vertigo, an abyss that each person has in his heart, an incomparable and bottomless abyss! For many days and nights, we will vainly wonder in our agony, "What are these words: God, Eternity, Infinity?" We spin around in that circularity, blown away by the wind of death like the leaf tossed by the storm. You might say that the infinite takes pleasure in deluding us in this immensity of doubt.

But we always tell ourselves, "After many centuries and thousands of years, when everything is used up, there will have to be a limit." Alas, eternity rises before us and we know fear—fear of that thing which ought to last for such a long time, whereas we pass so quickly.

Such a long time!

I wish I could live after the demise of humanity and live without nature or mankind—what grandeur that emptiness would offer! There will likely be shadows; the earth will be reduced to a little burned ash and perhaps a few drops from the sea. My heavens! Nothing more than . . . the void that spreads out through the expanse like a shroud.

Eternity! Eternity! Will it last forever? Endlessly?

But what remains will be the slightest piece of the world's clutter, the last breath of a dying creation. The burden of existence will tire the void itself. Everything will call for annihilation. Alas, this idea of something endless makes us blanch. And we who are now living will be taken into that immensity which rolls over us. What will we be then? Nothing, not even a breath.

For a long time I have pondered the dead in their coffins . . . the long centuries that flow thus beneath the noise and bustle on the world's surface, whereas *they* repose calmly between their rotten boards in a gloomy silence occasionally interrupted by a falling hair or a worm slipping over a bit of flesh. What a silent sleep they have under the ground, under the flowered field!

Still, they must be cold under a winter snow.

Oh, if they awoke and returned to life, and if they could see all the tears that garnished their shabby winding-sheets, all the stifled sobs, all the grimacing expressions, they would be horrified by this life which they left tearfully, and they would quickly return to the comforting truth of emptiness.

Of course, it's possible to live and even die without wondering a single time what life and death are. But for the one who watches the leaves trembling at a gust of wind, rivers snaking through the plain, the agony of life's vortex, the good and evil in a life span, the sea wave's roll and the sky deploying its lights; and the one who wonders, "Why those leaves, why does water flow, why is life itself such a terrible torrent which the boundless ocean of death will engulf? Why do men move and work like ants? Why are there storms? Why is the sky so pure and the earth so squalid?—those questions lead into shadows with no promise of return.

Doubt sets in later. It is something more felt than spoken. Here man is like a stranded traveler, looking everywhere for tracks that will lead to an oasis but finding only desert. Doubt is life. Doubt pervades action, speech, nature, death!

Doubt is death of the soul. It is leprosy that claims spent humanity, a sickness brought on by knowledge and leading to madness. Madness is doubt that comes from reason. Perhaps it is reason itself.

You be the judge.

TWENTY

There are poets whose souls are replete with fragrances and flowers and who see the world as a great dawn; others see only gloom, bitterness, and anger. There are painters who see everything as tinted with blue; others, as entirely yellow or black. Each of us has a prism through which he sees the world; happy is the man who discerns bright and gay colors. Some men see the world only in terms of titles, women, banks, a name, destiny; follies! I know some who see only railroads, markets, cattle; some discover a sublime plan, others an obscene farce.

No doubt some would ask you what is meant by *obscenity*? Like other probing queries, that's a troubling question to resolve.

I would sooner use a mathematical definition of an excellent pair of boots or a beautiful woman, two important subjects. People who see our globe as a large or small clump of mud are unusual, or else are difficult to take.

You have just spoken with one of these sordid characters, people who don't label themselves as philanthropists and who, without fearing that people will go so far as to see them as supporters of Don Carlos of Spain,[10] don't vote for the demolition of cathedrals. But you soon stop in your tracks or admit you are beaten, for those are unprincipled people who consider virtue a word and the world a clown show. They go on to see everything from a disgraceful perspective; they smile at the most beautiful things, and when you talk to them about philanthropy, they shrug their shoulders and tell you that philanthropy consists of pledging money to the poor. What's the point of having your name appear in pledge lists in the newspapers?

What a strange diversity of opinions, systems, beliefs, and follies! Certain people you speak to are gripped by fear when they ask, "What! You deny that? You doubt it? Do you think you can revoke the grand design of the universe and mankind's obligations?" And if by mischance your gaze happens to betray your soul's dream, they stop in their tracks as if their logic had triumphed, like children frightened by a ghost who close their eyes tightly for fear of seeing.

Open them, you weak and prideful man, you pitiful ant who struggles with a speck of dust; you declare yourself free and great, and you hold yourself in high regard—you, so wretched during your lifetime—derisively celebrating the transience of your rotting flesh. And then you imagine that such a splendid life, caught between a touch of pride which you call greatness and that base self-interest which is the essence of your society, will be crowned by a kind of immortality. Immortality for *you*, who are more lascivious than a monkey, meaner than a tiger, and creepier than a snake? Come on! Show me a paradise for the monkey, tiger, and snake, for luxury,

---

10. *Carliste:* an adherent of Don Carlos de Bourbon-Molina, the pretender to the Spanish crown. The concept of "Liberalism" arose in Spain among certain opponents of the Napoleonic occupation. The term then passed to France, where it denoted opposition to royalism after the restoration of the Bourbons in 1814.

cruelty, lowliness, an Eden for egoism, an eternity for this speck, immortality for this nothing. You boast about your freedom to choose good and evil? Probably to make everyone denounce you right away, because what good could you possibly accomplish? Isn't your every reflex aroused by pride or calculated out of self-interest?

You free? From birth you have been subjected to all possible paternal weakness; from birth you have been seeded with all your vices and even your stupidity, everything that would equip you to judge the world, yourself, and your surroundings according to that measure, that term of comparison which you harbor within. You were born narrow-minded, with fixed ideas about good and evil which conventional wisdom will continue to reinforce. You will be taught to love your father and care for him in old age; you will do both without any reminding, won't you? That's instinctive behavior, like the need to eat; whereas, beyond the mountains that mark the border your brother is being taught to kill his father when old age sets in, and he will do so, since he won't need to be taught that this killing is nature's way. When you are growing up, people will tell you that you must avoid a physical love for your sister or mother, whereas like all men you are the product of a primal incest, for the first man, woman, and their offspring were brothers and sisters; whereas the sun sets on other peoples who consider incest a special virtue and fratricide a duty. Are you already freed from the principles that govern your behavior? Are you in charge of your own education? Did *you* want to be born with a happy or sad disposition, consumptive or healthy, kind or cruel, moral or vicious?

But first of all, why were you born? Did you want to be? Were you consulted? You came about by fate, because once upon a time your mother took advantage of your father's return from an orgy, fueled by wine and debauched conversation; she brought to bear all her womanly wiles, driven by the instincts of her flesh and by the animality with which nature endowed her soul; she must have aroused that man who had wasted himself through carousing since his early teens. No matter how big you are, you were first of all something as dirty as saliva and as rank as urine; then you metamorphosed like a worm, and finally you reached the world, practically lifeless and bawling, screaming with your eyes shut, as though out of hatred for this sun that you have invoked so many times. You are fed, you begin to grow like a leaf; you're lucky if the wind doesn't soon blow you away, since you are beset by countless forces—by air, fire, sunlight, day and night, heat and cold, by all of surrounding existence. All of that dominates and excites you; you love plants and flowers, and you are sad when they wither; you love your dog, and you cry when he dies; a spider approaches you, and you recoil in fright; sometimes you tremble when you see your shadow, and when your thought itself delves into the mysteries of nonexistence, and you are frightened by doubt itself.

You say you are free, and each day you are impelled by a thousand things. You see a woman and love her, you die for love; are you free to calm your coursing blood, to calm your beating mind, to squeeze your heart, to calm the flames that devour you? Are you freed from thinking? A thousand chains restrain you, a thousand spurs goad you, a thousand obstacles hold you. You are shocked by a trait of a man you meet for the first time, and all your life you have an aversion to him, whereas you might have liked him if his nose had been a bit smaller. If your stomach is upset, you brutalize the person you would have greeted with good will. And from this state of affairs other circumstances flow inevitably, and from the new situation comes a new string of events. Are you the maker of your physical and moral constitution? No, you would be fully in charge only if you had fashioned it with yourself as the model. Do you think you're free because you have a soul? First off, you are the one who made this discovery that you are not able to define. A small voice tells you so; initially, your lie is that a small voice speaks of your weakness, and you feel an enormous emptiness, which you try to fill with all the things you throw in. Even if you believed it, are you sure of it? Who told you so? After being battered by two opposing feelings, and after hesitation and doubt, you incline toward a feeling that you believe stemmed from you; but dominance of thought requires having no inclination. Can you willfully do good when your heart harbors the taste for evil and when the flaws in your character have been fostered by your training? And if you are virtuous, can you still commit the crime that horrifies you? Are you free to do good or evil? If the instinct for good guides your every move, you can't do evil.

This is the struggle between two inclinations; if you do evil, it's because you are motivated more by vice than by virtue and the more intense fever won. When two men fight, it is certain that the weaker, the one less fit and able, will be beaten by the stronger, fitter and more adept. However long the battle lasts, there will always be a victor. The same is true of one's character: even if your sense of right wins out, will the triumph be just? Is the good that you value goodness in an absolute, unchanging, and eternal sense?

Everything human is surrounded by shadows. Mankind aspires to stability in the face of emptiness. He himself is adrift in this vague immensity where he would like to find safe harbor. He clings to everything but retains nothing. He has seized country, freedom, belief, God, virtue, and it has all slipped through his fingers. He is like a madman who drops a crystal glass and laughs at all the shattered fragments.

But man has an immortal soul made in God's image. He has spilled blood for two ideas to which he clings without understanding: a soul and God.

This soul is an essence around which our physical being revolves like the earth around the sun. Since this noble soul is a spiritual principle without any earthly limitations, it is in no way lowly and abject. But doesn't thought drive our bodies? Isn't that why we lift our arm when we want to kill? Isn't it thought that quickens our flesh? Could mind be the principle of evil and the body its agent?

Let's see how pliant this conscience of the soul is, how soft and workable it is, how easily the soul bends to the weight of the body or else leans on it, how venal, low, creeping, flattering, lying, or deceiving it is! It betrays the body, hand, head, and tongue. It insatiably seeks blood and gold, always desiring everything ad infinitum. It haunts our very core like a thirst and vague fervor, a devouring fire, an axis that spins us.

How mighty is Man! Not in body so much as in mind, which you claim has made you nature's king. You are great, strong, the master.

In fact, every day you overturn the world, dig canals, build palaces, dam rivers, harvest the earth, mold and consume its bounty. You admire the way the keel of your ship splits the waves. You believe that you are better than the wild animal you eat, freer than the leaf that is carried off by the winds, loftier than the eagle who soars over battlements, stronger than the ocean you ply, than the earth from which you extract your bread and diamonds. But alas! the earth you stir returns and revives by its own powers. Rivers burst the canals and flood fields and towns, castle stones dislodge and fall from their own weight, ants scurry over crowns and thrones. No more than a drop of rain or the beating of a bird's wings, the passage of your flotillas will leave the ocean's surface unmarked. You too traverse this ocean of the ages without leaving any more of a trace than your ship leaves on the sea. Your self-styled greatness comes from your unrelenting work, but this labor is proof of your weakness. You were condemned to learn a useless lesson at the cost of your sweat; you were a slave before birth and unhappy before your first breath. You contemplate the stars with prideful satisfaction because you named them, calculated their distance, as if to measure infinity and enclose space within the limits of your mind. But you're wrong! Who is to say that beyond this world of light there are not other comparably infinite expanses? Maybe your calculations are limited to a few feet, after which a different scale of phenomena begins. Do you even grasp the meaning of the words you use . . . "expanse," "space"? They surpass you and all of your globe.

You are great and yet you die more sorrowfully than a dog or an ant; and then you rot. When the worms have eaten you, when your body has dissolved into the damp of the tomb and your dust vanishes, let me ask you: where are you and where is the human soul that spurred your actions toward hatred, envy, all the passions? Where is that soul which sold you out and led you to so much sordidness? Is there any ground hallowed enough to receive you? You respect and honor yourself like a God, you invented the idea of the dignity of man, an idea which, by the sight of you, would occur to nothing in nature. Needing honors, you honor yourself; and though your body was so disgusting in your lifetime, you want honors bestowed on it when it no longer exists. You want respects paid to your carcass, which in its corrupt rot is yet reborn purer than when you were living. Is that your greatness? The greatness of ashes, the majesty of emptiness!

TWENTY-ONE

I returned two years later to you-know-where. She was no longer there. Her husband was alone, having accompanied another woman, and had left two days before I arrived. I returned to the beach, but how empty it was! From there I could see the gray wall of Maria's house. What isolation!

I reentered the room I mentioned earlier. It was full but none of the familiar faces were there, and the tables were taken by people I had never seen. Maria's was occupied by an old woman who leaned on the very spot where *her* elbow had rested so many times.

I stayed like that for two weeks; a couple of days brought rainy weather, so I remained in my room, where I heard the rain fall on the slate roof, the far-away sound of the ocean, and from time to time a few shouts from the sailors on the dock; I recalled all the things that the sight of the same places inspired.

Once again I saw the same ocean with its same waves, still immense, sad, and bellowing as it struck the rocks; this same village with its clumps of mud, its shellfish trade, its multistoried houses. But everything I had loved, everything that surrounded Maria, this beautiful sun filtering through the transom to gild her skin, the air surrounding her, people who passed near her, all of that would return no more. Oh, how I would like just one of those incomparable days! To go back without changing a thing!

What, will none of that return? I feel my heart's emptiness, for the humanity that surrounds me makes me into a desert where I am dying. I remember those long, warm summer afternoons when I spoke to her, when she knew of my love; her detached gaze penetrated me like a ray of love that reached the bottom of my heart. How could she have actually seen that I loved her, for I didn't love her then, and I lied about everything I told you; it was *now* that I loved her, desired her, and recreated her in my imagination, while she conversed, returned my gaze, and accompanied me through field and woods. I thought of her when I slept on the grass and watched the blades bend with the wind and the surf beating on the sand. In my heart I reshaped all the scenes of her actions and speech. Those memories were passionate.

I frequented the places where I had seen her walk. It was impossible to rediscover the timbre of her voice and use it to charm myself. How many times did I pass in front of her house and look at her window!

I spent two weeks rapt in my dream of love for her. I recall heart-rending things. One day I returned toward dusk, walking through cattle-covered pasturage; and as I picked up my pace I heard only the sound of my stride through the grass. I kept my eyes on the ground. Somewhat lulled by this regular movement, I imagined Maria walking beside me; as she held my arm, she turned her head to look at me. It was she who was walking through the grass. I knew that I had staged this hallucination for myself, but I couldn't help smiling and feeling happy. I raised my head to the gloomy weather. On the horizon a magnificent sun was setting into the waves, while bands of rays rose from a fiery sheaf until they disappeared into a heavy, black cloud that laboriously engulfed them; behind me a reflection of this setting sun reappeared in a corner of the clear blue sky.

When my eye returned to the ocean, the sun had almost disappeared. Its disk was half submerged, and a slight trace of pink rose skyward as it steadily faded.

Once as I was returning on horseback along the beach, I instinctively watched the foam from the waves soak the legs of my mare. I watched her hooves kick up stones as they dug into the sand along her way. The sun had quickly disappeared and the sea was overcast, as though a darkness had smothered the waves. Sea foam that was lodged between rocks trembled at a gust of wind, making a sea of snow; gulls passed overhead and I saw their white wings dip toward that dull and dismal water. Nothing can describe the beauty of the scene, with its sea, shore, shell-strewn beach, its rocks covered with wet seaweed and topped with foam that shifted in the breeze.

I could surpass the tenderness and beauty of those things if I could relate all the love, ecstasy, and regret I felt. Can you portray the beating heart? Can you describe a tear and paint the way its crystalline nectar bathes the eye in amorous languor? Can you explain everything you feel in a single day?

Oh, you pathetic human frailty! How you speak and stammer with your words, languages, sounds; you define God, heaven, earth, chemistry, and philosophy, yet your speech can't capture all the joy you are made to feel by a nude woman . . . or by a plum pudding!

TWENTY-TWO

Oh, Maria, Maria! Goodbye, dear angel of my youth, whom I saw when my emotions were fresh, when my love was so sweet and redolent of tender dreaming!

Goodbye! Other passions will be born, and perhaps I will forget you. But you will always live deep in my heart, where each passion is overturned and broken down so that new passions may grow. Goodbye!

Goodbye! Oh, how I would have loved you, kissed you, held you in my arms! My heart melts with delight at the thought of all the madness that my love imagines. Goodbye!

Goodbye! And yet I'll always think about you. I may die when I am thrown into the whirlwind of the world, crushed beneath the trample of feet, torn to shreds. What will become of me? I would like to be a white-haired old man. No, I'd like to be handsome as an angel, crowned with glory and genius, and place everything at your feet so that you could walk over it. But I have none of that, and you looked at me as coldly as though I were a humble servant or a beggar.

And do you know that I haven't spent a day, a night, a single hour without thinking of you, without imagining you emerging from the waves with your black hair resting on your shoulders, your dusky skin beaded with salt water, the rustle of your clothes, and, imprinting the sand, your white foot with its lightly painted nails. Will that vision always be with me, resonant in my heart? No, it's all emptiness!

Goodbye! And yet if I had been bolder and four or five years older when I saw you . . . might it have? . . . Oh, no. I blushed each time you looked at me. Goodbye!

TWENTY-THREE

When I hear the bells ring and the clapper send out its vibrations, my soul is overcome with a vague sadness, something dreamy and undefinable, like a dying reverberation. The mournful drone of the bells that are rung for the dead opens my heart to a succession of reflections. I imagine the height of festive celebrations, with floats and crowns amid triumphal shouts, overseen by an eternal majestic silence.

At the sound of that harbinger of death, my soul rises toward eternity and infinity, hovering over an ocean of doubt.

The voice is as cold and unarguable as the tombs, and yet it chimes for all festivals just as it weeps for the dead. I love to become bemused by its harmony, which stifles the city's sounds; when I stand atop a hill that is gilded by ripe wheat, I love to hear the trailing sounds from the town clock singing out over the countryside; at the same time, the insect whispers in the grass and the bird coos in the tree.

When the sky filtered out color on those sunless winter days, I stayed for a long time listening to the bells mark the church's ritual hours. Voices from everywhere rose skyward in collective harmony, and I focused my mind on this gigantic instrument. It was huge, infinite; in my heart I felt sounds, melodies, echoes of another world, immense things that also met their end.

Oh, bells! You will also sing out at my death, and a minute later you will announce a baptism. This makes you derisive like all the rest, as much of a lie as life itself, whose every phase you announce: baptism, marriage, death. Pitiful brass, your knell wavers and disappears as it rings out; it would serve equally well to pour molten fury on a battlefield or to shoe horses!

Smarh

An Old Mystery

Unpublished until now, this work did not win the Montyon Prize.[1]
This will surprise the unfortunate curiosity seeker who opens it, since its stupidity would seem to deem it worthy of such an honor.

Mothers may allow their daughters to read this material.[2]—THE AUTHOR

Shapeless chaos.[3]—OVID

At the time of Christ's coming, the Archangel Michael had defeated Satan.

Christ had appeared on earth like an oasis in the desert, like a gleaming in the shadows; the oasis dried up, the spark of light died, and everything was reduced to shadows.

---

1. The literary prize founded by Jean-Baptiste Montyon of the Institut de France was awarded annually for work demonstrating traditional virtues and the highest classical values. The origin of the satirical reference may be the preface to Balzac's *Père Goriot* (1835) or the preface to Théophile Gautier's *Mademoiselle de Maupin* (1836): "Instead of offering a Montyon Prize as the reward of virtue, I would rather . . . give a large premium to anyone inventing a new pleasure" (cf.13:554). Until a year before his death, Flaubert combined the Montyon reference with the borrowing from Sade/Piron (see note 2 below) as an ironic touchstone for comment on his work and on that of others. Rote repetition of the idea, however, reduces its original wit to a cliché—the linguistic reflex that drew Flaubert's barbs against other writers for their use of language as a template. To Ernest Chevalier (March 18, 1839), Flaubert wrote: "I am writing works which will not win the Montyon Prize and which *mothers will not allow to be read to their daughters;* I will look for the chance to use this felicitous phrase as

For an instant, humanity had raised its head but then let it drop to the ground; it resumed its old life, and only the sound of crumbling stone marking the collapse of empires disturbed the temporal silence within the eternal calm of oblivion.

The races of mankind were seized by a leprosy of the soul, and everything became degraded.

Laughter was shaded by anguish, men were weak and malicious, humanity was mad, slobbered and foamed; it ran through fields like a child, sweated from fatigue, and went to its death.

But before returning to the void, it wanted to consummate its final minute; the orgy had to be ended before humanity fell down drunk, vile, dispirited, with its belly full and its heart empty.

Satan had only to nudge the wheel of evil that had pulverized mankind since the dawn of creation, so it too would finally wind down, as worn out as the raw material it devoured.

And as the triumphal shout rang through the air, the red mouth of hell seemed to open and proclaim its victories.

It made the sky shudder. Was the earth asking for a new Messiah? In its agony, was it directing its final hope toward Christ? No, the voice repeated several times: "Michael, answer me!" That voice was triumphant, full of anger and joy.

THE VOICE: "Your foot once pinned me down, and I felt your heel grind into my chest, for Christ had solidified the earth in its youthful purity,

---

an epigraph" (12:355); then, on April 15: "Yesterday I finished a mystery that will require three hours to read. . . . Mothers will allow their daughters to read it" (12:355). As evidence of art imitating life, in 1856 he closed a letter to Madame Roger des Genettes: "A fickle lady told me that she would not let her daughter read my book, from which I concluded that I was extremely moral. The worst farce that could be played on me would be to award me the Montyon Prize." To George Sand in 1875, (15:431), he declared: "I am now writing a piece of fluff that mothers will allow their daughters to read"; and in 1878 he wrote to Emile Zola: "I would not advise my daughter to read it [Zola's *A Page of Love*] if I were her mother" (16:43).

2. Flaubert took this epigraph from *The Bedroom Philosophy* (1793) of the Marquis de Sade, who in turn borrowed the phrase from Alexis Piron's *Métronomie* (1738), 3.7, where it stands as an admonition to virtue over wit.

3. From *Metamorphoses*, v.8, where Ovid describes the artful formation of the world from chaos.

where you later trampled me; now that it is old and worn out, your foot would dig into ashes.

"My pride devoured my heart but I sowed the blood from this ulcerated heart, and this scattered rain of malediction bore fruit.

"Now there is not a single virtue that I have not eroded with doubt, not a single belief that I haven't brought down with my laughter, not a shopworn idea that hasn't become reduced to a cliché, not a single fruit that is not bitter. What a beautiful work!

"Oh, how I plied and shaped this loving and happy earth, made for man's delight, how I battered and sapped it, how I champed hard at the bridle of pain!

"If the earth had not drunk all the blood I scattered, it would have made a broader ocean than all of the Creator's seas. All the maledictions born from the heart would make a beautiful concert in praise of God.

"And then I gave them chimeras they didn't have before; I scattered words to the wind which they took for ideas and chased after them to puzzle them out; they wracked their little brains, they wanted to peer into the bottomless pit, they approached the edge and I pushed them in.

"I thank all of you who seconded me! All honor to the vanity called greatness, which handed over to me poets, women, kings! Honor to drunken anger, which breaks and kills! Honor to jealousy, to deceit, to the luxury called love, to the flesh called the soul! Honor to that beautiful thing which claims all of a man's faculties and opens him to surrender . . . what greatness!

"Long live hell! Give me the world until its final hour! I raised, nursed, and mothered it and rocked it in its childhood. I was its consort. How it loved me! How it took me!

"And with what passionate love I gave my fiery kisses!

"Until the world's final hour, I will watch over its fondest days, I will close its eyes, I will lean down to its mouth to receive its final gasp and see if its last thought will bless its Creator.

"And now, Archangel, I have defeated you in turn; each day I insult you, each day I take Christ's empire, each day entire souls give themselves to me.

"There is an old relic of a man who lives in supreme saintliness. In a few days you will see me plunge him into evil within the space of a few hours. Then you will tell me if virtue still exists and if my hell did not long ago melt the ice that imprisoned it.

"You'll see that such works made me well worthy of creating a world, and that they make me the equal of the one who created them!"[4]

(*It is evening in Asia Minor, where a vale shelters a hermit's cabin, near a small chapel.*)

A HERMIT: "Go, my children, return home with the Lord's blessing; the man of God has just blessed and purified you. May his blessing be eternal and his purification withstand time! Go, and don't forget me in your prayers, for I will think of you in mine." (*After dismissing the faithful:*) "I love all those men, and my heart opens when I speak to them of God; those women are like angelic sisters to me, and how I adoringly kiss those small children!

"Oh, thank you God for making my soul tender like yours and capable of loving. Blessed are those who love! Considering the long fasts I undertook, when I decked your altars with flowers picked from the valleys, when I kneeled in prayer at length, contemplated the sky while thinking of Paradise, consoling those who come to me, it seems to me that my heart is accommodating and that this love is a force which would create something.

"I am happy in this retreat; I love to see the river wind along the valley floor, to see a bird spread its wings, to see the pink splashes of the setting sun. With its starry diamonds and its moon resplendent against the blue sky, the beautiful night will deepen my admiration to the point of love; and when I think of the blessings of the afterlife, my soul melts in ecstatic revery.

"Thank you, thank you, dear God! What more do I need, now that your

---

4. The temptation of Christ by Mephistopheles reproduces the comparable scene in the prologue to Goethe's *Faust* (vv.245–353), while his seduction of Martha in the garden (vv.3076–3203) anticipates Yuk's conversation with the woman (below; 11:517–22). The cosmic flight of Satan and Smarh (see further below and 11:561) recasts the flight in Goethe's drama (vv.4399–4404) as well as Delacroix's famous engravings in *Faust* (Paris: Motte & Soutelet, 1828), plates 1 and 16, indicating how much these tableaux in Flaubert are of their time. In *The Family Idiot* (p.265) Sartre says of the battle between the two monsters in "Dream of Hell": "Obviously, it is inspired by the first part of *Faust*."

gift of love has gladdened me? When you summon me, I will die with a blessing on my lips and I will pass from this world to an even better one. Happiness, joy, love, ecstasy, you are all of this!" (*He kneels in prayer.*)

SATAN (*dressed as a doctor*): "Excuse me for interrupting your pious thoughts, sir."

SMARH: "The man of God serves everyone."

SATAN: "I am a Greek doctor who has crossed deserts in order to sit at your feet and to discuss destiny's grand design with you. A man like you is well versed; we are both sages, aren't we?"

SMARH: "What knowledge do you mean?"

SATAN: "It is greater than you suspect. Still, your holiness, through deep inner reflection we have succeeded in solving daunting problems. Nothing is obscure to me." (*Aside:*) "All is black."

(*A married woman enters to speak to Smarh.*)

YUK: "What do you want, my sweet one?"[5]

THE WOMAN: "To consult with the holy father on religion."

YUK: "At the moment he is busy contemplating, conversing, holding forth, and expatiating with that holy man over there in the doctor's uniform. He mustn't be disturbed."

THE WOMAN: "A doctor! Is he a papal nuncio or a Greek theologian?"

YUK: "Both. He has strong ties to the papacy and monastic orders, and he has recommended wonderful tricks for their enjoyment. He is steeped in theology. You know your household, and, like you, he muddies clear waters and does the devil's work there."

THE WOMAN: "What do you mean by that?"

YUK: "Just that you are extremely nice, charming, and have the kind of bosom that would make a whole classroom of schoolboys faint."

THE WOMAN: "Get along with your naughty remarks! Leave me alone so I can speak to the hermit."

YUK: "Don't worry, I'm an old-timer who is slow on the draw. I used

---

5. Many accounts of Yuk have been advanced with equal certainty. Jonathan Culler: "In fact, Yuk is really the God of Language, which is both grotesque and creative, the true form of immortality in that nothing exists outside it," in *The Uses of Uncertainty* (Ithaca, N.Y.: Cornell University Press, 1974), p.52. René Dumesnil, in his edition of *La Tentation de saint Antoine* (Paris: Belles Lettres, 1940), p.xxiii, astutely proposed Flaubert's mythical demiurge *le Garçon* (Old Boy) as a model; René Descharmes, in *Flaubert* (Paris: Ferroud, 1909), pp.116–21, nominated Edgar Quinet's "Mob" from *Ahasvérus* (1833), which Flaubert read in 1837, as a likely prototype.

to be good at it and could have populated an entire desert, but now I have given myself over to religion and follow my holy master everywhere; he lets me do most of the work, such as lighting candles or cooking dinner, hearing confession, preparing the eucharist plate, cleaning, scouring, and scrubbing. In short, I am his unworthy servant. You see, you mustn't be afraid of me. I am gleefully diabolic in my pronouncements but levelheaded in my actions. And who might you be, mother? You strike me as a good woman. From what I can see, I can tell that you are married to a worthy man. Oh, a most excellent man, but (between us) a rather simple sort. I know him; on your wedding night you had to teach him certain things that women usually know all too well but pretend not to. I have known some of them to swoon out of modesty. They have practiced their craft since the age of nine, while asking, 'What are you doing?' But *you* have remained as discreet in your marriage as the Virgin. You have charming children who resemble their mother."

THE WOMAN: "You must be from around here if you know that. Yes, I love those poor children!"

YUK: "And you're happy that way?"

THE WOMAN: "Quite happy, my lord, what more do I need?"

SMARH *(answering the doctor):* "To tell you the truth, I have never sought happiness in knowledge, I haven't worked, read, or pondered."

SATAN: "Neither have I. That entails vanity more than anything else. But I am not talking about knowledge from books, sir, but rather from the heart and from nature."

SMARH: "Of course! I have spent many years of my life in mature reflection."

SATAN: "So I was right in saying that you are a scholar. That observation ought to apply to a man who owns a veritable library, rather than to another who possesses God, for God is true knowledge."

SMARH: "Yes, God is the sole aim of my study."

SATAN: "More than a sage, you are a saint. What a blessed life! To pray to God all day long amid nature's beauties, to be respected by all around, because people consult you constantly on all manner of subjects, on religion, life, death, and eternity. Men, women, and children flock to you. You are the patron angel of the region, drying all eyes, comforting every misery and disappointment; in your saintliness you reconcile families and shore up households!"

SMARH (*humbled*): "You flatter me, my brother!"

SATAN: "No, I am delighted by that charming picture. You tell loose women: 'Go on, return to your family, love God and your children.' You say to children to practice their religion; to servants: 'Serve your masters in love'; to thieves: 'Be honest folk.' When a pauper comes begging, you say prayers for him."

SMARH (*astonished*): "I'm befuddled."

SATAN: "And when you confess young ladies alone in the privacy of your cell, apart from prying eyes, has it never occurred to your holiness to slightly lift the veil that filters vague shapes and deftly smooth out that skirt hiding a calf where your prying eyes move upward? . . . And when you tell those women to love their husbands, don't you ever think that they love others and that their husbands are going to fornicate with the Devil's daughters? When you tell those men to love their children, haven't you ever considered that those aren't their children, and that when they are ready to go to bed they find their place taken by another and the hole closed?"

SMARH: "No, never! But who ever told you such things? I don't believe I was thinking that at all. You open up a new world to me."

SATAN: "So you still don't think (what *are* you thinking of?) that the honesty you preach to the thief would cause him to lose his status; that lost women would wither on the vine of virtue; that a valet who didn't thoroughly hate his master would no longer be a servant, and that the master who didn't beat a servant would no longer be a master?

"There are even more surprising things, for every day you say openly: 'Do good, avoid evil, love God, we have an immortal soul,' without knowing what good and evil are, without ever seeing God, without knowing whether he exists, and all the while taking as your guide a mumbling old priest who knew no more than you. You are so certain, so convinced and persuaded about the soul that you would shed your blood for it; on whose authority? Do you feel your soul the way you feel your stomach when it cries out its hunger, the way your tired eyes ask to be closed, the way your stomach harangues you: 'Comfort me or else I'll make you pay for it.' Really, is your soul hungry? Does it sleep? Do you feel it within?"

SMARH: "Those are tough questions. I've never thought about them."

SATAN: "You're disturbed by trifles! It's as clear as day that you widely portray the nature of that soul, its needs, its suffering, destiny, its punishment . . . and you are disturbed by trifles! Really? My friend, I would have thought you more intelligent for a man of God. You fortunate man! You haven't a conscience, since you teach and demonstrate things beyond your ken."

YUK *(to the woman):* "You're happy with such a man?"

THE WOMAN: "Oh my goodness, yes, you have to be."

YUK: "Yes, you have to resign yourself, don't you? But it weighs on your heart. While doing the housework your sadness fills your eyes with big tears. 'If only fate had been different, I would have been someone else. My husband would be tall, handsome and dashing, with black eyebrows, white teeth, and an inviting mouth. Why didn't I experience this happiness?' Then you lapse into daydreams, you get bored, your drunken husband returns, stinking of wine. What a man!

"You wonder if it will always be that way. You feel alone, unloved and isolated in the world, yet you need love in order to live! Once you saw a handsome young man who kissed your hand, and soldiers often pass under your window. At the public baths you blushed right away at the sight of naked men. How funny! And, my little one, you dream about all that. You are very sad when you go to bed, and you fall asleep thinking about the men in the baths, about your young lover, about soldiers and the like. Your mind is a battleground of fleshy thighs. You tell yourself, 'If only I had a pair against mine,' and your dreams are delightful."

THE WOMAN: "What an evil man!"

YUK: "For a long time you have limited yourself to dreams, reveries, and wishes, but you have long been captivated by the itch of the flesh, and each day you ask yourself: 'When will that happen? Will it be soon?'"

THE WOMAN: "That's regrettable, I must say. But I resist, struggle, and I even came to consult . . ."

YUK: "How simple you are! Do you need an ascetic to teach you what you ought to do? If virtue exists, each creature by itself ought to be able to distinguish and practice it."

THE WOMAN *(aside):* "I never thought of that." *(aloud:)* "Yes, you're right. Besides, I'll resist alone; I'll drive off those obsessive ideas by myself."

YUK: "You say they obsess you? On the contrary, you like them. How pleasant it is to think about that all day long, to imagine an attractive companion who wraps his arms around you!"

THE WOMAN: "Every day I reproach myself for those thoughts as though they were crimes. I kiss my children in order to cling to something of surpassing saintliness, but unfortunately that tender, confusing, and veiled image always passes before my mind's eye."

YUK: "And isn't it when evening falls and the sun's rays die upon the flagstone, orange blossoms exude their pungency, roses close their petals as everything goes to sleep, the moon rises amid white clouds? . . . Isn't that when the form approaches you to utter, 'Love me, Love me! Come to me and learn all the delights of a night of love! If only you knew how it enlarges the soul, and how on that wonderful day our two naked bodies, kissing on a carpet . . . if you could but imagine how I'll clasp your hips and kiss your breasts, how I'll nestle my head against your heart, and how we'll be happy, how we will revel in our voluptuousness!' Isn't that right? Isn't that what you think about, what you hope for, and that's why desire consumes you?"

THE WOMAN: "That's enough! You sear me with your reminder of everything I feel; those thoughts make me blush with shame."

YUK: "Why? Aren't they as lovely, sweet, and smiling as roses? Don't you have a kind of thirst? An impetuous force in your heart that drives you headlong?"

THE WOMAN: "I can't resist it."

YUK: "Don't you often like to admire your body when you look at yourself naked? And you say: 'What a lovely thigh, beautiful body, what a well-turned bosom . . . and what a waste.'"

THE WOMAN: "Oh, yes! My eyes have often been met by a man's long gaze; some seemed to blaze forth, whereas others inundated my being with a flood of loving tenderness."

SATAN *(to Smarh):* "Knowledge will teach you all of that, learned master."

SMARH: "What knowledge?"

SATAN: "Mine."

SMARH: "Which is that?"

SATAN: "Knowledge of the world."

SMARH: "Will you show it to me? What are you, angel or devil?"

SATAN: "Both."

SMARH: "And how do you get that knowledge?"

SATAN: "You'll find out!" *(Satan disappears.)*

YUK: "Well, take the first man you happen to meet, even if he is a fresh and fair sixteen-year-old. Take that child to your bed, and that night you'll see how he will love you, how you will feast with delight on that love. Yes, it will be the voice of your dreams and that angelic body which haunted your dreams."

THE WOMAN *(bemused)*: "Bring him then, let him come! I'll shower him with fiery kisses and unimaginable pleasure. I must have been crazy to grow old without experiencing love. Now the delights of the most torrid nights are mine. Let me get my fill of passion and satisfy my desires! Long days and nights given over to kisses! Ah, my whole life condensed to a sigh, all my dreams realized! Oh, how happy I'll be! Meanwhile, I tremble at the thought that this will be my happiness."

YUK: "Isn't it a pleasure when your thought creates all such desired satisfactions, and when you tell yourself, 'If only he were here in my arms right now, with his mouth touching my lips and our eyes transfixed!'"

THE WOMAN: "Enough! Stop it! Something has been burning my heart as you were speaking, and I am overcome by the fire burning beneath my breast. I crave all of that! I have to leave, oh, yes, I must go!

"What a gorgeous spectacle!" *(She leaves.)*

YUK *(laughing)*: "Before tomorrow morning that old biddy will take on all the kids in town, as well as all the farm boys."

(It is night. The moon and stars are shining. The countryside is hushed.)

SMARH *(leaving the isolation of his cell and beginning to walk)*: "What is this knowledge I have been promised? Where can you find it? Who will confer it? Where does it begin and end? Where does it take you? Unfortunately, I find everything chaotic and see only shadows.

"Where am I heading? I don't know, but I want to explore it. Everything I know seems small and trivial. Unfamiliar needs well up from my heart. If only I were to plumb infinity, to know the world I walk on, to see you, O God whom I adore!

"What *is* it? My mind gets lost in this abyss.

"Didn't my saintly life please me, praying to God and helping mankind? Why do I need anything else? Man must have been made to learn, since he wants to.

"I have nothing to do with what most men know, and I despise their books as being mere testimonies to their errors. I need divine knowledge that will lift me above humanity and draw me near to God.

"My heart expands, my soul opens up, and my mind is engulfed; I feel a change coming on, perhaps death; maybe it is the onset of that blessed eternity which has been promised to saints.

"A century has slipped by since I began thinking, and ever since that stranger spoke to me I have been feeling larger. My soul is slowly expanding the way the horizon does during my walks, when I feel that it can shelter all of creation.

"My long nights used to be filled with sleep and rest, given over to vague and gilded fantasies; I often fell asleep dreaming of that heavenly ecstasy; my fellow saints came to admonish me to pursue my life, directing me toward the distant future of bliss and the road leading to it; but no sooner did I close my eyes than passion began to torment me, so I got up and came here.

"The night air used to refresh me, and I enjoyed that soft languor it brings to the senses; my ear was seduced by the sound of the wind when it makes the leaves rustle, and I listened to the water rush through the valley. I loved the way moonbeams turned the mossy woods to silver. My head lovingly turned toward the intense blue of the star-studded sky, and I told myself that eternity must be sweetly calming in its silent expanse, entirely dispossessed of valleys, trees, leaves, and even more beautiful than this expanse beyond my sight. My thought plunged on as far as humanly possible, and I felt that this harmony of sky and earth was made for the soul.

"Yet this night is as beautiful as all others, these flowers are as fresh, the sky is as blue, the stars are quite silvery. That's certainly the same moon whose rays I saw dancing on the flowers. Why doesn't my heart open any more to the redolence of everything? I am overtaken by pity for all that and feel a jealous envy toward it.

"Just look at me, now that I have risen to some particular stage from which I can plunge into the infinite. Oh, who will spare me from this anguish and tell me what I'll be doing an hour from now, where I'll be and what I will have learned!

"Where is the unknown being that overthrew my soul?"

SATAN *(suddenly appearing):* "Here I am. I have returned as I promised."

SMARH: "What for?"

SATAN: "For you, my teacher!"

SMARH: "For me! What do you want with me?"

SATAN: "Didn't you want to learn knowledge?"
SMARH: "What knowledge?"
SATAN: "But there is only one true knowledge."
SMARH: "What's it called?"
SATAN: "Knowing."
SMARH: "I'm not familiar with it. Where do you find it?"
SATAN: "In infinity."
SMARH: "Is that what infinity is?"
SATAN: "And the one who knows it knows everything."
SMARH: "But God is all there is."
SATAN: "God? What's that?"
SMARH: "God is God."
SATAN: "No, God is this infinity, this knowledge."
SMARH: "So is God everything?"
SATAN: "Hold on, you're wandering. Your limited mind cannot rise higher. You're like other men; the world is beyond your grasp, its countenance is too lofty for your child's reach, and you would kill yourself trying to reach it. I am the one who can lift you to the height of those things."
SMARH: "And what will you teach me?"
SATAN: "Everything!"
SMARH: "Come on!"
(Satan and Smarh soar through the air into infinity.)
SMARH: "We have been rising so long that my head is spinning and I feel I am going to fall."
SATAN: "Are you frightened?"
SMARH: "No one ever flew higher; my body can't stand any more, and vertigo has gripped me. Help me."
SATAN: "Come closer to me. Here, take hold of my feet, if you're afraid."
SMARH: "What a strange sight! In a single glance I can take in the planet there in front of me. It seems to be surrounded by a blue halo, and the stars appear attached to a black background."
SATAN: "Had you dreamed of anything so vast?"
SMARH: "Oh, no! I didn't believe that infinity was so huge!"
SATAN: "Yet you claimed your thought could enclose it, because every day you said: 'God! Eternity!' And you lost yourself in the grandeur of the One, in the immensity of the Other."

SMARH: "That's true. A view like this surpasses the limitations of your soul. You'd have to be a God to grasp it. How big it is! How small the oceans seem to us. *(They continue to climb.)* What? Are we still climbing? Where?"

SATAN: "Why ask such a childish question? Do you need your bearing before taking off? Is there a motive to your actions? What makes the world go around? Why do you see this small globe spinning so fast on its axis, making its inhabitants dizzy?"

SMARH: "How vast creation is! I see the planets rise, I see the fiery stars driven along. What hand guides them? Space opens out as I rise, worlds revolve around me, and I am the center of this bustling creation!

"Oh, how expansive my heart is! I feel superior to that miserable world which I have outdistanced beyond measure. The planets dance all around me, comets flash by, trailing streaks of flame, and in future centuries they will return like galloping mares in the fields of space. How this immensity soothes me! Yes, that's designed for me; infinity surrounds me, and I devour it at my leisure." *(They continue to rise.)*

SATAN: "Are you satisfied with my promises?"

SMARH: "They exceed the limit of everything; I have to fight for breath as the air whistles past me. I am drifting aimlessly."

SATAN: "Are you complaining?"

SMARH: "I don't know whether it's pain or joy."

SATAN: "Look how beautiful everything is! What is its purpose?"

SMARH: "Isn't it for me?"

SATAN: "For you alone, isn't that right?"

SMARH: "Is all that eternity, infinity?"

SATAN: "Rise some more."

SMARH: "Mercy!"

SATAN: "Why mercy? Aren't you the king of this creation? This eternity surrounding you was created for your soul."

SMARH: "But this creation crushes me under its weight; this eternity overwhelms and kills me."

SATAN: "What's gotten into you?"

SMARH: "My head feels weak."

SATAN: "Really? Man's greatness! Yet if I wanted to, I could let you go and you would fall; your poor human carcass would be undone before you ever smashed into another world somewhere!"

SMARH: "When will we stop? This immensity tires me so much that I'm going to die."

SATAN: "So you're already tired of eternity? If you were like me, you'd see!"

SMARH: "Oh, eternity! Is that it? Is that the promised happiness?"

SATAN: "Living forever is some happiness, isn't it? And that's what you want! You aspire to eternity, and you're already tired of that! And that's what you hope for! You want eternity, and life tires you? Haven't you already longed for nothingness a hundred times, to stay calm in the void, even to be somewhat less than dust in the tomb, since a child's breath can disturb it? Your prideful nature: too tired to live for a few minutes, yet you would like to endure forever!

"You see, eternity has been made for us, for those sparkling planets, for those golden stars, for that silver moon, for everything that moves and trembles, for me . . . and for everything that eats incessantly.

"If only you were big enough to see everything, you would see that everything is only a tear! If you could hear everything, you would hear only a single cry of pain: the voice of creation blessing its God."

SMARH: "Who created that? Did he die on the Mount of Olives? When the evening breeze mixed the Lord's words with indistinct desert sounds from afar, was it he who spoke to the armies of Israel? Who originated all that? And have all those worlds gone with the wind, the way sand slips through your fingers? Is that the voice which rumbles in the storm and sings among the leaves? Are those the rays of the sun that gild the clouds? Is he recessed somewhere in space?"

SATAN: "What would you say if you saw him? Why do you need to know him? What madness eats at you?

"You have to know everything! That's enough about the creator of those shining specks of dust. He now pities his creation, caring little whether a tiny worm eats or dies. He sits there far above us, overseeing the vast expanse, covering it with his raiment as if it were a death shroud, and watching worlds revolve in space. He sits alone in his timeless immovability. He was a great creator whose creation is misfortune."

SMARH: "Are you saying that he doesn't worry about his creation and that he doesn't guide eternity?"

SATAN: "Yes, but in order to disturb it, the way a giant's foot makes the sand quake."

SMARH: "I believed that he controlled all things with his will, that his word directed worlds and that the stars bowed down in his presence."

SATAN: "No! You see, everything adheres to laws that were irrevocably established on the accursed day when all was created. A ponderous destiny shapes eternity as it fashions human existence, unable to escape the fate of its own work."

SMARH: "But wasn't there a time when none of that existed? What was it then?"

SATAN: "Emptiness!"

SMARH: "The void must have been even emptier! This infinity where we roam was even more vast! Wasn't it bigger and more beautiful?"

SATAN: "Much more beautiful, because we two were asleep in the death that would bring us into life."

SMARH: "And its limits were still farther off?"

SATAN: "I already told you there were no limits at all."

SMARH: "But who made the existing chaos? It required a God."

SATAN: "He generated himself."

SMARH: "When? Oh, the abyss! I would like to have been alive then, swimming in the midst of it. How my soul would have adapted to the immensity of that eternal night!"

SATAN: "Unfortunately, the mechanism has been set up to grind on eternally and pulverize."

SMARH: "Won't it ever wear down?"

SATAN: "I hope so, because eternity . . ."

SMARH: "Oh, that's a frightening word, isn't it? Even if there were only emptiness, it would make you tremble."

SATAN: "Oh, yes! All those worlds will grow weary from spinning and shining; they will turn to dust, worn out like old bone fragments. Yes, some evening this sun will be extinguished in darkness. Oh, yes! Tears will dry up, everything will be decrepit, and he perhaps . . ."

SMARH: "He, the Supreme Being, will die like his work?"

SATAN: "Why not?"

SMARH: "What? Can eternity be limited?"

SATAN: "Oh, what a supreme joy to realize that it too will perish and that one day this essence of evil, this breath of life and death, will pass away like the others! What a joy to think that the awesome voice will be quiet, the blinding light will be gone forever! Oh, you too would wander about like dust until a speck of my ashes came across your speck right here where the remnants of your work stood! We would be equals in the emptiness from which you have conjured me! As a powerful spirit, born to create and kill, to give birth and destroy, you too would be annihilated! Just imagine that nonexistence would also claim this name that stirred the seas, the world, the stars, and the boundless expanse! Oh, blessed death! When will you come? Oh, how I envy the pleasures of sepulchral dust!"

SMARH: "Do you mean to say that the creator would also be subjected to something? I thought he was the master of creation."

SATAN: "No, he isn't the Lord, because I curse him as I wish. No, the Lord couldn't destroy himself."

SMARH: "So, we are free."

SATAN: "Do you think that freedom belongs to us? What freedom?"

SMARH: "We are free, aren't we? When I was on earth I felt completely chained down and blocked by a thousand restrictions; whereas my mind flew off to ethereal regions, my body couldn't rise an inch above the ground I walked on. But now I feel larger and freer, and I breathe more easily. My mind opens up to all mysteries, and here we are at the very limits of creation, which I may surpass. What grandeur there is all around us! Everything illuminates us with its glow. Can't we wander as we wish in this immensity? Can't we stroll at will through this eternity that contains the entire past and future, both seeds and rubble?

"Look how those clouds softly unfold beneath our feet, how gently and expansively they billow! See how the stars wander and shine against the deep blue sky, how white the moon is and how the sun sends out its golden shafts below! Why would all that exist if it weren't made for me? Creation must have some other purpose than its own life."

SATAN: "You're free? sizeable? Not really. Freedom is neither for those stars wandering daily up a path marked out in space, nor for you who have been born in order to die, nor for me who was born and perhaps will never die. How great it is to wander in this void, to be dust in the wind, emptiness, a man in the infinite!"

SMARH: "But how many things we have passed as we moved along on our voyage! The world will be too confining if I return to it now; I who abide in the infinite will be constricted by its atmosphere fit for insects. But where are we going? Who drives us aloft without our seeing anything?"

SATAN: "Well, you would go on for centuries, eternities, and this void stretching before you would enlarge. Yes, nonbeing is greater than the mind of man and even all of creation. It surrounds and devours him as it spreads out in front of him. Eternity belongs to nothingness, whereas man lives for only a single day."

SMARH: "So everything, unfortunately, is only an endless gulf!"

SATAN: "And gods would waste away in attempting to measure its depth."

SMARH: "Do you mean that 'never' is the only word that rings true?"

SATAN: "Yes, it's the only one that exists, an eternal challenge thrown in the face of all living things. Yes, you see these yawning chasms beneath you, this immensity that is swallowed up below that surrounds us and extends over our heads? Well, just examine your heart and you'll see still deeper abysses, more terrible fissures."

SMARH: "You mean in my own heart? It never occurred to me. I know there are men who have been frightened by their own thoughts, and who have feared themselves, as I am afraid of these immeasurable precipices."

SATAN: "Yes, if you examine your thought, each idea will reveal horizons beyond its reach, heights it can't attain, and, even more than that, crevices that will frighten you and move you to fill them in. Escape will be futile: at every moment you'll feel your foot slip and you will wander around in your soul, a broken man!"

SMARH: "Do you mean that man's soul and God's nature are both hidden in shadow?"

SATAN: "Both are incomplete and flawed."

SMARH: "I thought both were great and true."

SATAN: "So you thought you were well off on earth?"

SMARH: "Yes!"

SATAN: "You were actually a saint . . ."

SMARH: ". . . Who invested everything in God."

SATAN: "Ah, I remember that being true! You were happy. You enjoyed a pure and eternal beatitude, whereas all around you everything living was contorted in an unlimited, eternal anguish. What! You had never sensed all life's falseness, narrow-mindedness, pettiness, and failures. Nature seemed beautiful to you with its wrinkles, wounds and lies; you thought the world's cries, its flowing blood, madman's drool, and rotten guts were full of harmony, truth, and grace. You thought this entire pile of ashes was great, this lie was true, and this derisiveness was good!"

SMARH: "But all that has changed since you have been with me, master! I don't know how many things have come out of me, how many things have been taken in; ever since, it has seemed to me that the measureless expanse has enlarged but has grown more shrouded."

SATAN: "That's right; as we go forward the horizon expands: we continue, but the desert extends in front of you, the chasm opens more. Truth is a shadow; man reaches out to grasp it, it eludes him, yet he continues his pursuit."

SMARH: "I thought I had comprehended it fully, that there was only God."

SATAN: "You mean you had never heard of the Devil?"

SMARH: "Yes, from sinners who approached me, but I was so pure that he was always far from my heart."

SATAN: "Pure? But there is nothing that a demon's breath can't wither. You didn't know that he stirs everything with his clawed hand and that he rips apart everything he stirs—souls, bodies, and the earth in perpetuity? The power of evil is everywhere; it blankets everything, and man throws himself into it, eager to feed on its errors."

SMARH: "The demon's power extends only to evil, since he spawns it; but what about goodness?"

SATAN: "Where is it? Can you tell me something that is good? What's good about it? Who set up the laws of good and evil? Can you show me something in creation that is made for your happiness, something true, holy, happy? Haven't you ever felt your will stop at certain limits it couldn't breach? Haven't you ever felt your tears flow, sadness flood your heart, mystery rise up to engulf you? Have you never contemplated the blank look of a skull and the way the demeaning emptiness of those hollow bones negates everything? Why do those flowers you smell wither in the evening? Why does a snake bite you when you hold it? Why does a man you love betray you? Why does the ground sink beneath your feet when you walk, why do you sink and drown when you want to walk over the waves? Why do you have to clothe and feed yourself, why do you need anything, why do you sleep, walk, and eat? Why do you feel a dagger enter your flesh, why has everything around you been created to make you suffer, and why do you live in order to die?"

SMARH: "Yes, respite is found in the grave."

SATAN: "No! *I* disturb the peacefulness of tombs! No! Death brings forth life, creation is corruption, manure fertilizes, and life emerges from the mire."

Smarh: "Isn't that the permanence and immortality of existence?"

Satan: "Yes, the immortality of worms in the rotting grave. Everything must live, be reborn, and suffer again."

Smarh: "Why is that a failure, as you put it? Why does new life spring from the breath of evil? Why aren't things the way I thought? Why did you come along to disturb me in my blissfulness and wake me from my dream? From this infinite perspective I feel my soul falter in sadness and bitterness."

Satan: "That's the mystery of the lie we call life. Truth is only the vulture that devours you from within."

Smarh: "Do you mean to say that God is malicious? And I had blessed Him!"

Satan: "You can't tell whether his work is good or bad, for you haven't lived; you are scarcely out of diapers, with your childlike acceptance. Yes, the creator of all that may be a devil from some lost hell, greater than the one who is roaring now, and creation itself is perhaps only a hell that punishes everything for having lived, with him playing the part of God."

Smarh: "Oh, my God, my God! I wanted to believe, to dream of your paradise with its promised joys. I loved to pray to you, to love you. This faith filled my soul, and now it's emptier and more deserted than the abysses lost in the immensity that engulfs me. I loved to see the roses graced by your dew, which condensed their fragrance into falling teardrops; I loved to gather them, to bathe in their scented aura . . . to scatter flowers on your altar."

Satan: "Come now, the most beautiful flowers are those growing on tombs; they pay homage to the majesty of oblivion and they perfume the carcasses under the coffin lid, beneath the capstone."

Smarh: "In my mindlessness I thought that everything was great! How foolish my heart was! That was the happiness of an animal. Happiness was made for the ignorant. Now that I know it, I see there is nothing, and yet I am frightened. So, is it the evil of hell that created all beautiful things? Oh, no, no. My heart still swells with love. Yet the one who leads me here is strong and true. Could he have done so otherwise?"

Satan: "Yes, your guide who plays with you and makes the world tremble is strong enough to smash everything, and his suffering makes him true." *(They continue to climb.)*

SMARH: "Oh, mercy, mercy! Enough, enough! I'm trembling with fright; it seems to me that this dome is going to collapse on me, that infinity is going to eat me up, that I am going to annihilate myself at once!"

SATAN: "And you felt so big just a few minutes ago! Your initial stupor gave way to an intoxication with knowledge; you viewed yourself as a God for having climbed so high in the unlimited expanse, and you were afraid of what made you glorious!"

SMARH: "The more you approach infinity, the deeper you penetrate terror."

SATAN: "What terror can attack God's creatures? You were so large, so happy, and now you are so small, so reduced by your fear and trembling! Is that what being a man means? Greatness and pettiness, insolence and stupidity! Your existence amounts to pride and nothingness."

SMARH: "No, no! The source of my trouble is that I know nothing; I know nothing, anxiety eats me, whereas you *do* know! But why are there these worlds? . . . Why anything? . . . Why am I here? . . . Oh, there are two infinities that confuse me: the one in my soul devours me; the one around me will crush me."

SATAN: "Ah, your ignorance weighs on you and the shadows horrify you? That's what you wanted!"

SMARH: "What do you mean by that?"

SATAN: "Knowledge. Well, knowledge is doubt, oblivion, lying, and vanity."

SMARH: "Nonexistence would be better!"

SATAN: "Nothingness exists, since knowledge does not. Do you want to climb higher? Do you want to go farther ahead? Oh, if you only knew the horrible mystery of it all, your skin would chill, your hair would stand on end, and you would die frightened by your thoughts!"

SMARH: "Oh, no, no, I'm afraid! This boundlessness eats and devours me; I tremble feverishly at the thought of being engulfed, of wandering like those planets impelled by the winds, and of burning with their illuminating fire; enough, mercy!"

SATAN: "And yet I would have taken you much farther into the immensity."

SMARH: "But always into nothingness. No, no, take me back to earth, back to my cell, to my wooden cross, my flowered valley. Give me back peace and ignorance. *(They descend.)* Thank you! Instead, introduce me to the world, show me life. You showed me God, so now show me men."

SATAN: "Yes, come and follow me; I'll show you the world so as to make you recoil in horror. Come along and I'll show you life's hellish tortures, tears, and lamentation; come along and I'll dust off and spread the shroud, spread the tablecloth for the orgiastic feast. Approach, creature of God; receive the embrace of the demon, who will rock you to sleep."

(The ocean, plains, high cliffs; gentle weather; the sun sets beneath the waves.)

SMARH: "Finally, I'm back on earth! This is man's birthplace and natural habitat."

SATAN: "Then why does he always curse it?"

SMARH: "It suits me fine. How beautiful nature is!"

SATAN: "Oh, and I suppose you understand it, do you? its mysteries are open to you?"

SMARH: "You can't fool me with your tricks and sophistry. My head isn't in the clouds any more, where all those wandering worlds frightened me. No, I was made for this one, and I must live here."

SATAN: "And die here too, isn't that right? You've been breathing here for a long time, in your suffering humanity. Go ahead and explain to me the mystery of one of those grains of sand beneath your feet, or the meaning of a single drop in the ocean."

SMARH: "But just look yourself at how calm the sea is and how the sun's rays give it a pink hue beneath its green waves! Do you smell the sea spray soaking the sand, and do you see the way those big waves keep rolling and breaking? Look at how that stretch of spent sea foam strews the beach with shells and water plants. Just look at how widespread that beauty is! Can you deny that my heart opens up to the spectacle of the far-off roaring sea, reaching out to lap at my feet, of the vast expanse that I take in at a glance?"

SATAN: "Yes, as far as *your* eye can see. You see into infinity as far as your mind will take you, and you believe you have grasped it when you only brush against it."

SMARH: "No! It's all too beautiful to have been made merely for man's joy and happiness. Just look at those high chalk cliffs, while overhead you hear the cries of the soaring, black-winged gull. Look beyond to the abundant fields, lush with bounty and rife with blooming flowers."

SATAN: "And just look how small you are at the base of the rocks, even how small you are beside the blades of grass that pop back up after the oxen trample them. Yes, you are weaker than these pebbles tossed around by the sea, howling as if it were tightly bound with chains."

SMARH: "But the pebble doesn't move, and my foot pushes it."

SATAN: "And how about you? Isn't there also a foot that crushes you under its invisible heel? Go ahead and crush a grain of sand, my strong fellow!"

SMARH: "But I move over the ocean without needing a path for guidance."

SATAN: "From among a thousand flotillas, just show me a single wake that marked a path lasting for more than a second."

SMARH: "I avoid his anger."

SATAN: "Create your own."

SMARH: "I escape his punishment . . ."

SATAN: ". . . when it stops."

SMARH: "I'm telling you: all of that was given to me by God. Hasn't my intelligence made me the king at the top rung of creation, there to master and silence nature as its sovereign? Am I not the one who shakes the earth, builds cities, determines the course of rivers? Tell me now, can you deny man's power?"

SATAN: "No! All honor to man who builds, destroys, and alters, who scurries, builds, and dies! And all honor to death, which reduces everything to rubble and ash, which swallows the past and brings down the palaces that soared! All honor to nature, which brings forth man, guides him with brazen reins, controls all his senses, torments him in every imaginable way, and kills and dissolves him before receiving him back into its bosom! Eternal power to man who lives and suffers, power to his indestructible art forms and endless works, to his immortal dust!"

SMARH: "The short life of our works doesn't disprove their power."

SATAN: "In other words, your strength proves your weakness; you are eternal and you die, you are strong and subject to everything, your works endure and perish; the palace you inhabit is outlasted by the tomb that encloses your dust, and both become dust in time; then, like you: nothing."

SMARH: "Man's works have changed the face of the globe."

SATAN: "Yes, the earth was forested but you harvested it; the fields were abundant and flocks fed; the earth enclosed a creative principle but you exploited and exhausted it. You believe that artificial means and the wretched fertilizer you spread will bring forth some kind of fruitful creation. Oh, no! Cast into the world, your immense pride led you to tame this nature around you; you wanted to appear mighty beside its grandeur; you thought yourself immortal next to life, and you have only weakness and nonexistence."

SMARH: "You liar! I feel strong!"

SATAN: "Really! How so?"

SMARH: "I have sovereignty over everything, beginning with the animals."

SATAN: "Through your guile. You picked up a stone, raised and built on it, but it tumbled down, and the fields are empty where towers once stood. The grass reaches above buried pyramids. You harnessed rivers but they overflowed their banks; you tried to confine the ocean at dockside, and you prided yourself that each day its smashing waves stopped at the same place; but slowly it ate at the land, and every day it eroded its limits."

SMARH: "On the contrary, isn't everything in creation ranked on a scale of forces and calibrated intelligence?"

SATAN: "Yes . . . and a scale of miseries. Go on."

SMARH: "Am I not superior to the horse, and the horse to the ant, and the ant to the pebble?"

SATAN: "Yes, since you are on horseback as a burden, and the horse crushes the ant, and the ant works the ground."

SMARH: "Don't I have an understanding, seeing, and feeling soul?"

SATAN: "One that suffers, too! Yes, your misfortunes make you greater than all that surrounds you, a greatness worthy of envy! The giant suffers more than insects! You believe you are master of land and sea, you smelt metal, chisel stone, and ward off the waves. Well, when the cauldron boils and the red swells of bronze shimmer, when the stone sings beneath the chisel's bite, when the earth groans under your blows, when the waves murmur as they hit the bow of your ships . . . yes, all of that suffers less than you do in your solitary idleness, without having your skin grated and torn or your innards ripped out. You need only raise your eyes toward the abyssal sky and wonder why all these things exist."

SMARH: "True enough, but why?"

SATAN: "It's because the heavens show you the lightning that scorches you; because the sea spreads out before you, parts, and swallows you; because your intelligence serves you but then betrays you and makes you suffer; and because the limitless expanse opens up its immensity in front of you and engulfs you."

(Nocturnal birds, vultures, and gulls leave their craggy lofts and soar all around. From time to time they dive to the strand in flocks and hunt through seaweed and debris in the surf. The roar of the crashing waves resounds through the caves of the escarpment.)

SMARH: "That nature is bleak."

SATAN: "A while ago you found it so pleasant."

SMARH: "That's what happens when the sun no longer shines and shadows shroud the earth."

SATAN: "Like swaddling clothes."

(Spray leaps over the rocks at sea level, and silence falls when the surf ebbs, leaving only the diminishing slap of the last wave as it sloshes between boulders, which is answered in counterpoint by a muffled roar far away. Birds of prey renew their piercing cries.)

SMARH: "O power of God, how great you are!"

SATAN: "And terrible, wouldn't you say? Don't you feel anything in your heart yield as it cries out your weakness and humble stature in the face of everything that exists?"

SMARH: "Yes, nature is frightening. Do you mean that everything here is only fear and dread?"

SATAN: "When man walks, his foot slips and he falls; when he thinks, he also slips, he falls again, and he wanders about aimlessly."

(The stars disappear, massive clouds shroud the moon and filter its white glow. Shadows soon cover the sky, and darkness is interrupted only by white lines made by the waves as they break over the reef. The furious waves cry out wildly.)

SMARH: "How terrible is the anger of the roaring sea!"

SATAN: "Those are the works of God, which smash, rip apart, and erode. Look how the rocks are smashed. Do you hear the ocean as it subverts them, attempting to uproot and sweep them into its midst, along with the grains of sand?"

SMARH: "How big the waves are! *(He approaches one.)* This one swells up to catch me and carry me off in its net of spray . . . Ah, it falls and dies . . . help! help!" *(He tries to escape, but Satan stops him.)*

SATAN: "What are you frightened of, my strong fellow? Try to kick the ocean, and your anger will only splash up a little water."

(Smarh tries to run, stumbles, and falls on the rocks. Satan tries to pull him up to his feet. The vultures slap wings against the rocks and cannot rise higher. Large black waves swell silently and ebb, leaving the sea looking spent.)

SMARH: "Mercy, mercy!"

SATAN: *(pulling him along on his knees):* Get up, get up, oh mighty man. Raise your head high against the storm! Is that what you are afraid of? What's a wave? Isn't your soul immortal? What can life do to you?"

SMARH: "Have pity! Have pity!"

SATAN: "Come on now, you image of God, be as big as the stone that resists you."

SMARH: "I have nothing. If that sea were to advance more . . . if those rocks were to move toward the shore . . . the sea is going to sweep me away! What horrible cries!"

(Uprooted sea plants float on the foamy swells, the powerful waves move in cadence. A gurgle is heard when the surf recedes. The sea seems to dig at the shore, to cling to pebbles before slipping away.)

SMARH: "How malicious creation is! Did existence always have so much anger, did strength have so much cruelty? Have mercy, master! Tell me if all that lasts forever, if that anger is eternal."

SATAN: "Of course it does! Didn't I tell you, Smarh, that evil was infinite?"

SMARH: "No, man doesn't consist of *that*. His body is beaten down, and pain crumples his heart."

SATAN: "Because his body isn't made of steel, but his heart is bronze on the outside and mud inside. Oh, you poor man! You are molded from the earth; water and sun comfort and harm you."

SMARH: "Why is there so much evil? Why is life filled with suffering that way?"

SATAN: "Why does life exist in the first place? Why the storm, unless it is intended to create and smash?"

SMARH: "And even though that's been going on for centuries, the earth is not yet worn out!"

SATAN: "No, but every foot that has walked on it has left its mark. The imprint of evil has pierced the earth to its core."

SMARH: "The ocean is the biggest thing there is."

SATAN: "Yes, it is the emptiest thing there is. Its jealous anger has been directed toward the earth since the day it was driven back to its sandy bed where it writhes, held in check in the abyss where waves and armies are swallowed up. Before that, the unlimited impact of its undying waves had no restraining shoreline; the surf didn't reach toward land, and a single wave could move endlessly for centuries over an unvaried surface of water. A huge calm ruled this immensity."

SMARH: "Aren't you speaking of epochs that are unknown to mortals, where embryonic creation first stirred, where the sea moved over valleys and the earth was covered with oceans?"

SATAN: "Yes, at that time the waves stirred the mud on which empires would be built."

SMARH: "So it was calm then? Was chaos good?"

SATAN: "It was the other eternity, which in its sleep pulverized nothing."

SMARH: "And wasn't there a single sound spread over so much surface? Was there no torture in its bowels?"

SATAN: "No, earth and sea were leaden and seemed mixed up, like saliva on dust."

SMARH: "And when creation appeared, the earth came forth and the ocean's fury was checked; ever since, the ocean has moved about as it does now."

SATAN: "But one day it held sway."

SMARH: "During the Flood, as I understand, when men were wicked and all hearts had been won over by corruption."

SATAN: "Then the rivers inundated fields; the plains were their bed; the sea drew entire oceans from itself. At first it rose higher than usual, reached cities, entered palaces, lapped at the root of thrones and carried off their velvet trappings. The thrones thought it would stop there but it rose higher, reached the deserts before coming to the pyramids. The pyramids believed that the waves would die at their feet, but the water surmounted their summits before reaching the mountaintops. It rose constantly, like a traveler climbing steadily. The waves swept away cities, towers, and tearful mankind. Then strange noises and cries were heard, sufficient to overthrow the world. You would have seen people cling to existence as it slipped away from them; they climbed mountains, but the sea rose behind them and swept them away amid the dusty rubble. When pyramids, forests, and mountains were uprooted, and when a jumble of tombs and thrones in a green plain spread out in all directions, the waves smashed, the storm rose, and the immense joy of death spread through this solitude."

SMARH: "Unfortunately, that didn't last forever. Creation is thus made only to rise from its own death and suffer from its own life. What a horror that flood was! Why is there so much misfortune?"

SATAN: "But the flood is still going on."

SMARH: "How is that?"

SATAN: "All hearts have bathed in the ocean of iniquity, and hasn't the enormity of evil covered the earth? At first, it swept away a few men before reaching the cities; it rose to power as it swept away palaces and took possession of cities! It reached the countryside, the forests, and each day it reaches out like a new deluge, like a rising sea."

SMARH: "Is that ocean you speak of as strong as this one?"

SATAN: "Bigger still, and its storms do more damage."

SMARH: "And where can one find refuge if everything is unessential and corrupt—a bottomless pit?"

SATAN: "That's just it: where? Who knows?"

SMARH: "Do you mean that happiness is only a lie?"

SATAN: "No, it exists."

SMARH: "Isn't it in joy, fame, ambition, in the passions that stir your heart and enliven it?"

SATAN: "Yes, your heart swells and comes alive in all of that—joy or pain, delight or suffering."

SMARH: "Yes, but I'd like to see the world, since I know nothing of life."

SATAN: "It's easy to teach you all about that. I'll take you there."

(He calls out "Yuk, Yuk!" Yuk appears.)

YUK: "Yes, master?"

SATAN: "He wants you to tell him what life is."

YUK: "Who's that? Who asks such a question? *(Satan points to Smarh.)* Really! *(laughing:)* Life? For God's sake, or for the Devil's, it's very ludicrous, very amusing, very entertaining, very true; farce is fine, but comedy is long. Life is a death shroud spattered with wine, an orgy where everyone gets drunk, sings, and then gets sick; it's a broken glass, a barrel of sour wine, and the one who tilts it too much before drinking often finds dregs and mud in it.

"Do you want to get to know that? Naturally, it's easy! But you'll be seasick every five minutes, wanting only to sleep because the spectacle will tire you quickly. For existence will seem like a bad boardinghouse stew that disgusts everyone from the first excessive spoonful slopped on their plate; for women will seem like fragile little larks, and men will seem like peculiar sparrows; thrones will tremble like jelly, power will seem like an undercooked custard and voluptuousness like a pathetic dessert.

"Master, setting our table with the finest fare in the world makes you a master chef. Leaving the sallow worthies for the angels, you reserve the prettiest sinners for us. At death's extensive feast we sit on thrones and pyramids, overlooking our tablecloth made from the shrouds of kings. We drink the best blood from battles, gnaw on the heads of the loftiest kings; sated by empires and dynasties, peoples and criminal passions, we return every day to watch men move about like puppets, gesturing as we pull their strings. We laugh as we watch centuries stack up in front of us, as we view the sad face of history with its rags streaming in the wind and see time eagerly playing the role of the grim reaper with its iron claws and eternally hungry tooth. For us, that entire scene turns about, pulsates, edges forward, writhes, and dies. We see the farce begin, candles flicker and die out, and everything returns to restful emptiness where we are all drawn like the damned, laughing, biting ourselves, shouting and crying.

"Ah, my strong-willed novice, so much the better. We have a lot to show you. First, a little history; next, a bit of anatomy; and we will end with gastronomy and geography. What should we do? Climb a mountain to see town and country? All right, let's find a high spot where we can get a good perspective. I can actually accompany you because the God of the grotesque is a good interpreter for explaining the world."

(A savage and his family inhabit mountain and forest. Stretching to the horizon there is a vast plain covered with pyramids and nourished by rivers. Farther on, one sees a city with marble and gold roofs gleaming beneath a torrid sun. The man and woman are naked; their brood plays

on straw mats near his horse. The savage looks at his mate with sadness and love.)

THE SAVAGE: "Oh, how I love the moss in the woods, the rustle of the leaves, the beating of birds' wings, my mare's gallop, the sun's rays, and the look in your eyes, Haïta, your black hair trailing down to your waist, your white back, and your neck, which dips and rises when my lips imprint long kisses. I love you with all my heart. When my beautiful mount runs and jumps, I let her mane blow wild, listening to the wind's whispered speech and the snapping of branches beneath her hooves. I see the dust rising from her flanks, mixed with the spray of her lather. As her hocks rhythmically contract and expand, I reach for my bow, drawing and bending it right to the breaking point until the bowstring trembles. And when the arrow cuts the air, my horse neighs, stretches its neck, springs forward, and its pounding hooves propel it ahead.

"The bowstring's vibration sings to the arrow: 'Fly, my slender daughter.' And already it has struck a leopard or a lion, floundering on the sand as its blood stains the dust. I love to embrace it, body against flesh, to stifle it as I feel its bones snap in my hands. When I skin its beautiful pelt the vapor of blood steaming from its body makes me proud.

"Some of my brethren put bark on the muzzles of their horses to guide them, but I let her roam free. She prances on the grass, jumps rivers, climbs rocks, and fords torrents with water soaking her hooves as they dislodge stones."

HAÏTA: "From the day I first saw you I remember that I loved your large, fiery eyes, your hairy, muscular arms, your broad chest where black hair hides bluish veins, your strong thighs that stay as hard as iron, the beautiful flow of hair crowning your head, your smile, and your beautiful teeth. You approached me. As soon as I felt your lips on my shoulder a shiver ran through me, and I felt an unknown scent flood my heart. It wasn't the pleasure of sleeping amid flowers alongside a murmuring brook. Nor was it the scene in the woods on a starry night when white clouds surround the moon and diamonds stud the entire blue garment of the sky. Nor round dancing on the grass, with bodies adorned by chains of roses! No, it was . . . I can't really say.

"And then to feel something stir in my womb, giving me an infinite hope of happiness and the chance to dream freely.

"And when twins came, I bore them lovingly to my breast. When I watched them sleep in our woven hammock, I wept with joy."

THE SAVAGE: "Yet I feel the ponderous sadness of my heart like a heavily laden boat crossing a lake whose rising waves make the bridge shudder. Long ago (my white hair shows how pain has aged me) an unknown enemy pierced my heart with a poisoned arrow, and I am dying.

"Yesterday I was wandering about as usual, but I didn't goad my mare's flanks with my knees and didn't draw my bowstring. I sat in the middle of the forest and listened for raindrops on the leaves.

"What was I thinking then? I looked at the pearls of dew on the grass. The tiger passed me by without incident, the eagle vainly pounced on the trunks of old oaks. I lowered my head as tears furrowed my cheeks. At midday the sun's rays gilded the trees as it passed through the foliage, and I saw that light without a smile. Oh, no! I was saddened.

"And yet Haïta is beautiful, I love no other woman, my children are beautiful, my horse runs well, my bow shoots its arrow, my shelter is fine, and when I return, there is always freshly picked fruit and milk from my white cow. Alas, I thought of unknown things and believed that fairies came to dance before my eyes and showed me golden palaces where I was master. The fairies trod the grass with their silvery legs; their smiles were sad and their eyes welled up with tears. What did they tell me? I've completely forgotten those things that once thrilled my soul. And then at nightfall, when vultures shot from craggy aeries with ferocious cries, when jackals and wolves stealthily crept along, when the birds stopped their singing, everything was black. At that moment I was frightened and began to tremble as if I were dying or as if the night were going to bury me in a shadowy world, and yet my quiver is well stocked, my arm is strong, and my mare was there, walking over the dried leaves yet ever ready to leap like an arrow skipping across a lake.

"And last night, as I lay awake while my wife still clutched my hand to her heart, sleeping like our children, violent desires beset me. I wished for unknown happiness, imaginary raptures, and wanted to sleep and dream in paradise! My heart seemed compressed, and yet Haïta loves me with all her might!

"Whether in a dream or in my waking mind, the leaves of the trees suddenly became shrouded one day, and I saw an immense red plain before me. In the distance there were piles of gold over which richly appareled men walked. A chilling snow fell on my weak and naked body, yet I had only to put on clothes to be warm. When I look at myself, I blush. Why is that?

"Other women might love me more than Haïta . . . how can anyone love more than she does? Her kisses are always loving! But why couldn't there be other loves within love itself?

"And then the woods, lakes, mountains, torrents, all these voices that spoke to me in great harmony now seemed empty and deserted. Life on earth is stifling, my constricted heart swells with my tears to the point of bursting with anguish. Why couldn't there be more attractive shelters than mine, woods even ampler and with more inviting shade? I want other drink, other food, other loves.

"And then I am eager to leave my surroundings and move forward, following the path of the sun, ever forward until I reach the noisily bustling cities that export armies, commerce, and people. They contain something magical and supernatural. As I cross my threshold, I imagine that I would be frightened to enter them, and yet I am compelled to head toward them. An invisible hand pushes me forward, like the desert sands driven by the wind. Seeing the yellowed autumn leaves spin, I longed to join them in their dance through space. I fought with one of them and urged my horse to pursue them, before some became lost in the clouds and others fell into the torrent. For a long time I stared at the gulf where they submerged amid the swirling moss, equally rapt by their rise until they disappeared in a cloud.

"Will I be like Saharan dust and like the autumn leaves? If only I could drown myself in the spiraling depths! If only I could rise eternally in the heavens!

"Why do inner voices call me? When I listen I seem to hear someone in the distance telling me to 'come, come!'

"Will there be a battle, covering the plain with thousands of warriors astride chargers with flowing manes, bows pulled taut with death-dealing arrows? Oh, how the air will ring with cries, while the ground flows red!

"No! Maybe it's a long voyage, like the squadrons of birds that cross oceans. And I have to depart alone! . . . But where? I don't have their wings.

"So I'll say goodbye to my wife and children, to my shelter and hammock, to my dog and the crackling fire of my hearth, to the lake where I often saw my reflection, to the woods where I drew proud breaths. Goodbye to those stars, since I will see others . . . and my mare? Must I leave her? But if she died on the way, wouldn't the vultures eat her eyes? . . . And then when my children are older they will mount their horse as I did and will go hunting to feed their aging mother . . . but the poor beast will be dead, the shelter will be destroyed by a storm, the grass will wither, and my surroundings will vanish and die!"

SATAN: "Hurry! Hurry up! Don't you hear voices on the wind telling you to leave? Well, go!

"Are you afraid of leaving Haïta? I'll give you other wives. Are you afraid of leaving your horse? I'll give you carriages. Instead of your shelter you'll have palaces, instead of the woods you will have cities . . . cities, clamor, gold, whole battalions, a burning furnace, frenzy and wild intoxication!

"Oh, you don't know what joys, delights, and exquisite pleasures there are! Your soul will expand doubly, and entire worlds will enter and revolve within you.

"Do you hear the dancing of naked women who call you with their smiles? Oh, if you knew how beautiful they are, how their bodies contain love! They will take you and coddle you on their panting bosoms.

"Do you hear the rumor of war and the brazen chariots rolling over the marbled cities? Do you hear the extended clamor of civilized peoples? Blood is flowing, so come to the war!

"And they will raise you on a throne; in other words, you were free and will be king. You will find armies and nations at your feet, and when you kick, you will grind men underfoot. You will have vast feasts where drunkenness will overcome your soul. There will be new dishes, new wines, unknown frenzies.

"Come on! Do you hear the golden chalices being brandished and teeth clacking on crystal goblets? Do you hear the pleasure, power, ambition, all the delights of body and soul which speak to you, which await, jostle, and surround you?

"Night approaches, the stars rise in the sky, the wind picks up, leaves blow over the grass . . . go!

"And you will go ever forward until you fall down at the door of a golden palace."

THE SAVAGE: "Goodbye, farewell! I am leaving for the desert, driven by sand and wind.

"I already see the oasis and hear the festive singing.

"Farewell, Haïta, children, mare, goodbye woods and torrents!

"A voice told me 'Set forth!' leaving me under its seductive allure. Goodbye again!"

THE SAVAGE SPIRIT: "Stop, stop!

"No, no! Just keep rocking in your woven hammock, keep riding your horse, relieving the leopard of its bloodied fur. Look. The lake's water is pure, the oaks are tall, and isn't your wife fair? Don't you remember those delicious nights in the flowered meadow beneath the leafy trees, beside the moonlit brook, as the mysteriously redolent night winds dried the sweat on your tired limbs? Come on! There's the same sun setting on the horizon, redder than usual against a bloody backdrop and portending misfortune. . . . how fresh the green moss is, how the torrent groans under its load of foam! Do you need any flowers other than the forest's, any music other than the waterfall, any other love than Haïta's kisses, other happiness than life?

"No! You are filled with molten lead and your heart is afire, so take care! Before your body turns to ashes, it will rot from pride.

"Others like you have unfortunately headed toward the city of men. One evening they bade an eternal adieu to their wives and homes. They left valley, mountain, and the bank that is kissed each day by the waves' foamy lips. Their wives cried, the hearth turned cold, the dog at the threshold barked at the moon, the mare whinnied on the grass.

"And then they were gone! A demon took them and made them founder in their hope, like fire dropped into a river. They were gone for a long time and covered untold ground! They left behind all the lands they crossed. The road led on, the desert stretched to the horizon, and the mirage of happiness eluded them. Frequently glancing back to behold only dust storms, they were soon sated with the bitterness of a slow agony of despair unto death.

"No, don't abandon the woods where the tiger recoils from the bitter tip of your arrowhead, nor the murmur of the lake where deer come to drink at night, as their hooves disturb the moon's silver shafts, or the torrent splashing over rocks, or your sleeping children and your wife, who looks at you through her tears as her heart breaks. Your thatched hut is better than their marble palace, your freedom than their power, your innocence than their voluptuousness. They lie and delight in mockery, their intoxication is that of a bemused idiot, their greatness is prideful and their happiness a lie."

(The savage did not listen to the Angel's voice and left. Satan began to laugh, seeing humanity follow its fatal path and civilization spread over the plains.)

Yuk said, "But that's not all. Now let's enter the city, and let's not bother with trifles around the city gate."

At night not a single sound came from the sleeping city except for a muffled humming like the end of a chant. They went in. The streets were deserted, boats bobbed and rubbed their hulls against the stone quays, the breeze played in the rigging, water flowed under the bridges, the moon lit up palace domes, and the stars sparkled. The squares, streets, broad walkways, open squares, all were empty, and a white glimmering illuminated everything and made shadows dance. Not a cloud.

Yuk was with them.

It was warm, the air was trapped between the houses, and often warm gusts seemed to rise from the lead domes and run through the air like an invisible ember. Some men were stretched out on the ground in a drunken sleep, while others were dead or at least seemed to be sleeping. Something dark and bitter invaded the city's sleep.

Walking ahead, Yuk guided Smarh in this profaned labyrinth. Along the way he pulled some sort of powder out of his pocket and threw it in the air. It rose in a spiral, then fell down the chimneys until the walls soon came apart, and capacious horns grew to a full wingspread, while one woman turned her back to one man and offered her front to another.

From Yuk's mouth came slander, lies, poetry, chimeras, religions, parodies, all of which multiplied in their flight, stretched out and regrouped, braided and curled, until they finally streamed into someone's ear. Or else they planted their seed to germinate in a fertile mind, or built something by destroying something else, buried and unearthed, lifted up or knocked down.

Each movement of his face was a grimace, whether in front of a church or a palace, cabaret or hovel, pauper or king. If he stuck out his foot, he sent a crown flying, knocked over a belief, a pure soul, a virtue, or a conviction.

Afterward, he chortled with the long laughter of the damned, Homeric and unquenchable, a laugh as indestructible as time, as cruel as death, as expansive as the infinite, as enduring as eternity itself. And one dark night on a boundless sea, sustained by an eternal gale, within that laughter there floated empires, peoples, worlds, souls and bodies, skeletons and living corpses, flesh and bone, truth and falsity, greatness and debauchery, mud and gold. Everything was there, riding the ebb and flux of eternity.

Then it seemed to Smarh that the world had been skinned and left bloody and palpitating in its nakedness. His eye plunged deeper into the shadows. For a moment he thought he saw stars, but the shadows prevailed.

"Let's go in here," Yuk said.

And a palace door opened in front of them. They climbed a marble staircase splattered with blood on each step. Their every step ground golden goblets and human heads underfoot, and at each step they could feel the texture of flesh giving way under their weight and causing sighs to be heard.

They found themselves in a throne room. At the foot of the throne there was a pale, emaciated man in a purple wrap. *That* one had sleepless nights. His life was an ordeal, reduced to the pathetic piece of gilded wood that he clutched with both hands. Carefully hedging around his throne, he shored it up as it was about to topple and weighed it down with corruption, gold, and skulls that he gathered from the crowd.

And on bended knees all those vices trailed at his heels, all those virtues bowed as he passed, and his smile melted all those convictions like lead, while the capital sins harassed him by tugging at his purple shroud and pulling away some threads.

And Ambition told him, "Look, over there you have empires, mankind, laurels, glory, gunpowder, battles, cities. The spent powder of the battlefield is still swirling. On to war!" And he leapt on a horse bareback, spurring it with both feet as he galloped over men, and he burned cities as his horse smashed both heads and crowns. Red-stained uniforms and bloody hands appeared through the gory mist of the battlefield, and he called that glory.

And Luxury told him, "Look, over there you have women and voluptuousness, and it's all in your domain. Will any of them disobey their master? If one did, you could smother her in your arms, and right there you would have her warm and palpitating corpse. Don't you have women who are bent on devising exotic pleasures for you? Don't you have poets who will wrack their brains for the most exquisite refinements? And behold those naked women wreathed in incense and recumbent on a bed of roses. Through the night, their voices charm you like the sweet strains of a flute." And like a wild animal he leapt at the throats and stomachs of courtesans and highborn ladies. He growled with pleasure and wallowed in the mud like a pig. His wealth only made him worthless; for all his glory, he was vile.

Day and night, from dawn to dusk, he was surrounded by a host of beautiful women. While naked slaves danced and sang, the flourish of trumpets reverberated against the gilded domes. Meanwhile, a pair of white arms twined around his neck as his mouth passed from one beautiful pair of lips to another. A parade of fathers, husbands, brothers, and sons came to sell their daughters, wives, sisters, and mothers. Blonds and brunets, tawny Andalusian types with black hair, Oriental women with pendulous breasts hanging free, blue-eyed Greek virgins with immaculate shapes, and Nordic girls whose blond hair rivaled the autumn sun, as white as milk from the highlands—all were at his immediate disposal, whether adorned or nude. All flowers, scents, delights, and loves were his.

He became absorbed by this sea of flesh until he was sated, discarding some only to take on others. He enjoyed the whispers of confidantes, their savory mouths and white shoulders, wrapped in cascading black hair. When he felt a pair of knees brush his legs and arms draw him toward bare breasts, he fainted dead away. He was mad, idiotic, and stupid. He was involuntarily rapt when a woman's bead of sweat measured the length of his body. He fell to his knees, bemused by other delights, other dreamy morasses.

And Greed told him, "Gold, gold!" leaving him in the grip of insatiable desire. *Gold*. The word evoked satanic frenzy. He massed and piled his treasure, gathering from everyone and everything. His hands clutched so ravenously that they sweated gold. Overseeing factories to produce it, he could have filled an ocean in which he would bob and declaim, "I'm rich!" He was fitfully jealous of a scrap, to the point of stealing it. He had a thirst for everything, like poison coursing through his veins.

Pride told him, "Just look at your armadas, your oceans and empires, your enslaved masses. It's *all* yours." Seeing himself big, strong, and handsome, he had altars built to himself to satisfy his pride. More and more his pride choked him, like a gathering storm on the point of raging out of control in his soul.

Scurrying from treasury to harem, from his slaves to his mistresses, he himself became enslaved by his vices, irritated by a rose petal on his throne. But then an unexpected visitor kicked at his door until he dislodged it.

Everything collapsed, the lights went out, the wind blew away the throne, the palace was razed, the king and his empires, his delights and crimes, all of that was in his crypt, everything reduced to dust and oblivion.

Yuk began to roar with incessant laughter. Satan declared himself bored by all he had seen.

"Something erotic and ludicrous, pastoral, sentimental, and elegiac. Come on, Yuk, literature watered down for the taste of a consumptive reader!"

YUK: "What do you expect us to show the novice? Betrothal and marriage or death? A lie or a promise?"

SATAN: "Yes."

YUK: "You mean together, don't you? Because a pledge and a lie are synonymous, just like husbands and cuckolds, fiancés and corpses."

SHORT BOURGEOIS COMEDY
Scene 1

(A mother in lace mitts is knitting in a comfortable salon beneath a shaded lamp. A young man and young woman exchange glances.)

YOUNG MAN: "Well?"

YOUNG WOMAN: "Well?"

YOUNG MAN: "Mademoiselle!"

YOUNG WOMAN: "Sir!"

YOUNG MAN: "My dear, I love you *(kisses her)*, I love you with all my heart; if you knew . . ."

The young woman glances up, the young man sighs, and the mother looks at them with a smile.

The conversation continues, as they discuss marriage plans and the decor of their home. The young woman insists on exercising economic restraint, whereas the young man is making lavish plans.

Each one becomes bolder. Each morning the young man arrives with a large bouquet. When he leaves her apartment, he visits his doctor, who completes the cure for an inconvenience that would be annoying on his wedding day and would be dangerous for his wife.

He was a good boy; he had studied law and profited nicely from his three years as a student. He had ravaged a regiment of shopgirls, exclaiming as he abandoned them, "So what! Women like that!" He no longer knew what to do with himself and wanted to reform his ways, to pay his debts, and to settle down and get married.

His wife-to-be was pleasant, a tall eighteen-year-old blond who had been raised under her mother's wing to be chaste, withdrawn, and timid.

He finally convinced himself that he loved her. With a little more imagination, he would have appeared like the lover in a drama. Still, it seemed a bit odd to him.

But the wedding day arrived; the bride was as beautiful as an angel, the young man as handsome as a gendarme. The young woman dreamed of a thousand confused instincts—that poor little dove locked in her cage. Through the bars of social custom and the dark veil of decorum she had glimpsed only a small corner of that blue heaven called love. The young man thought about the upcoming night: "A virgin, a woman like that!" He couldn't get over his astonishment.

Scene 2

A church, guests, beggars. Priests are in their regalia, money clinks in the offertory plate, and the scene is set with many candles. The betrothed are kneeling; the bride trembles with pure joy. The young man has had his hair done and is wearing white gloves; he took an hour to wash his hands with different soaps and exudes their scents.

When they ceremoniously exchange their vows at the City Hall, everything is concluded.

Yuk's well-known laughter begins to peal. He is right, since the young man is facing a half-century of married life.

Propriety forbids us to dwell on their wedding night and to describe everything that went on then. It would be interesting, but decency—that impotent pimp—forbids us. Let's go on to . . .

Scene 3

. . . the honeymoon (see Mr. Balzac's *Physiology of Marriage* for the successive phases of wedded life).[6]

---

6. *The Physiology of Marriage* (1829) is a satirical caricature that sold widely and generated minor scandal. Its Meditations recount the history of love, marriage, family, and women in French society from its earliest roots. The narrator counsels fiancés and husbands about how to avoid the pitfalls of marriage, yet he also blames men in turn. The fifth Meditation

The woman realizes that her husband is much stupider than she had thought. He had seemed so witty when he was just her fiancé (to use the poetic expression), her match (to use the social expression), a good friend (as the cooks put it), and a gleam in her eye (as we would say)!

Moreover, she loved poetry and dreams, capricious, hazy, and wandering thoughts; and her husband tells her that Lamartine is incomprehensible, that dreamers are crazy, and that only money and geometry are true. Her heart was filled with a crown of fragrant flowers, flowers of poetry and flowers of love. Her soul was filled with a serene, pure, and religious joy; and proceeding leaf by leaf, day by day, and with the raucous laughter of a triumphal man, of reason crushing poetry, he trampled her illusions and childlike thoughts. She had to bid farewell to all those translucent reveries where her mind was softly lulled in a boundless heaven, in an ocean of limitless delight and ecstasy! She had to abandon the authors she enjoyed reading on a summer day, seated in the shadow of an elm with her favorite poets and their airy verse, who were treated like idiots by a supposedly witty man!

She was annoyed at first but then persuaded herself that she was wrong. She began to love social life and wanted to go to the ball. Her husband gave his consent. He was proud to make his wife sparkle and to show off her diamonds. Watching other men squeeze her half-bare frame as they flashed the most dazzling smiles they could muster, he said to himself, "That woman is mine. You have her smile, but I have her kiss; you have her gloved hand, her slippered foot, her veiled bosom, and I have her bare hand, her naked foot, and her bare breasts. I have the pleasure that you only dream about. That sparkling beauty, the eyes that look at you, and those glittering diamonds are mine. I have all the treasures you covet!" Thus did pride creep into that love and take it over completely.

Scene 4

She had the most beautiful son in the world. She loved, caressed, and

---

furnished Flaubert with the model for Djalioh's stab at playing the violin ("Whatever You Want," sec. 5).

kissed him every hour of the day. Her happiness was endless because that child contained all her joy and her love.

Her husband found that her childbearing had made her lose her looks. He was annoyed by his son's crying. It was only later that he loved him, at the time when the son's reputation might reflect on his father.

He went back to his whores, however, and resumed the ways of his bachelor life. His wife spent her evenings beside the cradle, praying to God and crying. From time to time the child opened his arms and stammered. His small, dimpled hands stroked his mother's cheeks, which had become reddened from her large tears.

Scene 5

Thus, on her side of things, she led a life of devotion, sacrifice, and fighting. Her husband led a life of pride, money, vice—a cold and gilded life, like the decoration on a valet's old coat. They remained strangers to each other, living under the same roof, joined by the same law but disjoined in their hearts.

On the one hand, there were tears, sleepless and desperate nights filled with anguish and love. On the other, there was a rich and miserable life with its worrisome cares, envy, hatred, regret, insomnia, and lies.

Like everything else, both their lives ended in the grave. The woman died first, alone with a priest and her son. The husband was informed that his wife had died. He dressed in black and ordered a coffin.

Scene 6 is filled with the laughter of Yuk, who ended the bourgeois comedy by adding that people had a lot of trouble burying the husband because of two frightening horns, which rose in spirals. How the devil had he gotten them with such a small, virtuous wife?

They continued walking, rummaging back and forth in every stream in search of a virtue, trying to discover gold in every lump of mud. Cries of joy and shrieks of woe came from every house they looked in. Here there was a casket, there an empty barrel.

Day broke and the town began to stir. Men filled the streets, some returning from orgies while others cried from hunger. Some fell from exhaustion; others, besotted with wine, were crushed under cart wheels.

You could hear the sound of horses' hooves on pavement and the steps of men hastening over cobblestones. Gold was already spilling on the tables, whips were snapping on the shoulders of slaves, prostitution was opening its venal portal, vice was awakening, crime was honing its dagger and starting up its machines. The day was about to begin.

The morning breeze was chilling the skin of a tattered man. When the sun appeared, he shivered with pleasure, began to exercise his shoulder, and smiled stupidly. You would have thought that he wanted to open himself to the sun's warmth. His yellow skin, black beard, and dark hair were covered with dust and pieces of straw; hunger showed in his hollow eyes, and from his half-open mouth came the cold laughter of a famished wild animal.

(Yuk, Satan, and Smarh, dressed as workers.)

YUK: "What's the matter with you, my friend?"

THE PAUPER: "What's the matter with me? But how about yourself? Until now, no one has asked me such a question. Everyone just looks at me when they pass by. But you aren't from around here. Yes, I can see it by your clothes. Oh, if you're from the beautiful country of Germany, tell me if the Rhine is still flowing, if Cologne Cathedral with its stone saints is still standing. Tell me if the trees still have their leaves, because as far as I am concerned, nature has changed since I have been in this hideous city."

YUK: "Let's see, tell all that to these comrades of your own social standing and region."

THE PAUPER: "My standing? I don't have any. My region? I no longer have one. Do the unfortunate have one? It's the happy ones who have a homeland, but the only native land for the poor is the anguish in their hearts. What do you want me to tell you? All I know is that I'm hungry and hate the rich. I left my country because I was driven off by shouts and stones, for my rags were bloody and there was a scandal in my family. Ah, but the scandal is to live the way I do. I don't know exactly where I have been, wandering at random over roads and through fields, living on a stolen apple, a piece of fruit, or a scrap of bread. People always drove me off, saying that I was ugly."

YUK (LAUGHING): "Ha, ha, ha!"

THE PAUPER: "I didn't learn any trade; I only knew how to eat, and I had nothing to eat. At times I was seized by great anger, and it seemed to me that I could have smashed the world with a single kick. In the evening I had to fight with the dogs for garbage scraps by the side of the road and for rags thrown into the mud. Yet some people are happy, eat big meals, and when I ask why, there is a huge gap that I can't cross."

YUK: "Ha, ha, ha!"

THE PAUPER: "Don't laugh, for goodness' sake! Just listen. No one has loved me, whether man, woman, or dog. One day a dog approached me, but since I couldn't feed him, he bit me and went away. But one time in a town somewhere I was able to work on the scaffolding of a church and save a sack of money so that I could get married. Martha loved me. Twice she came alone to the riverbank to tell me that she loved me. She wore flowers in her hair and was singing. Then, somehow she no longer wanted me and was taken by a rich man."

YUK: "That's the way it is, buddy. Girls love handsome, rich gentlemen and velvet doublets."

THE PAUPER: "Don't speak to me about rich people again. I hate them! While I die of starvation at their palace gates, my heart holds treasures of hatred for them. And when I am cold, hungry, unhappy, and wretched, I feed on that hatred and it makes me feel good."

SATAN (WHISPERING INTO THE EAR OF THE PAUPER): "That one *(indicating Yuk)* has a purse with him. Kill him and you'll have it. No one will see you. But if someone should see you, kill him too out of spite. Why did he start laughing at you when you told him about your troubles? He's a hardhearted rich man."

(Yuk appears, showing a magnificent outfit; a diamond-studded purse hangs from his belt.)

THE PAUPER (TO HIMSELF): "Oh, my God! I've never had such thoughts. Suppose *I* were to become rich, happy, have servants, horses, a sumptuous table, and be served like a prince . . . but to kill a man!"

SATAN: "Bah! A man! No one will know. Hurry up, there's no one coming in the street right now."

(He slips a dagger into his hand. The fascinated pauper turns on Yuk, who falls to the ground with stab wounds.)

SATAN: "Help, police! . . . A man has been stabbed! Grab that bum!"

(The body of the worker lies wounded on the ground, but Yuk gets up.)

YUK: "Did you really think I was dead? Oh, good heavens! If I stopped living there wouldn't be any more world or creation. Me, die! But I am reborn from death itself. I am reborn with life because I even live in the dust of tombs. It's impossible.

"Whoever says that I no longer exist lies like the Gospel. Die? But there wouldn't be any more government, religion, virtue, morals, or laws. Who, then, would hold the crown, the sword; who would wear the mantle? Who would be a doctor, poet, lawyer, or priest? Would there be anything to do? Life would become boring and stupid like an old woman. Die? But what would become of families—who are the guarantors of conjugal faith?

"Oh, do I get angry at that horrible idea of social anarchy: public morality. Public morality, customs, philanthropic institutions, virtues, systems, theories. Think about it: if I were to die, all of that would die too. How would things be then? How can you conceive of the world without me, without my occupying two-thirds of it, without me to make it fully alive?"

(The authorities come for the pauper.)

SATAN: "So much the better. That rogue was boring me to death. But besides, it would be inconvenient to kill him so soon. Let's hold him back. He'll have to stew in prison, violate six nuns, and slaughter about thirty people before he gives up the ghost."

(The pauper escapes from the grasp of the officers.)

Yuk rubs his hands, stretches out in the sun, spits in the face of the magistrate, and urinates on the church.

It was a tall church with a blackened porch, and spires and pyramids of stone. It was old and venerable. They entered.

The nave was high, empty, and solitary. The shadows from the slender, handsome columns fell on the worn flagstone. Shadows were growing long, yet the rays of sunlight filtering through the red stained-glass windows cast a glow that seemed to spread like that of the hanging lamps. There was something sad and imposing in that church. It was so large that men seemed quite small when seen from its heights. There was no longer any incense at the feet of the Virgin or flowers on the altar. The voice of the organ was silent. Deep in the background there was a black cloth, a shroud, and a mass for the dead.

The person stretched out in the coffin had never killed, pillaged, or raped. He had never been sent to the galley or had any run-in with the police. He was an honest man. When he left the church and was carried through the street, everyone doffed his hat. They saluted the corpse.

But the priest hurried things and quickly dispatched the corpse into the ground. The poor priest! That day he had already blessed six unions, done three baptisms, and buried four Christians; as for communions, well, they're countless. He was prompted by the idea of his mistress awaiting him. She was getting bored, waiting so long in that warm bathtub. He left, tossed aside his white gown, and began dreaming of adultery.

Oh, how empty that church was! There were no more chants from the people, no more voice of the priest, no prayer intoned by the organ.

But it must have been beautiful on winter days with its thousand candles lit, its congregation singing as it paced in the galleries. Everything sang and resounded with love; from the vault to the tombs, from glass to stone, everything was a single song of joy! Yet how beautiful it was, also, on those summer days when the harvesters covered with sweat entered to have their wheat sprouts blessed. Then the ladies of nobility came, with their entourage of pages, knights, kings, emperors, popes. All came to pray, weep, and love. Before leaving for the Holy Land, the knights in armor said last goodbyes to the great portal bathed in sunlight, to the slate belltower where the bronze voice sings and prays in its stone cage! . . . All gone! As empty as a skeleton!

When a man's steps are heard, they seem like groans or sighs. Draped in their granite cloaks, you can see bishops, cardinals, and dukes stretched out on stone slabs with their mouths gaping; they seem to sleep like the dead. All around the church there is such a torrent of heavy, cold rain that the greenish walls sweat. The worn-out grounds are stuffed with cadavers, the earth echoes, the dead are heaped, and the living generation walks above the extinguished generations. As they go on, the living continue to sink into the earth around the tombs, while their successors begin to walk over their heads.

Everything is used up, withered, and tired. Plaster has eroded between the stones, the faces of the saints are grayed and eaten by time. The flowers in the rose window have become discolored. And the vault itself is caving in, overburdened and frightened by the abyss beneath.

Then Smarh began to weep bitterly and said:

"Alas! Has some conqueror come along and taken all the gold vases to shoe his horses? Have they carried off the holy relics? And the consecrated wafers? Why has the singing stopped? Why is the incense burner empty? Why are the tombs overrun with worms? Why are the walls within so moss-grown and falling to seed outside? The candles are cold and the flowers are faded.

"On past Sundays, children used to come, brimming with joy as they knelt to the Virgin; as they sang, they watched the candlelight flicker over the starry dress of the Virgin.[7] But the children no longer come, and some of them even turn their heads when they pass by.

"When snow covered the ground, when rain fell, when hail beat on the stained glass, everyone used to seek refuge in the vault spreading over them like the wings of a dove. When misfortune struck someone, he drew near the altar cloth to dry his tears and assuage his ills. I have seen people beat the ground with their foreheads and soak the marble floor with their tears; and when they arose, there was a smile of hope in their souls! They had glimpsed heaven in the midst of misfortune, happiness in faith!"

THE CHURCH: "They don't want me any more. Tomorrow the masons will assault my foundation in order to topple me and demolish me stone by stone."

THE FONT: "They came for my water so they could wash their hands. I foamed and boiled, but they spit in my wave and enjoyed watching the circles they made in the water."

THE NAVE: "Everything has taken place beneath me: weddings, funerals, the dead and the living. I echoed the chants, sighs, and cries of pain. The incense, the fragrance of the flowers, the voices of prayer, and candle smoke all rose up to me. How many times have I resounded resplendently! But I am sad and want to lie down on the flagstone at my feet."

THE COLUMNS: "People used to gird us with garlands, but now we are bare. For six centuries we have been standing apart from one another, but now we are sinking into the ground. The whole church seems to be sliding into a mire, as if a demon were crushing its roof with his weight."

THE WINDOWS: "How many times has the sun made our colors translucent, but our refractions no longer illuminate anything. Every day, people

---

7. This description of the Virgin Mary recalls comparable ones in Flaubert's other writing and travel diaries; cf. *Madame Bovary*, 1:III.

in the street throw stones at us, and the winds dislodge the fragments. All our flowers and colors will have to be laid at the feet of God."

THE FLAGSTONES: "We have been used up, and are shot through with holes. We are tired of being trod by impious feet. The dead beneath us seem to be pushing up against us. Why were we quarried from the side of a mountain, where we were so content in the bosom of the earth?"

THE BELL: "I have been silent for a long time, since no one comes to begin sounding the clapper of my great bell. Is everyone dead?

"My bronze voice used to sing madly, so that I made my fragile bell-tower tremble. The tower wavered drunkenly and shuddered under my weight. I filled the air at the top of my voice as I looked out upon the countryside, men, women, old people and children, all hastening and crowding to file through my portal. From the day I was hung here, I have been celebrated and honored as the queen of the building and the head of the cathedral. Wasn't it I, in fact, who gathered the prayers of everyone in my spirals of harmony? But today I am silent and bored in my isolation, gripped on high by vertigo. I believe that I am going to crumble and take my steeple with me. I would rather be melted down into cannonballs and fly across the field of battle."

THE GARGOYLES: "We have been here for a long time, standing straight up or cantilevered. People are not frightened when they look at us from below. Rainwater used to stream from our mouths, grimacing so as to frighten onlookers. Now they sneer at us from below. Oh, how I would like to detach myself from this stone, leap up and go away. I stretch out as far as I can, but my feet are stuck in the church wall. If we all try together, maybe we can break free or drag it behind us. Let's all try to push forward, extend our legs, and let our shaggy hair bristle. We want to slither along the ground like snakes, to run and jump, instead of remaining suspended in space, watching the crowd mill about below and owls beating their wings around our flanks."

And Satan answered the church immediately:

"No, I don't want you any more! You have been impeding my progress for a long time. I'll knock you down, for you are beautiful but old, and I hate you with an eternal hatred. I'll flatten you because you are obstructing my path, and coaches will be able to proceed better when you are no longer in the way.

"You can no longer rally the love of the faithful or of artists in your defense. My mind has insinuated itself into your veins, from the bottom of your deepest column to the air above your highest spire. Vice oozes from your stones, and doubt erodes your facade, eating away at your face. What are your plans? You are going to fall flat, where the grass will cover you for all time.

"Since you are made of solid white marble, my holy water font, you will be the chalice from which I drink blood, and your water will be used to wash the legs of a war-horse somewhere.

"Your nave will fall to the ground, and the vault will tear open like a full belly on the point of bursting.

"Your fragile columns will soon break like reeds under the weight of their cathedral. They will crash like a sea wave that has swollen beyond its limit, only to fall to the empty, flat surface.

"And as for you, my old flagstones, your flat, square faces will be used to pave streets. And the courtesan's foot, the mule's hoof, and the wheels of carts will wear you down so much that you will end up as dust blown away by the wind.

"And you, my great bell, you're going to be melted down. You'll do your bounding and resounding in the open field; each time you sing, you will kill men as you pass by.

"My dear spectrum of stained glass, you will be broken and can delight in seeing your fragments glance off the wall in their fall and smash to bits.

"The gargoyles will fall stone by stone, killing victims in the process. But you'll be carefully picked up, recut, bleached, and reused in some emporium or in a brothel, where I'll see you often."

He spoke, and the entire church crashed in a heap. The vault met the foundation in a horrible tangle. But the fall was met with great laughter, and philosophers applauded. But another laugh drowned them out completely. As you might imagine, it was Yuk's laughter.

Smarh found himself alone in a desert expanse, up to his waist in ashes. The more he tried to free himself, the more he sank in. Everything around him was dreary, inert, or destroyed. He said:

"Where am I? *Where*? I rose into the infinite expanse and was overcome with disgust for infinity. I returned to earth and quickly became sated. Well, what now? I find man and nature hateful. Oh, what a pitiful creation!"

And he too began to laugh.

"I am tired of everything, so I must die. What are those spirits who led me to the places I saw?"

Satan appears to him and says:

"It is I. It's I! I am the Devil!"

Smarh was so amazed that he nearly died.

SATAN: "What's the source of your dread? Why do you fear me? If I wanted to, I could take you straight to my hell; your flesh would be renewed only to be roasted again, because you gave yourself to me long ago. Didn't you curse life? Didn't you laugh at creation? Aren't you imbued with doubt and a slack spirit? Bliss is reserved for those who find solace in the joy of their faith. Did you understand a single thing you witnessed? Have you felt everything that you claim to find disgusting? What do you know about life?"

SMARH: "I thought I knew it. But I really see that I hardly glimpsed it. I still believe that I see the light, until you come along and plunge me in darkness. No, the only thing I see anymore is an obscure, inky horizon.

"Just look! The ashes reach my stomach, the sun has set, and a sullen red aura blankets this waste like the glow emanating from smoldering ruins. Tell me, will the horizon brighten, or will the sun continue to sleep in the shadows? Where am I supposed to go, and what can I do? Will you give me fruitful plains, calm seas, and a life without bitterness and vanity?"

SATAN: "No! On the contrary, I want the gales and vanities to blow into your existence the way wind fills a sail, and to sweep you toward something immense and unknown except to me."

SMARH: "But haven't I already been made to bend like a reed? Do you want the storm to continue until it makes me completely disintegrate?"

SATAN: "Yes! And to abandon you on the sands of a desert where despair will come to eat your soul like a vulture."

SMARH: "That way I'll move from one disgusting experience to another, sated by an endless succession of feasting! You're going to lead me from world to world! Enough, please! Enough of this perpetually dark and dreary ennui! Doubt continues to gnaw at my guts! Have pity on me!"

SATAN: "No! No, I don't want you to doubt any longer. I want your thought to stop going in circles, like the earth in its wobbly and drunken course."

SMARH: "And what will you do to me? Are you going to change me and give me another body, since mine is already old? I contain the memory of ten prior existences, and I've already tangled with so many things that if I keep doing this I'll end up as dust."

SATAN: "You say your blood is old? I'll make poison flow in your veins to nourish your tired flesh. I'll help you along until you can go it alone, and on that day I'll let you out of my clutches.

"Now go on, run and leap into vices, crimes, and passions. Am *I* going to shake up your existence! I'm going to make your heart swell until it bursts; I'll keep plying you continually until you can't take it anymore. Under a molten sun you will taste of life as you cross oceans of blood and seas of mud. Don't you have a goal? Aren't you destined to accomplish a mission and undergo suffering and anguish? When your legs are worn out and your feet have been ground into dust, I'll keep driving you toward a realm of limitless pain until you are reduced to absolutely nothing. Do you understand what I mean?

"Did you believe that you could look at life directly, that you could creep right up to the edge and then back away? Not at all! I'm going to make you swim through it for a long time, plunge to the bottom of the slime and drink in all its bitterness.

"Tell me what you want. Give particular shape to a dream, probe an idea, want something, and immediately your dream will become a reality that you can touch with your hands. I'll take you right to the bottom of the chasm of thought, and I'll fulfill your desire."

SMARH: "What do I know?[8] For I have a thousand aimless passions and confused instincts. My soul contains the ruins of twenty worlds; there's no sign of a breeze to revive all those flowers that have become withered from belief, love, and lost illusions. My storm-tossed heart is as dry as a rock

---

8. Flaubert frequently cites Montaigne, with or without acknowledgment, throughout his correspondence. Here he quotes the famous "Que sçay-je?" (What do I really know?) from the "Apology for Raimond de Sebonde," as he did in the "moral" to "Rage and Impotence," in "Passion and Virtue" (sec. 8), and again in a letter dated Dec. 18, 1839 (12:365); cf. "Diary of a Madman" (sec. 1).

bleached by the sun. I am as exhausted as if I had walked for centuries over an iron road.

"And yet I still need to live! In the depth of my soul, there is still something stirring that struggles for life, something calling for me insistently, like a baby crying for its mother in the night. At times my blood boils as if my veins were made of heated bronze.

"If only the heavens could bathe my heart in a misty dew and let it drowse in the natural aroma. If only the refreshing breeze of a summer night could liven my worn-out eyes, exhausted from their sleepless vigils!"

SATAN: "Come, come along, my master, your journey isn't finished. You can complain when you're old. Be steady, steel your heart for a long life, and don't lose hope in the future if you want to be happy. Look at the world: it has been sweating for more than six thousand years of hard labor, plodding in an endless circle which it thinks is progress.

"Come on now! All this is yours, and hell is there to serve you. The world spreads its tablecloth for your pleasure. What would you like to eat? What will you use to sustain yourself? Glory? Delight? Crimes? Everything, it's all yours!"

Satan whistled and two winged horses appeared. Their long backs undulated like serpents, their long, black tails slapped the ground, and their manes floated and whistled in the wind. Their wings served them like bat wings, and when they flew away all you could hear was the sound of their wings beating the air and the steam shooting from their muzzles. They galloped over the world in giant strides, ravaging cities, fields, battlements, belltowers, and oceans. In their hellish flight they crossed empires like a sandstorm, seeming to get caught up themselves in the storm, along with the sandy remains. Satan stood straight and still, full of majestic pride. He beheld everything disappearing behind and appearing ahead of him. Smarh nestled into the mane of one of the horses, holding on to steady himself.

They went from one end of the world to the other in their wild flight. As they were driven along by their horses, everything passed by in front of them: pyramids, armies, tombs, kings in purple mantle, empires—all sped by as they cut through space. Their steeds beat their wings and lowered their heads to increase velocity, as Satan continued to whip their flanks, saying:

"Let's go, faster, faster! Or else I'll tie you to the tail of a passing comet that will wear you out in its eternal flight. Faster! Fill your mouths with the rush of air! Are you tired from the several thousand leagues it took you a whole hour to cross? Let's go faster or else I'll crush your head with a kick! Clouds are rolling by, snow is falling in the mountains, the sea writhes and groans, and the air whistles by. Stretch out your neck even more and vault that mountain in a single bound, span that ocean with a single beat of your wing. When you're tired you can go rest on a patch of cloud, and when you are hungry I will feed you with the marble from someone's tomb."

And they returned to their flight, faster, longer, quieter, and more terrible. From a distance you could see them in space, crossing the void and galloping into infinity.

When the horses were exhausted and their manes had whipped their flanks, now covered with lather and blood, they began to glide in spirals and finally alighted on earth.

It was evening, and the copper tints of the setting sun lay over the hills. The site was a village cemetery, amid the grass and grayed stones. The chargers plodded over the earth, scraping their wings on the ground, which was strewn with rock fragments. They were panting as they dragged their bellies over the surface, like lizards.

The church was old, gray, wrinkled. Through its stained glass you could see a few candles being lit and extinguished. Peasants were playing and conversing in front of its porch.

Smarh and Satan were seated at the foot of a yew tree whose branches spread all around them like a green rose. Silence fell, voices were hushed, and the wind stopped blowing. As night approached, Satan and Smarh sat there and looked at each other for a long time without saying anything.

Satan was stretched out on the ground, surveying the horizon with his wild stare, while his claw mechanically slipped into the crack of a tomb to stir the ashes a bit. Smarh watched him with dread; trembling like a leaf, he had never felt so enfeebled.

The approaching night was splendidly illuminated. Red and blue lights emerged from the ground and then returned. The earth rumbled and shuddered like ocean waves. Men began to flee, but the ground around the cemetery rose up to swallow them. The stained-glass windows of the church began to shake by themselves and come to life, while behind them the flickering lamp flames made them shimmer as if their painted flowers were fresh and an infernal wind had made them tremble.

The two protagonists had begun to walk together when Smarh saw Christ in the desert, all alone. Suddenly the monstrous head of the Devil emerged, sneering so frightfully that Christ was afraid. Satan opened his mouth, stretched out his hands, and snapped his claws.

Smarh turned toward him quickly, and seen this way, Satan seemed even more horrible. He was walking in fire, sweating blood all over his body. Amid the green waves of grass the tombs seemed to bob about like the refuse from a ship, revealing parts of skeletons and cadavers as they softly swelled. The winged horses would unearth them and casually feed on them.

Then everything vanished. The shadows returned, and all you could hear was the eternal rain of blood, boiling, frothing, and scalding the earth as it fell. Suddenly Smarh saw Yuk balancing on a rope that extended from heaven to hell, convulsed by immense peals of laughter.

They started out again into the dark night, until they finally changed worlds and came to the bank of a river.

You could hear the water rushing through the bamboo, whose heads bent with each gust of the breeze. The blue waves rolled on, lit by the moonlight reflected in them. While clouds surrounded the moon before changing shapes in their wandering passage, the current carried the river off through a silent countryside in full flower.

The surface was so calm that you could have taken the current for a monstrous serpent slowly winding itself through the grass to bite the ocean far away. Slipping across the shimmering shadows you could see stars and masses of black clouds. Frequently the white wings of a swan disappeared into the green reeds.

The warm, clear night was steeped in tropical fragrance. Its transparent blue atmosphere seemed to be illuminated from behind by a blaze of stars. The great, broad horizon bestowed a loving, voluptuous kiss on the sky.

Smarh felt his strength returning. His soul was awakened to a new perception, as though nature had endowed him with a sixth sense. It was intimate and unobstructed enjoyment, beyond which he saw giddy thoughts mill about in confusion, tender, vague, and indeterminate images. For a long time he was swept away in blissful ecstasy, surrendering to the intoxication of everything, letting the harmonious delight of the broad, pure, and limpid sky soak into his soul through every pore. His soul was also opened to the way the grass in the countryside swayed with the aromatic breezes, when flowers cradled their calyxes to let their scent escape to the passing zephyr. His mind's eye took in that soft and murmuring wave of milk as it moved through the rushes, and the swans whose webbed feet softly trod the still waters sleeping in the stream bed, making them spread out in circles to plant a steamy kiss on the gilded sand with its scattering of white shells.

As his soul expanded, it swam effortlessly. It spread its wings and soared through the midst of creation, light-headed from the scented atmosphere, drowsy and indifferent like a sultana on a bed of roses. You could feel the warm earth growing in beauty as it slept.

The waves stop, looking like silver swords planted in the grass. The reeds hush, flowers open, the night becomes even clearer, longer, more delightful. And while Smarh stood there, passing shadows could be seen to rise up, materialize, appear and vanish. Vague forms of pale, naked women surrounded him, walking barefoot on the fresh green carpet. They surrounded him, stared at him, called to him, then ran away very quickly. Some were bent down to the ground like flowers in a stiff breeze, and you could see the black hair covering their white backs; others stretched out on his knees, hanging their heads well over so that their tan, palpitating bosoms could be seen. They were lively, capricious, flighty, and as indecisive as a series of images in a dream of love.

They came to cast flowers before him as they danced all around. With their round white arms around one another's marble hips, they formed a chain. Their swan's necks reared back and their breasts shuddered as if they were singing. They were, in fact, singing so low and indistinctly that Smarh heard only soft, weak sounds like those of a flute when its last strains die away. They plunged into the river, reemerging with their bodies soaked and their wet hair lying over their breasts. The blue wave would often sweep them in front of its course, as though they were held by invisible, perfumed arms.

Then Smarh felt something rising within him like a giant wave. Various illusions played before his eyes, lighted his heart, and impelled him toward a future replete with delight. He wanted to run after them, but they vanished as he chased them headlong.

They were so beautiful! Some came down on a gray cloud, others were brought by the waves, while still others arose from the earth among the grass and flowers and seemed to ride on a moonbeam or on the fragrance of a rose. How beautiful, elegant, and transparent they were, so much so that you might have taken them for the most beautiful dreams of a poet! Some were white with golden hair, while others were dark and fiery, with black eyes that seemed to shoot flames.

It was so beautiful to see that garland of naked women, interwoven and animated, that Smarh was consumed with frenzy as he chased after them. They eluded his grasp, and then they were back dancing in front of his eyes. He was gripped with boundless desire; his soul was a hot cauldron in which a gigantic, tormented passion simmered. A devil was in his flesh, urging him forward, telling him a hundred endless things and singing songs without words, without phrases or ideas; but it was something of scope: ardent, devouring, brimming with anger and frenzy, airier than dust, and more fiery than a flame. He darted this way and that as his blood began to boil. His flesh trembled and seemed to be reformed by that passion. His bones seemed to fragment, his sick thought was enclosed in a tight circle against which he smashed his head when he tried to break out.

Satan finally took pity on him. He kicked the ground and a palace came forth.

Smarh found himself in a large room, seated at a table covered with a wondrous array of delicacies. He pounced on them, delightedly savoring the first mouthfuls and drinking a few drops of the most aromatic liqueurs. The white marble paneling and the gold tiles were sculpted and finely chiseled. Here and there were naked women as beautiful as statues and just as interchangeable! The whole scene was illumined by shimmering lights.

There were endless chants, as soft and pure as the swallow in the fields and as the voice saying "I love you" with a kiss. Everywhere there were roseate forms, alabaster breasts, countless beauties, endless intoxication.

Now, just imagine something more tender than a loving glance, more fragrant than roses, more beautiful and resplendent than the starry night: it is voluptuousness in all its forms, under all its masks, with all its ravishment and rapture, its racing pulse, its intoxication and delight.[9] Think

---

9. This is an excellent example—emphasized here by Flaubert's aside to the reader "Now, just imagine"—of the way he occasionally repeats a fragment from other writings in excep-

of the most beautiful shapes and love-filled nights. Let your imagination run wild with a poet's delirium and with the most arrogant and titanic recollections of Rome; imagine a night of wild orgy, awash with naked women as beautiful as Venuses, attended by choruses of voices, gold chalices, the most exotic delicacies, and the headiest drink. And now imagine, if you will, a palace made of marble and gold, lit by the brilliance emerging from its walls, and girded by trees with pink foliage; and imagine the sea churned by waves of milk from which arise crowned and garlanded nymphs, and then dances and exotic ecstasy without end, madness, and women assuming the most exquisitely erotic poses on pedestals. With your miserable words, limping style, and your stammering imagination, do you believe that you could capture a fraction of what went on that night?

Your impoverished language has been castrated by grammarians, although it is chaste enough by itself. Will it enable you to describe the fragrance of a flower, the green shade of a grassy field, or even let you paint a pile of manure or a drop of water? Will words capture an entire thought, or can't the expression embrace it with its own powers? Thought used to be free, immense, unsubstantial, and it would be up to you to seize and hold it, to nail it down to a miserable sheet of paper with a dry, sober word. Come on, now! With words, sentences, and style, give me an exact description of one of your memories, of a countryside, or of just any old shack!

That's what makes me despair. You know I dreamed of that wonderful orgy for a long time. I'm tired of facing the fact that I've tasted none of it, so I can't tell you the least thing about that idea or thing called voluptuousness. It's such a delicate, gossamer thing, an insubstantial pink haze where your soul drifts in its oppressed confusion.

Some day I'll include the best page ever written, if I can just get enough imagination to sit down and ponder about Nero surveying the ruins of Rome or about pirates on the banks of the Ganges. But I warn you in advance that it will be haughty, monstrous, and immodest to the wild-

---

tionally dense contexts; cf. "Dance of the Dead," sec. 5. In both cases, I have translated *suave* as "tender." (I have rendered *voluptés sans fin,* later in this paragraph, as "exotic ecstasy without end" in order to temper the repetition.) In the *Sentimental Education,* the hero is drawn to the *suavité infinie* emanating from the maternal eyes of his forbidden love goddess (3:261–62). Since *suavitas* is the essential attribute of the Virgin Mary, cf. the voluptuous "transfiguration" of Emma Bovary and her death (1:239, 326; cf. 11:455).

est extent. It would affect you like a slice of bread covered with jam and heavily laced with an aphrodisiac, and if you're a virgin, you will learn some new tricks; if you're decrepit, your youth will return. Yes, that page will be more lavish than the poetry of Mr. Delille, will be more interesting than the tragedies of Mr. Delavigne, will exceed the exuberant style of J. Janin, and will surpass the florid style of P. de Kock.[10] This will be a page, then, that would heat the walls if it were posted as a bill, making the people stampede to the nearest brothels and overrun them. Men and women would be forced to couple in the streets like dogs and pigs—a race vastly inferior to the human race, I admit, which is the sweetest and least offensive race of all.[11]

In the meantime, I'll stop here because the most poetic thing I have to offer you is silence.

But now there is Smarh getting up from his bed of roses because he has grown tired of them. He sits down on the white marble tiling encrusted with diamonds, panting as the sweat runs down his face; his great sad and empty eyes look around slowly and nearly close, having been emptied of their tears. His eyelids grow heavy, his arms and legs are weary, and his soul has been shredded by bitterness and disgust. Why is that?

Beckoning women parade before him, gyrating to display their buttocks clad in scarlet and white, and their lustrous hips. Their hair spills over their white shoulders, their breasts tremble, their pearly teeth give the suggestion of a smile, and their eyes hold him fast, radiating the warmest and tenderest expression imaginable, bathed in an amorous torpor.

After a while he took off after them, running, jumping, and snorting with pleasure before nearly fainting dead away. Once he is glutted, he throws them aside, and turns away to go to sleep.

On a gold tray, they serve him tasty morsels that it has taken twenty

---

10. For Paul de Kock, see note 4 to "A Lecture on Natural History," above. Casimir Delavigne (1793–1843) was a poet and playwright (*Sicilian Vespers*, 1819), whose patriotic elegies led to his classification as a "liberal," according to the nineteenth-century understanding of the term. Father Jacques Delille (1738–1813) sang the pleasures of country life and attacked the Revolution; he became a patriarch both of neoclassical writers and young Romantics. Jules Janin (1804–74) was influenced by the Gothic novel and fantastic tales, but he made his mark as a journalist, becoming the drama critic of the *Journal des Débats* in 1830.

11. Cf. the distribution of prizes in the "Comices Agricoles" of *Madame Bovary*, 1:180.

slaves three days to prepare. Cargo ships are dispatched in all directions to get whatever is desired. Instead of fruit, meat, or fish, it's some unheard-of creation, something to make you die from pleasure. No sooner does he lodge it in his palace than he discards it. In a goblet of cut diamonds he is offered an azure wine crushed from clusters of Oriental grapes, redolent of the most exquisite perfume, a wine so delicious that you'll never again taste its equal. No sooner does it moisten his lips than he vomits and throws it away.

He used to adore the sweet nothings of love, the locked alcove, the woman trembling to the point of fainting as she offers her breasts. He loved the sighs, the kisses, and the extended raptures that filled his eyes with tears. He loved wild, intoxicated dances, swaying back and forth with many arms linked. He adored dazzling lights and the way the moon overlays green lawns with silver. He loved the mystery of the woods and the scent of flowers. He loved heart-rending things that can also make you dissolve in ecstasy. What was going on with him?

All of that was so beautiful, coveted by him with great desire. How many times in his dreams had he conjured that superhuman and impossible creation! He gets weary. His soul is expansive and yet empty, like a ball filled with air.

No! He wants no more of that, no more of all those countless beauties, all those contrived pleasures. He lies there slumped on his side, nearly dead drunk, while his heart is riddled with disgust, his body is overcome with fatigue, and his dreary eyes stare vacantly. Carnal pleasure has spent, stirred, itched, and irritated him before snapping him like a reed and then throwing him into cloying boredom, the kind of naked, deathly ennui that weighs down on your soul like a leaden hood and finally crushes it.

And Yuk is still there with his disgraceful expression. He slobbers on sovereign dignity; he smashes the marble statues and melts down the gold; he drinks the wine and spits on the delicacies; he grabs the women, uses them up from head to toe, from laughter to tears, body and soul. He stains everything and makes it ugly; he ages the young, makes beauty ugly, abases whatever is noble, turns sweet into bitter, and degrades honor. You can see him claiming the title of king of pleasure and of whatever makes things venal, unworthy, dissolute, and true.

Smarh himself begins to laugh and to despise the flesh. He rises, squares his jaw, and exclaims:

"Satan! Satan! I want something other than your joys. Come on! Give me a horse! An army! Battles! Blood! I want to drown the people in all that. Do you think it is in my nature to fall asleep in downy softness or to give myself over to animalistic pleasures? Get that out of my sight! I'm after huge scope. I want to linger in people's memories, to mold them in my hands, and to maul them continually with all four feet of my horse."

And he took off like an arrow shot by a bow. The army he led marched triple-time to catch up with him. But by then he is past the Alps, the Himalayas, crossing oceans and deserts in a flash.[12]

Far above, a vulture soars on spread wings. Sometimes it alights on his crown and squawks when it sees blood flowing and the armies covering the plain as they are transformed into cadavers, like freshly mown wheat. He continues on.

He goes ever forward, leaving nothing behind him but vast ruins; the earth has become so crusted over and swept by dust clouds that grass can't grow anymore, rivers are clogged with corpses, and blood stains the mountain snows.

All along his way dying men extend their hands in supplication, but the breastplate of his war-horse knocks over pyramids, while its hooves demolish cities. And still he goes.

All that can be heard behind him is a huge sigh, a final death rattle, a last throb. The former blaze is now reduced to smoke, the corpses are rotting, and the bones have been bleached by the rain storms. On he goes.

He has come across the small town where he was born, the simple house where his mother gave birth to him; he has torched the harvest and ripped away the roof of his father's house. He has come to plains marked only by a trail of blood. He has put conquered nations in chains, adding, "I'll be back!" And he then is gone, leaving them all to die in slavery. Look at those rusting leg irons and skeletons creaking in the wind.

He has razed so much that you think he intended to transform the earth into a mausoleum to house his name. Is there no stopping him? He has worn out twenty generations who tried to keep up with him. Yet he con-

---

12. It appears that the following description is derived from the famous but barely translatable definition of the Romantic hero in Victor Hugo's *Hernani*, 3.4.992: "Je suis une force qui va" (I am an irresistible force); Flaubert cites the play throughout his letters. Here I have modified his formulary wording *il va* to suggest the expression's amplitude.

tinues to go onward so quickly that eagles can't catch him and vultures don't have time to finish their generous meals. His cape billows in the wind, his sword is broken, he whips his horse with his scepter and digs his spurs into its belly. His horse's mane stands on end, its mouth is white with foam, its shoe is worn out, and it lifts its head to pick up the scent of blood.

He never stops and never looks back. With his head thrust forward and his brow knitted, his eye eagerly devours the horizon. As he strides into the future, he dreams of conquering another world. A winged demon cries out to him as it leads the way, with a voice that rings with the clash of arms: "There's another one, one more! There's an ocean you haven't crossed, one more empire! Have you had enough? Well then, keep going!" The wind ruffling his clothes drives him on. He wishes the world were larger so that his conquests would be that much greater. He would like to carry a cannon with him in order to hasten the advent of death and nothingness.

Since his bed of laurel wreaths is too cramped, he launches fleets upon the oceans and leads armies against empires. On he goes, smashing, pulverizing, and carrying off a distressed populace in his arms and leading an enslaved world behind his horse.

When his ship founders on shoals, the keel stirs up the flotsam and the corpses bobbing in the swells. When his horse is at full gallop, it often cuts through blood clear up to its breastplate as its hooves disembowel the dead. When he lifts his head, he sees a sky reddened by the glow of a fire.

He went on for a long time, so long that the earth was deserted from north to south. He went beyond Asia and Europe, the Old and the New World. He crossed ice floes and the South Seas where the water steams and bubbles over fiery sand. Deserts and forests alike showed the bloody boot print of the conqueror who had crushed something with every step.

And on he went. He saw many fresh streams and many mossy woods with lavish foliage and beautiful roses. Although his throat was dried out from all the dust, he didn't stop to slake his thirst at a stream, nor did he wash his hands or sit beneath the green growth to watch the clouds float by.

Nothing pleased him. His soul was as empty and insatiable as the desert. The more he went on, the more his ambition grew. The mountain always rose faster than the traveler could climb.

Then it was all over. One day his horse spread destruction across the globe until he came to the Ocean that no man can cross; there he stayed, looking around for another mare to continue his flight and a star to guide the way. The only thing left to do was to scavenge fragments of seashells and sift the grains of sand.

Was he all through? What could he do and where could he go? The world was barren, emptied of slaves and armies. He lifted his eyes to heaven, was gripped by unlimited desire, and exclaimed:

"What is the world? How small it is! I'll suffocate if this earth doesn't enlarge for my use! Broaden the seas, and make these confines give way. Expand the atmosphere where I breathe. Is that all? Does life end there? I consume the world and want more: eternity, eternity!"

And he tried to heap all the dust he had made into a big pile, building a pyramid of skulls that were dried by the wind; he used torn battle flags to sweep spilt blood into a ditch, repeating, "Glory, glory!" But it crumbled so fast, the dust blew away, bones covered everything, and the earth drank the blood. He heard a voice behind him:

"Eternity, glory, and immortality are all mine!"

But he got up slowly, like a shadow leaving a tomb and wearing a long, worm-eaten shroud, which served to wrap a skeleton in strips of flesh that were as green as the cemetery grass. His yellowish head bore the cold smile of a courtesan. His mace was a golden scepter on which you could see a plowshare.

He arose, full of anger:

"Who dares to claim that immortality exists?"

YUK: "I do."

"Do you know who I am? Look at my feet, covered with the dust of empires, and see how the fringe of my coat is soaked with the tears of generations."

The ghost shook red dust from its shroud, adding:

"That's history. Just dare to claim that there is any immortality except mine."

YUK: "And mine."

DEATH: "And who are you?"

YUK: "And you?"

DEATH: "I am death! And you?"

YUK: "Just look. My head pierces the clouds and my feet stir the ashes in tombs. I speak with the world's voice, and when I do, it is the voice of creation at work. I am past, present, and future, the world and eternity, this life and the next, body and soul. You can destroy pyramids and kill insects, but you won't deprive me of the smallest fragment of anything.

"I sneer at your winding sheet and your sepulchral joys. I laugh in your face, which has always slipped off me like water over marble. Your yellow head, your belly in shreds, all the dust around you, the tears of blood and the sobs, all that magnificent cortege you revel in, the ruins, the past, history, all those grains of sand that formed your throne, the world that is the wheel you turn through all time, from the widest oceans to the tears of a dog, from the Atlas Mountains right down to a manure pile, from a tree trunk to a blade of grass, I tell you that all this is within your domain. It's your glory, your kingdom, and more than I could describe, everything you eat and consume, everything that lives and dies, begins in order to die, and do you realize that I take pity on all of it? It makes me laugh louder than the noise your foot makes when it smashes the world with a single kick!"

DEATH: "Who do you think you are?"

YUK: "Why, haven't you ever seen me? Wasn't I the one sleeping on the black cloth at the funeral of emperors, the one who led the horses in the procession? Wasn't it I who dug the grave and made the jumbled corpses of heroes rot in their marble mausoleums, just as the bodies of wolves decompose in the woods beneath a bed of leaves?

"When you entered a church and set about mowing the way you do elsewhere—old glutton that you are, eating dirt and bronze indiscriminately—didn't you notice that Christ was broken by my eternal hand, as I polluted the altar?

"Look here: when the dawn begins to reflect off windows as you are leaving an orgy, when you swill wine from golden goblets and use regal linen to dry your mouth hiding its rotten teeth, haven't you heard my buzzing song as it threads among the sounds of shattering glass, playing counterpoint to the blow-flies flitting over the blue lips of the corpses?

"When you lean all the way down to the ground in order to mow more effectively, don't you glimpse something through the dust clouds of falling kingdoms? In the midst of falling ruins, haven't you heard the rumble of pyramids collapsing, adding one more ruin to the pile, another voice to those voices, inserting a grimace among those faces?

"Didn't you see something stronger than time, something that guides and impels it, and sates to the point of intoxication? Didn't you see another eternity in this one?

"Do you believe that everything ends when you pass by? Do you think you are infinity and that you establish limits wherever you happen to stand? Just because your cart toils everywhere, do you feel that you lay the seeds of total destruction? As though ashes didn't remain after a fire! Doesn't the cadaver breed rot? Doesn't eternity follow time?"

DEATH: "What's your name? Answer me! Speak!"

YUK: "So! You want to know my name? I tell you that I am eternal truth, the clown, the grotesque, the ugly. I am what is, was, and will be. I am all of eternity itself. Really, you know me well, since I have kissed your face and gnawed your bones more than once. We spend wonderful nights together, wrapped up in your torn shroud."

DEATH: "That's true! I had forgotten about it, or at least had tried to, because you irritate and nag me, exhaust and beset me. You want to take everything I have for yourself alone. When you're through with me, I don't think a single thread of my coat will be left over."

YUK: "It's true, I'm a rather tyrannical spouse, but I'm such a good provider that you have no cause for complaint."

DEATH: "That's true, too! We'll make a great couple, since we can live without one another. After all, you still eat the crumbs that fall from my mouth and the dust stirred up by my heels."

Then, in a flash, all of Smarh's life passed quickly before his eyes, like a stroke of lightning. The first thing he saw pass by in his mind's eye was his hermit's lodge with his wooden crucifix, and his saintly life with its pure days and calm nights. He remembered that someone had come to speak with him, leaving his soul immensely confused and spinning in a chaos of ideas, and that he had departed with that creature in order to climb endlessly. He didn't know where they were going or how they would reach immense heights so lofty that thought itself can't reach that high. And he was so extremely fearful that his mind snapped like a reed, smashed by the tempest of infinity.

Then a storm arose, and he felt weaker than a fly's wing when he confronted nature. And again he sensed something weighing on him heavily as though his wings were covered with lead, and thus he lay there in a heap, imprisoned by the weight of that invisible chain.

He observed camel trains carrying Bedouins toward a city, yet in the heart of the city itself were all those fragile things: king, church, virtue—in short, everything that withers and rots.

At that particular point, he had a lapse of memory.

Then all of a sudden, as if by magic illumination, he witnessed the parade of all those women of his imagination who beckoned to him with a smile. He recalled all his sensual delights and the disgust that went with them as an integral part of life! He remembered his wild rides on horseback, against a backdrop rumor of war, when his mount was lathered and spattered with the blood of the dying; then, there was only a barren waste covered with ashes. He was overwhelmed and tortured by those memories, as if he were in an arena locked in combat with his own mind, which used its iron claws to fight him, to shake, maul, and knock him down before he fled in terror. With his mind in hot pursuit, he couldn't escape. The chase seemed to continue until he fell down, light-headed and spent from fatigue.

His agony endured longer and more cruelly than Christ's, because it was bereft of hope. There was no horizon to open up at the end of this long, empty, and painful road, no sun to break through the clouds, no dawn to follow the night. He too sweat tears and peppered the ground with drops of blood.

Oh, yes, it was worse, because the cross he had to bear was the dead, pulverizing weight of his soul. He had borne it all his life, and now that he had climbed to the top of his Calvary, he dropped it out of weariness.

He didn't spend three days in the tomb, and his crypt had no stone sarcophagus; rather, the living corpse, twisting and contorting beneath the sepulcher of life's end, was thought itself.

But in his weariness, in the midst of his silent tears when everything weighed heavily on him, he rose up like a final sigh, a last kiss, something infinitely loving yet insubstantial. He revived, opened his eyes, looked around for something he had never seen, and longed for whatever didn't exist. He raised his arms to the endless expanse and began to dream of unknown beauties. Like an old veil ripped apart by the storm and dropped to the ground in silence, his weather-beaten soul began to flutter as though billowing in a tropical breeze bearing perfume and soft, muffled echoes. His taste for life was reborn, as his heart opened up to hope like flowers to the sun.

What sort of day lay ahead of him? What tempest would lie in wait to destroy it? The poor flower! Poor soul! It was a small baby, still pink all over, its soul endowed with love, dreams, and ecstasy.

He left in the morning but didn't head for the fields where his father was working or for the shore where his older brother's boat was tied up. He loved to watch the fleeting clouds, the rolling wheat fields as they bent to the wind like waves at sea; he wandered in the woods and listened to the rain falling on leaves, the birds cooing in the flowering hedge, and insects buzzing in the air as they played in the sun's warmth. He watched the snow fall and listened to the wind howl.

He continued toward the sea, his only love. He ran until he set foot on the beach, where the wind skipping over the waves dried his blond hair, which was soaked in sweat. The sun scorched his white skin, the rocks tore at his feet. What did he care, as he listened to the waves break and ebb on the sand, and watched the sun bathe in the ocean spray.

He perched on another rock, like an eagle in its nest as it surveys both sun and sea. He scanned the green plain stretching out before him, dotted with foamy trails and rippled here and there by a gust of wind. He studied the shadows of rocks as they elongated over the sand and then diminished. He stood motionless for a long time as he watched the same wave, the same blade of grass, the lines of water running off the same rock covered with seaweed, a speck of foam driven by the wind onto the strand.

Frequently he scooped up the fine sand in both hands and delighted in watching tiny streams sift through his fingers at different points and then spin and dance in the passing breeze. In the evening he watched the sun dip below the horizon and beheld its beams as they joined the reflection from the waves and together formed an immense concentration of light rays. The gulls skimmed the waves, and small clouds of sand, carried along as the wind picked up, were scattered all along the beach. Beneath the starry moonlight the green waves were patched with silver strips.

He lived his finest years that way. He grew into a life of complete contemplation, tears, ecstasy, revery, and idle comfort. He lived like the flowers themselves beneath a sunny sky. Everything that sang, flew, pulsated, and beamed, birds in the woods, leaves trembling in the wind, rivers flowing through brilliantly colored fields, dry rocks, storms and hurricanes, foamy waves, sweet-smelling sand, autumn leaves when they fall, snow-covered tombs, sunbeams, moonlight, the whole chorus of voices, all the smells, and everything that joins the vast harmony called nature, poetry, and God—all of that echoed through his soul and resounded within him in a long chorus that came to life in the form of scattered and fragmented words. But the finest and most sublime beauty never came forth; when you come down to it, the inner music of thought and poetry itself is only a weak echo from the other world.

During one summer sunset when he was returning home, the sun was red, and white gossamer strands floated in the air. On that day he had watched the regular rhythm of the sea, the grass trembling in the gentle wind, clouds unfolding and rolling about like ideas in the limitless blue sky. He looked at all that with unseeing eyes because other storms raged in his soul, other clouds than those in the sky.

Poor child, why was he already weary of all that? He had hoped for a broader horizon than the one spread out before his eyes, something brighter than the sun. On beautiful summer evenings he had admired the fragrances released by roses and jasmine, when gusts make them twist their flowery heads, the same breeze that stirred the delicate folds of the leaves and conjured up distant echoes of love and perfumed aroma. That was when the moon shone bright and calm, silently bathed in its reflected radiance, when the clouds spread out like mountains on the move, like waves from another ocean. But he felt something in his soul that was sweeter than all that perfume, more tender[13] than all that brightness, as though there were an eternal source of voluptuousness in his soul with worlds of light shining from within it.

He couldn't be satisfied any longer with just relaxing in the bottom of a boat, asleep on a torn fishing net, and letting the slap of the rising tide lull him as the sun glinted off the whitecaps and the keel of his boat grazed a sand bar, dislodging a few stones. He was tired of seeing waves rolling at sunset, when the sand crabs pepper the shore like rain falling on the sand; tired of feeling the autumn wind blow through his hair, just as it blew the yellow leaves and ruffled the feathers of a dove—the same wind that seemed to sob silently amid the dead branches. He didn't want any of that!

Does that mean that he was immune to the kisses of that dark-haired girl waiting for him each evening in the chapel of the Virgin, waiting each night in the brush, scanning the mist to make out his emerging form, and

---

13. Cf. note 9 above and the emanation of sweetness (again, *suavité*) and poison from the same sacral locus in *Salammbô*: "Something that was softer than wine, more terrible than death, flowed up from her. . . . 'It stifles me, and I feel that I am dying; and then something sweet flows from my brow to my feet'" (2:65, 76).

listening for his whisper? And what about his humble lodging and its roof of rotten straw, the one that is covered with snow in winter but blanketed by white flowers in summer? A stretch of fresh lawn stands in front of the house, wherein his mother is knitting at the fireplace. When he was a child, he slept outside in the sun; as a boy, he played at knight errantry with his grandfather's sword; he played on the grass with his old helmet and wore his shield to bed. There's the old bed he was born in.

You can't see the sea from the window, because it's hidden by that hill. But you can hear the waves, and in the winter the sea overflows into the swamp over there on the right.

His mind shifted to the present, still lulled by his cadence, listening to the sound of his footsteps in the grass, watching the sun sink into the horizon, and taking in the sight of the cattle sleeping in the shade and moving their heads only to chase away the horseflies.

Suddenly he saw a form pass by near him, like a mouth grazing his cheek. A sprite appeared to him wearing a gold diadem, strewing his path with flowers, diamonds, and an assortment of laurel branches blown down by the wind. The apparition disappeared in a cloud of dust.

He went to the city brimming with confidence, joyful and full of himself, striding toward a future that he himself endowed with boundless happiness and enormous enthusiasm. Impelled continuously by his soul and stirred by its muted cries, he determined to become a poet.

Being a poet means to have your hair turn white before your time; to shift from one misery to another; to reach out your arms as you chase an eternally fleeting illusion throughout life; to be tortured by an endless hunger and thirst, like a fabled creature; to feel yourself lose all the fruit you had hoped to pick, even though you were close enough to enjoy the scent of its nearly ripe fragrance. You live with your jealousy, with rage, love, with your soul, facing an indifferent and sneering world. More costly than spilling your blood, you spill the contents of your heart; you decant it into crystal goblets that have been chiseled like marble. And all of that just to have your work trampled by the unruly mob, broken and ground underfoot, to have it satirized, and have mud spattered on the white wings of those poor angels that arose from your heart.

"A poet! Ah, yes, a poet!"

He repeated that word like a beloved tune whose melody lingers in your ear to whisper its notes of love.

Oh, to be a poet! To feel yourself larger than life, to feel that your soul is spacious enough to accommodate the dance and speech of everything, like God holding his creature in his hand. To give expression to the entire great chain of being, from a blade of grass to eternity, from a grain of sand to man's heart; to have everything that is the most beautiful, the softest and most tender; to have the most expansive loves, the longest kisses and nocturnal reveries, conquests, applause, gold, dominion, immortality! Wasn't it all for him, for the poet: the moss in the burgeoning woods, the beat of a dove's wing, the sand adding its fragrance to the shore, the lush breezes from southern seas, all concerts of the soul, voices of nature, and the voice of God himself?

Write me some verse, relate something to me, sing me a ray of sunshine or a woman's sigh, but let her voice be soft, have her lull me to sleep under a blanket of roses, let her break my heart and kill me with delight and ecstasy.

When I see you, my poet, I'll know all the secrets of your soul; and when I recall the strains of your verse, I'll fall to my knees. You will be my God, since I don't have any. I'll spread my royal cloak at your feet. I will melt down all the crowns to make you a footstool.

One day when he was gripped by inspiration, he took his pen in hand and, with tears of joy and pride, dashed it across a piece of paper. With fiery eyes, breathless, he grasped at the onslaught of ideas passing through his mind, alert for anything born from his heart that he could externalize, strip bare, and offer undisguised to the public.

His soul was spinning within as if in a giant chasm. He wanted to stop it, but it was swept away in the vast gulf. When he began to feel weak, he said to himself:

"Oh, what misfortune! What's happening to me? My heart is burning, yet my head is frozen. My mind used to be rife with ideas, but it no longer has any. All I feel is the passion flowing in me endlessly, like waves slapping together on a gloomy night. Is there anything else I can say or do? No.

"What misery! I won't be able to whisper a single sigh without having everything crack, break, and come crashing down on me. My soul expands until it suffocates me, and will destroy the body housing it like a swollen hand that tears the glove covering it. Why is that? What a curse!

"Write then, you wretch, since the Devil drives you to it!

"Yes, I am filled with thought that contorts within me like a serpent. I imagine it as broad as the horizon when it spreads out at dawn, and when the sunshine begins to dissipate the fog, it rises, grows, reaches toward me until I seize it and exclaim, 'You're mine, all mine!'

"How beautiful and sublime that is! Am *I* a genius? Alas, no!

"So are you flying off, my dear illusion? And you, my pride, are you leaving me too? What will become of me?

"And yet . . . not everything has been said! Let's persevere, continue, explore my soul, even if it should turn to dust in my hands.

"Love! What about love? Oh, but what miserable vanity! Can poetry ever describe the miracle of a smile or the delightful joy in a glance? Love! Even though I repeat that many times, have I actually said anything? No!

"Take glory, for instance. Let's see: Alexander, Caesar, Napoleon . . . how's that! Armies on the move, gunpowder, and blood—how stupid! Glory? Greed devours me, and I can't express a thousandth part of the anger welling up in my heart.

"Would you like me to speak about death instead? It reveals the truth about nonexistence. But my thought is getting sidetracked; the more I think, the less I speak. If I were a resurrected corpse I could explain many things: whether worms devouring your belly bring joy or agony, and whether the tomb is as dark as they say. But what can I say? Does art extend that far? Is the world of poetry as much a lie as this one? Can't we ever go beyond?

"And yet I do feel the traces of dominant genius, spilling over within me. No, that's pride! . . . pride, the blood of poets!

"There is nothing for me to do but stand here silently in the face of that idiotic world, staring at you with its stupid grin as though you were a tattered clown who cries behind the mask of his laughter and seeks just one more beautiful thing to please the crowd.

"But I haven't a single letter to write about love, glory, death, pride, and all those meaningless notions that surround and plague me!

"What about God? I used to believe in him. My mind goes back to the time when I prayed to the Virgin on bended knee, when my mother taught me my prayers. If I were to return to my faith, at least I would have some passion and conviction and thus could move others. But I am too proud to lie and couldn't do it, *I* who laugh when I pass a church and who spat on the Cross one day when I was hungry.

"But how can you love something, have faith and believe, since everything is so horrible here and doubt abounds every time you breathe a word, since the relentless hunger of misfortune and despair have devoured every belief? In this world and in poetry, in the finite and the infinite, within my soul and outside, everything deceives me with its lies, everything runs away and makes fun of me, and here I am writhing in an ocean of slime and being dragged under. I should laugh at all that and then go off to a tavern to get drunk, or else run to the whores to wallow in the misery of sensual delight.

"So much the better! I can't sink any lower. I don't have much of anything left, and I'm afraid that my misfortune would increase and that I might fall farther still, but here I am at the bottom . . . unless there are more infernos beneath hell, and more despair following despair.

"Can I stay like this forever? But the ills besetting me would not be enough for me, and my heart will have to double its size so that I can find a continuing place for all the disgust in my heart.

"And to think that I used to be satisfied with a sunbeam, with the golden harvest, with beautiful moonlight in the woods; to think that it filled and satisfied me when those echoes were captured by my sonorous and well-turned verse! How long ago all that seems now! I was so young, so innocent, and so happy!

"But after dwelling on nature I wanted to capture my heart; after the world I wanted infinity, and I drowned in that bottomless pit and am still spinning. I wanted to probe and dissect the passions, to reduce them to marvelous skeletons, but death seized my soul. I had wanted to tame the passions and make them obey and shape them to my designs, but they swept me away in their stormy passage. I believed that nothing was too big or too strong for me, and here I am at the heart of the void, weaker than a broken reed.

"Farewell, then, to all those beautiful dreams, to those lovely days that the deceitful dawn said would be bright and shining. They led me to seek a world of enthusiasm and rapture. My path was supposed to be lit, but it left me in shadows, beneath a paradise of thought from which the cold sword of reality keeps me forever separated.

"Oh, prison of flesh, how I curse you! What accounts for you? What's your purpose, you wretched, living carcass, dragging your rottenness through the streets, eating, drinking, and reveling? Why am I attached to this corpse that drags me around the world, *I* who want to fly to heaven and then set out for infinity?

"What crime did you commit, my poor soul, to be imprisoned in this body where you flap your wings in vain and break them on the walls that contain you? I have a deep sense that you want to leave your vale of tears, that when I look at the stars you stream toward them. When the sea lies before me, you outrace my eyesight, and when I see tombs, isn't that you who reaches for them with open arms, whereas my body wants to live?

"You are one note of the melody, a sigh . . . no, that's not really it! You are my heart when it's full blown, you are that voice which is speaking, asking, sobbing, and twisting inside me while my lips pretend to smile.

"Oh, you poor eagle locked in a cage. Through your bars you still see the high reaches you have lost, there among the clouds where you were born, and you search for the open sky where you soared. But the bars hold you in, and all you can do is tuck your head under your wing and die. You're already strangling and soon you will be just a tepid body called despair."

Then Smarh left the city at the evening hour when everything sparkles and bustles in the cool of the growing mist. He walked barefoot in the muddy path, yet everywhere around and behind him, matter pulsated with life force, and it energized things, built kingdoms, spawned philosophers and sectarians. Poets were driven off, scorned and humiliated. He wasn't wanted, and thus was exiled. When he left, everything behind him fell to ruin, punctuated by enormous laughter.

He came to the plains alone. In the midst of the shadows in that open stretch, he began to weep. Immense depression swept over him like a vulture on its dead prey. It extended its broad black wings and began eating while it filled the air with raucous cries.

He wept bitterly at great length, and each one of his tears was a curse lodged against the earth. Each was a piece of his heart which was swept away into oblivion. It was the agony of hope, faith, love, beauty, everything transitory and moribund that aspired to eternity. Rising up from the ground, the wind of eternity tore away the sap of life, all its freshness and heady aroma, all its illumination and heartbreak, everything charming and voluptuous, beliefs, passions. It scorched the earth and withered flowers.

Thus, everything would come to its end. Fissures marked the death rattle of the exhausted and dying world. His soul was driven mad by the anguish it endured, enclosed tightly within an iron ring.

An eternal night was about to fall, without stars or light. Already Satan was eagerly covering the world in order to rip out its last word and thought.

Smarh was still drowning in his misfortune. His head was buried in his hands, and the dust flew off his hair when it flapped around his teary eyes.

The only thing heard was the immense rumble of the storm of time coming to an end, shuddering with its last sob on the threshold of death. The earth was dislodged from its axis; it wobbled in a weary, exhausted stupor, as if a hurricane had tried to knock it down. The sun set slowly, as though it wanted to say an eternal farewell to the earth and give a long, final kiss to the woods, fields, forests, vales, and deserts it had lighted, to the ocean above which it had rolled for countless hours. In the sun's absence, the stars no longer shone, having gone on to illumine higher worlds.

Why, then, does Smarh lift his head? There is a woman standing next to him . . . no, she's an angel. She wipes his tears with the tip of her white wing. She lifts him to his feet and draws him to her heart. She too has been crying and her feet are bloody. She says to him, "Oh, my beloved, come to me. They have driven me off into exile. Love me, for I am so beautiful."

And Smarh gave a final cry of joy as he grasped for the same branch from which the hurricane had torn him. Suddenly, he exclaimed:

"Yes, I love you! I love you! You see that I am reborn to life. You see the sun returning, the grass growing on the hills, and the river flowing again. Yes, I love you! Oh, my God, my God! In my doubt, my despair, my cursing, and my ignorance, the passing world appeared to me like a chain of skeletons in an infernal dance. But Providence unfolds before my eyes, I see the dawn breaking and the horizon beginning to unfold, revealing a luminous, eternal presence in its deep recesses. Yes, I love you! If only you knew how much! Just listen! Am I the one who lived so long and strode through so much dust and plowed through so many ruins? No, you can see the dust rising to heaven and the ruins are still there. What was I? A poet? Yes, yes! I will continue singing forever! Yes, I love you!

"When I was in the tomb a while ago, the marble slab weighed heavily on my head, and I was confined by the planks of my coffin. But now I'm in heaven! My love for you is eternal! You are mine through all eternity!"

He was on the point of extending his open arms to the angel of Truth and embracing her. Already their eyes had met, their tears had dried, and the atmosphere became flooded with hope for creation. But then the world returned to its old bed of woes, and he squinted his eyes to glimpse the last star; he had inhaled a breeze from heaven, but then he fell back asleep in the ashes.

Satan reappeared in a small patch of light to declare:

"Stop, she's mine! Smarh, I'm telling you to stop!"

SMARH: "Yours? Get thee behind me, spirit of darkness!"

SATAN: "I'll squash you, you arrogant insect. You're nothing but a soap bubble that is kept aloft by my breath alone."

SMARH: "Aren't you all mine? My heart is all yours!"

SATAN: "No! I offer you everything."

Spending its last strength, the earth cried out, "Love him! Love him!"

Rising above its ashes, an angry hell fumed, "Love *him,* love *him!*"

But laughter ripped through the air; Yuk emerged to speak these words: "She's mine. Eternity is for you!"

And eternity confirmed this, repeating, "He's the one! It is he!"

Smarh continued to wander aimlessly through the void.

Satan shed a tear.

Yuk began to laugh as he pounced on her and suffocated her with such a powerful and terrible kiss that she choked to death in the arms of the everlasting monster.

G.F.

Here is the reflection of a man who was not involved in this matter, and who reread it a year later with the following judgment:

It's allowable to write miserable stuff, but not this kind. Whatever you admired a year ago is very bad today. I'm very annoyed because I had spotted you as a person with great promise, and you saw yourself as a minor Goethe. That's no small illusion. You have to begin with ideas, and your renowned mystery is devoid of them. My poor friend, you'll chase your dreams enthusiastically but will be disgusted by whatever you write. You just have to accept things the way they are. Do you know what I like best about your work? It's this very page, which next year will seem to me as stupid as the rest and will prompt another series of bitter reflections. In a year I might be dead; so much the better! And still you are afraid, my idiotic friend. As I bid you farewell, the best advice I can give you is to stop writing.

JASMINE